A *Heartbeat* in Danger

Charles
Thank you
Dan Morrow
James 4:10

DAN MORROW

ISBN 978-1-63844-293-6 (paperback)
ISBN 978-1-63844-294-3 (digital)

Christian Faith Publishing, Inc.
832 Park Avenue
Meadville, PA 16335
www.christianfaithpublishing.com

Printed in the United States of America

Acknowledgements

This project would not have been possible without the support and prayers of the following people—

Sonja N; Dan & Diana E; Brad & Teresa B; Carla S; John & LeeAnn H; Tracy M; Michael & Amy D; Karen W; Charlie & Elaine R; Matt & Leisa H; Phil & Kathy R; Zeke & Trisha F; Roger & LeeAnn B; Chris & Belinda B; David W; Crystal A; Patrick & Emily H; Trent E; Serena D; William C; Thomas C

Extra Special thanks to my wife, Nicki, for her unwavering love and support. All my dreams would still be dreams if there hadn't been you. Let me say once more that I love you.

And, of course, to my Mother and Father. I cannot express the depth of my gratitude for being encouraged from a young age to write, to express my thoughts and emotions in words. I hope I am a tribute to the sacrifice and love you've shown me throughout my life. I am eternally grateful for you both.

Chapter 1

The lights from R. Wilson Stadium shone against the evening sky, the newly remodeled scoreboard reflecting the final score of a hard-fought football game: Oakwood High Eagles—37, Westland Warriors—36. A late October mist crept in from the surrounding open fields, covering the field turf in an almost ethereal glow. The empty bleachers on both sides of the field were littered with streamers, paper cups, and popcorn boxes—typical of another boisterous Friday night crowd. The cleanup crew would take three hours, if not more, to return the stands to their usual pristine condition.

At the south end of the stadium stood Baker Fieldhouse, named in honor of famed Eagles halfback Quincy Baker. He had graduated from Oakwood High School in 1936 and led the state in rushing yards, as well as total touchdowns, two years in a row. He went on to be an all-American in college, then was drafted in the Marine Corps during World War II.

After the war, he was posthumously awarded the Medal of Freedom for his bravery at the battle of Bastogne. To say he was the most celebrated alum in the city of Blackburn was an understatement. To this day, his relatives lived off Quincy's fame, using it to curry favor with local restaurants and car dealerships.

The crowd that gathered outside the Eagles locker room brought their fervor, as each player leaving the building was greeted with spirited cheers and congratulations. After all, winning the conference title and advancing to the high school playoffs was certainly cause for celebration, especially when the victory came at the expense of the Eagles' primary rival in the last game of the regular season.

A horde of students, faculty, alumni, and parents had formed outside the locker room. As the players walked through the waiting crowd, they chanted the names of each player, sharing celebratory high fives with each other as they passed. Parents and girlfriends waited patiently toward the end of the line to give their congratulations once the player had made their way through the mass of revelry.

Standing among the crowd was Stacy Kent, a senior cheerleader. Wearing a pair of thick, black sweatpants and a red letterman jacket, she shifted nervously, waiting to see her boyfriend, Tucker Hamilton, emerge from the locker room.

A beautiful blond, blue-eyed girl, she'd made the squad partly because of her looks but mostly because of her determination to be the best at her chosen sport. She took cheerleading seriously enough to be considered for competition teams and had been offered spots from various teams around the state. She graciously declined each offer, opting instead to focus all her attention on the opportunity to attend UCLA after graduation.

When she learned that Tucker had been granted a full scholarship to her school of choice, she chose to follow him there. Her cheerleading coach was a former Bruins cheerleader who told Stacy she would put in a recommendation for her to join the squad.

Standing nearby was her mother, Tori Butler. One look at her and it was obvious where Stacy got her looks. Clad in a pair of designer leggings, a pair of black designer boots reaching midcalf, and a black leather jacket, she made every effort at looking young enough to pass for being a student.

As a newly divorced woman, she reveled in the attention she received from men in general, but specifically from the young, virile male students at the school. To say she pushed the limits of decorum when it came to meeting Stacy's friends was an understatement.

Stacy would have chosen to wait alone in this phalanx of raucousness, but she promised her mom they would be together for at least one game. The longer they stood together, the more Stacy regretted her decision.

"When is Tucker coming out?" Tori asked, her tone exposing her displeasure.

She reached in her small purse and pulled out her compact mirror, opened it, and began primping her long, dark hair. Stacy sighed, not turning to look at her.

"I don't know, Mom. He'll be here whenever, okay? I told you, you didn't have to wait with me."

"I don't mind, honey," Tori said, putting the mirror back in her purse. "It's just getting late, and I told Rick I'd meet him at the bar after the game. Now I'll have to call and tell him I'll be late."

Stacy sighed heavily, closing her eyes. She turned to look at her mom.

"I told you we'd be here for a little while. You chose to wait with me, so please stop complaining."

"You don't need to talk to me like that, young lady," Tori said, placing her hand on her hip. "I don't appreciate that tone of voice."

Stacy shook her head and closed her eyes, turning away. She prayed Tucker would appear from the locker room, and soon.

The players continued to straggle out, the crowd thinning as parents and girlfriends met each player and headed off to celebrate the victory elsewhere. Stacy grew more anxious as time passed. This wasn't like Tucker to take so long in leaving the locker room. The longer she stood, the more concerned she became something was wrong with him, especially after what happened to him on the field.

Early in the third quarter, he'd taken a pitchout and was running along the far side of the field. A Warriors linebacker angled his pursuit perfectly, squaring up to the runner and lowering his shoulders, preparing for the collision. As all football players are taught, the low man wins the leverage battle, but in this case, it led to a heart-stopping moment.

As Tucker was hit, his head snapped back sharply, his body falling nearly limp to the ground. He remained motionless for some time, as the trainers and doctors rushed across the field to attend to him. The longer he lay prone on the turf, the more it became clear to everyone this was a serious situation. Several of the players from both teams had taken a knee, some with heads bowed, seeming to be in prayer.

The Warriors linebacker who delivered the blow was in obvious distress, standing at a close, but safe, distance from Tucker, hands on hips, watching intently as the scene unfolded. More than one of his teammates could be seen leaning in close to him, offering words of encouragement and providing a reassuring slap on the back. Several of the Eagles players approached him as well, a clear sign there would be no ill will between the combatants for the remainder of the game.

After a short time, the trainers were able to roll Tucker to his back and raise him off the turf to a seated position. He stayed this way for several more minutes, the doctors and trainers continuing to ask questions and probe his body for any tangible injuries. Several long minutes passed before he was helped up off the field to a standing position. The trainers placed Tuckers arms around their shoulders and helped guide him slowly toward the sideline.

In an act of sportsmanship, the Warriors linebacker who delivered he hit, trotted over. He spent a few minutes talking to Tucker, who nodded his head. After a brief conversation, the Warriors player gently tapped Tucker on the helmet and headed back to the huddle.

As he hobbled off the field, everyone in attendance rose to their feet and cheered. Tucker gave a slight wave of his hand to the crowd, acknowledging their support. The trainers guided him to the bench, where they helped him gently sit down. He spent the remainder of the third quarter seated, as the doctors continued their examination, almost assuredly checking for any possible serious concussion signs.

As the doctors and trainers were conducting their exam, Stacy remained motionless, hands clasped together close to her mouth, her gaze never wavering from Tucker. More than one of her teammates came over and offered a hug of comfort and reassurance.

Early in the fourth quarter, Tucker reached for his helmet on the bench beside him, put it on, and stood. He made his way to the edge of the sidelines, standing next to Coach Dyer, indicating he was ready to go back in the game. Once Tucker stood and made his way off the bench, Stacy let out a heavy sigh and clapped her hands, a look of concern never leaving her face.

The rest of the game was a blur, as Stacy robotically went through the motions of the cheers with the rest of the squad. When she wasn't cheering, her focus was on Tucker. She felt like she didn't breathe until the game was over and she saw him jog off the field with the team.

Now her nerves were still evident as she waited at the end of the line, absentmindedly biting her fingernails, her feet shifting constantly. Finally, she caught a glimpse of him coming out of the locker room, but walking slower than normal.

His brown hair was still wet from showering, his Eagles Football sweatshirt hiding his well-proportioned physique. The remaining crowd let go a loud cheer as the star halfback appeared. Several alums gave him a pat on his back, while more than one parent pumped their fists in joy as he passed. A few of his close friends exchanged hand slaps with him. He managed a weak smile, acknowledging the praise, but it was clear from the way he walked, this game had taken a toll on him.

He looked up and caught sight of Stacy, a wry smile coming to his face, a twinkle lighting up his brown eyes. He hurried his pace now, giving just a passing acknowledgment to the accolades being heaped upon him. After a few minutes, he stepped to where Stacy was, pulling her close to him as he did. In return, she threw her arms around his neck and began to cry.

"I love you," she whispered, the words almost lost in the noise around them.

Tucker kissed the top of her head and leaned down close to her ear.

"I love you too," he whispered.

The two took a step back from each other, still holding hands and smiling. Tori cleared her throat loudly, shaking the pair out of their wonderland. Stacy turned to look at her as she put her arm around Tucker's waist.

"Sorry, Mom. I just needed a second," she giggled.

Just then, Coach Dyer appeared from the locker room and spied Tucker. Hurriedly, he pushed his way through the humanity and made his way to where Tucker and Stacy were.

"Tucker!" Dyer shouted. "Tucker!"

He continued pushing his way past the students and parents, all excitedly milling around the Fieldhouse exit. Tucker heard his name and turned, just in time to see Dyer stepping near them.

He had a smile affixed to his round, chubby face, complimenting his slightly rotund body. Though only thirty-three, he'd been in coaching for nearly ten years at some level, be it peewee leagues or working as a coordinator at other high schools around the state. He'd landed the head coaching job at Oakwood a little more than three years ago and taken the program from also-ran status to the heights of making the playoffs.

Tucker's smile got wider as Dyer stepped in and hugged his star running back.

"Son, you put on a hell of a show tonight," he said, wrapping Tucker in a tight bear hug.

The two held each other this way for a few moments as they slapped each other's backs repeatedly.

"Thanks, Coach," Tucker said.

He stepped a few paces away from Dyer, the smile never leaving his face.

"Listen, you need to get home and get some rest tonight, okay? I know you fooled the doctors so they could clear you from a concussion, but I've been around long enough to know the symptoms. You've got 'em now," Dyer said.

"Coach, I feel fine."

"It's false hope, Tucker. Trust me. I know you wanna go celebrate with your girlfriend," he said, pointing at Stacy, "but you need to get home, get yourself in a dark room, and lie down. Don't go partying or anything, you hear me? I need you for the playoff run, and I need you at your best, understand? We've got the team to win state, but that means we gotta get healthy. So get home and get some rest. You can take practices off this week."

"I understand, Coach, but what about film work? Do we know who our opponent is yet?"

Dyer got a serious look on his face, his hand rubbing his chin rapidly.

"Mmhm. Westview."

"Are you serious? Westview?" Tucker said, his eyes growing wide.

The Westview Cougars were one of the most dominate teams in the state. They'd won multiple state championships and feared no one. They'd gained a reputation as being arrogant, but when a program attained the level of success this school had, it could afford to be cocky.

"Yeah," Dyer nodded. "So now you know why I need you at your best."

"Okay, I get it, Coach. I'll be ready to go Monday."

Dyer's eyes got narrow. "Did you hear me? I said, you're gonna have practices off this week."

"But, Coach, I need to get practice reps. I need to stay in game shape," Tucker said, pleading his case.

"Son, listen to me," Dyer said, leaning in close and lowering his voice. "I don't say this to just anybody, but you've got talent I haven't seen in a long time, understand? I can't explain what it is, but you've got what it takes to make it at UCLA. Hell, maybe even the NFL. I'm not blowing smoke up your ass, son. It's the truth. We don't need you during practice. We'll let Adams take your reps this week. I still want you in the film room as much as you can. But I don't need you exerting yourself. You take the week off, watch tape when you can, and be ready to go next Saturday. Got it?" Dyer's smile was as wide as ever now, and he gave a wink as he spoke.

Tucker looked down at the ground, his head still woozy from the effect of the blow he took earlier. He raised his head and looked into Dyer's eyes, nodding.

"Okay. I'll take it easy this week, Coach. I trust you."

Dyer was beaming. "Great," Dyer said, grabbing Tucker one more time and slapping his back as they embraced. "All right, you need to get home and get some rest."

He turned to look at Stacy. "Young lady, just make sure you take good care of this man the rest of the week. We're gonna need him."

"Yes, sir," Stacy said, giving a smile and a quick salute.

"You kids have a nice night," Dyer said as he turned and walked back to the locker room.

Tucker watched as Dyer became lost in the crowd, then turned to Stacy.

"Well, you heard Coach. I need to get home," Tucker shrugged.

"Well then, let's get you home," Stacy giggled, then turned to Tori. "Um, I'm glad you were here."

"Why wouldn't I be here?" Tori said indignant.

"Do I need to go over your history, Mom?"

"No."

"Okay then. Tucker and I are gonna go, okay?" Stacy said, looking first at Tori, then to Tucker.

Tori looked at Tucker, a devilish smile crossing her lips.

"Well, dear, that's fine. I need to go too. Rick's waiting for me at the bar."

She extended her arm out to Tucker and stepped in to embrace him. He, in turn, wrapped an arm around her shoulders.

"Congratulations, Tucker. You were magnificent," she whispered, a hint of seduction coming through her tone.

"Thank you," he said, suddenly feeling the awkwardness between them.

After a few moments, he loosened his grip, but Tori seemed intent on extending the hug. He furrowed his brow, and his eyes began darting around, looking for a way to escape. It was obvious she didn't want to let him go.

"Mom!" Stacy said, nearly shouting and slapping her arm.

Just then, Kim, one of her teammates, ran up to Stacy. The two girls locked in a warm embrace and began chattering on about the game and what they were doing later, among other topics.

Pretending not to know what she was doing, Tori let go of Tucker and stepped back from him.

"Oh. I'm sorry, dear. I didn't realize we were hugging that long," she said, her hand drifting slowly up and down Tucker's arm. "You didn't mind that, did you?"

She gave a quick wink as Tucker stepped further away from Tori.

"Uh, no. No, I didn't. It's okay, Ms. Butler," he said sheepishly.

She stepped in close to him again, a beguiling look in her eyes.

"You know, I need some help around the house in my home gym. Maybe you could come by and show me how you train for football. I'd like that."

Tucker could feel himself becoming both weak in the knees at the thought of what Tori was proposing and a little repulsed that his girlfriend's mom was coming on to him.

"Uh, I don't know. It depends on when Stacy would be home."

"We don't need her. We could do this together, just you and me. I know I'd really enjoy it."

If it wasn't clear what Tori wanted, this last statement made it glaringly obvious. Tucker reached over to Stacy, still engaged in conversation with Kim, and shook her arm.

"Hey! We need to go. Come on," he said.

Stacy looked quickly at Tucker.

"Oh yeah," she said, turning back to Kim. "We're gonna go. Call me later, okay?"

"Okay. Love you. Bye," Kim said, bounding off to find another friend.

Stacy turned to look at her mom. "Okay, well, Tucker and I are gonna go. Did you say you're meeting Rick at the bar?"

Tori blinked rapidly, shifting her thoughts from Tucker to her for-the-moment boyfriend.

"What?" she said, composing herself, straightening her coat, and primping her hair. "Yes. We're supposed to meet at Louie's. It's close to the mall. What are you two doing?"

"Well," Stacy said, looking at Tucker, "you need to get home, right? Isn't that what coach said?"

"Yeah," Tucker nodded.

"Then I'm gonna make sure he gets home. I'll be home later, okay?" Stacy said.

"Fine, dear," Tori said, moving to hug Stacy. "Just be careful."

She gently wrapped her arm around Stacy and gave a quick hug. She stepped back and looked at Tucker, the lustful gleam in her eye coming to the fore.

"And you," she said, moving to embrace him again, leaning in close to his ear as she did, "you remember I want to see you for a private session in my gym. Got it?" She patted his shoulder and stepped back. "Okay. I'll see you both later. Be careful. Love you."

She put a hand to her lips and gave an air kiss as she turned and walked away. Stacy and Tucker stood with their arms around each other and watched as Tori disappeared in the crowd.

"Your mom scares me," Tucker said.

Stacy looked up at him. "Why do you say that?"

"Because," he answered, shaking his head, "she comes on to me every time I see her. I swear, she's a cougar in every sense of the word. I'm afraid to be alone with her."

"Yeah," she sighed. "It's embarrassing that she's my mom. I hate it when she tries to act like she's still in high school."

"Just don't let me be alone with her, okay?"

She moved to face Tucker and put her arms around his neck as she did.

"So did you wanna go home, or maybe we could… I don't know. Go someplace else?"

She turned on her brightest come-hither smile for him and gave a lustful sigh as she spoke. A sheepish grin crossed his face.

"I like the sound of that."

"Yeah, me too. I mean, if you're okay," she said, brushing her fingers across his forehead. "I don't want you to get sick on me or anything."

He closed his eyes and exhaled heavily. "No. I should be fine."

She leaned up and pressed her lips to his, an exhilarating bolt of electricity shooting through their bodies as they became locked in a passionate moment known only to lovers. She leaned back from him after a moment or two longer.

"Okay. Let's go."

"Right," he answered.

She moved beside him, clasping her hand in his, their fingers intertwined tightly, as they began to walk slowly to his car. The shouting from the thinning crowd hadn't subsided, and there was a sense this party would last well into the night, if not until the break of dawn. It was clear this victory meant a lot to the students at

Oakwood High, and the entire student body wanted to make sure the world knew it.

Stacy and Tucker were breathing heavily in the back seat of his 2012 four-door sedan, the windows fogged over, the sweat from their bodies dripping onto the cushions. Tucker caught a glimpse of a stain on the seat and suddenly became aware he needed to find a shop to detail his car. He found it odd he would realize this in such a passionate moment.

They had driven to Melrose Park, their usual make-out spot, and found a dark corner of the parking lot far removed from the single light pole near the entrance. Though this was the only light, it was able to illuminate most of the parking area. The only dark corner of the lot was now occupied by Tucker's car.

Stacy lay on her back, her breathing coming in short, quick bursts. Her eyes were closed, and it was obvious she was allowing every ounce of ecstasy to course through her body. She made no effort to move, lying motionless, completely overcome with joy.

Tucker had managed to wiggle his way to sitting upright in the back seat, wiping his eyes from the sweat dripping off his forehead. He pulled the blanket closer to his waist and looked over at Stacy.

"You okay, babe?" he asked.

"Yes," she said in a whisper. "Are you?"

"Uh huh."

"That was amazing," she giggled.

"Yeah, it was."

"Why haven't we ever done this before?"

"I don't know," he shrugged. "We just didn't."

"Well, I regret that. We'll have to do it again. Soon," she said, giggling again.

He leaned his head back on the rear headrest.

"Yeah. Sometime in the future," he said wistfully.

Her ears perked up, and she gave him a curious look. She cleared her throat and looked up at him.

"Do you ever wonder about our future?"

"What do you mean?"

"I mean, our future. You and me, together. Do you ever think about that?"

He sighed, reached for his sweatshirt, and picked it up off the floor of the car. "Yeah, sometimes," he said, pulling his sweatshirt over his head and slipping his arms through the sleeves.

He reached down again, grabbed Stacy's bra, and handed it to her. She took if from him and held it in her hand.

"What do you think about it?"

She shifted herself to a semisitting position and began putting on her bra, straightening it as best she could. Tucker fumbled with his pants, managing to get one foot in the pant leg, before stopping.

"What should I think about? Why don't you tell me what our future looks like," he pushed his other leg inside the opposite pant leg and was able to pull his pants to his waist.

"Well," she started, "I see us with two little kids, one boy, one girl. I see a nice yard where we can have a picnic with our kids, or with just you and me. I see a dog running around in the yard, licking our kids' faces and making them laugh."

He was busying himself with putting on his shoes at this point and stopped.

"You seriously think about all that?" he said, sounding surprised.

"Uh huh," she said. "I see a nice backyard with a firepit, maybe a patio where we can cook s'mores."

He shook his head.

"You've got it all figured out, don't you? You think about this way too much."

"Of course, I do. Don't you?"

"No. I tend to think more like, I hope our kids won't be criminals or homeless or somethin' like that."

"Well, that's important too. But there's so much more."

"Like what?"

"Like vacations," she said. "I've always wanted to see the Grand Canyon, go to Vegas, maybe go to Florida. I'd love to see the expressions on our kids' faces when they see the ocean for the first time."

"You're sounding crazy."

"Hey," she said somberly, "I have a question to ask."

He sighed, his hand rubbing his forehead. "What?"

She inhaled deeply, summoning as much strength as she could to ask the question. She exhaled slowly before she spoke.

"What would you say if I got pregnant?"

The question hung like a weight in the air, dampening any shred of bliss they just experienced. Neither of them were prepared to offer a solution, only possibilities. Tucker rubbed his eyes, feeling himself become warm. He shivered ever so slightly from the chill in the car.

"I don't know. Probably take you to get an abortion."

"Why?"

Tucker slapped his hand on his leg. "Stacy, you and I aren't ready to have kids. We can barely take care of ourselves. What makes you think we can take care of somebody else? Besides, why would I want to bring a kid into this sick world, huh?"

"Yeah, Tucker, it might be sick, but there's a lot of good too."

"You mean like your parents' divorce?" he said, his voice edging close to anger.

"You know that was my mom's fault. My dad is a good man, sort of. He didn't deserve what happened."

"How do I know you wouldn't do that to me?"

"What?" she said, incredulous.

"You told me your mom screws around all the time, how she's never home. According to you, it's a miracle she came tonight."

Stacy balled up her fist and slammed it into Tucker's shoulder. He winced, rubbing the spot where she hit him.

"I would never do that to you! How dare you say that about me."

"Look," he sighed, "I need to get home. I don't need to sit here and answer questions about you being pregnant."

"But what would happen if I do get pregnant?"

"Like I said, you have an abortion. I don't want to be a father, and you couldn't be a mother on your own."

She took a deep breath, closing her eyes. It required every ounce of self-control to not be angry at what she just heard.

"Why don't you think I could handle a baby on my own? Am I stupid or something?"

Tucker rubbed his temples, feeling his pulse getting stronger.

"No, I didn't say that. I mean..." he paused, trying to rid himself of this burst of pain he was feeling. "I mean, you're the kind of girl who needs a husband. I'm certainly not husband material."

"Yes, you are, Tucker. You're everything I've ever wanted. I love you, and I want to spend the rest of my life with you."

Tucker closed his eyes, exhaling loudly. "I... I just don't think I could handle being a father when I've got a scholarship waiting for me to play at UCLA. All I need to do from there is impress the scouts just enough to get to the NFL. I don't need the hassle of a kid."

Stacy felt a tear forming in her eye, but she wiped it away. She stared at the ceiling of the car, her eyes darting around looking for something to focus on and help make sense to her.

"Well, now's a good time to tell me, right after sex."

He turned to look at her. "I'm sorry to say this, but I don't need to deal with a kid right now, okay? Maybe that could wait."

"You're saying maybe you'd want to have kids someday?"

He chuckled. "Yeah. Maybe."

His voice sounded thick, as he took his fingers to rub his temples vigorously, trying to rid himself of what felt like the onset of a severe headache. She looked at him intently.

"Are you okay, Tucker? For real?"

He suddenly felt himself getting warmer, his face becoming flush.

"Yeah. I think so."

He closed his eyes, his body shivering in earnest now, and buried his face in his hand. He stayed like this for several minutes. She pulled herself upright, pushing the blanket away from her body, leaned over, and kissed Tucker's cheek, her lips lingering for several minutes. She put her hand around his head and pulled him close to her. She gently ran her fingers through his hair.

"I love you," she whispered.

He slowly turned his head to hers and kissed her forehead.

"I love you too."

He shuddered in the chill of the cool October air permeating the car. She moved back from him, resting her back against the car door.

"Are you sure you're okay?"

He kept his eyes closed, his head turning slowly, as if he were trying to clear his mind.

"Yeah. I just feel a little woozy, that's all," he said, his words labored and drawn out.

"You're not acting like you're okay. I saw the hit you took in the game tonight, and I was worried about you. I didn't want to make anything worse for you by coming here."

"The trainers said I was okay. They wouldn't have let me play in the fourth if I weren't ready."

"But Coach Dyer said something about a concussion. Is that what you're feeling now?" she asked, curious.

He smiled weakly. "No, I'm okay. I just need some water."

"Don't you have some in the trunk?"

"Oh yeah," he said, trying, and failing, to snap his fingers "I do. Let me get dressed, and I'll get some. Where are my clothes?"

He fumbled around the back seat, searching for his sweatshirt first. He reached up and turned on the overhead light in the car and started searching for his sweatshirt again. Stacy was silent as he fumbled around, uncertain what he was thinking.

"Okay, where are my shoes?"

His words came out thick and slurred. Stacy gave him a curious look.

"You're wearing them. Are you sure you're okay, Tucker? You sounded funny just now."

"Huh?" he said, looking at Stacy through half-open eyes. "What are you talking about?"

Again, his words sounded heavy, only this time they were nearly indecipherable. She noticed his head began rolling back, falling on the rear seat headrest. His breathing suddenly became labored and heavy.

"Tucker! TUCKER!" she shouted. "You're scaring me. Tucker! What's wrong?"

She began to shake him, trying in vain to get a response from him. His breathing came in short, quick bursts, his body seeming to convulse.

"Tucker! Tucker!" she screamed. "What's wrong? Talk to me, Tucker!"

She felt herself careening over the edge of terror, her voice panicked and shrill. His body suddenly heaved, his breathing shallow and labored the longer he sat, until finally, a low gurgle emanated from his throat. His arms went limp, and his head rolled slightly to the left, turning away from Stacy.

She frantically searched for her phone, fumbling to pull it out of her pants pocket. Her fingers didn't seem to obey her mind in trying to swipe her phone on and dial 911. She managed to find a moment of calm during the horror welling in her mind and pressed the numbers on her phone. She pulled the phone to her ear and waited.

The parking lot and surrounding woods were awash in red and blue lights, flashing from the emergency vehicles filling the lot. EMTs and police officers milled around the area, engaged in conversation, and taking inventory of the contents of Tucker's car.

She stood alone near the ambulance, arms folded across her chest, pulling the letterman jacket tighter against her body. Her eyes were red and swollen from crying. The buzz of activity around her seemed almost dreamlike, as each of the first responders appeared to move in slow motion from their fire trucks to the car and back again.

Tucker's body had been placed on a gurney near his car, a white sheet pulled up tightly above his head, covering his face. She found herself transfixed by the sight of her boyfriend's lifeless form, regardless of how desperately she wanted to avert her eyes.

A police officer touched her shoulder.

"Stacy?" he said, his voice somber.

She jumped in fright, closing her eyes and turning away from the officer. She took a few moments to compose herself before turning back to look at him.

"What?" she said, the fear evident in her voice.

"My name is Officer Thornton. I'm sorry to scare you, but I'd like to ask you a few questions," he said. "Can I do that?"

"Yes," she said, almost in a whisper.

"What were you two doing out here tonight?"

She shifted her body nervously, looking down at the ground. She shook her head. "I'd rather not say."

"Listen, I know this is hard to do, especially right now. But I need to find out what happened. You're not in any trouble, okay? I just need to know what you were doing here. That's all."

She sighed, bringing her hand to her eyes and rubbing them.

"We...we came here to have sex."

"Uh huh. Did he seem like he was sick to you?"

"Not at first.

"What do you mean, at first?"

She wiped her forehead then began chewing her fingernails.

"I mean, when we started having sex, he was fine. He didn't seem like he was sick or anything. I mean, he took a really hard hit in the game tonight, but I didn't think anything about it."

"He played for Oakwood?"

"Yes," she nodded.

"You said he took a hard hit tonight. What happened with that?"

"What do you mean?" she asked.

"I mean, how hard was the hit?"

"Hard enough to take him out of the game. He came back and played in the fourth quarter though."

"Okay, well, we'll have to interview the trainers and doctor at the school and see what they say. Now, what did he seem like before he, uh, died?"

The question was direct, almost cold. Thornton's body language belied the pain he felt in asking someone as young as she was such a horrific question though. Tears began flowing down her cheeks again, and she sniffled loudly as she tried to form coherent words.

"I... I don't remember."

Thornton reached out and placed a comforting hand on her shoulder, giving a slight squeeze.

"Listen, I understand how hard this is for you, and you're doing great. Like I said, you're not in trouble, okay? I just need to ask a few questions to understand what happened."

Stacy nodded. He peered at her intently.

"Did someone call your parents? Do you need a ride home?"

"My mom is on her way. I interrupted her date, so she wasn't happy about that," she said.

"Well, I'd hope she understands if her daughter's in trouble. I would think she'd want to get to you as fast as possible."

She looked up at Thornton. "You haven't met my mother."

She turned back and fixed her eyes on the gurney where Tucker's body lay.

An EMT had moved to where Tucker's head was and placed his hands on the gurney. He was engaged in conversation with several other EMTs. Slowly, he began pushing the gurney toward the ambulance.

Stacy felt her knees become weak, her stomach convulsing in fear and rage. She felt a scream work its way from the pit of her soul, into her heart, and finally finding release in her throat.

Thornton reached out and wrapped his arms around Stacy, pulling her into his body in a bear hug, as she struggled to move toward the gurney. She needed to touch his body, kiss his lips, and see his face one more time.

But it was too late. The EMTs loaded the gurney into the back of the ambulance, shoved it inside, and closed the doors. One of the EMTs started toward Stacy, a mournful look in his eyes as he approached. He paused in front of her, reaching out and placing a comforting hand on her shoulder.

"Ma'am, I know this is the hardest thing you've ever had to deal with in your life. My nephew is on the team and always talks about what a good man Tucker was. He was always helping the younger guys, teaching them, and making sure they did the right thing. You've got a lot to be proud of in saying he was such an important part of your life. I'm deeply sorry, but I wanted to tell you what my nephew thought of Tucker," he said, leaning in and wrapping Stacy in a warm hug. "I'm very sorry, ma'am."

He kissed the top of her head, then moved on to the passenger side of the ambulance and got inside.

Stacy watched as the ambulance crept its way past the line of police cars and the single fire truck, heading to the road leading out of Melrose Park.

There was no siren, no flashing lights as there would be under normal circumstances. Instead, the dull thud of the engine punctuated the grip of anguish locked inside her heart.

As she watched the ambulance exit the parking lot, she caught sight of her mother's sports car pulling in. She closed her eyes, her insides trembling at what she expected would be a harsh tongue-lashing from her mom.

Thornton let go of her shoulders and stood beside her. He looked down at her carefully.

"Would you like me to stay here with you for now?"

Stacy shot him a quick glance and nodded. "I'd like that."

Tori stopped her car approximately five feet from where Stacy and Thornton stood. The driver door opened, and Tori got out, a mixture of anger and sadness on her face. She walked toward Stacy her arms open.

"Honey, I'm so sorry," Tori said.

She embraced Stacy warmly, pulling her into her body and resting her cheek on Stacy's head.

"I'm so sorry," she repeated, gently stroking Stacy's hair.

"I'm sorry I ruined your date with Rick."

"It's okay. I took him home and told him he needed to sleep it off. I don't need to deal with a drunken jackass like him right now."

"Okay."

Tori kept her hands firmly on Stacy's shoulders, but then she stepped a few paces away from her.

"What were you two doing here anyway? I thought you said you were going to take Tucker home."

Stacy looked down at the ground, a sheepish expression on her face.

"Uh, ma'am," Thornton stepped in, "if I may. Your daughter told me they were out here walking the trail along the ravine when it happened. Apparently, the young man was injured in the game tonight. We won't know if that had anything to do with his death until we interview the doctors and trainers at the school. Once an autopsy is done, we'll know the cause of death for sure."

Stacy looked up and over at Thornton, a slight smile crossing her lips. She mouthed the words, "Thank you," as her smile grew wider. Thornton gave a slight nod and winked.

"Oh well, if that's all it was, then that's okay," Tori said, turning to Thornton, extending her hand. "I want to thank you for helping my daughter tonight, Officer..."

"Thornton," he said. "Kelvin Thornton."

"Well, Officer Thornton, if I ever need someone to pat me down properly, I'll be sure to call you."

She flashed her best seductive smile and winked as she held his hand a little too long for his liking.

He withdrew his hand, forcefully, and smiled. "I'm glad your daughter's all right. She's been through a rather traumatic experience, and she's gonna need help to recover. I hope you realize that."

Tori blinked her eyes rapidly, her head recoiling slightly.

"Oh. Yes, yes, of course I'll get her the help she needs. I've got a great therapist she can go to. I'll set up an appointment as soon as I can."

"Good to know," Thornton nodded. "Well, listen, you're free to go. We just have some cleaning up to do here, so you don't need to stick around, okay?"

Stacy removed herself from her mother's arms and walked slowly to Officer Thornton. She wrapped her arms around him and squeezed. He returned the favor, though with slightly less force.

"Thank you," she said.

The next several days seemed to meld together in a morass of emptiness and pain. Though she had the option to take time off from school, she chose to attend. She took pride in her perfect attendance and planned on keeping intact her streak of not missing a day since kindergarten.

Her friends and fellow cheerleaders were all supportive, offering hugs at every opportunity, sitting with her at lunch and walking with her between classes. Stacy found great comfort in this and, more than once, had friends stay at her house to help work through the nightmares she was having.

She'd started therapy almost immediately and was told the night terrors wouldn't last for long. At least she hoped not. As a precaution, she'd been prescribed medication to help offset the terror. Sadly, the positive side effects of the medication seemed to be sporadic in nature.

Since the team made the playoffs, that meant extra practices not only for them but the cheerleading squad as well. The girls would gather in the auxiliary gym every afternoon between three and four and rehearse their routines until they all could be performed from rote memorization. Stacy found this daily routine becoming a great comfort, and it helped alleviate the pangs of guilt lurking in the shadows of her heart.

Stacy kept in touch with Officer Thornton, answering any additional questions he had about what happened the night Tucker died. He soon became a source of understanding and comfort during this time, and she opened herself up to him frequently about her guilt over witnessing his death. At one time, she blamed herself for causing this tragedy by asking him to have sex. Thornton did his best to work through this pain with her. He was a reliable resource, bolstering the weekly therapy she started.

In turn, he kept her apprised of the ongoing investigation into Tucker's death. The interview with the doctors and medical staff at Oakwood resulted in the same conclusion. The autopsy revealed an undetected blood clot formed in his brain, caused by the blunt force trauma of the hit. The determination was, the clot moved faster than expected, causing Tucker to have a fatal stroke.

At the time, the hit was treated as nothing more than a regular football play. After all, the doctors on the sideline were entrusted with the safety of all players and rapidly performed the mandated testing to ensure nothing further was medically wrong. It was with a heavy heart that all parties involved agreed it was simply a series of unfortunate events that led to this tragedy.

"Stacy, honey? Are you ready to go?" Tori called out from the kitchen of their two-bedroom condo.

Built in the '90s, it had begun to show its age, as some of the moldings and baseboards were cracking. Tori hired a maid to come in once a week to make sure the dust didn't become a problem and keep the house looking meticulously clean. However, based on the frequency Tori found herself staying out, it didn't require much upkeep. More than once, Stacy gave the maid a day off, with pay, and cleaned the condo herself.

"Yeah, I'm almost done," she said from the bathroom.

Straightening her black dress to smooth out any wrinkle, she looked carefully at the makeup on her face. In her estimation, the mascara would disappear from the expected tears that were sure to come during the funeral. Tori walked up the stairs from the kitchen and down the hall, stopping just outside the bathroom.

"Oh, honey," she said, stepping behind Stacy, "you look beautiful."

She reached out, placing her hands on Stacy's shoulders, and leaned down to kiss her cheek. For a moment, it felt like Stacy had a caring mother, one who fawned over her dress and gushed about her makeup and hair.

"Thanks," Stacy said. "I just hope I can make it through the service without crying too much."

As she spoke, she felt a tear forming in her eye. She reached up and wiped it away quickly with a makeup cloth.

"Don't worry about that, dear. Everybody cries at funerals. We'll get through this together. How about that?" Tori smiled and looked at her daughter in the mirror. "You haven't changed a bit from when you were a baby. You look so much like your mom," she said under her breath.

"What did you say?" Stacy asked, scrunching her nose.

"Oh, uh, nothing," Tori said. "I meant you look so much like me when I was a baby."

Stacy turned to face Tori. "No, you said something about 'your mom.' What did you mean by that?"

"Nothing, okay?" Tori said, her eyes darting around the room. "Just drop it. I was talking about myself when I was little."

"Whatever," Stacy said, rolling her eyes.

She reached over and flipped the light switch off and stepped out in the hall, following her mom back downstairs to the kitchen.

"Okay, do you have everything you need?" Tori said.

"Yeah. Let's go," Stacy said, following her mom to the door leading into the garage.

Tori opened the door from the kitchen to the garage, and they both walked to get in the car. Tori had already pushed the garage door opener, and the unmistakable creak and clack of the chain engine prattled about loudly in the confined space of the garage.

Both ladies now seated and buckled in the car, Tori fired up the engine, engaged it in reverse, and backed out, pushing the remote in the car to close the garage door. Safely away from the garage, Tori engaged the car in drive and steered them toward Memorial Funeral Home, over on Twelfth Avenue.

Due to the compressed football schedule and the team wanting to attend en masse, Tucker's parents, Greg and Brenda, agreed to hold the funeral the Wednesday prior to the game. Out of respect for one of their own having died, the school decided to close for the afternoon, allowing anyone from the student body to attend and pay their respects.

As they pulled in the parking lot of the funeral home, Stacy's eyes grew wide at what appeared to be most of the student body milling about outside the home. She put a hand to her mouth in shock and surprise that so many people would want to be a part of this somber occasion. She remained this way until Tori found a parking spot and pulled in, put the car in park, and shut off the engine. The two of them remained silent for a moment before getting out.

"Stacy, listen to me. This is going to be hard. Just be ready for it, okay? I'll be right by your side the entire time, so you're not alone."

She glanced back at the students just now starting to file inside.

"Looks like I'm not the only one here for you," she said, reaching over and squeezing Stacy's hand. "I'm so proud of you, honey. Let's go."

For a moment, it felt like Stacy had a genuine relationship with her mother. In that split second of Tori squeezing her hand, it was if all the memories of their arguments disappeared, relegated to the fire of forgiveness.

She smiled, wiping the tears from her eyes. "Okay," she said nodding. "I'm ready."

The two got out of the car and began walking to the funeral home entrance. As they approached, several of Stacy's friends and members of the cheer squad ran to her. The girls began throwing their arms around her in a warm embrace. It was in this moment Stacy realized she would be in tears the entire service.

After too many hugs and kisses on the cheek than she could count, Stacy finally made her way inside the home and to the front of the massive room, filled to overflowing with the student body. Already seated at the front were Greg and Brenda Hamilton. As soon as they saw Stacy, they both stood and walked to her, wrapping their arms around her, weeping with and for her.

"I'm so sorry this happened, Stacy," Brenda said, kissing the top of Stacy's head. "He loved you so much."

"Thank you, Mrs. Hamilton," Stacy said.

Brenda stepped back from Stacy.

"I want you to know, you're welcome at our house anytime. We consider you part of our family now. Don't be a stranger, okay?" she said through an encouraging smile.

Stacy wiped her eyes and sniffed loudly.

"I won't. Thank you."

She reached out and squeezed Brenda's hand then turned to sit next to her mom.

As she glanced toward the front of the room, she felt herself becoming weaker than she already was. Front and center at the head of the room lay the casket, the top closed per the request of Tucker's parents. Rumors circulated they didn't wish to inflict any more emotional trauma on Tucker's classmates. It was bad enough they collectively had to face this tragedy. His parents didn't wish to add to their misery.

Behind a small podium to the left of the casket sat the funeral director, Coach Dyer, and someone Stacy didn't recognize. Judging by the large Bible he was clutching, he must have been the pastor of the church Tucker and his family attended. At this moment, nothing mattered. She was devoid of emotion and just wanted to get through this as best she could.

After a few moments, the funeral director stood and walked slowly to the podium.

"First of all, I want to thank each of you for coming today. It's a testament to the character of this young man how much of an impact he made in his community. I'd like to introduce two people who played a prominent role in Tucker's life. His football coach and his pastor. First, Coach Dyer would like to say a few words."

He stepped away from the podium and returned to his chair. Dyer trudged slowly to the podium, a piece of paper in his hand. He leaned his hands on either side of the podium, head down, took a deep breath, and sniffled. He reached up and wiped his eyes, then forced himself to look up.

"You know, in football, we talk a lot about dealing with adversity, about dealing with pain and overcoming obstacles. We try to teach our men to be the best they can be, not only on the field, but in the classroom and in the community. My staff and I spend time with each athlete and stress the importance of doing the right thing, being the right person, of helping others when you see them struggling. And I've watched so many of my players live this out and make their communities better than before."

He paused, bringing his hand to his mouth, clearing his throat more than once. He sniffed again as he continued, "If you ask any one of Tucker's teammates, they'll tell you the same thing. He was a young man of integrity. It's a testament to who he was as a person that the entire Eagles team is here today to show their support to you, Greg and Brenda. They loved him, and I know they love you too."

He motioned his hand in their direction and gave a nod of his head. Greg and Brenda forced a smile and nodded back.

"I wanna share with you one story that tells me all I need to know about who Tucker Hamilton is as a human being."

He took a deep breath, the tears falling feely from his eyes now.

"A year ago, our last game was against Ridley High, one of the top programs in the state. Well, we got embarrassed in that game, and we lost. A lot of it was my fault. I was outcoached. But when we got in the locker room, I saw everybody's heads down, and the kids were cussing and yelling at each other. I stood there and shook my head, not knowing what to say.

"All of a sudden, Tucker stands up from his locker and yells out really loudly to get the team's attention. He spent about ten minutes, by my guess, encouraging his team, telling them to learn from that game and remember how it felt to be that embarrassed. He made every one of the returning players swear to come to camp in the summer and work harder than ever before. And then he said this: 'I promise, I won't let you down with how I play next season. Follow me, and we'll get where we want to go.'"

Dyer paused and turned away from the podium. His body shook as the tears came faster and harder now. He wiped his face and looked out into the crowd, then to each of his players.

"Men. This might be the hardest thing you'll ever have to overcome. This might be the biggest obstacle you'll ever face in your life. But let me tell you this: 'I promise, I will not let you down with how I coach this game on Saturday. I guarantee it.'"

Dyer pounded the podium for emphasis and raised his fist in the air.

"This game is for Tucker. Let's go get this victory for him!"

This brought cheers from the players as well as several of the other guests. It was the perfect antidote to the misery everyone in the room was dealing with.

Dyer sat down, leaning his elbows on his knees and burying his face in his hand. The pastor seated next to him put his arm across Dyer's shoulders and gave a few pats on his back. The funeral director stood once more and came to the podium.

"And now, Pastor Mathis would like to say a few words," the director said.

The director quickly made his way back to his seat as Mathis came to the podium, opening his Bible and placing it down. Mathis gave a quick smile and wink to Greg and Brenda, took a deep breath, and exhaled quickly.

"Well, I may not have anything as inspirational to say like Coach Dyer, but I'll do my best," he said.

He looked down at his Bible, leafing through it absent mindedly. He sighed and rubbed his forehead.

"You know, as a pastor, I'm charged with performing a lot of different tasks. Funerals, for instance. I've got a lot of notes and suggestions that help me formulate what I want to say. But this..."—he turned to look at the casket and shook his head—"this isn't something anyone can prepare for on the day of the funeral. I mean..."

He looked down at his Bible, almost willing it to speak to him in this moment and help him get through the service. He sighed again, his anxiety level rising. It was clear Mathis wasn't handling this moment well. He looked up at the tear-stained faces of the people gathered in the room.

"I need to be honest with you. I don't have anything prepared for this, so instead, I want to tell you something that meant a lot to me," he said, clearing his throat. "I'd like to share a memory of Tucker as well. This happened about, oh, three years ago, I think.

"He and his family were new attendees at Gracepoint Church, and I was talking with Greg and Brenda, getting to know them and their story. In the middle of our conversation, I look behind Greg, and I see Tucker playing with a couple of the younger boys from our elementary level classes. They took turns chasing each other in the lobby. They wrestled around on the floor, and Tucker treated them like they were his brothers. It was beautiful. He must've played with them for at least twenty minutes, maybe more.

"But what made that moment even more meaningful was, those two boys lost their father in Iraq. He was deployed for a year prior to his death and was about one month from coming home. Now these two boys will live without their father. Tucker showed me that if I spend time with someone, even if it's only a few minutes, it can make a difference.

"I want to challenge any of his teammates to step up and take his place. Whether it's at church, a community center, or wherever kids are, make a difference in their lives. Spend time with them. Listen to them. Encourage them. We need more of that influence in this world. Tucker lived out the axiom 'Love thy neighbor as thyself.' I would encourage all of us to do the same."

Pastor Mathis turned, wiped his eyes, and returned to his seat. Dyer reached over, slapped Mathis's back, and shook his hand. The two remained this way for several minutes as the funeral director set about giving the needlessly boring details of forming the processional to the cemetery.

Stacy sat through the service with a tissue covering her eyes, the tears flowing hard and fast. Tori put an arm around Stacy's shoulders in a show of support. Greg and Brenda never looked up from the floor, their faces red and puffy from crying. It was clear: this wasn't an isolated incident, as everyone who gathered had the same reaction at hearing the kind words Coach Dyer and Pastor Mathis spoke.

The mood would remain somber and quiet for the remainder of the afternoon and into the gathering at the Hamilton home after the graveside service. The usual fare would be consumed, and everyone would speak in hushed tones, as expected. If there was laughter, it would be short-lived and die out quickly.

Stacy was sitting on a couch in the Hamilton household, leafing through a scrapbook of memories his parents had cobbled together for this occasion. She smiled often, seeing Tucker at various stages of his life, an ever-present smile on his face. She would miss his smile, but more than that, she would miss her one true love. At this moment, it seemed no one would ever ascend to that level of trust and love again.

Chapter 2

Stacy's dreams had become more surreal and slightly tinged with fear over the last several weeks. It had been almost five weeks since Tucker's death, and she was coping as best she could. The twice-weekly therapy sessions seemed to be helping, and she was told to prepare herself for the worst of her nightmares to begin during this time.

Her dreams didn't disappoint.

On this night, deep in her subconscious, she found herself wandering in a forest, a thick fog covering most of the surrounding area, her visibility severely diminished. She wore a long silk gown, red, with a silver crown affixed to her head. As she walked, the beasts that roamed the woods would stop when they saw her, bowing as she passed by. She never acknowledged their presence but knew they understood her intent.

Up ahead, there was a clearing in the middle of the woods, a wide swath of sunshine filling the meadow occupying this space. This beauty was surrounded by the trees of the still, gray forest, forming a near-perfect circle around the meadow.

The grass of this meadow was as lush and green as she'd ever witnessed in her life, the air filtering along the pathway as fresh and brilliant as anything she'd ever experienced. As she neared the meadow, she heard the laughter of children and craned her neck, trying to see them.

She wondered what game they were playing, what delights they found in such a beautiful setting. A smile graced her mouth as she neared the clearing. She raised her arms, feeling the gentle breeze blowing from within the meadow toward her.

She paused for a moment, a strange familiarity washing over her. She recognized this place. She knew she'd been here. She couldn't remember the name of this place, but she knew her parents had taken her to this exact spot when she was a child herself. She laughed at the memory of running, jumping, and tumbling in the grass and feeling the beautiful sunshine and cool breeze cross her cheeks.

Where had she been taken when she was a child? What was this place, and why would she remember it? Was there something significant about it? What was it that drew her here, especially if she was dreaming?

She started walking again, slower, and more cautious. She wasn't sure why she would be afraid, only that she needed to see this place again. Whatever the reason, it had to be important enough for her to be here again.

She closed her eyes as she reached the edge of the forest, where the trees gave way to the meadow. She stopped, her smile wide across her face, her arms fixed close to her side. The laughter was louder now, musical in nature, the squeals and shouts bringing much-needed delight to her heart.

Slowly, she opened her eyes, the expectation of what awaited her filling her soul with joy.

Her mouth fell open, her gaze turned quizzical, and she shook her head. There were no children in the meadow. There were no games being played, no running or jumping and clapping of hands. The meadow was completely devoid of anyone having been here.

"Looking for the children, are you?" a voice said, breaking the silence.

Rather than be frightened, she turned to look at a Being standing next to her. Though it was shrouded from clear sight, she saw a bemused smirk on his face, rubbing his chin in a way that villains do in children's fairy tales. She was startled by his presence but found it most odd she wasn't scared of him.

"Yes, I was. Do you know where I can find them?" she asked, sounding more like a queen requesting an audience with a rival.

"The children aren't here. Only their memories stay behind. They're taken far away from this place, to somewhere they can never be hurt again. Somewhere the evil one can never search for them and steal them away," the Being said.

"Why is that? Why should children be taken away? It is nonsensical," she said, her face a mask of questions.

The Being sighed and closed his eyes. "Because the evil one made the choice to capture them and inflict the worst imaginable pain upon their souls. They were cast out of their shells and sent to be with him. But somewhere between being harvested and cast out, love saved them and brought them to this place of beauty."

"But why are they someplace else? Why can they not remain here?"

She marveled at how regal she sounded in her dream like state. The Being's face became grim, his eyes dark and cold.

"Because evil visits the children. Always. Even here. They are hunted like prey, treated as so much excess chattel and wheat. They are harvested when the hunters have their feast. It's more like an orgy, really, a selfish, disgusting affair, unsuitable for any right-minded person."

"Why does this happen?"

The Being closed his eyes and began to meditate, his lips moving without making a sound. After a time, he opened them and looked directly at her. "It happens when life is no longer considered precious."

He moved close to her, his eyes cutting deep into her soul. He stopped about one foot away from her and sighed.

"And I believe it's time for you to go home now."

He waved a hand over her face, causing her to gently rise from the ground. She felt herself begin to float toward what seemed like a black hole. Embracing the sensation of flying, she closed her eyes and held her arms away from her body as she drifted through the darkness.

Suddenly, her eyes shot open, a gasp escaping her lips. Her breathing came in short, quick bursts. Her heart began pounding hard against her chest, keeping perfect time with her breathing. Her mind felt thick and became more disoriented the longer she lay still. Her eyes darted across the ceiling, a vain search for...what exactly?

It was as if she were waking up in her bedroom for the first time in her life.

Confused, she quickly sat up straight in bed, clutching her blanket tightly to her chest. She brought her hand to her forehead, rubbing it across her skin, trying to rid herself of this ache in her mind.

She tried, and failed in her attempts, to make sense of her dream. What was it the Being said? Something about the children were gone or missing from the meadow. That an evil one was hunting them. Was that it?

Her breathing slowly returned to normal, and she inhaled deeply, letting out the air in her lungs just as slowly. Suddenly, a wave of nausea washed through her, and she leaped out of bed and ran to the bathroom, turning on the light as she did. Flipping up the toilet seat, she knelt in front of it and steadied herself for what she knew was coming.

Her breath came in short waves, the nausea creeping up her insides, until resistance was rendered irrelevant. Her vomiting came in loud, short bursts, her stomach tightening with each wave of spittle. It only lasted a few moments, but the fatigue it caused was relentless. She spit out the last vestige of whatever globule remained in her mouth and leaned on the toilet, eyes closed and praying she was just sick.

The vomiting had become more frequent in recent days. Though she tried to pass it off as the flu, there was a nagging feeling it could be something more. She hadn't had a period since before Tucker died, and there was a small, lingering doubt in her mind she tried to dismiss as often as possible.

Maybe she was pregnant.

She shook her head, a smile crossing her lips.

No, she thought. *We only did it once. How could I have gotten pregnant from having sex once? What are the chances of that happening?*

She managed to laugh a little at this seemingly absurd thought.

After regaining some semblance of normalcy, she reached up to the toilet handle, pulled it down to flush it, and lowered the seat cover. She moved to sit on the bathroom floor, her arm propped up on top of the toilet seat. She rubbed her eyes trying to calm her nerves, hoping she could stave off whatever nausea might come next. When, or if, it would happen, she couldn't be sure.

She needed to see a doctor. Soon.

She eased herself off the bathroom floor, stepped to the sink, and turned on the faucet. She cupped her hands under the rushing water, adjusting the faucet to achieve the perfect level of warm and cool temperatures. Finally reaching that point, she let her hands dangle, watching as the rivulets of water cascaded from her fingers. It was almost mesmerizing.

She washed her hands, scrubbing them vigorously, rinsed them off, and leaned her face closer to the sink. She rubbed water over her cheeks, her forehead, and her lips, the soothing calm a minor respite from being sick. She turned the faucet off and shook her hands a couple of times in the sink.

She reached for the towel hanging on the rack behind the toilet to dry her hands. She then held it to her face, eyes closed, lost in the sublime comfort of darkness it brought. She took a deep breath and let it go quickly, dried her face, and replaced the towel on the rack where she got it.

Just then, she heard the door to the garage slamming shut loudly.

"Dammit!" her mom shouted.

Stacy sighed, turned off the bathroom light, and walked to the stairs. She tried to remain as calm as she could but knew this conversation would be all about her father and how terrible he was. It was almost a daily routine.

Once at the bottom of the stairs, she turned to walk the short distance to the kitchen. She stopped before entering the room and saw her mom holding onto one of the table chairs, her other hand covering her face.

"What's wrong?" Stacy asked.

Tori looked up, the rage in her soul evident in her eyes.

"Your father is a no-good, lying son of a bitch, that's what. He was supposed to send money this week to add to your college fund, but instead, he's spending it on a golf trip with his office buddies this weekend."

"Mom, it's okay. We've got plenty of money in there now. He can miss a couple payments, and I'll still be okay."

"That's not the point, honey," Tori said, slamming her hand on the table. "The point is, we had an agreement. He signed paperwork saying he would pay his share each week. And he's found a way to avoid taking responsibility for his own daughter. That's why I'm so angry."

Stacy moved toward her mom, holding out her hand.

"Mom. It's no big deal, okay? I've got more than enough money to cover my first year. I'm gonna be working at the country club again next summer, and the money from that will be more than enough to cover me my freshman year. I'll be fine, Mom. You don't need to be hysterical about it."

Tori wiped a hand across her face as tears began to form in the corners of her eyes. She sniffled and looked at Stacy.

"Honey, I hear what you're saying. But you don't know your father like I do. He's a lying, cheating bastard who doesn't want to support his family. And I hate him for it."

Stacy sighed, closed her eyes, and shook her head. She felt a smile cross her mouth.

"You know, you say this all the time. You realize I spend time with him on the weekends, and we have a rather good time together. You know we talk to each other. And he never says anything bad about you, do you know that?" Her eyes pleaded with her mom to stop.

"Ha. That's just because he wants you to think he's something he's not. He wants you on his side so he can make me look bad. He's fooling you, Stacy, can't you see that?"

Stacy laughed.

"You know what, Mom? You made yourself look bad when you cheated on him, okay? Dad didn't need your help with that. That was all you."

She was surprised how angry she sounded but felt proud of herself for finding the courage to say what was on her mind.

"Don't you talk to me like that, young lady!" Tori shouted. "Don't you stand here and accuse me of this divorce being all my fault. How dare you presume to know what happened in our relationship. You don't have any idea how lonely I was, how much I wanted your father's affection, and he never showed it. You don't know what you're talking about."

"Maybe I don't, but I'm old enough to see what you do when you're around my friends."

"What's that supposed to mean?" Tori said, a look of semishock on her face.

"Oh, please. You flirted with Tucker all the time. You flirt with my other male friends all the time. You can't hide it, Mom. I've got eyes, and I see what you do when they come over. You're almost begging to get them into bed. You're practically a slut, okay?"

Tori stepped closer to Stacy, cocked her right hand back, and swung it hard through the air, hitting Stacy's left cheek with a thunderous sound. Stacy yelped in pain, grabbing at her cheek and recoiling from Tori.

"Don't you ever call me a slut again, do you hear me?" Tori said, seething with rage. "You need to show me a little respect, do you understand me? I work hard to provide a roof over your head. I'm the one paying the bills and buying the groceries. I'm the one driving your ass all over town for your little parties and get-togethers. And you have the nerve to call me a slut? How dare you! You better be grateful I don't ask you to leave this house. You'd be homeless if you ever walked out of here."

Stacy looked up at Tori, her eyes glazed over with tears.

"I hate you," she whispered.

"Get out of my sight! Now!" Tori shouted.

Stacy turned and walked hurriedly out of the kitchen, then practically ran upstairs to her bedroom. By the time she reached her bedroom door, tears were falling hard from her eyes. She slammed the door shut behind her as she fell onto her bed and sobbed.

As was her routine, she reached over and pushed Play on her phone. It was hooked up to a set of high-quality speakers. She turned up the volume, trying to become lost in the anger of the music.

It was moments like this she missed Tucker the most. He always had a way of calming her down, of helping make sense of the world around her. Without him, everything felt a little more hopeless and dark.

And she realized what Tucker meant by telling her the burden of being a single mother was too great for her to handle. If she couldn't rely on her own mother to help raise her child while she worked her way through college, who could she rely on?

She remained in this state for what seemed hours, lying on her bed, face buried in her tear-soaked pillow. And her thoughts never strayed far from wishing Tucker would call her phone so she could talk to him just one more time.

She desperately wanted to tell him his memory helped push the Eagles to the state championship. She wanted to tell him she was so heartbroken over his death that she didn't cheer in the game, instead watching it from the stands with friends. She wanted to embrace him as the team had embraced her, calling her on to the field to help lift the championship trophy. She was part of the team now and would be forever. Somehow she sensed he knew.

The sobs came more frequently now, as she felt herself consumed with pain, wishing he were here to console her and tell her everything would be okay.

"I think we missed our turn," Stacy said, peering out the windshield.

She sat in the passenger seat of her friend Tonya's two-door sedan. It was an older model, but it was in remarkable condition, as expected from a company that built quality cars.

"What was the address again?" Tonya asked.

She was a curvy, dark-haired beauty, her tan skin accentuating her round face. Her deep brown eyes were seductive and more than once caused several athletes to fall prey to their charm.

Stacy checked her phone app again. She'd mapped out the directions to the clinic and thought they followed them precisely. She swiped her phone on, punched in her password again, and waited the split second for the map to come back on her screen. She looked at the ubiquitous blue line showing her coordinates as her fingers tapped the passenger side door.

"Yep. We missed the turn back there," she said, pointing behind them. "But if you make a right turn up here at Maple, we can circle back to it."

"Okay," Tonya said, giving a quick glance behind them and into the right lane.

She flicked her turn signal on, indicating she was changing lanes. Not seeing any traffic close to her, she eased the car smoothly into the right lane and looked for Maple.

"How far is it?"

"It's a couple more streets," Stacy said, looking at the map. "It'll be like a main intersection or something."

"Okay," Tonya said. "Hey, um, do you mind if I ask you something?"

"Sure."

"Are you sure you wanna go through with this?"

"It's only an exam, Tonya. Right now, all I'm gonna do is talk to them about what I wanna do. It's not like I'm going to do something today. I told them first, I need to know what to expect if I get it done. Then I'll make the decision on what to do next."

"Yeah, but, Stace, this is huge. I mean, I've never known one of my friends who have actually done this, ya know? This is freaking me out."

"Would you calm down? It's not a big deal. Lots of girls go through this, you know that."

"Yeah, just not any of the girls I know, all right? What did you tell your mom you were doing?"

Stacy shrugged.

"I told her you and I were going shopping. She doesn't need to know."

"How did you hear about this place?"

"I looked it up online," Stacy sighed. "It said it's one of the best clinics in the city. I read up on them a little bit. It seems fairly good to me."

"Yeah, but can you just walk in there and talk about your pregnancy with them? Aren't they gonna want to do anything else today?" Tonya asked, genuinely confused.

"I don't know. But I'm not ready to do anything yet. If they ask me about it, I'll just tell them I'm thinking about it, and I'll come back if I want to get it done."

Stacy's eyes suddenly lit up.

"There's Maple," she said, pointing at the approaching street.

Tonya flicked on her turn signal and eased the car around the corner.

"Okay, where do we go from here?"

"Let's see," Stacy said, looking at her phone again. "Stay on Maple for about six blocks, and turn right on Green. Then a left on Woodward, and it'll be on the corner of Woodward and Eastview."

"Thanks," Tonya said. "Hey, I want you to know, I'm not trying to talk you out of this, okay? I just want to make sure you know what you're doing."

"I know," Stacy said, her voice low. "That's why I need to talk to someone before I decide."

"Couldn't you have gone to your regular doctor and talked to them?"

Stacy laughed.

"No way. She and my mom are best friends. They hang out at the country club all the time and flirt with all the men who come in. She'd tell my mom I was pregnant, and I don't want to have that conversation with my mom."

"Maybe, but don't you think she deserves to know?"

Stacy looked out the passenger side window, her thoughts suddenly racing back to when she and Tucker had sex.

Before it happened, she was hesitant at first, but her choice was made easier by the connectedness she felt to him. Something in her heart and mind knew, beyond a shadow of doubt, they would end up getting married and raising a family.

She'd had the conversation with her mom about sex and knew from a clinical viewpoint what to expect. It wasn't until she met Tucker that she wanted to put that knowledge into practice. She shook her head at the idea she would get pregnant the very first time she had sex.

What are the odds? she thought.

She laughed at this prospect and passed it off as bad timing. She turned to look at Tonya.

"Listen. I know I might be breaking some sort of moral code by not telling my mom, but I don't think she'd understand. Well, maybe she'd understand, but she'd never accept it. How do you think she'd act around me if she knew? She already treats me like crap now. How do you think she'd treat me if she knew?"

Tonya adopted a look of resignation on her face.

"Yeah. I guess maybe you're right. Where am I turning again?"

Stacy looked at her phone app once more.

"Green. It's up here on the right about two blocks away," she said.

She glanced up intently at the street signs, reading each name as they passed. Suddenly, she saw the street they were looking for.

"There it is," she said, pointing at the sign.

Tonya steered the car around the corner, following the precise directions Stacy provided. Within ten minutes, maybe more, they found themselves in the parking lot of the Sanger Rose Clinic.

Straddling the line between the lower- and middle-income homes of the city, the building itself took up half a block of space. The exterior of the building was well lit and clean; the only hint there might be any trouble being brought upon the building were the wrought iron rails covering the windows.

Stacy heard rumors there were sometimes throngs of protesters who lined the opposite side of the street. She heard they usually held up posters showing horrific images of aborted babies and could be quite boisterous.

But on this day, there were less than ten people milling about on the opposite sidewalk. From their appearance, the group gave the impression they would be more suited waiting in line at a coffee house for their Grande lattes than standing on a street opposite an abortion clinic.

Stacy surveyed the group of people, gauging their level of hostility. The last thing she needed was someone shoving a pamphlet into her chest or shaming her as she attempted to make her way to the front doors. She seemed to remember hearing city council passed an ordinance forbidding any protesters access to within fifty feet of the clinic. By her estimation, the people across the street were taking great liberties with interpreting what constituted fifty feet.

Tonya chuckled, pointing at the group of protesters.

"Typical religious idiots."

"Why do you say that?"

"Isn't that who they are?" Tonya said, looking at her friend. "Don't you watch the news?"

"I mean, I pay attention, but those people don't look violent to me," Stacy shrugged.

"They never do, Stace. They always show up in their nice button-down shirts and neatly pressed slacks and try to come off as these holier-than-thou freaks. But whenever someone walks in, they jump on you and shout all kinds of nasty things at you."

"You really believe that? The cliché about church people? Tucker went to church. He wasn't like that at all."

"He's the one who told you to get an abortion, wasn't he?" Tonya countered.

"Yeah, but that was only because he wanted to focus on football and not being a father. He didn't think he was ready. I think he was, but we'll never know."

"Yeah, well," Tonya laughed, "you still should get ready to be shamed while we walk inside. Don't say I didn't warn you."

"There's only one way to find out. Let's go," Stacy said.

She took a deep breath and pulled the car door handle, pushing the door out wide. Tonya had gotten out quickly and slammed her door shut, already heading to where Stacy was. She wasn't about to be separated from her friend in a potentially hostile situation.

As the girls exited the car, the slamming doors gained the attention of the small group of people across the street. Almost as one, they collectively turned their heads in the direction Tonya and Stacy were coming from. The girls tried to keep their heads down as they walked quickly to the front entrance, but they kept glancing up to see what the group of people would do.

As expected, they raised their placards, flashing horrendous pictures of post-aborted babies. Some signs had large lettering splayed across them, each a variation of the girls entering the clinic being a baby killer and going to hell because of their choice. The screams of anguish began and grew louder as the girls got closer to the front door.

No one was brave, or stupid, enough to cross the street. Despite giving a generous definition to what fifty feet meant, the protesters weren't about to jeopardize themselves by instituting a physical confrontation.

The shouting continued, even as the girls swung open the front door of the clinic and sought refuge in the small foyer. They entered another set of doors that led inside to the main lobby and away from the group of protesters. The girls walked a few paces inside and stopped.

The interior lobby was rather cozy. To the right of where they stood, leather couches adorned the front wall, an additional love seat sitting on the opposite side. A large fish tank occupied most of the space on the far wall, the low hum of the motor adding a touch of calm to the room. Directly opposite of where they stood was the receptionist desk, occupied by a distracted middle-aged woman with dark-rimmed glasses dangling on the tip of her nose. She glanced up and saw the girls frozen near the front door.

"Can I help you?" she said.

It was obvious she wasted no time in doing her job, as the tone of her voice had just the right inflection of fatigue and annoyance.

Stacy walked to the desk. "Yes, my name is Stacy Kent. I'm here to see Dr. Rose."

"Fill out this form, and have a seat. Someone will come get you when she's ready to see you," the woman said.

She produced a clipboard from seemingly nowhere, with a form attached. She clanked it against the top of the counter and never looked up from what she was doing.

"Th-thank you," Stacy said, her words halting and soft.

She took the clipboard and walked to the leather couch and sat down next to Tonya.

"What's all this?" Tonya asked, pointing to the clipboard.

Stacy glanced at the form, furrowing her brow.

"It looks like just some general information about me."

"Oh. Okay. Hey, do you want me to come back in the room with you?"

"No. I think I'll be okay."

"All right. I'll be here if you need me though," Tonya said, rubbing Stacy's arm.

She gave a smile and turned away, pulling out her phone. She busied herself with checking social media pages as Stacy set about providing the required information on the form. After a few minutes, she was done with the form and stood up, walking it back to the receptionist.

"I'm all done, ma'am," Stacy said.

The receptionist glanced up long enough to grab hold of the clipboard and pull it down onto her desk. "Have a seat. The doctor will be with you shortly," she said.

She seemed robotic in her motions and speech, causing Stacy to feel a little more than nervous. Stacy turned and walked back to the couch, sitting down next to Tonya. She pulled out her own phone, and soon, she too busied herself scrolling through her own social media pages.

After what seemed like hours, the door leading to the exam rooms opened. An attractive young nurse stood in the doorway holding a clipboard.

"Stacy?" she said. "Dr. Rose is ready to see you now."

Stacy looked up, her nerves suddenly kicking into overdrive. She glanced at Tonya, who was equally as nervous.

"You got this, Stace," Tonya said, squeezing Stacy's arm.

Stacy nodded, stood, and walked cautiously to the door. Her feet seemed encased in cement as she moved in slow motion toward the nurse. She tried to project some semblance of confidence, but it seemed to have abandoned her in this hour of need.

The nurse smiled and reached out her hand.

"Hi. My name's Beth. I'll be checking you in."

Stacy reached out and took hold of Beth's hand, more for stability than of courtesy.

"If you'll follow me, we'll be in room 12 down the hall."

Beth led the way down the sterile-looking hall, her ponytail bouncing as she walked. Her brand-new tennis shoes squeaked against the floor as they passed by several other exam rooms. She turned to look at Stacy.

"How are you today?"

"Nervous," she said.

"You know what? It's okay. Lots of girls feel the same way when they come in. Just relax though. You're in good hands," Beth said, doing her best to allay any fear Stacy may have.

She stopped outside the exam room and waved her hand toward the door. "Here we are. You can have a seat on the table."

Stacy moved to the exam table, stepping up and sitting on the paper covering the leather surface. She shifted nervously as she watched Beth move to the computer in the corner. It was attached to the wall by a movable metal arm. Beth swung the computer toward her and began typing on the keyboard.

"Okay, Stacy, I'm just gonna ask you a few questions before Dr. Rose comes in, okay?"

"Sure," Stacy responded.

"Now, do you know when your last period was?"

Stacy thought for a minute.

"Uh, maybe five, six weeks ago, I think."

"Okay. And how did you find out you were pregnant?"

"I bought a test at the pharmacy. It came back positive."

"Any morning sickness?"

"Yes," Stacy said, managing a slight chuckle. "Just this morning, in fact. I was in the bathroom vomiting."

"Okay, so you're in the very early stages of pregnancy right now, which helps determine how we want to handle this issue."

"Well, that's what I needed to know. What are my options?"

"Dr. Rose will go over those with you. Right now, I just want to get an idea where you're at with this. Once we know, that will help the doctor decide what to recommend."

"Well, I've thought about it, and I'm thinking I want an abortion," Stacy said.

She recoiled in surprise and shook her head at how casually she could verbalize what she'd been feeling for some time. The words sounded hollow, devoid of emotion.

"Well, there are several ways to handle this, and Dr. Rose will go into more detail with you. Right now, let me get your blood pressure."

Beth moved beside the exam table, took the blood pressure cuff off the wall, and attached it to Stacy's arm. The rest of the exam was almost identical to her being seen by her primary care doctor. Her temperature was taken, and her height and weight were measured. The more she went through the motions of the exam, the more she relaxed, feeling herself become somewhat calm.

"Okay, well, I've got what I need. I'll let Dr. Rose know you're here, and she'll be in to finish up with you, okay?" Beth smiled, standing at the door ready to exit.

"Okay. Thanks," Stacy said.

"Don't worry. You're gonna be okay," Beth said, giving a wink as she stepped out of the room.

Stacy looked at the now closed door and sighed. The only sound in the room was the paper on the table being displaced as she moved, trying in vain to get comfortable on the leather covering. She pulled out her phone, absentmindedly scrolling through her messages, not pausing long enough to read anyone's posts. Her mind raced at a speed she'd never encountered before, and she wasn't sure how to slow it down.

She put her phone away and closed her eyes, feeling her heart rate increase. She took a few deep breaths, exhaling slowly. She'd learned this technique through cheerleading. It was one of the exercises the squad practiced for calming their nerves before a competition. She sat up straight and felt her body regain composure the longer she concentrated on breathing.

What will it be like if I do get the abortion? she thought.

Her eyes popped open as she stared at one of the posters on the wall, asking for help in a clinical trial on pregnancy. She didn't bother reading the details as her mind began anew its acceleration in thought. She suddenly realized she'd never considered the ramifications of her having this procedure done.

What would her mom think? What would her friends say if, and when, they found out? Would a boy want to date her after knowing what she'd done? Would they accept her for who she is? Could she have a normal relationship again? Could she get pregnant again and have a family like she'd wanted to do with Tucker? Would she feel guilty after going through this?

A tear formed in her eye and started tracing a line down her cheek, inexorably making its way to her chin. She looked over to the small counter next to the exam table, saw a box of tissues there, and pulled one out. She wiped her cheek and closed her eyes again.

So many things she hadn't considered, and here she was, in a clinic to discuss the possibility of altering her life forever. The weight of her decision was too much for her, and she wished she'd asked Tonya to join her in the room. She briefly entertained the notion of texting her to come back, but the knock on the door startled her out of her thoughts.

The door opened, and an attractive, young-looking doctor stepped inside, a coy smile on her face. She carried a clipboard and a small pad of note paper in her hands.

"Hi," she said, stepping toward Stacy, shifting the clipboard and notepad to her left hand to extend her right hand. "I'm Dr. Rose."

Stacy reciprocated by shaking the doctor's hand.

"I'm Stacy."

"Stacy, it's good to meet you," Dr. Rose said, moving to sit on the portable stool resting near the computer. "How are you?"

"I'm okay, I guess," Stacy sighed.

"You guess?"

"Well, I mean, this is, like, a little scarier than I thought it would be."

"Well," Dr. Rose smiled, "I'm here to help you, okay? Hopefully, I can make this as easy as possible."

"I hope so," Stacy chuckled.

"I just have a few questions to ask, and we'll go over what options you have available to you. I'm here to help find the best solution for you, okay?"

"Okay," Stacy nodded.

"Now, I see you're a cheerleader. How exciting!"

"Yeah, it's been fun. I enjoy it."

"How long have you done that?"

"This is my third year."

"Wow. Now, do you cheer only at football games, other events, or what?"

"Yeah, we cheer at all the football games. I don't do all the basketball games. We kind of rotate girls to do those."

"Mmhm. Are those the only times you cheer?"

"No. We go to competitions around the state too. Those are really stressful," Stacy said laughing.

"Stressful, how?"

"I mean, the teams are really good. You really need to be on top of your skills when you get to that level. The tension is unreal."

"I can imagine," Dr. Rose said. "So tell me, what else do you like to do?"

"Well..." Stacy thought, "I like to go shopping. I spend a lot of time with my friends. Uh, I read, but not as much as I'd like."

"What do you like to read?"

"Mostly thriller books, some romance, but like I said, I don't read as often as I should."

"Well, Stacy, I'd like to get into what brought you here today. I know this must be exceedingly difficult to deal with, but I want to understand how you got to this point in your situation."

Dr. Rose took out a pen, clicked the end of it, and began jotting down some notes on her pad.

"Well, there's not much to tell. I mean, I'm pregnant, and I'm not sure if I can handle having a baby right now."

"Why is that?"

"I'm supposed to go to college next fall," Stacy said, fidgeting with her tee shirt. "But I'm not sure about that right now. I'm busy with school and cheerleading, so that takes a lot of my time. My mom wouldn't be much help if I had a baby. Of course, she doesn't know I'm pregnant, and I'd like to keep it that way, if possible."

"Of course," Dr. Rose said. "Why wouldn't your mother be much help?"

"Because she's always at her boyfriend's house or going out drinking," Stacy said, brushing the hair away from her eyes. "She's hardly ever home. When she is home, we usually fight all the time. I'm afraid she might freak out if she knew I was pregnant."

"Do you think she would support your decision?"

"What decision?"

"Any decision you make. You can choose to be a mother, choose adoption, or choose abortion. It's up to you."

"That's not the point. If I have a child, it's going to make things worse for everybody. It'll be a huge problem."

"And that's what I want to help you with. How to make this not be a problem for you. I want you to feel comfortable with what you choose, so you know it's the best decision for you."

"Well, right now, it seems like not having a child is the best solution," Stacy said, fidgeting with her shirt again.

"I understand. Now, do you know what to expect by going through with this procedure? Have you read any information about it?"

"It seems kinda simple, really. I mean, how hard can it be to do this?"

Dr. Rose leaned forward. "It is rather simple. I want to ask you a couple of more questions though. How far along are you?"

"About three, maybe four weeks. I think."

"Did you take a pregnancy test or go to your primary care physician?"

"I took two pregnancy tests. Both came back positive."

"And what does your boyfriend think of you being here?"

Stacy's eyes began tearing up, her body becoming tense. She could feel the swelling in her throat nearly prevent her from speaking.

"He…he died," she whispered, forcing the words out of her mouth.

She buried her face in her hands and began weeping. Dr. Rose stood, placing her clipboard down, gathered several tissues from the box near her, and walked to Stacy. She put a hand on Stacy's back, practically shoving the tissues into Stacy's hands.

"I'm so sorry. I had no idea."

"Of course you wouldn't know. I didn't tell you," Stacy said, her words tinged with sadness.

"Would he have supported your choice?"

Stacy looked up at Dr. Rose.

"He's the one who suggested I get an abortion. He said he wasn't ready to be a father, that he was only thinking about football. He got a scholarship to play for UCLA, and he wanted to focus on that. He told me he wasn't husband material, but I know better. He was the love of my life," she said, sobbing, the tears falling hard and fast down her cheeks.

"Stacy, we could hold off on talking for a few minutes if you'd like. I'm sorry to hear this. I know this is a lot to deal with for someone as young as you are. You're very brave."

Stacy looked up, wiping her eyes with the tissues and sniffling loudly.

"Thank you," she said softly.

She took a few moments to wipe her eyes and regain her composure. She practiced her deep-breathing exercise to calm herself. Within five minutes, she was back to her normal self.

"I'll be okay to talk now. I see a therapist once a week now about what happened, and that's been going well. I'm gonna keep seeing him for a few more weeks, so that's a big help."

"I'm glad to hear that," Dr. Rose said, returning to the stool.

She picked up her clipboard and began jotting on her notepad.

"So your boyfriend was the one who suggested you come here, right?"

"Yes."

"Well, Stacy, there are a couple of ways we can go about this for you. Since it's still early enough, I can either prescribe medication to induce the extraction of cells, or I can perform the procedure myself. Either way you decide, it will only cause minor discomfort for you. I want to assure you, either method you decide upon is perfectly safe."

"So how does it affect my baby?"

"Have you been to your ob-gyn?" Dr. Rose asked, her eyes narrowing.

Stacy shook her head, still sniffling from her outburst earlier.

"Well, right now, it's still too early to know what's going on inside. It's an amorphous mass of cells, hardly anything to be concerned with, really. That's why I wondered how far along you are, so that lets me know which method is the best one to treat this."

Stacy sat rigid on the exam table, head down, still wiping her nose and sniffling.

"I don't know what to do, Doctor. I mean, I read it costs a lot of money to do this. What I have in the bank, I was saving to pay for school in the fall. So I either pay for this or I pay for school."

"But, Stacy, think about this," Dr. Rose leaned on her knees as she spoke. "You're young. You're highly active and have a vibrant life outside of school. You have so much of life ahead of you to live, and that includes college. There are plenty of programs you can look at for grants and loans to help you. You have plenty of time to be a mother years from now, when you're in a more stable situation with your life. Right now, I know this is difficult for you to deal with, especially not having someone to support you. I'd like to help alleviate this for you as best I can."

Stacy rubbed her forehead, her eyes closed. She found herself wishing her father were with her right now. She'd always relied on him to help her through any tough situation she faced, even though he didn't always agree with her. Ever since her mom decided to ask the court for sole custody and restrict visitation, Stacy felt cut off from her father. Her heart begged for his advice at this moment.

"Stacy?" Dr. Rose said. "Are you all right?"

"I just need time, Doctor."

"Time for what? To think? I understand, and I want to help you, I really do. But if I could give you my input, I think you've made the right choice in coming here. I know I couldn't handle being in your situation."

"Listen, can I come back? I need to go right now and just think about what I want to do, okay?"

Dr. Rose sat back, shook her head, and sighed. She brought her hand to her eyes and massaged the bridge of her nose gently.

"I understand, Stacy. I just don't want to see you make a mistake and wait too long before you feel free of this burden. It's a lot to carry for someone as young as you."

"Please. I just need time to think about this, that's all," Stacy said resolutely.

Dr. Rose held a finger to her mouth, studying her patient. She looked down at her clipboard and jotted something on her notepad before looking back up at Stacy.

"Okay. I understand," she said standing up.

She walked slowly to the exam table and stood in front of Stacy. She reached out and put a hand on Stacy's forearm.

"Just remember. The longer you wait, the more agonizing it will be to move forward. If we do this today or tomorrow, it will last only about ten, maybe fifteen minutes. I could do this procedure and take away that concern you have over what to do about your future. You'd be free of this burden forever."

Stacy inhaled deeply, letting her breath go slowly. She was back to her breathing exercises she learned.

"I know, Doctor. I appreciate you taking time to talk to me. It really has helped a lot. But I need to make sure I do the right thing, okay? I just want to be sure it's the best decision for me."

"And that's what I want too, Stacy," Dr. Rose said smiling.

She reached inside her coat pocket and produced a business card, handing it to Stacy.

"Here's my information. Please call me as soon as you make up your mind, okay?" she gave a wink. "But don't wait too long."

"I will," Stacy said, a weak smile on her face.

"Okay then. You're free to go. Enjoy the rest of your afternoon."

Dr. Rose moved toward the door, pulled it open, and waited until Stacy had stepped off the exam table and walked into the hallway. Dr. Rose followed Stacy out of the room and extended her hand as they stood just outside.

"Thank you for coming in today."

"You're welcome. Thank you for your help," Stacy answered.

"Give me a call as soon as you can, okay?" Dr. Rose winked again as she spoke, an almost-devilish grin coming over her face.

Stacy felt a shiver go up her spine as she saw this. "Okay. Bye."

She shook Dr. Rose's hand and turned to walk to the lobby, collect Tonya, and leave.

As they left the clinic, Tonya and Stacy managed to avoid the crowd across the street, which had grown in numbers, and made it to the car relatively unscathed. They drove quietly for several blocks, neither of them sure how to ease the tension between them.

"Can I ask you something?" Tonya said, finally breaking the silence.

"What?" Stacy said in a whisper.

"What did you talk about?"

Stacy sighed, collecting her thoughts. She didn't want to regale her friend with all the details, although there weren't many to divulge.

"The doctor told me I could do one of two methods in ending my pregnancy."

"What were they?" Tonya said, glancing at her friend.

"Since I'm early in the pregnancy, I can either take some pills or I can have the procedure done."

Stacy suddenly felt uncomfortable talking about her desire for an abortion. Why she felt this sudden conflict in her heart, she couldn't explain. She simply wanted to find a way to get beyond this with as little frustration as possible.

"You can take a pill for that?" Tonya asked.

"Apparently," Stacy answered.

"So what are you gonna do?"

"It's expensive, Tonya. I could either pay for it or go to college, but I can't do both. And I can't ask my parents for the money. They'd hate me if they knew I was pregnant."

"I don't think they'd hate you, Stace. At least your dad wouldn't. Your mom, on the other hand, you just might send her over the edge if you tell her."

"Yeah well, as much as we don't get along, I couldn't do that to her."

"So what are you gonna do?"

Something in the way Tonya asked the question hit Stacy hard. Her mind filled with millions of thoughts, all fighting for supremacy. She turned to look out the passenger side window, allowing herself to become mesmerized at the buildings and houses passing outside. At least it was a distraction from the decision she had to make. The longer they drove, the heavier the weight on her heart became.

She buried her face in her hand and sighed heavily.

"I don't know, Tonya. I don't know."

Chapter 3

A week later, Stacy sat on the leather couch in Dr. Sims's office, nervously playing with a fidget spinner she'd brought from home. Sure, it was considered a toy, but at a moment like this, it was a perfect way to deflect her nerves. Her eyes never strayed from the perpetual motion of the spinning orb, feeling her anger and pain releasing incrementally in every cycle it turned. She was happy she brought it with her.

"Stacy, why did you decide to go to the clinic without telling your mother?" Sims asked.

He sat with his left leg crossed over his right, his dark glasses adding a cold sense of acceptance to the session. His thin build was offset by a full head of hair, as unkempt as the beard and mustache splayed across his face. He chewed the end of his pen as he looked across at her, the customary air of expectancy filling the space between them.

"You know my mother," she sighed. "You've talked to her, so you know how she is, Doctor. She'd never support me if I have a child. I can't go to college and expect her to help. I can barely afford to pay for school. How could I afford a babysitter too?"

"Hmm," Sims said, jotting some notes on his yellow legal pad.

He shifted his weight and uncrossed his legs.

"Have you at least told her you're pregnant? I mean, since the last time we talked?"

"Doctor, I'm not gonna tell her I'm pregnant, okay, so you can stop asking me that," she laughed. "She doesn't need to know. That's why I went to the clinic."

"Did you decide what you wanted to do?"

It was her turn to shift in her seat this time, giving the spinner one more whirl with her finger.

"No," she said, her tone flat.

"But you told me you were set on getting an abortion. What changed?"

"Nothing's changed. I'm just not sure yet."

Sims tapped his pen on the legal pad, looking over his notes as he cleared his throat.

"Stacy, you've been back and forth on this since the first time we met together. I'm certainly not able to tell you what to do. I just want to help you decide the best course of action. But it seems you've suddenly become confused in making this decision."

She stopped the spinner and shoved it in her pocket.

"Look, I don't feel like I'm ready to be a mother, okay? I don't have a boyfriend, the person I wanted to spend my life with is dead, my mother won't help me, and my dad isn't a big part of my life either, although he'd probably be more understanding. I can't pay for college and day care. I can't take classes all day, work all night, and try to take care of a baby by myself. You tell me why I shouldn't have an abortion."

The anger surprised Sims, who stared at her wide-eyed. He spent the next several minutes taking in this sudden outburst, unsure what to ask. He spent a minute or more alternately looking at his notes, out the office window, and back again, trying to find the right words to say.

"Yeah," she laughed. "Can't think of anything, huh?" She shook her head. "This is a waste of time. I'm over Tucker's death, as much as I can be, I guess. But I'm stuck. No matter what I do, I'm on my own. I can't rely on anybody but me right now, so I'm the one that's gotta make the choice, not you."

"Stacy, can I ask you something?"

She rolled her eyes, shook her head, and leaned back on the couch, crossing her arms. "Sure. What?"

"Do you think by telling your mother about your pregnancy, it might be the remedy to heal your relationship with her?"

She was taken aback by this question. In every scenario she played out in her mind, she'd never considered this a viable possibility.

"What do you mean?" she said.

"I mean, right now, the two of you are broken people. You both want love from each other, but you don't know how to ask for it. You both blame the other person for your misfortune, but you don't consider it just might be your individual choices causing the rift between you."

"Have you met my mother? Are you kidding me?" she said, sarcasm dripping from every syllable.

"You forget, I counsel her every week too. I hear her side of the story, just like I hear it from you. I think you need to consider this from her perspective, Stacy." He gave a semistern look as he said this.

She looked down at her feet, at a loss for words. She searched her mind for any shred of truth to what Sims was telling her. Could it be as simple as telling her mom about the pregnancy? Could it really change things?

Did she want to risk everything by telling the truth?

"Stacy, I know this is difficult. I'm proud of you for working through the death of Tucker so quickly. I know that was devastating, but you're making remarkable progress in dealing with that. But this is a separate issue that must be dealt with head on. There's no getting around it, Stacy. Sooner or later, your mother will find out. Do you want to deal with the aftermath then or take care of it all now?"

"I thought an abortion would end the conversation for good, Doctor. If I'm not pregnant, there's no problem to talk through, nothing to worry about. That's why I went to the clinic."

"True, it would solve the problem of being pregnant. But would it solve the problem of being at war with your mother?"

Stacy laughed mockingly at this question, looking out the office window.

"Doctor, I came here because I was dealing with watching my boyfriend die right in front of me. I still have nightmares about that. From what you've told me, that's not gonna go away anytime soon, if ever. But this talk about my mother is getting ridiculous. She's a slut. She was a slut when she and my dad were together, she was a slut when they got divorced, and she's an even bigger slut now. She's never going to change."

"I prefer to view that behavior as a result of being starved for affection," Sims said.

"Am I supposed to support her decision to sleep with almost every guy she meets?"

"No, but you could at least try to see things from her perspective. Perhaps there's something in her past that's causing her to act out. In my opinion, there's nothing wrong with a healthy libido finding satisfaction in others. There's nothing morally wrong with finding acceptance and love from numerous partners. It's a sign of a healthy sexual appetite. Don't you think that's something to be celebrated as well?"

"Doctor," she said in disbelief, "with all due respect, I don't believe you."

"Why not?" he said, clearing his throat.

Stacy chuckled. "I've watched my mother date one guy after another. I've seen her flirt with my male friends. I've listened to her cry at night, asking why she can't find love with one man. I've grown up in a home torn apart by anger and cheating. After what I've seen, I'm not sure I believe love exists."

"Perhaps it exists in the form of many different men. Don't you think this is what your mother is exploring? And don't you think your mother deserves your love and support, regardless of her actions?"

"Do you ask her that same question about me?"

Sims paused, his eyes darting around the room.

"Well, what your mother and I talk about is, uh, confidential," he said, clearing his throat. "Just as what you and I discuss is confidential. I'm not at liberty to say."

Stacy leaned forward aggressively.

"You know I could just walk out in the waiting room and find out, don't you? She brings me here every week. I could walk out there right now and get the answer."

Sims looked down at the floor, his deflated persona on full display now.

"Okay, I'll tell you," he said, clearing his throat and straightening himself in his chair. "I've never asked her that question."

"Why?" she asked, venom lacing her words.

"Well, we never really got around to…it's just…" His voice trailed off as his eyes fell to the floor again.

Stacy blinked, threw her head back, and laughed mockingly. "Well, I'll be damned. You're sleeping with her too." She rubbed her hand across her forehead. "You bastard," she said in a violent whisper.

She stood up, paced the floor in front of the couch a few times, then stopped, looking directly at Sims, her eyes burning a hole in his skull.

"I don't ever want to see you again, got it? This is my last session. I'm never coming back, not even if it's free. How could you do this to me? I trusted you. And this is what I get for coming to my mom's shrink? Screw you, jackass. I'm done."

She turned and walked to the door, opening it swiftly. Stepping into the lobby, she walked in a huff past her mother and headed toward the car. Tori looked up from the magazine she was reading and noticed her daughter racing out the door. She tossed the magazine back on the table in the middle of the waiting area, stood, and half ran, half walked to catch up to Stacy. Once outside, she tried to get her daughter's attention.

"Stacy!" she yelled. "Stacy, slow down."

She pulled the key fob for her car out of her purse, pushing it to unlock the doors.

Stacy was near the car by now, noticing it was unlocked. She reached for the passenger side door, opened it quickly, got in, and slammed it shut as hard as she could, settling into the passenger seat.

By now Tori was in complete confusion over what had set off Stacy.

She arrived at the car, her mind racing with questions, opened the driver door, and got in. She closed the door, straightened herself in the seat, and pulled the seatbelt across her body, clicking it properly in place. She turned to Stacy, who was staring out the passenger side window, her breathing heavy.

Tori moved to speak, took note of Stacy's angry posture, and thought better of starting a conversation. Instead, she put her foot on the brake and pushed the button to start the car. She glanced over at Stacy one more time and decided to wait until later to find out why she was so enraged. She put the car in drive, pulled out of the parking space, and headed for home, both occupants remaining silent for the entirety of the trip.

The silent treatment continued when they got home, as Stacy made her way to her bedroom, slamming the door shut for maximum effect. Tori knew better than to try and talk to her daughter when she was in a mood like this. Previous efforts resulted in the two combatants hurling curse words at each other and vowing never to speak to the other again.

While Stacy did whatever she did upstairs to work through her anger, Tori busied herself making a salad. As she poured the bagged lettuce into a bowl, she took note of the age of the leaves. They appeared as if they were bordering on not being edible, but they would have to suffice for now. She added some sliced tomatoes, croutons, a sliver of onion, and bacon bits, topping it off with Italian dressing for good measure.

Returning the lettuce and dressing to the refrigerator, she reached on the bottom shelf and pulled out a bottle of red wine. She retrieved a wine glass from the cupboard and poured the liquid inside. Her lunch complete, she sat at the small dining room table and lazily ate her salad. Surprisingly, it was unusually crisp, and she savored every bite.

As she ate, she strained her ears listening for the unmistakable sound of music from Stacy's bedroom. Knowing this was her daughter's outlet when she got angry allowed Tori to feel somewhat calm about their frequent altercations. It was a habit Tori had grudgingly accepted as normal at moments like this. Not hearing the usual thump from Stacy's speakers, Tori knew this wasn't a good sign.

She finished her salad, setting the bowl in the sink with the other dirty dishes and took a deep breath. There was only one way to find out if Stacy was okay. She had to break the silence between them. She took a long, slow drink of wine and set the glass on the counter.

Slowly heading for the stairs, she strained her ears again for any hint of music playing, hopeful to avoid a confrontation. Still no sound. She crept up the stairs, careful not to make too much noise, straining to hear something, anything, from behind Stacy's closed door.

A sudden wave of panic washed over her.

What is she doing? she thought, stepping closer to Stacy's room.

As she arrived, she placed an ear on the door, listening for even a muffled sound, or heavy breathing, some sign Stacy was okay. She knocked softly on the door.

"Stacy?" she called. "Stacy, are you okay, honey?"

No answer.

She knocked again, this time a little harder.

"Stacy! Honey, what are you doing in there?"

Her voice registered her panic, although it bordered on fear now. This wasn't like her daughter to ignore her. Normally, she would've given some acknowledgment by now. Consumed by fear something wasn't right, Tori placed her hand on the doorknob, turning it ever so slowly.

Good, she thought, *she didn't lock her door.*

She turned the knob all the way and pushed the door open gently. She stepped inside Stacy's room and gasped, her eyes wide and frightened.

Stacy lay on her right side on the bedroom floor, eyes closed, her right arm outstretched away from her body. An open bottle of pills lay just beyond her fingers, as some of the contents spilled out onto the carpeted floor.

Tori rushed to her daughter's body and knelt on the floor. She placed her fingers on Stacy's neck, hopeful she'd find a pulse. It was slow and weak, but Stacy's heart was beating. She reached a finger and placed it under Stacy's nose, feeling the air exhaling softly from her nostrils. She was alive but needed help. Fast.

Tori stood up, pulling her phone out of her pocket. She dialed 911 and waited, trying to remain calm, but not taking her eyes off her daughter's limp body lying on the floor.

Once again, Stacy found herself walking slowly through the forest she had visited before. She wore a green dress this time, regal and beautiful in its opulence. The crown on her head was much bigger now, and she felt the weight of it digging into her skull. If she could, she would've taken off the crown and left it behind. For reasons unknown, she kept it on her head.

She stopped walking and surveyed the beauty around her. The sun was floating in a perfectly blue sky, the clouds only teasing they were still in existence. The birds in the trees set about exchanging their chatter, an unseen maestro orchestrating their every note. It was a serenity Stacy hadn't experienced in quite some time.

She smiled, gazing upon the sheer beauty of the forest around her, this time bathed in the warm glow of the sun. The leaves seemed brighter, the grass greener, the dirt pathway she stood upon cleaner and more orderly than before. If she could, she would visit here as often as possible. She might even consider living here, if she only knew where here is and what significance, if any, it held. She couldn't shake the feeling she'd been here before, but she didn't know when, or why. Yet it was all strangely familiar.

"Quite a bit better this time, no?"

The male voice startled her, and she caught her breath for a moment, turning to see the same Being who visited her previously was back. She laughed.

"Yes. It's lovely," she said. There was that regal, queenlike voice again…

The Being looked over the forest and sighed heavily. "Too bad it doesn't last," he said, a forlorn look coming to his eyes.

"What do you mean?"

He glanced over at her quickly, then to the ground, and finally off into the distance of time.

"I mean, beauty only lasts for those who seek its comfort. It will thrive, always, if it is tended to and cared for properly. If not, it becomes like a nightmare, much like it was the last time you were here."

She looked at him, puzzled. "But I had nothing to do with the sadness that surrounded these woods. I only heard the music of children but couldn't find them. You told me they had been taken away to be safe."

"Yes, that's true," he nodded.

"So why am I here now? Have the children returned to play?"

She glanced around, expecting at any moment she might catch a glimpse of children running and leaping for joy.

The Being walked a few paces ahead of Stacy and stopped. He straightened his shoulders and pulled himself upright, almost towering over her. He scanned the horizon; for what, she wouldn't know. After a time, he turned to face her.

"You love the children, don't you?"

"With all my heart."

"And you would do whatever you could to ensure their innocence and dignity would remain intact, would you not?"

"Of course. Why wouldn't I?"

He stepped in close to her and leaned his head down.

"Because the child you carry in your womb is in danger. And yet here you stand, expecting to see others laughing and enjoying their freedom."

She recoiled at hearing this, stunned at the Being's abruptness.

"You presume to know everything about what I will do, is that it?"

"I presume nothing, madam. I know the secret you harbor in your heart. You wish to rid yourself of the responsibility of being a mother, of nurturing a child and seeing them take flight on their own path. Tell me I'm wrong."

"You..." she started, then paused a moment, shaking her head. "You don't know what I'm dealing with, do you? You have no concept of the hell I'm going through right now. I would rather die than accept the burden I carry."

"But you still entertain the thought of letting your child pass into the nether world, don't you? You still wish to never see them grow, never hear them cry for a love only a mother could give, don't you? This is the danger your child is in. This is what I know of you. Do not question my motives, dear child. I know of what I speak."

He sounded stern, almost angry, as he spoke.

She remained silent, weighing her options on what to say or if a response was necessary. So many questions arose in her mind now. How did this Being know anything about her? Why would he say her unborn child—little more than the size of a peanut at this stage—was in danger? What danger could he be referring to? She wasn't sure how he could know what she harbored inside but was certain she didn't wish to find out how he gained this knowledge.

The Being peered intently at her, studying her eyes that so carefully betrayed her false bravado.

"You're wondering what having a child would be like, aren't you?" he smiled.

"What do you mean?" she said. "I'm merely disturbed by someone who presumes to tell me what I feel, or think, when you know nothing about me."

He stepped beside her, sighed, and gently placed his arm on her shoulder. "Stacy. Do you see that playground set over there?" He pointed to a large playground apparatus resting in the middle of the field, its gleaming railings sparkling in the sun.

She suddenly recognized it as the one from the campground her parents used to take her to when she was little. "Yes. I see it. What about it?"

"You were running on top of it when you fell and scraped your knee. Your mother ran to you and helped you down, then very gently carried you to the tent your family occupied. There she cleaned your scrape and put a Band-Aid on it, then leaned down to kiss it and make it better. Do you remember that?" he said, smiling warmly.

She was stunned, silenced by the clarity this stranger had in describing her childhood. The memories of days spent at the lake in these woods came rushing back to her, and a smile began to grace her lips. She forced herself to stop, convinced it would only encourage the Being to talk more about her childhood.

He looked intently at her, searching her face for evidence his comments hit their mark.

"You resist the truth, no? Why do you fight this, young one?" he asked, shaking his head.

She turned to look at him, straightened herself, and jutted out her chin.

"You speak foolishly of my past. You have no real knowledge of what took place, nor do you understand what I am coping with now. My mother is emotionally distant. My boyfriend is dead and will not be with me to raise a child. My father is busy with his life and has no time for me, except on the weekends, and even then it's not consistent. You may speak as if you know my life, but you have no knowledge of the pain I'm confronting now. I was supposed to go to college and be with my boyfriend, but now that can't happen. I cannot have a child right now. It will ruin my life. I have no future if I have a child. I have no choice." She exhaled loudly, content she'd stated her case for the Being to be silenced.

A coy smile crept across his face, his eyes dancing playfully.

"You don't think I understand?" he laughed. "My dear, I know far more than you realize. What would you say if I can show you the future? Would you like to see what your child could become? If you allow it, I can show you what may, or may not, happen to your child."

"What would that do?" she said, wrinkling her nose. "Why would I want to see a future that will never exist? It is pointless to show me because the future has been decided."

The Being slumped over, his shoulders seeming to indicate he was defeated.

"So that's it then, is it? All this time, this so-called 'confusion' you say you have over what to do is just a lie, is that it?"

She turned away, averting her eyes before she allowed him to see a tear falling across her cheek. "It is the only way," she whispered.

"The only way," he said mockingly. "Is it? Are you sure?"

He studied her body language, looking for an indication the truth of his words had been acknowledged. He closed his eyes and shook his head at not seeing his desired intent.

"Young one, I can show you the possibilities if you allow it. You must trust this is for your own good."

She turned to him, anger in her face. "And why would I want to witness this future? Why would I subject myself to something I know will not happen? Why would you mock my pain by doing that?"

The words fell hard out of her mouth, spewing forth in rage. He pursed his lips and held up a hand.

"Because you believe in the truth of your child's life being precious."

Something in his voice and the way his eyes seared into her heart caused her to look down at the ground. Suddenly, she felt herself confused, lost in a maze of wondering what could be and what was now. She shook her head.

"I don't understand. Why would you do this?"

"Because you love your child," he said. "And despite saying your decision has already supposedly been made, you still harbor a wish to know what will happen."

Stacy moved to a wooden bench nearby, her feet moving in halting steps, her hand clutching her stomach. Slowly, she lowered herself to sit, her mind devoid of reasoning. After a time, she looked up through tear-stained eyes at the Being.

"How can you show me what I don't wish to see?"

"Ah," he smiled. "But the better question is this... How willing are you to perceive the truth of this mystery?"

"Ms. Butler?"

Tori jolted out of her semisleep and looked up to see a doctor and nurse standing next to the chair she occupied in the hospital waiting room. Somehow she'd managed to fall asleep, though she didn't know for how long. She rubbed her eyes.

"Yes?" she said, her voice low.

"My name is Dr. Blanton, and this is Nurse Green," he said, his hand extended.

He was a short balding man, his thick glasses resting gently on his weathered face. They accented his gray hair perfectly. Nurse Green was a heavyset woman, with straight, auburn hair reaching down to the middle of her back. Slowly, Tori reached up and shook the doctor's hand.

"May we sit down?" he said, waving his hand in the direction of the chairs to her left, positioned at a ninety-degree angle from her own.

"Of course, please," she said.

She straightened herself in her chair, yawned, and stretched a little as Blanton and Green sat down.

"First of all, Stacy is doing fine. We've managed to stabilize her vitals, and we're assessing her for any serious injuries that may have occurred when she swallowed the pills."

Tori breathed a sigh of relief.

"Oh, thank God," she rubbed her face with her hand. "I've been so worried."

"I understand, ma'am. But I'd like to ask a few questions, is that okay?"

"Sure."

Blanton sighed.

"Ms. Butler, do you know how she got ahold of the pills? Were they prescribed for her, or did they belong to someone else?"

"I don't know. I certainly don't take them, so they're not mine. She must have gotten them from a friend at school," she said, confusion in her voice.

"Is everything okay at home? Any signs of depression or change in behavior?"

"No, nothing like that. She's a great kid."

"Has she been through any traumatic events that may have triggered this, something like a breakup, or you and your husband divorcing, something like that?"

"Her father and I have been divorced since she was little, but she never really told me she had a problem with it. She visits with her dad on the weekends, but otherwise, she seems normal to me. Well, as normal as a teenager can be, you know?" Tori managed a slight chuckle as she said this.

"Well, emotional scars may take some time to manifest themselves. Have the two of you talked through her feelings about the divorce?"

"I never really thought it was an issue. I mean, when I told her what was happening, she didn't seem out of sorts about it. Like I said, it's been quite some time and I tried to explain it as clearly as I could when it happened. I never really thought she'd react this badly about it. Could that be why she did this?"

Tori was genuinely curious to know the answer, as she leaned forward in her chair. Blanton adjusted his glasses and sighed.

"Ms. Butler, teen girls often mask their emotions for the preservation of those around them. I've dealt with this sort of thing before, and almost always, it's because of them not opening up about what they really feel. Sometimes it's hard for them to verbalize what's going on internally."

"Yeah," she nodded. "I can see that, I guess." She reached up and rubbed the last vestiges of slumber from her eyes. "But if she had a problem, she would've told me. Like I said, she's a good kid. We talk all the time."

"I don't doubt that, Ms. Butler, but I need to know. Have there been any signs recently of a change in her behavior? Has there been a change in her friends or who she associates with after school?"

"No, not that I've noticed. I mean, her boyfriend recently died, but she's been going to a therapist for that. It seems to be helping her, so I don't think that's a problem anymore."

"I'm so sorry. I had no idea. You said this was recent, correct? Do you remember when it happened?"

"It's been a little more than a month, I don't really remember. I'm sorry, it's been a busy fall for us."

"Well, listen, like I said, she's in stable condition, and we're running a few tests right now. We want to know how high the levels of toxins were, and that will help us decide the best course of treatment. She's in a medically induced coma right now, but I think she's going to be okay. I'll let you come visit as soon she's more stable, okay?" he smiled.

"That would be fine, Doctor," she said, reaching out and squeezing his arm.

He patted her hand and chuckled. "I'm glad I could pass along some good news. I'll get back to her and see how she is and then let you know when you can come back and see her, okay? Oh, and this shouldn't affect the baby at all." Blanton stood, reached up, and straightened his glasses again and let go a heavy sigh. "We'll keep a close eye on that for you too."

Tori's face suddenly froze in shock, her eyes blinking rapidly.

"Her…what?" she said, softly.

Blanton looked quizzically at her. "Her baby. You didn't know she was pregnant?"

"No. I had no idea. How far along is she, do you know?"

Blanton stroked his chin the way villains do in children's fairy tales. "My guess is only about a month or so, we're not sure. We'll look at that more in-depth as we go."

Tori stared at the floor, suddenly wishing it would open and swallow her whole. She propped her elbow on the arm of the chair, burying her face in her hand. She sighed heavily. "Why didn't she tell me?" she whispered.

Blanton leaned down closer to Tori. "I'm sorry you had to find out this way. I thought you knew. I realize this is a shock to your system, but please understand, we'll do everything we can to make sure your daughter and her baby are safe. I promise." He reached out and patted Tori's shoulder. She pulled her head up and stared at him, a blank look on her face.

"I… I appreciate that, Doctor. I'm just shocked, Stacy never shared this with me."

Blanton chuckled. "Well, in my experience, it's not the first time a teenage daughter would hide something from their mother. But we're going to do everything we can to make sure she's okay."

"Thank you, Doctor."

He smiled. "You're welcome, Ms. Butler."

He gave a wink and turned, following the nurse back to the operating room. Within minutes, they disappeared behind the automatic opening double doors leading back to the patient rooms.

Tori looked from the doors to the television in the far corner of the room, her mind in disbelief at the news of her daughter's pregnancy. She smiled, briefly, at the thought of being a grandmother, surprisingly at ease with this idea. However, anger replaced her bliss, and she shook her head.

Why couldn't she tell me? she thought. *Doesn't she trust me?*

She exhaled loudly, rubbed her forehead, and stared at the television. A rerun of a '90s sitcom about nothing was on, and she soon became lost in absentmindedly watching the show.

Hours passed, and Tori returned to the waiting area from the hospital café, coffee cup in hand. For being in a hospital, the food was surprisingly above average quality. She took two steps inside the room and stopped. Her heart jumped out of her chest at the sight of her ex-husband sitting alone, alternating between typing on his laptop and watching TV.

At forty-five years old, Jason Kent was six years older than Tori. His rugged features and near-fanatical devotion in going to the gym enamored Tori when they started dating. This devotion lasted well into their first five years of marriage, although by then, she grew tired of his near constant absence.

If it wasn't him working out at the gym, it was a late-night meeting or an out-of-town conference that seemed to come up every two to three weeks a month. She used this vacancy as an excuse to find comfort in the arms of other men, neglecting her own lack of contribution to their marriage.

She gathered her composure, rolled her eyes, and sighed heavily.

Might as well get it over with, she thought, taking in a deep breath before moving to where Jason sat.

He glanced up from his laptop, noticing Tori coming closer. He gave a weak smile in her direction before training his eyes back to his computer screen, typing furiously as he did. Tori stopped near him, put one hand on her hip, and cleared her throat. He turned his eyes to look at her.

"Aren't you going to ask me to sit down?" she said, not bothering to mask the bitterness in her tone.

"You don't need my permission. Have a seat," he said, pointing to a chair opposite himself. He returned to typing on the keyboard of his laptop.

She flopped down in the chair and watched as he busied himself with whatever was more important than her. She placed her purse and coffee cup on the empty chair next to her, straightened herself, and folded her arms across her chest. After a few minutes, she cleared her throat again, a clear indication she was perturbed.

He raised his head, a look of confusion on his face. "What?" he asked, raising a hand, palm upward and shrugging his shoulder.

Tori snorted. "If I have to tell you, that's pretty damn sad."

He exhaled, rolled his eyes, and focused back on his laptop. He made a couple of clicks to save what he'd been working on and hit the off switch. He waited a couple of moments as it powered down, lowered the screen, shoved it back into his ever-present backpack and looked directly at her.

"There. Now what did you want?" he said, folding his arms across his chest.

"Well, your daughter tried to kill herself tonight by overdosing on sleeping pills. I thought you'd be a little more concerned than you are."

"Yeah. The doctor told me when I got here about fifteen minutes ago. Where'd she get the pills? From you?" he smirked, his brown eyes turning cold.

"Dammit, Jason, you know I put those in a safe place. There's no way for her to find them."

He laughed, seeming to enjoy this a little too much.

"You put them in the same drawer as the condoms you use with other men, didn't you?"

Her eyes narrowed, and if she could, she would've killed him with her gaze.

"You son of a bitch," she said, her tone bitter. "You have no right to talk to me like that. What I do is none of your damn business." She shook her head and sighed.

He laughed again. "You're right. It's none of my business," he waved a hand dismissively. "But, uh, how's this new guy, Rick, is it? Heard he's a real winner."

"Who told you about him?"

"Stacy did, told me he's a real piece of work. You deserve him though. You're both crazy," he said, laughing again, this time leaning forward, resting his elbows on his knees. "I don't care who you date, but when it affects my daughter, I have a real concern."

"Listen to me, you piece of garbage. Rick is a good man. He treats Stacy well. You think I'd let anyone disrespect her? I'm not the one dating some little twinkie."

"What's that supposed to mean?"

It was Tori's moment to laugh. "You know damn well what I mean. That little bimbo girlfriend of yours is barely old enough to drink. It's disgusting, is what it is. What kind of example does that set for your daughter, huh?"

"What the hell do you care?"

Jason was seething with rage, his teeth clenched and his face turning red. He sat back in his chair and tried in vain to distract himself with the TV. He glanced back at her for a moment before he spoke.

"You're the one who cheated on me, not the other way around," he said, pointing an accusatory finger.

"Ha," she laughed, "you're a liar."

"Am I?"

"Jason, how many times did I see lipstick on your shirt collar? How many times did I see pictures on your phone of whatever woman you were hooking up with at the time? You didn't do a good job of cleaning up your history on that, so I know all about who you've been with and how many different girls you've screwed. Don't act like you're innocent."

He looked at the floor, absentmindedly shaking his right leg up and down. He ran a hand through his hair a couple of times and shook his head. He finally looked up at her.

"Look. Can we just call a truce while we're here? I mean, Stacy's in trouble. Let's focus on her and not what happened between you and me, all right? Can we do that?" he pleaded.

She closed her eyes and wiped a hand across her eyes. "Fine."

"Is she still going to therapy?" he said, clearing his throat and straightening his tie.

"Yes. Once a week."

"How's she doing with that?"

"It seems to be going well. She's not having as many nightmares as she did right after Tucker died, so it's been helping."

"Why did she skip her weekend with me? Is that because of you?" There was a hint of sarcasm rising in his voice. He smiled, unnerving Tori as she glared at him.

"No. She didn't tell me. You'd have to ask her why."

"I thought she told you everything," he sneered. "When did that stop?"

"When you walked out on her."

"Seriously, Tori? You wanna have this argument again? I thought we called a truce."

"Yeah, well, maybe that can't happen," she said, standing up. "I can't do this right now, you jackass. I'll find someplace else to sit."

She grabbed her purse, slung it on her shoulder, and picked up her coffee cup. She took two steps away from him before stopping. She turned and walked back to stand in front of him.

"One more thing," she leaned down close to his ear to whisper. "Your daughter is pregnant." She stood back up, turned, and hastily walked out of the waiting room.

Jason stared after her his mouth open. He blinked his eyes rapidly and shook his head. "What?"

His voice registered his shock at hearing this. He was begging to know more details, but it was too late. She was already in the hallway by now, never acknowledging if she heard him. He closed his eyes, rested his elbow on the chair's armrest, and lowered his head into his hand. He rubbed his eyes and let out a slight laugh.

The Being was now pacing in front of Stacy, taking slow and deliberate steps, his hands clasped behind his back. He was calm and quiet, almost in a trancelike state.

The longer Stacy watched him pacing, the more she became unnerved at how little emotion he demonstrated. For her part, she sat quietly on the bench, thoughtlessly rubbing her hands up and down her thighs. She had been this way for some time, only glancing up at the Being occasionally. He was making her nervous the longer he stayed silent.

"Why do you not speak?" she finally said. "Why do you remain silent?"

He paused, turning his head slowly to look at her, a quizzical look on his face. "Do you not understand my proposal?"

Her eyes darted across the ground beneath her, searching for a way to avoid answering the question. "I-I guess I understand."

He stopped pacing and turned toward her. "So you're prepared to be taken into the future and see what may happen to your child? You're fully prepared to witness how their life may turn out?"

"I guess so," she said in a whisper, nodding.

"What was that? I couldn't quite hear you."

"I said, I guess so," she snapped, her eyes glaring at him.

"Excellent," he grinned, rubbing his hands together excitedly. "This will prove to be most informative. However, I feel I should prepare you for what you are about to see." He moved slowly to sit next to her as he continued, "During this journey, you will be able to see your child's possible future. You'll witness their potential, both good and bad. Mind you, you will only see a small portion of the entirety of their life, but I trust it will impact your decision dramatically."

"I will see both good and bad?" she said, the words coming slow from her mouth. "What does that mean?"

He turned his body to face her. "It means, you will see both their possible success as well as any possible failure. You will see what may, or may not, become of your child. However, you will not be able to intervene in any way. You will merely observe what happens. Simply put, I want to show you the result of your choices and how they may affect your child."

"My choices?" she said, confused.

"Yes. You see, as a mother, you wield a great deal of influence on your child's life. The way you think, the way you speak to others, your compassion or lack thereof matters to your child. All of who you are will influence how they perceive the world around them. Of course, there comes a time in every child's life when they are old enough to decide for themselves what they want their life to become. At that point, you are free from the constraints in teaching them. The hard work of laying the foundation of their life will be over.

They must strike out on their own and make a way for themselves. But the question will remain: What if the foundation you prepare in their spirit is not sustainable for their well-being? What then?"

Her eyes darted across the ground again, her hands moving faster up and down her thighs. Her heart began beating faster, her throat becoming dry and her tongue swollen. It was as if her entire body was conducting electricity as the sensation coursed through her veins.

"I don't know if I can do this," she shook her head. "I'm not sure I want to see these things."

Her words came in a defeated whisper. The Being stood slowly and smiled. "And why is that, my dear? Understand, when you become a mother, you realize you are stronger than you believe. When no one else can summon the courage and strength required to finish a task, a mother will not stop until the job is completed. That's what makes being a mother a divine privilege unlike any other."

All of a sudden, her hands stopped moving across her thighs. Though her head remained lowered toward the ground, she seemed to have an epiphany. She looked up at him, the curiosity evident in her gaze.

"So when my mother stayed up all night making my science project, then went to work all day afterward, that's the kind of strength you think I have?"

"Of course," he nodded a smile fixed to his face.

"I-I can't believe it," she said, the words stumbling out of her mouth. "I never knew."

He walked to Stacy and knelt in front of her. "Of course, you didn't know. What child bothers to think how often they inconvenience their mother? What child looks out for the best interest of their parents or takes into consideration that at one time, they were children just like you? You wouldn't be expected to think this way as a child. That's what age and experience will teach you. To appreciate what God gave you when you didn't know what you had."

Stacy looked at him, a tear forming in her eye. "Then I think I'm ready to face my future," she said, matter-of-factly.

He smiled, reaching up and gently placing his hand on her cheek. "Trust me. You won't regret this."

Tori found a smaller waiting area a short way down the hall from the one Jason occupied. Consisting of only a small table and two chairs, it wasn't much bigger than a walk-in closet. Still, it offered a chance for her to be away from Jason and space enough to calm her nerves. She took a sip from what remained of her coffee and winced. By now it was cold and tasteless. Looking around the room for a trash can, she found none were nearby.

She shook her head, set her coffee cup on the table, and propped her elbow beside her cup. Placing her head in her hand, she sighed heavily. Not having seen Stacy since she followed the ambulance, she was troubled in not being given an exact time when she would be allowed to visit. It was unnerving for her to feel so vulnerable at this moment.

She took some small comfort in knowing Jason had taken time to be here. Though her hatred for him remained, she knew he loved Stacy and that his love was reciprocated. She was overwhelmingly proud of Stacy in deciding for herself what to believe about her father, though she questioned the method in which Stacy reached that conclusion. In her mind, all the facts were there to prove him worthless, yet Stacy acted as if she wasn't concerned.

What am I gonna say about her being pregnant? she thought, shaking her head. *How are we gonna deal with that? I'm not ready to help Stacy become a mother. What was she thinking?*

In this moment, it was a challenge to entertain the notion of being considered a grandmother. Though it was a title she looked forward to attaining later in Stacy's life, the suddenness in which it came numbed her heart.

Why didn't she tell me? she thought, feeling a tear trace a line down her cheek.

Her thoughts turned to the days at the campsite by the lake, to all the times she and Stacy would play together on the playground apparatus. Through the fog of her tears, she smiled, even as they were streaming from her eyes. She propped up both elbows on the table and buried her head in her hands, crying in earnest now. Within minutes, she was bawling, her sobs coming in waves.

If their situation were better, she would run to Jason and fall into his arms for comfort. She needed him to hold her, to stroke her hair and tell her it would be all right. Instead, the tears stung her cheeks as they fell to the table.

What if her daughter never woke up? What if the last thing she remembered of Stacy was a silent scream for help and she never bothered to save her?

Chapter 4

Over the years, Riverview Hospital gained a reputation as one of the top medical research hospitals in the country. Situated in Beckton—about a twenty-five-minute drive from Blackburn—the hospital had grown not only in size but in notoriety for its cutting-edge research related to childhood cancer.

Of course, they were nowhere near solving the puzzle that is cancer—the sheer volume and variety of cancers one could be stricken with denied that advantage—yet they continued to forge ahead in their constant struggle. The lead research team at this facility was relentless, pursuing every opportunity they could find in ridding the world of this treacherous disease.

Wordlessly, the Being and Stacy walked the fourteenth-floor hallway, the tightly woven carpet muffling their steps. An unnerving hush filled the air around them as they passed by numerous doors, each adorned with a different doctor's name.

"Why are we here?" Stacy asked, softly. Even though it wasn't a possibility, she was concerned their presence might cause a disturbance.

"This is where your daughter works," the Being responded. "I brought you here to see what she's accomplished."

"A doctor," she whispered, a smile on her lips. "Who knew that was possible?"

He turned and looked at her. "I did," he said, sternly. "You did as well."

"I have a daughter?" she asked, trying to change the subject.

"Only if you agree to keep her from danger," he replied, his gaze fixed forward.

She felt herself recoil at this comment, her stomach nervously churning.

The Being stopped near the end of the hall, looking at the door to his left. "This is her office. See?"

He pointed at a small placard attached near the door. Stacy walked beside him and smiled as she read the name on the placard: "Dr. Olivia Hamilton, Pediatric Oncology."

"She kept his last name," she whispered.

She put a hand to her mouth and gasped with joy, then reached out to touch the placard. She brushed her fingers slowly across her daughter's name, a warm, contented smile affixed to her mouth.

"Of course she kept Tucker's last name. You taught her everything you knew about him. She's proud of her father, even though they never met." He turned to Stacy and waved his hand forward. "Come," he said, as he took her hand and led her into Olivia's office.

The two took a few steps into the office before stopping. Her eyes grew wide as she gazed around the spacious room.

It was a large corner office, dominated by floor-to-ceiling windows encasing a portion of the walls making up the corner. This offered a spectacular view of downtown Beckton and Fuller Square, a five-block-long green space in the center of town. Just in front of these windows sat a larger-than-expected oaken desk, sparsely decorated and gleaming bright in the reflection of the sun shining through the windows.

In a high-back leather chair behind the desk sat the beautiful thirty-two-year-old Olivia Hamilton, typing furiously on her computer. Her brown eyes were accented perfectly by a pair of black-rimmed glasses, and her dark hair was pulled back in a ponytail.

Stacy couldn't help but smile, a tear forming in her eye. Holding her hand to her mouth, she could feel the pride in her daughter welling inside. She sniffled as she watched her daughter's relentless focus on her computer, alternately sipping water from a plastic bottle and taking bites of a protein bar.

To the right and behind Olivia, various plaques were displayed on the wall, showcasing Olivia's degrees and certifications in oncology. Prominently displayed in a frame on the drawers immediately behind Olivia was a picture of a young woman with a small child. The faces were blurry and unrecognizable, causing identification to be impossible.

This scene was almost too overwhelming to behold.

The phone rang on the desk, breaking the near silence in the room. Olivia sighed, shook her head as she stopped typing, and reached over to pick up the receiver

"This is Dr. Hamilton," she said, a hint of annoyance in her tone. She sat motionless for a few moments, her eyes fixed on a distant point on the carpeted floor.

"Listen, I explained to the salesman I wanted it in maroon, not red. Can't they get that right? How many times must I complain about this before I take my business someplace else?" she said, clearly bothered. "Yes, and I want the heated leather seats, with a sunroof. Do you understand?"

She paused for a moment, obviously listening to the other person speak.

"Look, I don't have to tell you, I'm a very influential customer. I can tell half the city about my experience with you and tell them to go elsewhere to buy a car. I can purchase a Jaguar anywhere, not just at your dealership. I expect better service from someone with such a high rating."

Stacy was taken aback at hearing the venom and rage in Olivia's tone, shaking her head at the lack of manners her daughter was showing. How could Olivia have such a negative attitude about something as simple as choosing a new car?

"I'm sorry," Olivia sighed, "there's a call on the other line. I'll have to call you back." She reached over and pushed a button on the phone. "Hello?"

She put her hand on her forehead and began rubbing it vigorously. "Hi, Mom," she said, rolling her eyes.

Stacy watched intently, studying Olivia's facial tics and expression. She was stunned at how rude her daughter could be to her.

"No, Mom. I told you, I didn't want you to invite Grandma to my birthday party, okay?" Olivia said, pausing to listen. "Because she got drunk last time and embarrassed the hell out of me, that's why." She slammed her hand on the table.

"Then call her back and tell her I won't be there. I don't care how upset she is about it. I don't care to be in the same room as her, okay?" She sat back in her chair her face contorted in anger. "For the last time, Mom, I don't give a damn what she thinks or if she's sorry. I don't want her there, and that's final."

She listened for a few more minutes, then suddenly threw her pen across the room.

"Uninvite her then. I don't care what she thinks. It's my party, and I don't want her there, got it?" she screamed, slamming the phone down.

She buried her head in her hand, swiveling her chair in a slow half circle, exhibiting her obvious distress.

"Why is she like this? Did she not learn proper manners? Surely I would have taught her that," Stacy said.

The Being turned his head slowly to look at her. "Perhaps you did, my dear. But if she observed how you treated your own mother, she may have learned differently."

Before Stacy could speak, the office phone rang again.

Olivia picked it up slowly, shaking her head as she pulled it to her ear. "Yes?" she said. She paused a moment, reaching for her protein bar.

"I said my reservation was at 7:00 p.m., for two. How can you not get that right? I come in there every week. If this is how I'm going to be treated, I'll either speak to Henri about hiring someone more competent or take my business elsewhere."

It was obvious Olivia was accustomed to flaunting her prestige with everyone she came in contact. Still, her daughter's complete lack of decorum was stunning.

Maybe it would be better I don't subject the world to someone like this, Stacy thought.

"Thank you. I look forward to a lovely evening," Olivia said and hung up the phone.

Once again, she swiveled in her chair, only this time she turned to look out the windows. She found herself becoming lost in the mundane activity below. She gazed upon Fuller Square, letting out a deep sigh, removed her glasses, and rubbed the bridge of her nose.

Stacy looked at the Being and pointed toward Olivia.

"Can I go near her? Can she see me?"

"No, she can't see us. We are merely apparitions in her mind, nothing more. You can stand beside her if you wish, but she will not be able to acknowledge your presence."

Stacy walked gingerly toward Olivia, a cautious look on her face. Stopping at the edge of the leather chair, she leaned down, peering anxiously at her daughter. For the few moments she was there, Stacy tried to absorb as much of this moment as she could. She'd never seen anyone as beautiful as her, nor someone so accomplished.

Olivia seemed frail, almost childlike in this moment. The semblance of a tear formed in her eye, and she reached up to wipe it away. She let out a heavy sigh and leaned her head against the back of the chair.

What is she thinking? Stacy thought. *Did I teach her how to live properly?*

A knock on the door broke the silence, and Olivia turned in her chair, wiping her face and steeling herself for whoever was behind her office door.

"Come in," she said, clearing her throat as she did. She slid her glasses back on to maintain her professional image.

The door opened, and a ruggedly handsome man entered the room, carrying a folder and a yellow legal pad. Clad in what looked like the finest business casual clothes one could buy, he smiled as he closed the door and walked toward Olivia. His broad shoulders seemed unnervingly constrained by his navy blue polo shirt, his khaki pants accentuating his powerful thighs. It was clear this man spent an exorbitant amount of time at the gym.

For her part, Olivia leaned back in her chair, a sly, seductive smile crossing her lips. She removed her glasses, placing the end of the temple piece in her mouth.

"Sorry to bother you, Olivia, but I just got the report back from the lab," the man said.

He stopped on the opposite side of the desk and placed the folder in the middle of the desk.

Olivia broke her gaze from the man, glanced down at the folder, then back to the man.

"Is that all you had for me, Chad?" she said, her voice laced with seduction.

He broke into a lascivious smile. "No, it's not."

With that he moved behind the desk as she swiveled in her chair to face him. He pulled her up from the chair, wrapping his taut arms around her, and kissed her passionately. He leaned her onto the desk, and the two engaged in heavy kissing and panting.

Suddenly, the room became a blur as Stacy's head swiveled right to left. The air around her became dark, and she looked at the Being to her left. He was turning his right hand in a circle, finally stopping when there was only light covering both himself and Stacy.

"You don't need to see that," he said matter-of-factly.

"Who's Chad?" she asked, her voice soft.

"The two of them have some sort of understanding as to their involvement."

"Sort of?"

"Because she never saw what a healthy relationship looked like, your daughter has a fear of commitment. They've been seeing each other for quite some time, but she refuses to settle down with him, or anyone else."

"What happened to me? Don't I find someone to marry?"

"I can't tell you," he replied. "I can only show you what will happen to your child, not you."

"But I'm part of her life. I deserve to know what happens to me," she insisted.

He turned to look at her, a harshness revealed in his eyes. "And what do you care of your influence on your unborn child's life? You don't even want to give her the chance to see the light of day. Why should you be concerned with how she would live her life?"

She turned away from him, suddenly frightened. She did her best to gather her composure before she spoke.

"May I remind you, I was brought here by you. It was you who chose to show this to me. I only agreed to this arrangement out of curiosity. I don't understand why you only allow me to see my daughter and not myself."

"You wish to bring harm to your child in the present. You wish to rid yourself of any relationship with your child before one could even begin. And yet this curiosity drove you here. Why should you be allowed to see how you would interact in the future when there is finality in your present?" The Being was angry now, his tone combative.

"I just want to see how I treat my daughter, that's all. Is that too much to ask?"

"Yes, it is, because you've chosen to flee from this responsibility, young one. Why should you have the pleasure of seeing the two of you together if all you wish is a lifetime free of the constraints of raising a child?"

He studied her face carefully, addressing every nervous tic coming to bear. Closing his eyes, he exhaled slowly. He shook his head before speaking. "You've agreed to see something no one else has ever seen. You have a chance to see what your child could become. I told you before we began, you would witness both the good and bad of what your child could potentially become. If this is too difficult, I can end this now, and you'll never know what may become of her."

Stacy wiped her eyes, trying in vain to hide the tears rolling down her cheeks. She sniffled loudly and reminded herself of the breathing exercises she learned in cheerleading. She practiced that now as she felt her heart rate slow, returning to a semblance of normalcy.

"No. I'll be all right if we go on. No matter how I feel, I want to know what happens to my child," she said.

The Being relaxed his body. "Then we shall continue."

He waved his right hand again, and the air around them swirled with color, brightening as the clarity of another scene unfolded before them.

They stood in the corner of an elaborately decorated restaurant. Classical music played over the PA system, providing the right amount of ambience to an elegant establishment. Hues of peach and white, mixed with a hint of black accent, adorned the walls. The tablecloths and dinnerware gleamed brightly, the gold of the knives and forks shimmering in the soft lighting. Groups and couples sat at the tables dotting the main floor, all clad in their most elegant evening wear.

For the women, long dresses seemed to be the norm, silver and gold jewelry accentuating tan skin. The occasional small tattoo could be seen peeking up from the small of their back at the bottom of their low-cut gowns. For the men, it was either tuxedos or the finest haute couture suits. The air of sophistication oozed from every inch of this room, and Stacy found herself intimidated.

"Where are we?" she asked.

"The Medallion, one of the finest restaurants in the city. There's Olivia and Chad now," the Being said, pointing to a table sequestered at what appeared to be one of the quieter corners of the room.

The couple were laughing, both enjoying their dinners, Olivia choosing asparagus as a side dish to a filet mignon, Chad enjoying a couple of oysters, accenting his salmon filet. Anyone giving a casual glance would assume they were a happy couple.

Stacy smiled, absorbing the tableau in front of her. "Wow," she said.

"Why do you react this way?" he asked.

"Because look at her. She's a doctor, she has an amazing man, she's eating at an incredible restaurant. How could I want more for my daughter?"

"Come with me," he said, smiling, as he walked toward the table.

Stacy couldn't help but feel tension in the air as she passed by each table. Despite the outward appearance of happiness, it seemed there was an underlying sense of dread and emptiness permeating the laughter. She furrowed her brow at the juxtaposition of such emotion, wondering how anyone who could afford to pay for a dinner this elegant would be lacking anything.

They stopped a few feet away from Olivia's table and watched; for what, Stacy wasn't sure. But she remained quiet, taking her cue from the Being's silence.

Olivia opted to break from the appearances of other women, having chosen a dress stopping just above her knees. It was low-cut, providing just enough view of her cleavage to be enticing to any man with a wandering eye. For his part, Chad towed the line of wearing what must have been an expensive Italian suit. To Stacy, it appeared it would have to be custom made to fit his muscular build.

"I'm glad you stopped by earlier," Olivia said.

"Me too," Chad said, his eyes twinkling. "I should do that more often."

Olivia giggled. "Sooner or later someone will find out what's happening. I don't think that would sit very well with the board if they knew I was having sex with my assistant."

"Yeah," he laughed, "but what a way to go out, huh?" He smiled, lifted his wine glass, and winked, taking a slow sip before setting it back down on the table.

"I'm not even supposed to be here with you. I hate this sneaking around," she said, her eyes suddenly darting around the room.

Reading her concern, he looked around the room as he wiped his mouth with his napkin. Uncertain what he was looking for, he leaned in across the table.

"What are you doing?" he whispered.

"I suddenly realized Dr. Hawthorn dines here frequently."

He blinked rapidly, a confused look on his face. "Who's Dr. Hawthorn?"

"Only the head of the department. If he sees us together, it could be disastrous."

Chad suddenly laughed, leaning back in his chair, his arms outstretched. "Who cares?"

"I do," she said, angrily. "I worked hard to get where I am now. I work at one of the top research hospitals in the world, I've got a penthouse suite with a Jacuzzi tub, and I'm buying a new Jaguar tomorrow. If Hawthorn finds out about us, he could fire me, and I could lose all that."

Stacy felt herself awash in a mixture of anger and disappointment over hearing Olivia's selfishness.

How shallow is my daughter? Where did that come from? she thought.

Chad picked up his wine glass and took another drink, then set it back down on the table. His eyes never left Olivia's face.

"So why did you invite me somewhere you know we might get caught, Olivia?"

She toyed with the remaining bites of food on her plate, her mind racing to find a plausible answer.

"I don't know," she shrugged. "I heard he wouldn't be here tonight, so I made reservations for us. Don't worry about it. Nobody will find out."

"Yet we're sneaking around, is that it? At least that's how it feels."

She sighed, rubbing her forehead. "No, I didn't mean it that way."

"Then how did you mean it, Olivia?"

Running out of food to move around on her plate, she put her fork down and reached for her napkin. Softly, she touched her lips with the napkin, then placed it back on her lap. She cleared her throat as she looked at him.

"Listen, Chad, what we have is special. I love being with you, but we need to be careful. There are certain rules I can't break, and one of them is that Hawthorn doesn't like interoffice relationships. That's why we need to keep this a secret. I'm sorry if that bothers you, but that's the way it is."

Chad shook his head. "Just like your mother," he half whispered.

She froze. "What did you say?"

Stacy's ears perked up as she moved closer to the table.

"Look, Olivia, I like spending time with you. I mean, the sex is amazing, sure, but I love being with you. You're an amazing woman, and I'd like to see where this goes. I thought you wanted that too."

She reached over and picked up her wine glass, nearly emptying it in one swallow. Placing the glass back on the table, she closed her eyes and breathed in deep. Exhaling slowly, she looked at him directly.

"I'm not sure what you think of us or how serious you thought we were. I don't know where you got the idea this was a real relationship, because I never wanted that."

Chad felt her words viciously embed themselves in his mind. He sat frozen, studying Olivia's face for any signal she may change her mind.

"You're serious about this, aren't you?"

"I'm afraid I am. I have my career to think about, and I don't need to be weighed down with anything that will distract me from that. I'm sorry you misinterpreted my intentions." Her tone was flat, icy, and harsh. She crossed her arms, giving a sigh when she finished talking.

He reached up and scratched his head. In his disbelief, he laughed, shaking his head at what was fast becoming the worst date he'd ever been on.

"So tell me something. All this tonight, the fancy restaurant, the nice clothes, the expensive wine, what was that for? To soften the blow of breaking up with me?"

"Chad, I'm not breaking up with you. I'm defining the parameters of whatever this is between us. All I can tell you is, I'm not in a place where I can have a serious relationship yet. I'm sorry if that's not okay with you."

His eyes lost any sort of compassion. "You were only using me for sex? That's it?"

She laughed, waving a hand in the air. "I thought that's what all men wanted. Am I wrong?"

"Yeah, pretty much," he said. "Look, since all I am is your eye candy and we can't agree on anything, I'm just gonna go, okay? Or did you need me to pay the bill?"

She stared at him for a long, silent moment. "No. I don't need you to pay. I can take care of that myself."

He stood, straightened his suit coat and tie, and looked down at her. "Well going forward, you better get used to doing a lot of things by yourself. I'll be looking for a new job in the morning, so I won't be in the office. I'm not going to apologize for your need to get coffee on your own too. Goodbye, Olivia."

He stepped past her chair and headed for the exit, leaving Olivia at the table, baffled by this sudden turn of events. She put her hand to her mouth, her insides quaking in sorrow. She would have cried had she allowed herself to feel something more than pure arousal toward Chad, but the tears wouldn't come. This wasn't the first time she'd been through this though. She wondered if it wouldn't be the last.

Stacy began to cry watching her daughter's frustration. She felt a deep longing in her soul to reach out and hug her, to comfort her and tell her she would be all right. Somehow she knew, in Olivia's reality, she hadn't done that. Or she had and Olivia decided not to listen. Either way, Stacy would never find out how she raised her daughter. She was left watching Olivia's heart shatter, a hollow pit of sorrow that couldn't be filled right now.

The Being stepped beside Stacy. "Have you seen enough of this scenario?" he turned slowly to look at her.

She sniffed, watching her daughter reach into her purse and pull out her platinum credit card and lay it on the tray with the bill, then take another sip of wine.

"Why is she like this?" she asked, turning to face the Being. "How did she end up this way? She's so cold and uncaring, almost heartless. Where would she get the idea that this was acceptable?"

"I think you know, Stacy. Think carefully about how you've talked to your own mother, and you may find the answer."

Stunned at his blunt assessment, she fumbled to formulate a response, but none came. She could only watch as Olivia signed the bill and rose to leave the restaurant. All of a sudden, the two of them stood outside in the parking lot, watching Olivia trudge slowly to her car. Again, there was that maternal instinct to run to her and hold her until the tears disappeared.

"My daughter is a success whether she has a man or not. Who cares if she was using him for sex? Don't men do that all the time?"

"Is that what you wanted with Tucker?" he asked.

"What do you mean?"

He closed his eyes, exhaling in exasperation as he did. "You told him you wanted to marry him, to spend the rest of your life with him. You told him he was special to you. Did you mean that, or were you just looking to have sex and find out what you were missing?"

"You know nothing of what you speak. I loved Tucker more than anything in the world. We were supposed to share the rest of our lives together. I wanted to have a family with him because I knew he would be a good father someday. How dare you question my motives?"

"Then why fall prey to his suggestion about fleeing the responsibility of raising a child?" he said, staring at her, his eyes aflame and harsh.

She backed away from him, turning her head. "I-I don't know," she stammered.

She reached for her chest, her lungs weak from seeking oxygen. The Being smiled, his eyes suddenly turning soft and warm.

"There was so much more to think about before having sex with Tucker, wasn't there?"

"All I wanted was to be with him," she whispered, shaking her head. "Was that so awful?" She looked back at him, her eyes pleading for an answer.

"No. It wasn't. He was a good man, Stacy, you're right about that. And I'm sorry you never had the chance to see what he could become. Sadly, I will not be able to provide resolution to your wondering. I'm afraid all you can do is imagine what he would be like as a father. However, he is not part of this journey."

He looked at her, a sadness creeping into his gaze she hadn't noticed before. She stiffened, straightened her gown, and cleared her throat. She wiped her eyes and exhaled loudly.

"Then continue. Let me see what happens to my daughter if I may. I'm ready for it."

The Being cocked his head and grinned. "Are you sure?"

"Yes," she nodded. "Lead me."

He waved his hand forward as the air around them became aglow with bright colors.

"Then we shall continue."

Once the colors faded, Stacy found they had arrived in Olivia's penthouse suite. The building itself was built on a hillside, and more than one suite on the backside of the building had an extended balcony, like the one Olivia had chosen.

Situated on the third floor, the rear balcony peered out over a valley below, providing a beautiful view of the twinkling lights in downtown Beckton. The balcony itself was hidden by thick bushes and trees from the other suites. As the Being and Stacy walked slowly through the living room, they noticed Olivia sitting in the Jacuzzi, only she wasn't alone.

Stacy's brow furrowed as they got closer to the balcony, her mind straining to know the identity of the man Olivia sat with.

"Who is that?" she said, putting her hand on the Being's arm.

"A waiter from the Medallion," he answered. "He noticed she was upset, and the two began talking shortly before she left. He seemed charming and attentive, so that's how they ended up here together."

"But she just broke it off with Chad a few minutes ago. How could she do this?" she asked, the confusion evident in her voice.

"Loneliness can cause regret. It's amazing what lies a broken heart will believe."

"But she never loved Chad. You heard her. She was only with him for sex."

He let out a heavy sigh, shaking his head. "Sex is meant to be something deeper than what it has become. When you cheapen the true meaning of it, a part of your soul dies."

"What does that mean?" she said, clearly confused.

She looked intently at him, her eyes pleading for an answer. He returned her gaze, a softness covering his eyes. "Sex only means something when two hearts are connected at the most intimate level of the human soul. Pretending otherwise is a foolish game."

By now Olivia and the waiter had moved their activity inside, closing the bedroom door tightly. Stacy could only stand in amazement at how cavalier her daughter was behaving in this moment. How she wished she could suddenly intervene, to talk to her and warn her of the pitfalls of abusing this most precious gift of the soul.

How she wished she could see if her influence may have led to this moment. She could only shake her head, speechless at what she witnessed.

This is madness, she thought. She looked to the Being, unsure of what to do.

He turned to meet her gaze, then shook his head. "Oh, don't worry. There's no reason to go behind the doors. I think we both know what's going on. Best leave it alone," he said. "Besides, it's time to move on."

"To where?" she asked.

"You'll see."

The rhythmic beep of the heart monitor matched the incessant tick of the blood pressure cuff attached to Stacy's arm. An air tube was taped to her chin and protruded from her mouth, causing slight discoloration around her eyes. It all added to the appearance Stacy had been beaten.

Tori's eyes remained fixed on her daughter's face, tears stinging her own, as she leaned forward in the lounge chair beside the bed. Her elbows rested on her knees, her hands clasped together tightly as she held her fingers against her lips.

Stacy was taken to a recovery room, where she was placed for three hours, then transported to a private room. Once she was safely inside her single-person room, Dr. Blanton allowed Tori access to her daughter. She felt like it had been days since seeing her, but spending time in a hospital has a way of blurring the reality of time when waiting on a loved one.

Blanton already went over some of the details of what the staff was monitoring and cautioned Tori that most patients may never properly recover from a coma. This reality only served to heighten her own anxiety, leaving numerous questions unanswered.

"Stacy," she whispered, "don't leave me, baby. I need you."

Her words were soft, the compassion resonating in her soul. She lowered her head, closed her eyes tightly, and shuddered.

"I can't bear the thought of losing you, honey."

She looked back up at her daughter, reaching over and taking Stacy's left hand in hers. She squeezed it tightly.

"Give me a sign, honey. Let me know you're okay. Please," she begged.

She gripped Stacy's hand tighter now, hoping against hope she would receive some sign her daughter heard her. Giving a quick glance up at the heart monitor and the other machines on the wall, her mind was a blur of thought, not knowing what all the various numbers meant or why they may be flashing. She shook her head.

Finally realizing she wouldn't have the satisfaction of a response, she let go of Stacy's hand. The constant beeping of the heart monitor became oddly soothing to her, as it was the only sign her daughter was still alive. She felt a pulse of anxiousness as she pondered the idea of becoming a grandmother. Her tears came harder as the thought shattered her composure.

Why didn't she tell me she was pregnant? she thought. *Doesn't she trust me? I thought we could talk about anything.*

She shook her head at this, grasping at air to understand the secrecy surrounding this notion.

Suddenly, her mind flashed back to a memory of being in church when she was little. She remembered hearing a preacher saying something about God being near the brokenhearted, of giving comfort to the downtrodden, or something like that. Having not returned to church since well before high school, her memory betrayed the exact words, but the spirit of what the preacher said resonated with her at this moment.

She drew in a deep breath as she stared at Stacy, exhaling just as slowly as she breathed in. She closed her eyes and felt the presence of something she hadn't felt in a long time. She smiled.

"If you're there, God, I sure could use a sign my daughter's gonna be okay," she whispered. "You probably don't want to hear from me, and I don't know why you'd listen to me, especially after all I've done. But I sure could use you right now. Please. If you're real, let me know."

A peace she'd never known washed over her heart, spilling over into a slight smile across her lips. She remained this way for several minutes, not wanting to leave this emotion any time soon.

Just then she heard someone clear their throat behind her. Her eyes jolted open, and she turned her head to locate the source of the noise. Tori exhaled loudly and shook her head.

"Oh, it's you."

Jason stood in the doorway, his shoulders hunched, his backpack in one hand, the other tucked into his pants pocket. He stepped inside the room and made his way toward Stacy's bedside, setting the backpack on the floor beside the lounge chair as he passed.

"Sorry to disappoint you," he said, stopping next to Tori. "I didn't realize coming to see my daughter was that much of a burden to you."

"It's fine, Jason," she sighed.

"How is she?"

"Dr. Blanton said she's stable, but she's still got a ways to go in recovery."

"That's a good thing, right?"

"Yeah, it is."

Jason stepped closer to the bed, reached out, and touched Stacy's hand, gently caressing her fingers with his. He quickly cleared his throat, feeling a tear starting to fall from his eye. He reached up and brushed it away, as if scratching an itch.

"So…uh, how long will she be here?"

"They don't know. The amount of pills she took could've killed her, so she's got a long way to go before she's okay."

Jason glanced at her quickly, noticing her eyes were red from crying.

"Are you okay to stay here with her? Do you wanna take turns?"

She looked up at him, a slow warmth filling her soul. "I'd like it if we took turns," she said, reaching out to touch Jason's arm. "Thank you."

"For what?"

"For being so kind to me."

"It's what I'm supposed to do as her father, right?" he shrugged. "Protect her? Keep her safe? It's what any parent would do, right?"

As she stood, her legs made it obvious how weak she was from sitting too long. She leaned on the bed rail for support. "Yeah, it is,

Jason. I just thought, you know…" Her voice trailed off as she lowered her head.

He reached over and rubbed her back, slowly, gently. For a moment, it seemed they were still in love.

"Know what?" he asked.

She shook her head, never raising it. "Nothing. But that feels good," she said, slightly arching her back into his hand.

"Again. It's what I'm supposed to do," he smiled.

She became lost in the simplicity of her back being rubbed, and her mind wandered to thoughts of when they fell in love, to when they got married, and the weeks after Stacy arrived. The sudden familiarity of them being a couple washed over her heart, and she felt a sudden longing to forget about the past and try to make amends.

"How long have you been here?" he asked, causing her oblivion to disappear.

"About two hours straight."

"You sound tired. Why don't you go lie down over there." He pointed to the couch against the far wall. "I'll stay at her bedside and keep an eye on her, okay?"

She straightened herself, looked at him, and smiled. "I'd like that. You gonna be okay?"

Jason sat down in the lounge chair Tori had vacated, reaching for his backpack as he did. "Yeah. I'm good. You get some rest, okay?"

She moved toward the couch, then paused, a sudden wave of emotion overcoming her thoughts. She looked to Jason, who was now concentrating on his laptop. She hesitated before moving to the couch.

Why do I want to kiss him? she thought. She shook her head, closed her eyes, and chuckled.

Jason looked over at her. "What?"

Tori opened her mouth, stopped the words from coming out of her mouth, and shook her head. "Nothing. I'm gonna get some sleep. Let me know if you need me, okay?"

"Will do," he said.

Tori sat down slowly, reaching for the blanket and pillow already in place on the small table beside the couch. She laid out the pillow, unfurled the blanket, and lay down, pulling the blanket tight against her shoulders. She shifted in place, trying to get as comfortable as the hard leather surface of the couch would allow. She looked over at Stacy and Jason and took in a deep breath. She felt a smile cross her lips as she closed her eyes and drifted off into what she hoped would be a wondrously deep, restful sleep.

Chapter 5

"Now where are we?" Stacy asked.

They were walking through what seemed to be a deserted area of a city, one she didn't recognize. The night sky cast a pall over their steps as they wended their way through town, the occasional streetlight providing just enough light for suitable visibility.

Stacy turned her head in a slow semicircle, expecting a devilish creature of some sort to make a sudden appearance. Her apprehension and fear were evident as she began shaking. The deeper through the city they walked, the more she realized this was no place for anyone to live, especially her daughter. She glanced around at her surroundings, taking note of what to expect before she suspected they would find Olivia.

Warehouses lined the street, looking as if they suffered from the ravages of war. The windows of each building were caked in dirt, the panes of glass shattered in multiple window frames. Doorframes were either nonexistent or severely damaged. Piles of brick and stone were strewn about the base of most buildings, an indication the upper level had given up its structural integrity.

The Being finally looked at Stacy. "We're in Goldcrest very close to Blackburn, where you grew up," he answered.

"Why are we here?"

"To visit your daughter again," he glanced in her direction.

"But I thought…"

He held up a hand, stopping her before she completed her thought.

"As I explained previously, I will show you both the good and bad of what your child's potential life would be. You must trust me."

She nodded her head, then scrunched her nose.

"She lives out here?"

"More like, she lives over there," he pointed a finger to a cluster of dirty tents. "Cortez Boulevard. This is where the homeless population gathers."

"Homeless?" she said, her eyes wide. "My daughter could be homeless? That's crazy."

The Being shook his head, bringing a hand to wipe across his eyes.

"Not at all. I could provide you with all the possible bureaucratic answers as to why this would happen, but I would prefer not to bore you with details."

"No, I really don't care to know. But can't she just get a job and be done with living this way?"

"So naive," he whispered.

"What did you say?" she asked, annoyed.

He let out a soft laugh, waving his hand. "Nothing. Come. I want to show you where your daughter lives among the tents. I think you'll be surprised."

They walked past squalor normally reserved for a third world country that's been exploited by the news media. Human waste could be seen dotting the sidewalks, trash lay piled high in the gutters, wet and matted to the pavement. Needles could be seen strewn nearby certain tents, a clear indication drugs were highly prevalent here.

The stench became nearly unbearable the further they walked. Multiple people lay on blankets in the cool night air, exposed to the elements. Their hair was dirty and unkempt, their clothes even more ragged and worn than could be imagined. There were some who walked in a zombielike stupor, eyes half closed, feet shuffling and leading them nowhere.

Some were hyperactive, their arms and legs jerking about aimlessly, the occasional shout of nonsense emanating from their mouths. This was either a sign of mental illness or habitual drug abuse having finally conquered rational thought and movement.

Stacy found herself walking closer to the Being than before, forgetting she couldn't be seen or touched. She gazed in terror at what amounted to human waste existing in a city that had abandoned them. They stopped outside a tent situated on the corner of the street. It had been secured, rather ingeniously, between a lamppost and a doorframe.

"This is where your daughter lives," he said.

Stacy shook her head, her mouth open in horror. "No," she whispered in disbelief. "Why?"

"I told you. I would show you both the good and bad of what could happen. This is the bad, only this isn't the only time you'll see her in a negative light," he said, his voice low.

"Where is she? I need to see her."

"She's inside. Look," he said, waving his hand toward the tent.

Suddenly, the pair were standing inside the tent, looking down at a frail, dirty woman, her shoes tattered and worn, dirt smudged across her cheeks and forehead. The tent reeked of filth, a lone candle the only attempt to quell the stench. Stacy took inventory of her daughter's belongings and noticed, again, a picture of a young woman with a small girl, their faces blurred out. She shook her head, reaching out to touch the photograph, as if she were able to discover who occupied this frame.

Just then, Olivia stirred violently in her sleep, screaming in terror, sitting bolt upright from her bed of torn-up blankets. Her eyes remained closed as she sat up, and her body seemed extremely rigid.

Stacy recoiled at hearing this, jumping backward. Her heart rate accelerated as she tried to decipher what caused this sudden outburst.

After a moment or two, Olivia seemed to calm down, her eyes never opening. She lay down and fell back asleep, almost as gently as a baby being tucked into her crib.

Stacy looked over to where the Being stood. "What was that?"

"When you're forgotten by society at large, you lose the sense of connectivity needed to maintain healthy relationships and behavior," he said. "It's very common to see this sort of behavior happen out here."

She turned to look at Olivia, now smiling in her sleep.

"What is she dreaming about? What is it that brings her such happiness in her slumber?"

"That is not for you to know, my dear," he smiled. "The imagination is a wonderfully terrifying arena of thought and emotion. Some things are better left unexplained."

"She seems so fragile," she said, her eyes gazing at Olivia's frail body.

It was hidden under layers of dirty clothes, but her face exposed the truth.

"Fragile, you say?"

"Yes. Why does it surprise you I notice this about her?"

"Because you've shown a complete lack of concern for her in your womb."

The words fell hard across Stacy's ears, as if being forcibly shoved into her brain. She stepped backward from Olivia, clutching her stomach. Her breathing felt labored and heavy.

"Why do you say this?" she said in a whisper. Her words were laced in venomous hatred as they escaped her lips.

The Being moved to stand in front of her.

"Is it not true? Do you not wish to rid yourself of this responsibility? You have made this clear from the beginning that you feel as though the burden of being a mother would inconvenience your life."

"But why would my daughter live in squalor? Why do you show me such a horrible thing about her? Surely I would have taught her to be resourceful, to guide her to a better future than this," she said, her eyes pleading. "Wouldn't I have done that? Is this my fault?"

A smile crept across his face as he looked at her. "Young one, every mother has dreams about their child's life before they take their first breath, free of the womb. The expectations are enormous. But at some point, you must trust you built a solid-enough foundation for your child to strike out on their own to a life in which they can succeed or fail on their own merit."

"So this is my fault? How is that possible?" Stacy shook her head.

"My dear, this is but one of many possible outcomes," he sighed, "I never told you which of these scenes might come true for your child or even if they would be true at all. Merely, I wanted to impress upon you the importance of your influence on your child's life. You hold the key to her future. You help her decide what will or will not occur. This is the reason being a mother is so maddening."

She felt a steady stream of tears crawling across her cheek as she looked at Olivia. She sniffled loudly, wiping the tears from her chin.

"I would never wish this for her. I would never want my child to live in such a manner as this. She could die out here, and no one would even know."

His eyes became cold as he looked directly at her.

"All the more reason to be involved in your child's life and protect her at all costs, is it not?"

Tori opened her eyes, slowly, almost painfully forcing them to function. She smiled at the sound of the beeping and whirring of machines, their familiar sounds lending a sense of normalcy. She looked over at the hospital bed, hoping Stacy might have woken up during the night. Sadly, she remained in her comatose state.

On the other side of the bed, she noticed Jason had fallen asleep in the chair, his head bent at an awkward angle. She chuckled lightly, thinking of the muscle strain he would feel in his neck once he woke up. She breathed in deeply and pushed herself up off the couch, the blankets falling beside her on the floor. She stretched, yawing deeply.

Doing her best to straighten her clothes, she suddenly realized she hadn't checked her makeup in quite some time. Quickly, she stood to her feet and made her way to the bathroom, closing the door behind her, locking it. It seemed some habits weren't easily forgotten.

After a few moments in the bathroom, she opened the door to the room, washing her hands at the sink. Waving her hand in front of the towel dispenser, she tore off a portion and dried them off. Somewhere between the sink and the door, she determined makeup was superfluous. She took a few steps toward Stacy's bed, stopped, and looked at Jason.

For a moment, her heart was carried away to memories before they were married. There was the senior prom they went to, the after-party, and the two of them making out in his car before he took her home. She thought about the night he proposed to her at a concert, having prearranged it with the band to integrate this moment into the show. They received a standing ovation when she said yes.

She smiled, remembering their wedding day. Though it was planned for August—the hottest month of the year—the day was picture-perfect in every sense of the word. Low humidity, beautiful sun, everything going off without a hitch. Well, except for her father tripping over her dress as he went to sit down. She laughed, remembering how it lightened the mood for everyone.

And then she remembered the fighting, of seeing lipstick residue on his shirt collar, evidence of his cheating. She remembered him lying every time about how it happened, until one night she caught him. Opening the bedroom door, she was greeted by the sight of Jason and a petite redhead together in bed. In the moment, she wordlessly closed the door and left, her rage rendering her speechless. She'd never looked back since.

She threw the towel into the trash can outside the bathroom and walked further toward Stacy's bed, stopping next to the lounge chair. She reached down and nudged Jason.

"Hey," she said. "Wake up, Jason! Wake up." She pushed him harder each time she spoke.

He jerked his head up, his eyes blinking open rapidly. "What? Are you okay?" he said, rubbing his eyes. He yawned, letting out a heavy sigh as he did. He stretched out his arms and exhaled loudly.

"Has she woken up at all?" she asked.

He stood, extended his arms outward, and yawned again, his legs feeling wooden. "No. She hasn't moved all night. I was hoping she'd squeeze my hand or something, but she didn't respond," he said, leaning on the bed rails, letting go with another yawn. "I don't know what else to do right now."

"The doctor said she can recognize our voices if we talk, so he suggested we talk to her as much as we can," she said.

"Mmhm," he answered, closing his eyes again. He rested his head on his arms, stretching out his back a little.

She turned her head to look at him. "You don't think that's real?"

"What?"

"That she can hear us, even though she's in a coma."

"I don't know," he shrugged. "I guess so."

"You guess?"

He glanced at her, his eyes still adjusting to the daylight. "Look, I haven't had my coffee yet, so this is all too much to deal with. I'm gonna go to the café and get some. Do you want me to bring one up for you?"

"Yeah, that'd be nice. Don't forget the creamer."

"Of course," he smiled. "You want something to eat too?"

"Yeah, maybe an apple, or something light, I don't know," she said, raising a hand in the air.

He reached out and put his hand on her arm, squeezing gently. "I'll find something, okay? Trust me."

"Okay."

"I'll be right back," he said, turning and making his way out of the room.

Tori brought her attention back to Stacy. She sighed, the feelings of regret and loneliness convening in her heart, a mass of confusion overwhelming her. She shook her head and leaned down on the bed rail.

How long will this last? she thought, shaking her head.

"No, you don't understand," Stacy said, shaking her head. "I can make this all go away with one simple decision, could I not? If my child is never born, she will not have to suffer any pain later in life. She will not see the horror of the world in its present state. I would not want my child to suffer like this."

The pair had made their way outside of Olivia's tent, standing in the middle of the squalor and filth. A calm breeze swept across them, bringing a moment of false refreshment. But it also carried with it the stench of unwashed bodies, clothes, and decomposing food.

The Being shook his head, lowering his gaze to the ground. "Such naivete," he said.

"Why do you say such a thing?" she asked curiously.

He looked quickly at her, then turned his gaze upon the street. "You honestly believe your child would not suffer any pain if they were never to see the light of day, is that it?"

"It is not even a child right now. It is nothing more than a mass of cells," she said, defensively. "It would seem I would be doing it a favor if it were never introduced to the horrors of this life."

He turned slowly to her, a tired look in his eyes. "What does your heart tell you, young one? What does your very own body tell you about this 'mass of cells,' as you call it? Does it lie? Does it whisper to you of life or of nothing?" He seemed near tears as he spoke, then quietly shook his head. "You may never understand, even when we are finished here."

She took note of the resignation in his voice and turned away, watching the goings-on of the homeless. She was disturbed by the sight of them, not wishing to be close to anyone. Everything in her mind told her to run away, but somehow, she knew it was impossible to escape. Looking once more at the Being, she sighed. What was the ultimate purpose to this endeavor she felt ensnared in? And would it be of any consequence on her decision?

Just then, she saw Olivia emerge from her tent, shoulders slumped, a lost look in her eyes. Stacy perked up, leaning toward her daughter expectantly. A wistful smile came to her mouth as she watched Olivia gather a few plastic trash bags and push them into the pockets of her nearly threadbare coat. She glanced around the area, a suspicious look in her eyes. Stacy furrowed her brow and looked at the Being.

"Why does she do this?"

"You've heard it said, there is honor among thieves, no?"

"No, I haven't," she answered, shaking her head.

"There is a supposed code of conduct among thieves to look out for one another, to protect one another," he said. "However, no such code exists. Only in the minds of law-abiding citizens does this thought ferment. Out here, only survival matters. Those who cannot fend for themselves are left behind to die."

Stacy's eyes grew wide as she watched Olivia trudge up the street, a slight limp in her gait.

"Can she fend for herself, or is she one to be left behind?" she said, the fear in her soul causing her words to tremble.

"We can find out together if you like," he said with a shrug.

Stacy watched as Olivia made her way to the street corner, turn left, and disappear. Stacy blinked, unsure what she would prefer to do at this moment. Part of her wanted to remain outside of Olivia's tent until she returned, content in the knowledge her daughter had at least a modicum of safety here. The other part wanted to run after Olivia and make sure she wasn't getting into a bad situation. Either way, she had a feeling the answer to her questions about Olivia's motives wouldn't be welcome.

"You're not sure which direction you'd like to go, are you?"

"Where does she go?" she asked, her voice just above a whisper.

"Come. Let us see," he answered, waving his hand.

The wind began to swirl around them, the colors becoming bright once more as they were lifted from the pavement and drifted through time.

Within minutes, the pair stood outside a modest English Tudor home, hiding behind one of the four massive bushes lining the property line. To the right of the front door was a three-car garage, facing inward, the driveway passing directly in front of the entryway. There was a small courtyard between the driveway and front door, with a patio table and furniture tucked away for the night.

The soft glow of outdoor lights added a touch of calm to the property, accenting the wooden slats along the outside walls of the home. The landscaping was immaculate, with smaller bushes and flower gardens seemingly everywhere.

Stacy smiled at the home, shaking her head as she gazed upon its muted beauty. "Where are we?"

"Your home."

His tone was devoid of any emotion, a blank stare frozen on his face. Stacy's mouth fell open in amazement.

"My home," she whispered, "oh my gosh."

She held a hand to her chest, absorbing the subtle simplicity of such a cozy atmosphere. Blinking her eyes in disbelief, this brief glimpse into her future showed her precisely what she dreamed about. As if for the first time, she looked at Olivia, standing behind one of the bushes as well. Stacy shook her head, her face registering her confusion.

"Why doesn't she go inside? Doesn't she realize she can sleep here instead of on the street? Surely she knows she's welcome in my home."

The words seemed superfluous even as she spoke them.

"Does she? What makes you certain of this?" He met Stacy's astonished gaze with resolute confidence.

"She's my daughter," her voice wavered. "Why would I let my daughter sleep on the street?"

"Why would you want any unfortunate circumstance to happen to your child, even if they exist only in your womb?"

She closed her eyes and shook her head. "I told you, the doctor assured me, it's not really a person right now. How could I possibly inflict pain on something that's not real?"

His eyes suddenly became dark and furious, his face blanched and cold. "You wanted the truth. This is the truth. Watch!" he said, his tone commanding and harsh.

The lights inside went dark, save for the soft glow of night lights placed strategically throughout the home. Olivia smiled, a gleam coming to her eyes. She hurried as fast as her limp allowed to a small enclosure, consisting of two rails of fence post, just big enough for hiding two trash cans. Once there, Olivia pulled open the lid of one of them and began rummaging through the waste.

Staring in disbelief, Stacy shook her head. Tears came to her eyes as she watched this scene unfold: her own daughter resorting to picking through a trash can.

"Why does she do this? What is she looking for?" her voice wavered.

"Food," he answered.

Stacy began weeping in earnest now.

"Why can't she come inside? Why?"

The desperation in her voice begged for an answer. He sighed, shook his head, and closed his eyes. Opening them, he took a quick look upward and shrugged before answering.

"I suppose you deserve to know some of what happens." He sighed again, turning to face Stacy. "She rummages through your trash cans because she is not invited inside. I am not at liberty to expound on the reason why this is, but she is not welcome in your home."

The weight of his words fell hard on Stacy, causing her to fall to her hands and knees. Tears began falling hard and fast across her face as she felt herself begin to dry heave. The pain of seeing her daughter scrounging for food was too much to bear.

For his part, the Being alternated between watching Olivia stuff the plastic bags with half-eaten food and looking at Stacy sobbing in agony. If he felt any sort of compassion toward either person, it was not evident in his mannerisms.

The sound of a dog barking from inside the house broke the silence surrounding them, and Stacy looked up to see what was happening. She saw Olivia attempting to run away from the trash cans, her limp more pronounced. There was panic on her face as she clung to the plastic bags, nearly overflowing with scraps of food.

Stacy watched as Olivia passed directly in front of her and disappear into the shadows. She heard a door open and glanced over to see who stepped outside. She looked through cloudy eyes at the person's face, unable to decipher their features. Truth be told, she wasn't certain she could identify if it was a man or woman at this moment.

The person turned their head left to right and back again. They appeared to be holding a weapon—a pistol, from what little Stacy could determine—and they took a few steps away from the door. After several minutes of searching the immediate area, the person shrugged their shoulders and headed back inside. The dog barking continued for several minutes, then finally subsided. No doubt the person was able to comfort the dog into silence.

Stacy soon found herself and the Being following close behind Olivia, making their way back to the tent city on Cortez Boulevard. As they rounded the corner, they were greeted by two police cars parked in the street, lights flashing. Olivia stopped dead in her tracks, a sudden panic washing over her.

Two officers—one male, the other female—were standing outside their cars, talking to a couple of the homeless people. The officers listened intently as the homeless people gesticulated wildly and without purpose, obviously telling the officers a story. Suddenly, one of the homeless pointed up the street in the direction where Olivia stood.

Olivia was visibly agitated, her breathing heavy and labored. She dropped the bags she carried, her eyes growing wide with panic. She turned her head in all directions, searching for someplace to hide. She saw the entryway to an abandoned store nearby and ducked into the shadows, her back pressed against the entry wall.

The Being and Stacy stood close by, expectantly waiting to see what would happen next.

Both officers turned their heads, craning their necks to see what the homeless were pointing at, curious to know if they were crazy or being helpful. The female officer turned back to the people they were talking to, waving a hand in the air as she spoke. The male officer held up his flashlight and shone it in the direction where Olivia was now hiding.

Deciding he needed to investigate further, the officer began walking cautiously toward where Olivia stood. With one hand on his service revolver and the other on his flashlight, he turned the beam of light in all directions, wanting to ensure he wouldn't be surprised. He arrived where Olivia stood hiding, her back planted firmly against the wall, and shone the light on her chest, illuminating her face at the same time.

"Ma'am," he said, "I need you to step out here for a few minutes. We need to talk to you."

"Why?" Olivia said, her voice raspy and hoarse.

"Just step out here, and we'll let you know," the officer said.

By now the female officer had joined her partner, her hand placed on her revolver as a precaution as well.

"But I ain't done anything wrong," Olivia said, starting to cry.

"Well, let us hear what you have to say, and we'll work with you, okay?" the male officer said. "You're not in trouble right now, but you need to cooperate with us, all right?"

Olivia cautiously stepped out from the doorframe, taking a few halting steps toward the officers.

"Wh-what do you want?" she stammered.

"First of all, I'm Officer Kendrick, this is my partner, Officer Taylor," the male officer said, pointing to himself first, then the female officer.

"What do you want? I didn't do nothin' wrong," Olivia said.

"Take it easy, ma'am. We just need to talk to you," Taylor said. "We were patrolling through here, and someone stopped us to say there was a disturbance down here. Several of the people we spoke to said you were the one causing it. Is that true?"

Olivia looked at Taylor, the bewilderment in her eyes painfully evident.

"No. I wasn't even here."

"Where did you go?" Taylor asked.

Olivia looked wide-eyed from Taylor to Kendrick, then back again.

"I went for a walk," she said.

"Where did you take your walk?" Kendrick asked.

"None of your business," Olivia said, the indignance rising in her voice.

"Did anybody see you leave?" Taylor asked.

"No. I keep to myself. I don't cause no trouble."

Olivia was shaking now, her hands trembling.

"Well, one of your neighbors said you came into their tent and tried to steal their Coleman lantern. Did you do that?" Kendrick said.

"No. I've got my own lantern. I don't need nobody else's lantern," Olivia said, spitting on the pavement. "Who told you that?"

"Take it easy," Kendrick said, holding up a hand. "I'm just trying to figure out what went on, okay? Like I said, you're not in any trouble right now, but we need to find out what happened."

"Well, you can tell my neighbors they can kiss my ass," she said, her voice rising as she spoke.

She looked in the direction of the other homeless, rage boiling in her eyes.

"Ma'am," Taylor said, holding up her hand, "there's no reason to yell at them. They were simply telling us what they know, just like you are. Calm down, okay?"

"Why?" Olivia shouted, pointing down the street at the others. "They hate me. They take advantage of me. I try to help anyone I can with what little I have, and this is the thanks I get. Why don't they just leave me alone?"

The tears fell faster now as she spoke, her trembling increasing.

"Ma'am, we're here to help figure this out, okay?" Kendrick said. "You need to help us understand what happened. There's no need to get so angry right now."

"But you don't understand," Olivia shouted, moving closer to Kendrick and Taylor. "They hate me. They harass me all the time. I try to be helpful, but they always take advantage of me. I ain't causin' no trouble down here. Why don't you go arrest them? They keep stealing from me."

She moved in a circle between Kendrick and Taylor as she spoke.

Kendrick immediately pulled out his Taser and pointed it at Olivia.

"Ma'am. Ma'am!" he said sternly. "I'm gonna have to ask you to stop moving."

"Why don't you go arrest them? I don't understand this. This is crazy," Olivia said, still moving wildly in a circle. "Why don't they just leave me alone? Why can't you see they steal my things?"

She was nearly incoherent as she spoke, her sobs coming strong and hard now.

Stacy was frozen where she stood, tears stinging her cheek as she watched her daughter. She couldn't believe Olivia was so erratic in her behavior.

Please don't use the Taser on my baby, she thought. *Please don't Tase her.*

She shifted nervously in her stance as she watched Kendrick and Taylor moving backward from Olivia. Taylor had one hand on her revolver, the other on her radio calling for backup.

"Put your hands in the air," Kendrick shouted.

"Don't you understand? They're trying to kill me," Olivia said, her voice pleading. "They want to kill me." She continued to move wildly, her arms and hands jerking awkwardly as she spoke.

"Put your hands in the air, or I will Tase you, understand? Put them in the air!" Kendrick's actions revealed he felt threatened. He continued to point the Taser at Olivia, never wavering in moving it.

Taylor made a move toward Olivia, attempting to grab her arms, but Olivia swung wildly, hitting Taylor in the jaw. It was at that moment that Kendrick unleashed his Taser. The prongs hit Olivia in the abdomen, and she began to shake violently. She stood for only a few moments, before dropping to the pavement, hard.

"No!" Stacy shouted, moving toward Olivia.

The Being suddenly reached out and took a firm grip on her arm. She looked back at him, stunned he would do such a thing.

He glared at her. "You would be wise not to interfere. It would be useless anyway."

He lessened his grip, but only after Stacy eased her body backward. He sighed, letting go of her arm.

"Remember, they can't see you, and you cannot change what is happening. We are here only to watch."

Stacy's tears fell faster now as she watched her daughter helpless on the ground, both Kendrick and Taylor forcing Olivia's hands to her back, attempting to put handcuffs on her.

"But they're taking my daughter to jail," Stacy said, her body and voice trembling.

"And what does that matter to you? Why so protective, young one?" he asked, looking at Stacy.

She pivoted her stance to face him, tears clouding her eyes. "Why are you showing this to me? What purpose does this serve, other than being a cruel reminder of what may come in my child's life?"

He leaned his head back and laughed. "You've chosen to flee the responsibility of being a mother, yet you behave as one. Your desire to protect your child reveals the truth. What does that tell you about your circumstance?"

She looked at the scene unfolding now. Olivia had been placed in handcuffs and was being led to one of the squad cars. By now two other officers had joined Kendrick and Taylor and were milling about the area.

Stacy shook her head, burying her face in her hand. "You never told me I would witness such behavior. You never allowed me to know what to expect. You hid this from me on purpose," she said, her voice barely above a whisper.

"I did no such thing," he answered. He let out a heavy sigh as he stepped closer to her. "Young one, you've made it abundantly clear what you wish to do, yet you seem to waver the more we see. Why is that?"

She looked at him with venom-filled eyes.

"You are the most cruel, evil person, or thing, I've ever encountered. You led me here to convince me I should have this child, that I should be a mother. You did not tell me of the cruelty my daughter would face. You lied to me."

"Did I?" he said, a curious look on his face. "I think you need to remember what I told you before we started this journey. I simply said, you will witness the potential good and bad of your child's life. That is all. Obviously, you still have a decision to make. I merely wanted to let you witness what may unfold if you decided to keep your child. I did not lie, young one. I believe you're lying to yourself."

She sniffled loudly as she watched one of the squad cars pull away. As it passed her, she caught sight of Olivia in the back seat, utter desolation in her eyes. It was as if her daughter's soul had been crushed.

Suddenly, the pair stood in darkness again, with only enough light to illuminate them individually. Stacy shook her head, an attempt to clear her mind of what she watched unfold with her daughter.

"You still don't understand," she whispered, her head low. "If I have this child, it will only be a burden on everyone around me. It's too much for me. I can't take this suffering any longer."

The Being breathed in slowly, closing his eyes. He exhaled just as gently, his breath carefully crossing her face. Expecting the worst, she was surprised how refreshing it felt on her cheeks. She closed her eyes and felt a peace wash over her like none before.

"Stacy, my dear," he started, "you have been given this opportunity as a gift. Learn from it. Never forget what you see and hear as we go along. What I am showing you is beyond comprehension, yes, but you are only witnessing one small part of the entirety of your child's potential life. You still are allowed the freedom of whether she lives or not. I cannot change your mind. Only you have the power to know. All I can do is present to you what could happen. It is no guarantee any of this will come true, but again, that depends on you. If you decide to be a mother, you take on the full responsibility to lead your child, to love them, to nurture them, and to teach them the right way to live. If you don't believe you are able to bear such a burden—which I know you can—then you know what to do. Either way, young one, you still hold the power in your hands. Tread lightly, my dear."

She remained silent for some time her mind overwhelmed with too many questions to sort through. She kept her head low, her eyes fixed on a point near her feet. She shuffled in place nervously.

What would she say? Would she even respond? What would she ultimately decide? Had she settled on a resolution to her problem or not?

Tori and Jason had finished their menial breakfast in Stacy's room, wordlessly watching TV. Being that it was only basic cable, the selection of shows was severely lacking in variety, but they made do with watching a rerun of a '90s comedy.

Jason nursed his coffee and was obviously more alert than before. Tori nibbled on what remained of her Fuji apple, the ham and eggs they shared having been devoured earlier. She sat with her feet propped up on the couch, and he occupied the same lounge chair in the far corner he'd slept in the night before. It seemed the quintessential portrait of domestic bliss, albeit under stressful circumstances.

Jason stood and gathered his Styrofoam container and plastic utensils. He walked to where Tori sat and picked up her container as well.

"Thank you," she said smiling.

"You're welcome."

He carried the waste to the trash can by the front door and threw them away. He wiped his hands on his jeans and walked back to the chair. Sitting down, he reached over on to the end table beside him and picked up the remote for the TV.

"Did the doctor say when they'd be back?" he asked, muting the television.

"No. But I'll talk to the nurse when she comes in and find out when he's coming by," she said. "Why?"

"I just wanna know if she's getting any closer to waking up."

"Me too."

She glanced over and watched the line showing Stacy's heartbeat scroll across the screen of one of the machines, a small reassurance her baby was still with her. She drew in her breath and exhaled slowly, brushing the hair out of her face.

"Listen," he started, leaning forward in his chair, "I'm sorry for being so rude to you in the waiting room the other day. I just flew in from Phoenix, and I was tired."

"What were you doing out there?"

"Training," he said. "Don sent me and Walker out to make sure they were using the new system correctly."

Tori swung her feet onto the floor as she faced Jason. "Did you make sure they were?"

"Of course," he chuckled. "I don't always enjoy traveling for work, but in the end, it's not so bad."

"Well," she said, looking down at the floor, "you were always good at telling people what to do. It's a gift."

"Maybe," he said, waving his hands in the air.

"Jason? Can I ask you something?"

"I guess," he said shifting his weight in the chair.

She cleared her throat and brushed her hair again, more because she was stalling for time than anything else. She closed her eyes and shook her head, nervously shifting in her seat.

"Why did we, um…" she paused, exhaling, "why did we get a divorce?"

He looked over at her, a stunned expression on his face. He turned his gaze to the floor, shaking his head, clearly taken aback by the question. He shifted again in his seat, unsure if he could provide an answer.

"I-I don't know what to say," he replied.

He rose from the chair and started pacing in a circle beside it. He alternated between shaking his head and lightly grunting. She watched intently as he made another round of laps in front of the chair, wondering if he was going to answer. More than that, she wondered why she asked the question in the first place.

Suddenly, he stopped, inhaled, and exhaled deeply, closing his eyes.

"Do you really want to try and answer that question now," he said, "especially with what's going on?"

He looked over at her, a grim expression locked on his face. "I-I just thought we could talk," she pleaded, "you know, like we used to."

"Tori, what brought this on?" he said, raising his arms outward. "All of a sudden, you wanna try to resolve our issues? Are you nuts?"

"It's just been so nice the last couple of days with you here."

He held up his hand. "Stop it, right now," he snapped. "There's too much to go over, okay? This isn't the time or place."

She rolled her eyes and flopped her hand on the couch. "When is the time and place, Jason?"

"Not while our daughter's in a coma. Besides, I thought we decided this a long time ago."

"Well, maybe I want to reconsider," she said, standing from the couch. "Maybe I want to try again."

"You're unbelievable. It didn't work before. What makes you think it'll work now?"

"I don't know, Jason. Maybe I just miss having you around. Like I said, the last couple days have been nice between us. I miss that."

Her eyes begged him to respond, yearning to know if he felt the same connection she did. Although she couldn't explain it, she felt the pangs of renewed love flitting about her heart.

"Tori, there's no going back," he said, shaking his head. "We don't work anymore, okay? We're different people now, okay? This won't work, so forget it. When I signed the papers, I was done with this relationship. I'm not going back."

He glared at her, his eyes cold and distant. He put his hands on his hips, shaking his head. A slight smirk came to his face, and he began laughing.

"What's so funny?" she asked.

"You," he replied, waving his hand at her. "Do you really think this will happen again?" He laughed louder now, tossing the remote onto the lounge chair. "I need some fresh air. I've been cooped up in here for too long," he said, turning and walking out of the room.

She stared at the empty doorway and felt a tear trickle down her cheek. She reached up and wiped it away, sniffling. She closed her eyes and shook her head, suddenly feeling foolish. She looked at Stacy and was struck by how frail her daughter looked. She walked over to the bed and leaned on the railing.

Her tears came slow and steady as she reached down and took hold of Stacy's hand, stroking the back of it with her thumb. She tried to smile, but it felt forced and unnatural. She leaned her head down on her arms and cried, feeling more alone than ever.

"Why must she be in this cage?" Stacy asked, her voice low.

She was staring at Olivia through the bars of a dirty jail cell. She was sleeping on a cold metal bench inside the cell, appearing as if she were home in a comfortable bed. Stacy felt a smile forming on her lips, but not coming to fruition. Instead, she couldn't help but be angry at the conditions her daughter found herself in currently.

The metal bars of the cell were flaking and needed replaced. The floor of the cell was covered in multiple substances, both solid and liquid. Stacy refused to imagine what made up this disgusting filth.

She held a hand to her mouth as she spoke, causing her words to be muffled. Tears clouded her vision as she looked at her daughter—frail, confused, and completely abandoned by society. Nobody should be subjected to this kind of treatment, especially someone Stacy knew was capable of so much more.

"Painful, isn't it, young one?"

She looked at him, her eyes injured at hearing something so insensitive. "Why do you show this to me?"

"Because you agreed to see both the good and bad of what your daughter might go through," he replied.

"No," she shook her head, "not like this. I didn't ask for this."

"Yes, you did." His voice was firm and harsh as he spoke, causing Stacy to shrink away from him.

Just then, a guard came up to the cell, taking his nightstick from his belt and rattling the bars. The noise was louder than expected, causing Stacy to cover her ears.

"Hey!" the guard shouted, "Get up!"

Olivia's eyes opened wide, and she bolted upright off the metal bench.

"Shut up!" she screamed back at the guard. "I was sleeping. Why can't you leave me alone?"

The guard rattled his keys, bringing them to the lock. He smirked as he unlocked the cell door and pulled it open.

"You made bail," he said.

Olivia sat dumbfounded, rubbing her eyes and shaking her head.

"What?"

"I said you made bail. You get to leave."

"Who paid my bail?" she whispered.

"Your mother came down to the station and paid it," he said. "She didn't stick around though."

Stacy's heart leaped at hearing even the small part she could play in her daughter's life. Olivia's mouth began to form a smile at this thought, suddenly stopping as a mixture of joy and resentment washed over her. She rubbed her eyes, then looked up at the guard.

"My...my mother paid?" she said, her words halting as she spoke.

"Yeah. Now let's go," the guard said, motioning with his hand to get up.

Olivia sat for a moment, alternating between staring at the floor and the guard. She stood up, slowly, her legs appearing weak. She took a few halting steps toward the cell door, though it was more shuffling than walking. Her limp was more pronounced as she walked, no doubt sleeping on the metal bench exacerbating the issue. She paused at the door, reaching out to touch the guard's arm. She gave a smile as she looked at him.

"Thank you," she said. "Thank you so much."

"Don't thank me. Thank your mom when you see her," he answered. "Right now, it's time to leave." He pointed down the hallway toward the exit as he spoke.

Olivia patted the guard's arm again and shuffled down the hall. Stacy walked beside her, smiling through her tears. The Being simply walked in silence behind them, a wry smile upon his face. Stacy turned to look at him, mouthing the words, "Thank you," as they walked.

The trio continued down the hall, through the precinct office, and toward the entrance. Inside the main room, the sound of telephones ringing, the chatter of conversations, and the shouts of anger by several perpetrators combined in a cacophony of noise.

Olivia turned her head in all directions, staring wide-eyed at the spectacle around her. She adopted a fearful look as she shuffled past the officers' desks and chairs. Stacy could tell Olivia wanted to leave here as soon as possible. Truth be told, Stacy wanted out of this awful display of anger and rage without so much as a glance backward. She would feel better once they were outside.

Olivia stepped gingerly down the stairs outside the precinct entrance, holding the handrail as she did. Finally arriving on the sidewalk, she turned her head side to side, as if searching for something. Stacy watched as Olivia turned in circle after circle, seemingly hesitant on where to go next.

"Why does she do this?' Stacy asked. She turned back to look at the Being, who was a few paces behind her. "Can you tell me?" she asked.

"My dear, your daughter has lived on the streets for a long time now," he answered. "Disorientation is part of not having a home. You have nowhere to go, nowhere to lay your head. You have nothing to look forward to but sleeping on a mattress of concrete. Not much of a life, is it?"

She turned and watched as Olivia moved slowly into the shadows, moaning in imagined pain. Or was it imagined? Olivia continued shuffling along the street, until she disappeared in the shadows, lonely and afraid.

"But I bailed her out of jail. Why would I leave? Why would I not want to see her?"

The Being sighed, rubbing his eyes, his head lowered in exasperation.

"Tell me!" she insisted. "Why would I do such a thing?"

"Isn't it obvious? Can't you see what's happening here?"

She stared at him, utter disbelief in her eyes.

"What should be obvious?"

"You have an estranged relationship with your daughter."

"I...what?" she said. "Estranged? Why?"

"Only your heart can tell you the reasons. Ask yourself how you act toward your own mother, and you'll find the answer."

She felt a rage building inside her, consuming her mind. Her eyes turned to fire, and she walked aggressively toward the Being. When she was a few paces away from him, she swung her hand backward, then forward, the palm of her hand striking his face hard. The blow caused his head to turn to the side, the redness on his cheek becoming exposed almost immediately.

"How dare you say such a thing?" she said, her teeth clenched in rage. "I may dislike my mother, but at least we're not estranged. I grow tired of your condescension toward me. I deserve respect."

He rubbed his cheek slowly, a vain attempt at numbing the sting from her blow. He turned his head back to look her in the eye. He smirked.

"You don't understand the ramifications of your life, do you? You literally can't see how your life might affect others, can you?"

She was breathing hard, the anger still roiling in her gut.

"You're a despicable creature. You deliberately mock me, to provoke me into doing something I'm not capable of doing. You know nothing of what you speak."

He closed his eyes, smiling, and shook his head.

"Young one, we are only at the beginning," he said, finally opening his eyes to look at her. "We still have far to go. Remember what I told you. What you witness is a small portion of your daughter's life. I never said what we see encompasses the entirety of who she becomes or even these situations would be her final destinations."

"That may be, but you act as though my allowing her to live is a noble gesture. You try to convince me that letting her escape my womb is something amazing. I simply don't believe that's true. It will ruin my life, don't you understand?"

He stood silent, his eyes blinking, a mixture of confusion and calm on his face. He exhaled, shaking his head, groaned and lowered his head. He remained looking at the ground for several minutes, the silence between them deafening.

She inhaled slowly, pulling herself to her full height. She jutted out her chin, her confidence in intellectually overpowering the Being coursing through her thoughts. Her smile conveyed her confidence that she had found a way to rid herself of his continued badgering.

Cautiously, he raised his head, studying her for a few moments. The longer he looked at her, the more she felt uneasy.

"Why do you look at me that way?" she asked, her eyes narrowing.

He exhaled slowly, closed his eyes for a moment, then opened them again. "Perhaps this was a mistake. Perhaps I should return you to your miserable life and allow you to destroy your daughter. You have only seen two possible scenarios of your daughter's life, and yet you wish to run as far away as you can. You tell me your life will be ruined by this child. You continue to believe in the negative outcome of your being a mother. It's as if you see no future in having a child."

He stepped closer to her now, his eyes warm and soothing to her soul. He stopped a few paces from her.

"Young one, you have no way of knowing what your life will become, even by witnessing these events. You have so much to offer the world, so much good locked away in your heart. So much love. Why would you not want to share this love with someone biologically wired to adore who you are?"

He smiled, his eyes turning sad as he gazed upon her. She moved to speak, but he held up his hand, motioning for her to remain silent.

"There will be time for you to speak later," he said. "It is time to move on."

Chapter 6

Nightbridge, a nonprofit company, was a hive of activity on this resplendent morning. Situated in an abandoned warehouse, it utilized only one fourth of the area for actual office space, while the remainder of the building contained row upon row of shelving units. The racks were spaced just wide enough apart to allow a forklift adequate room to navigate each row.

Pallets of nonperishable food lined the shelving, each of them shrink wrapped and ready for shipping. Meanwhile, any foodstuffs needing to be kept cold occupied a large room at one corner of the building. Separated into a refrigerator and freezer, these rooms contained all manner of meat, poultry, fish, eggs, and vegetables needing to be kept cold.

The employees hustled from one activity to the next, each with a smile affixed to their faces. Laughter could be heard often as the atmosphere seemed to engender this jovial nature almost organically. In fact, it was an essential component intrinsically built into the fabric of nearly every move made by its CEO, Olivia Hamilton.

She had been at the helm of this venture for several years now and found a welcoming community in the city of Colchester. A midsized town overlooked in the Midwest by much larger cities, Colchester nonetheless maintained a proud tradition of being famously hospitable to one and all. Olivia had chosen to locate Nightbridge here for that very reason. Knowing those who would be in her employ, as well as volunteer, would further the outreach of the company, it made the choice in location that much easier.

The Being walked slowly ahead of Stacy as they both ambled through the warehouse. He seemed to be walking with purpose, calm and proud. Stacy kept pace with him, alternately watching the volunteers working in tandem, all while keeping an eye on the Being. She marveled at the expansive nature of the warehouse, shaking her head at the thought of how so few people could keep so much food in proper order.

The Being stopped walking near a long table, manned on both sides by volunteers. They busied themselves sorting through and packing boxes of various canned goods and fresh vegetables. He turned his head toward Stacy.

"What do you think?"

"Of what?" she asked, confused.

"All this." He waved a hand toward the volunteers. "What do you make of this?"

"I-I don't know. What should I think?"

"Your daughter is responsible for this."

"She is?"

"Yes," he said, sounding exasperated. "She became the CEO here. Didn't you see that as we walked in?"

"No," she shook her head. "I guess I missed it."

"Come," he motioned with his hand. "She's in her office now."

The pair walked toward the offices, passing more long tables where more volunteers sorted and packed boxes with supplies. Located in the opposite corner from the refrigeration units, the offices were walled and partitioned off from each other. A wall of windows exposed the interior to the main floor where the volunteers were working. Inside, the various locations of the offices and conference rooms were clearly marked and separated.

Entering Olivia's office, Stacy couldn't contain her surprise at the stark nature of the room. Olivia sat at a small desk, focused on her computer. The wall behind her contained numerous pictures of her with what appeared to be local dignitaries. There was a prominently displayed picture of Olivia with what must have been a state official, perhaps a senator. Stacy figured as much by the mechanical smile on his face.

Stacy glanced down at the filing cabinet directly behind the desk and saw the same picture of a woman with a small child. Again, the faces were blurry, but it was the same pose as the others she'd seen before.

The Being noticed her curiosity as she gazed at the picture and smiled.

"That's a good picture, isn't it?"

"Yes, fascinating," she answered. "But why can't I see their faces? Why are they blurry?"

He smiled. "Perhaps you should be asking the significance of why Olivia chooses to display that picture."

"What do you mean?"

"Why would your daughter choose only one picture to carry throughout her life?" he asked.

She opened her mouth to speak, but just then, the phone ringing on Olivia's desk negated any question that might have been asked. Olivia sighed, reached over, and picked up the receiver.

"Hello?" she said. She smiled as she listened for a few minutes. "Yes, thank you so much. I certainly appreciate it. Yes. There's a loading dock in the rear of the building where you can drop off your donation."

Stacy smiled as she listened to Olivia.

"Oh, of course. We'll find good use for your deer meat. We pride ourselves on supplying a variety of food for those in need," Olivia said.

The office door opened, and a stout gentleman entered, carrying a manila folder. He paused a moment as he entered, looking intently at Olivia. She held up a finger, nodding her head.

"Yes. Thank you. I appreciate it. Listen, I'm sorry to cut this short, but my assistant just came in, and we've got some things to go over. Yes, thank you. Have a great day. Goodbye."

She hung up the phone and leaned back in her chair, smiling.

"Tell me you have good news, Paul," she said, crossing her arms.

"I do," he answered, closing the door tightly and crossing to the chair opposite Olivia's desk.

"Great. Is it what we expected?"

She leaned in on the desk, clasping her hands together in front of her. Paul opened the folder and pulled out a sheet of paper.

"Yes. We were able to secure our connection with Mid State Charity. We've got our supply chain, Liv."

"Yes!" she clapped her hands. "Now we can distribute to more families across the county." She sighed heavily, shaking her head. "You have no idea how long I've been praying about this, Paul," she continued. "I'm so glad the Lord answered me like this."

"He's always on time, Liv. You know that."

"Yeah," she laughed. "He sure is, huh?"

He reached over and handed the sheet of paper to Olivia. "This gives the breakdown of the financials and how it will boost our revenue to purchase more food. Instead of relying on donations only, we'll be able to buy in bulk."

"I'm so happy, Paul. You have no idea."

"I think I do," he chuckled.

"So how soon can we start?"

"Well," he sighed, "I don't think it'll be until mid-October at the earliest. I talked to the director, and he said it would take time to divert their supply chains to help us out. He didn't seem too concerned it would be a problem."

"How are we on supplies until then?" she asked.

He opened the folder again and pulled out another sheet of paper.

"Well, we might be a little thin through the end of next month, but once November hits, we'll start swimming in donations again." He chuckled. "People love to give and feel like they're helping others around the holidays."

"That they do, Paul," she smiled. "But don't those donations last us through February?"

"Yes," he nodded. "I just wish it were more consistent. But now that we can tap into Mid State Charity's supply chain, we'll be in better shape to help."

"That's what I was hoping for," she said. "Hey, what are we gonna do with payroll? Gina said she crunched the numbers, but we might not be able to pay everyone next month."

"Yeah," he sighed, heavily. "I don't have an answer. It'd be so much easier if we were for profit and charged everyone to buy from us."

"Paul, you know that's not how I set this up. I want to honor my father's memory, even though he died before I was born. From what my mother says, he was a very giving person. He was always thinking of others first."

Stacy couldn't contain her tears at hearing Olivia say this. She held her hand over her eyes as her body shook from her soft sobs.

"Okay, I can respect that," he nodded, "but it would make it so much easier."

"But we wouldn't be any different than a grocery store, Paul," she said, waving a hand. "That's not what I want to be known for, okay?"

"I'm with you, Liv. I'm with you, all right? So spare me the holier-than-thou speech," he said, a hint of indignation creeping into his voice.

"What holier-than-thou speech?" she responded, an edge to her tone.

He propped his elbow on the arm of the chair and leaned his head into his hand, rubbing his forehead. "I'm sorry, Liv," he said. "I've just been on edge since Jackie left. It hasn't been easy."

"I'm so sorry, Paul. When did she leave?"

"Last month," he sighed. "I mean, we had problems, just like anybody. But I thought we were okay. I never meant for her to leave."

"Well, we'll have to pray about it and see what the Lord can do," she said. "Right now, we need to gather the troops and let them know we're expanding our outreach." Her smile was as wide as it could possibly be as she spoke.

Paul looked up and smiled as well. "Yeah. That should boost their spirits, huh?" he said.

The pair stood and headed for the office door. Paul opened it, motioned for Olivia to exit first, and followed her close behind.

"Where does this faith come from? Why does she believe in God?" Stacy asked, half whispering.

"How does anyone come to believe?" the Being answered.

"I don't know," she said with a shrug.

"It's through hearing and believing in the Bible, simply surrendering to a higher power."

"Did I become religious? How is that possible? I never grew up going to church," she said, bewildered.

He turned to look at her, a warmth in his eyes soothing her mind. "My child, everyone has the opportunity to hear this message. It's everywhere. Why, the rocks, the trees, the very ground you stand upon cries out the wonderment of a Creator who formed the fabric of life. It only requires a childlike faith to embrace this truth."

She turned to watch Olivia and Paul walking toward the warehouse, animated in their conversation.

"She certainly does have a lot of good qualities in her, doesn't she?"

"Of course. She learned everything in how to perceive the world from you."

Stacy turned to look at him. "Why is it I can see her life, but I can't see how I'm involved? I still don't understand. Why is it this way?"

He studied her face carefully, his eyes narrow, as if he were deep in thought. He breathed in and out slowly before he spoke.

"Young one, you have expressed to me, and the world, that you are incapable of raising this child alone. You have nearly convinced yourself you cannot do this on your own, yet you won't even reach out and ask for assistance. You've decided this without hesitation. Do you not understand how that might be selfish?"

She turned away, looking in the direction where Olivia and Paul had gathered the volunteers and employees in a large group, taking turns in speaking to them. Stacy watched as they gesticulated and motioned with their hands while they talked. The smiles they shared lit up the room, and soon enough the gathering of volunteers cheered the news of being affiliated with Mid State Charity.

Stacy turned away from watching Olivia and Paul and stared down at the floor.

"I have a right to live my life the way I see fit, do I not?" she finally asked, her voice low and impassioned.

"Of course."

"And I can decide for myself what's best for me. Is that right also?"

She turned slowly to face him, feeling more regal than she had in all her dream state.

"Of course. Why do you say such things, young one?"

"Because," she said, jutting out her chin, "it's my life. And I will live it the way I see as right. The advantage of becoming an adult is deciding on your own how to live. I no longer require someone telling me what to do and how to do it. Going forward, I will decide these things. Isn't that right?" She sighed, her confidence in having so eloquently laid out her reasons for independence. She stared directly into his eyes, almost willing him to back down.

"May I ask you something?" he said.

"Yes."

"This freedom in living you speak of, what does that mean to you?"

"I just told you," she sighed. "It means no one tells me what to do. I get to live how I want. If I don't hurt someone else, why should it matter what I do?"

"What have you learned in watching your daughter?"

"What do you mean?"

"I mean, how has she behaved in what you've seen thus far? Do you approve of her actions?"

"Well," she hesitated, "no, I don't approve of everything. Why?"

"If you could, what would you say to her? Would you tell her to change her ways?"

"I would tell her to live her life and make sure she's happy. Why does she need someone else to make her happy? Isn't happiness and love found from inside anyway?"

"Young one, you may choose what you will. You may do as you wish, yes. You certainly have the freedom to do whatever your heart desires. But tell me—what does your heart whisper to you about who your daughter might become?"

She stared at him, her eyes blinking. Clearly, she was stunned and confused by this. "What are you saying to me? I can force what I believe on my own daughter?"

The Being laughed, the sound echoing around them. "Certainly not. But tell me this. What is it you desire for your daughter to become?"

"That she is happy. That she can provide for herself. From what you have shown me, she is more than capable of taking care of herself."

"And are you disappointed in her choices?"

"Some of them, yes," she said, hesitantly.

"So her choices affect you negatively, even though she is pursuing her own lifestyle, correct?"

Her eyes darted side to side, nervously. "Y-yes. I suppose that's true."

"Tell me again, young one. How does one choose for themselves without hurting someone else? Is this possible?"

He looked at her calmly, his eyes warm, almost comforting in their gaze. She stepped a few paces away from him, a confused look in her eyes.

"You see, you may believe what you choose doesn't impact another life. But you have experienced for yourself the sorrow in seeing what could happen to your daughter. Through her own choices, she has done things that hurt you, that caused you to be confused. How is it possible to choose something for yourself and not cause pain in another's heart?"

There was a soft knock on the door, causing Tori to jolt upright from the chair. Jason had gone to the café to get some dinner, leaving her alone in the room. She rubbed her eyes and turned toward the door.

Tonya stood nervously in the doorway, clutching her purse strap on her shoulder, her eyes darting across the room. She shifted from one foot to the other as she hesitated to enter.

"Hi, Tonya," Tori said.

"Hi, Ms. Kent," she answered. "Can I… I mean, is it all right if I come in?"

"Yes, please," Tori said, standing and motioning her to come inside.

Tonya walked gingerly toward the bed as her eyes grew wider than before. Tori met her near the bed and put her arm around Tonya's shoulders. She gave a squeeze as the two stood silent, looking at Stacy's comatose state.

"Is she going to be okay?" Tonya said, her voice shaking.

"Yes. The doctor isn't sure how long she may be like this, but so far, she's okay," Tori answered.

"I'm sorry I haven't come to see her sooner. I've just been so busy with work and school."

"It's okay," Tori said, hugging her tightly. "I understand, honey."

"I just didn't know if I should come by or not, to be honest."

Tori looked at her a little surprised. "Why not? You're her best friend. Why would you feel that way?"

"I don't know," Tonya shrugged. "I guess I just didn't want to see her this way. I'm a little scared she won't come out of this."

Tonya's voice cracked as she spoke. She wiped away the few tears streaking down her cheek and sniffed hard. Tori's arm remained around Tonya's shoulders and the two stood in silence for several minutes, each not knowing what to say.

Finally, Tori looked over at Tonya. "When did you find out she was pregnant?"

"So you know about that, huh?" Tanya answered.

"Yes. The doctor told me right after we got here," Tori answered. "Why didn't either of you tell me?"

"I don't know," Tonya shrugged, her voice weak. "Maybe 'cause she was scared."

"When did she tell you?"

"She took a test and called me almost immediately afterward. I told her to take another one to be sure it was right. So after the second one was positive, we both knew for certain she was pregnant."

"Why would she hide it from me?" Tori asked.

"I don't know. I mean, I know she was scared about being a mother. She felt like she'd have to take care of a baby alone."

"Why would she think that way?"

"After Tucker died, she just thought she was all alone, like she wouldn't have any help in raising a baby. She was super worried about trying to pay for school and paying for a baby. She was so scared, Ms. Kent. I feel bad for her."

Tori shook her head, trying to clear her mind of the sudden jumble of thoughts that came washing over her. Had her relationship with her own daughter devolved into an irreparable mess? How did that happen?

"Here, let's sit down," Tori said.

The pair moved to the couch, sat down, and got comfortable, semi facing each other.

"Can you tell me why she thought she'd be alone in raising this child?"

"I mean, Tucker wasn't here to help, and she mentioned you two don't really get along. I'm sorry if I'm speaking out of turn, but that's what she thought."

"She thought we didn't get along?" Tori said, her mouth falling open in shock.

"I'm sorry, Ms. Kent. I didn't mean to say that."

"No, no, that's okay. I should know this about her. Is there anything else I need to know?"

Tonya looked down at the floor, her nerves jangling hard against her thoughts. She raised a finger to her mouth and chewed on her fingernail as she weighed the ramifications of disclosing any further intimate information to her best friend's mother.

"Well, there is one other thing."

"What's that?"

Tonya closed her eyes and breathed in and out heavily. "She asked me to drive her to a clinic to talk about an abortion."

Tori's eyes grew wide. "What?" she said, in a whisper. "Why would she do that?"

"I'm sorry, Ms. Kent. I swore to Stacy I wouldn't talk about it to anyone. But I've felt so guilty in taking her. I told her on the way she should talk to you about it, but she didn't want to."

"I don't believe this," Tori said, looking over at Stacy. "My own daughter not trusting me enough to talk about something like that. How could she do that?"

"Ms. Kent, please don't be mad at her," Tonya said, reaching over and taking hold of Tori's arm. "She was really scared when we went there."

"What did she say? Did she tell you if she would go through with it or not?"

"She really didn't say much. We left the clinic, and she seemed really depressed. Maybe more depressed than when we got there. But she didn't say what she told the doctor or even if she'd go through with it or not."

Tori sat back, her face a mask of confusion and disappointment. She stared wide-eyed at Stacy, trying to find a rational thought that would explain why her own daughter wouldn't tell her about this. She shook her head and let out a sigh.

"Ms. Kent, please don't be upset with Stacy. She was really scared about going."

"I'm not angry with her, Tonya," Tori smiled. "I just… I just think there's a lot we need to work through. Maybe we aren't as close as I thought."

By now Olivia and Paul had returned to the office, the afterglow of informing the volunteers the good news still burning bright. They sat looking at each other, the smiles affixed to their faces evidence of just how good this moment felt.

"That went well, Paul, just like I thought it would."

"Yes, it did. I'll talk to Davis in transportation and put together a plan for how we'll deal with that. We're gonna have a lot more activity around here, so I wanna get a jump on it before it gets out of hand."

"Good," she said. "Do you think we have enough space to handle the load?"

"What do you mean?"

"Well," she sighed, "this will increase our shipping and receiving loads. Do you think we have enough bay doors to handle all of it?"

"Liv, we haven't even started to look at what may or may not happen yet. We just signed the paperwork today, so this is literally brand-new."

"You're right. I guess I'm too excited right now. I want to be sure we have as smooth a transition as possible when we start working with them."

"We'll be fine, Liv. Don't worry about that. You've put together a good team of people here. They know what they're doing."

Stacy nudged the Being. "See, she can take of herself. She's smart enough to handle things like this."

The Being kept his eyes fixed on Paul and Olivia, not acknowledging her statement.

"Paul, there is one thing I'm concerned with," Olivia said, her face turning pensive.

"What's that?"

She closed her eyes, breathing in and out slowly. "What about my mother?"

"What about her?" he asked, raising a hand, palm upward.

Stacy stepped forward a few paces, waiting anxiously for what Olivia would say next.

"She's been alone for a while now. I know she's living with my grandmother now, but she's not happy. She hasn't been happy for a long, long time."

"What are you worried about, Liv?"

"I'm worried she might end up alone for the rest of her life. She told me once that a part of her died when my father did." She shook her head, burying her head in her hand. "I just wish I could've met him. He sounded like a wonderful man."

Paul shifted nervously in his seat, uncomfortable with the subject matter. "Look, I don't know what to say right now. I'm not good at comforting people. Guess you could say I'm a coldhearted jerk," Paul shrugged. "I've only met your mom a few times, and she seems like a wonderful woman. Strong, confident, just like you. But if you're worried about her, why don't you call her?"

Olivia leaned forward onto her desk, shuffling papers and moving various objects more than once around the surface. It was obvious she didn't want to discuss this any further, and her demeanor suddenly changed.

"Listen, you go talk to Davis and set up a plan for transportation. I'll work on the financials a little, and we'll meet in the conference room around three. Sound good?" she said smiling.

Paul blinked hard and shook his head. "Typical Liv," he said, standing up.

"What did you say?" she said, giving a curious, almost-threatening look at Paul.

"Nothing," he answered, a smile on his lips. "I better get with Davis and start working on this transportation. If we're going to have an increase in deliveries and shipments, we better be ready, huh?"

"That's fine. I'll see you at three, okay?"

"You got it," he said, pointing at her. He turned and walked to the office door, opened it, and exited into the hallway heading toward Davis' office.

Stacy watched as Paul left, then turned to look at Olivia, who had slunk down in her chair, a pained expression on her face. Stacy moved closer to where Olivia sat, a wave of compassion washing over her. She watched as Olivia started to cry, the tears flowing slow and steady down her cheek.

"What are you wondering, young one?" the Being said, breaking the silence.

Stacy turned her head slowly toward him. "Why does she say I'll be alone? Why is she worried about that?"

The Being walked slowly to stand on the opposite side of Olivia's chair, stopping when he stood next to her.

"It amazes me," he said.

"What amazes you?" Stacy said, the sarcasm evident in her tone.

"How you vacillate so wildly between claiming you don't want a child yet acting like a mother in every sense of the word. It's nearly comical."

"I'm glad my pain brings you laughter," she answered, crossing her arms across her chest. "I'm so happy I could bring you joy through my sorrow."

"Joy?" he asked, arching an eyebrow. "You think I find joy in this? I believe you have a misguided idea of what joy is, my dear."

Olivia remained silent, her tears tracing a line down her cheek and to her chin. She didn't bother wiping them away. She seemed perfectly content to allow them to fall from her face, a baptism of sorts for her sorrow. Finally, she reached up and rubbed the palms of her hands vigorously on her face, wiping away her tears. She sighed heavily and turned to her desk, looking at the assortment of papers littering the desktop. She reached for a small stack of papers and began sorting through them. For what, Stacy didn't know.

It wasn't important enough to know.

Shortly after six o'clock, Jason had returned with dinner, joining Tori and Tonya. He'd brought back a few slices of the school cafeteria style pizza the hospital served. It was the kind that leaves greasy stains on the paper plates holding them. The three barely touched the slices, still lost in the shock of Stacy considering an abortion.

"Ms. Kent, I didn't mean to ruin your evening," Tonya said. "I just thought you should know the truth."

"No," Tori said, looking at Tonya, "I'm glad you told me. Now we know what we need to do."

She reached over and squeezed Tonya's hand gently, a smile on her face.

"Well, I'm glad you two have it figured out. I don't know what the hell to think," Jason said. He sat in the lounge chair his half-eaten slice of sausage pizza resting on a small Styrofoam plate on his lap.

"Jason, we don't know what she decided, okay?" Tori said, looking at him. "All we can do is wait for her to come out of this coma and talk to her about it."

"That's a pretty big decision for someone her age," he said, shaking his head.

"I agree, but we need to find a way to help her, don't we? Whatever it is she decides, we need to be there for her."

"It's your fault, isn't it?" Jason said, the anger in his eyes evident.

"What do you mean?" she said.

"You heard me," he said, nearly shouting, as he stood from the chair. The remaining slice of his pizza fell to the floor as the plate landed on top of it. He took a few steps in Tori's direction, his face turning red as his blood boiled hotter.

"This is your fault, you slut," he said through clenched teeth. "You put her up to this to get back at me."

"No, I didn't, Jason, and you need to quiet down before someone calls security," Tori said, standing from the couch.

Tonya made every attempt to disappear into the couch as she averted her eyes, staring at the floor, the wall, anywhere but at the two combatants now standing close together.

"How dare you call me a slut, you jackass." She pushed on his shoulder. "How dare you!" Tori was close to matching Jason's rage, her eyes turning to fire as she glared at him.

"I'm not the one dating a new man every month, okay, so back off," Jason said, his tone rising.

As carefully and quietly as she could, Tonya stood from the couch, snuck past Tori and Jason, and into the hallway. She shook her head, catching a glimpse of what Stacy had told her about them being combative. She walked down the hallway, silently praying that her friend would find the courage to do the right thing once she woke up.

"And I'm not the one dating someone just a little older than our daughter."

"I happen to love this girl. She's different."

"Different?" she laughed. "How is it different when she's barely old enough to vote?"

"I don't need to explain myself to you," he said, waving his hand dismissively at her. "What I do on my own time is my business. It doesn't affect you at all."

"Everything about what you do affects me," she shouted. "Everything you do affects our daughter, don't you see that?"

"And what about you, huh? Nothing you do affects her, is that it? You're the queen who gets to do whatever you want without sharing any blame, right? Is that how you see this, Tori, 'cause that's pretty messed up."

By now two nurses had entered the room, quietly watching what was happening. The one nurse, her graying hair cut short and pulled back, moved closer.

"Excuse me," she said, sternly.

Tori and Jason turned to look at the nurse, now standing just a few feet away from them.

"If you don't settle down, I'll be forced to call security and have you escorted out of this hospital. For the good of your daughter, I would suggest you find a way to act peacefully with each other. Understood?"

For a moment, Tori and Jason felt as if they were in grade school being punished by the elderly principal. They sheepishly looked at each other and then down to the floor.

"Look, I'm sorry," Jason said, extending his hand toward the nurse. "I didn't mean to cause a problem. It's just, we've got a lot of things to work out here, and sometimes it gets the better of us."

"Well, I suggest you save it for a counselor's office. This is a hospital, and we've got other patients to take care of, okay?"

She gave them both a stern look that told them calling security wasn't an idle threat.

"I'm sorry," Jason said. "We'll keep it down, okay?"

"Thank you," the nurse said.

She turned around and walked briskly out of the room, the younger nurse following her into the hall. Jason and Tori stood silent for several minutes, both trying to find a way to apologize without losing the war they started.

"Where are we going?" Stacy asked the Being.

They sat next to each other in the back seat of Olivia's car, enjoying the view of the surrounding countryside.

"You'll see."

"You know where we're going?"

"Not for sure, but I have a good idea. Now just sit quietly, young one. I want you to absorb as much as you can."

They remained silent for the remainder of the trip as Olivia made her way through Colchester. The city was a throwback to what small town life used to be. Wide wooden porches graced the fronts of houses, small tables and chairs set up to engender conversation. Couples walked along the sidewalk, either hand in hand, or arms around each other's waists. A few people were out jogging in the crisp air, the sweat evident on their clothes.

Olivia made the turn onto the interstate and accelerated up the entrance ramp. Stacy caught sight of one of the road signs, reading, "Blackburn—ten miles." Stacy smiled, excited to know the purpose of Olivia heading in the direction of her hometown.

It took approximately fifteen minutes to arrive in Blackburn. Seeing as how Olivia loved speeding, it could've taken them less time. However, instead of turning into the city, she passed by and continued for several more miles, out into the wide open spaces surrounding the city.

Out of nowhere, the clouds suddenly gathered into a thick mass, turning the sky gray. The sound of thunder echoed in the air around them, as lightning flashed its jagged beauty. Soon enough, rain started falling, hard enough for Olivia to turn on the wiper blades. The rhythmic thump of the blades hitting against its mark made the ride appear slower.

About fifteen miles outside of Blackburn, Olivia slowed her car, engaging her turn signal. Stacy peered out the windshield and froze. The sign she read gave her an ominous feeling to what they were about to see. She was too fixated on the sign to notice the Being looking over at her, a grim expression on his face.

They were entering St. Luke's Cemetery.

As Olivia turned onto the gravel road entry, a knot formed in Stacy's stomach, becoming tighter the further Olivia drove into the cemetery. Stacy searched her mind in vain for why they might be visiting a graveyard. Was her mother or father buried here? Could it be Tonya? How would she have been connected to Olivia anyway?

Olivia turned the car down the narrow pathways, clearly indicating she'd navigated this way before. Finally coming to a stop near a small cherry tree and a row of bushes, she put the car in park. She reached behind her seat for her umbrella and opened the door. Flipping the switch allowing the umbrella to open, she stepped outside, the sound of the rain hitting the umbrella bringing a modicum of relief.

Stacy paused outside the car, transfixed by the Being who was standing at a distance beside a gravestone. She couldn't move, her thoughts consumed in fear at whose grave they were visiting. She watched as Olivia trudged toward the same gravestone the Being stood beside.

Olivia stopped and turned to face the gravestone. She wiped her eyes, and Stacy could hear her sniffling from this distance. The Being looked at Stacy and somberly motioned for her to join them. At first, she shook her head, but as he continued to motion, curiosity got the better of her.

She started toward the pair, her feet moving slower than expected. She felt herself floating more than walking. As she stepped near the gravestone, her eyes grew wide, and her heart accelerated its beat. As she looked at the name inscribed on the stone, her eyes filled with tears.

It read, "Tucker Hamilton."

"This is impossible," Stacy said. "He wasn't buried here. This is all wrong."

"In this reality, this is where his parents chose to bury him, far away from your memory," the Being said.

"Why would they do such a thing? I loved him. Why would they want him far away from me?"

The panic is Stacy's voice was clear, her voice cracking as she spoke.

"Think, young one, think. Who was it that told you to get an abortion?"

"Tucker," she whispered.

"I can't provide the reasons, but Tucker's parents decided to wipe his memory from your life. By choosing this cemetery, they knew it was far enough away so you wouldn't visit often, if at all."

"No," she said, turning away in disgust. "No, this isn't how it's supposed to be."

"And how is it supposed to be, young one?"

Stacy walked several yards away from the grave site, then turned to look at Olivia, still weeping as she stood silent. Her shoulders moved up and down, clear evidence of the pain she harbored in her heart.

"It was supposed to be Tucker and me forever," Stacy said. "It was supposed to be the two of us raising a child together, getting married and spending the rest of our lives together. This isn't what I imagined."

"Life is never what you imagine, young one. It will continually surprise you, bring changes and new phases to journey through. If it remained stagnant, how boring would that become?"

"But Tucker and I had something special, something neither of us could define. We were made for each other, I swear it."

"Oh yes," he nodded, "you most certainly were made for each other. And without you both, you would never know the joy and beauty that is your daughter."

He motioned his hand toward Olivia, who had now gathered her emotions together and was making her way back to her car. Stacy watched as Olivia opened the driver door, sat down, then wrestled with closing the umbrella and putting it away in the back seat. She started the engine, engaged the car in gear, and drove off slowly toward the cemetery exit.

The Being walked up and stood wordlessly beside Stacy. They both watched as Olivia's car disappeared around a curve in the road, hearing the engine noise fade away. They remained silent for several minutes, the only sound the rain falling effortlessly against the leaves of the trees around them.

"May I ask you a question?" he said, breaking the silence between them.

"Of course," she said, wiping the tears from her eyes.

"Do you think there are mistakes when a child is born?"

His voice was low, almost ominous, as he spoke, sending a slight shiver up her spine.

"What do you mean?"

"Do you think any child is ever born by accident?"

"Yes."

He was stunned, his face a mask of surprise, as he furrowed his brow and looked at her. "Why do you say this?"

"Tell me this. If a mother is raped and she becomes pregnant, is that not an accident?" she said confidently.

"Have you considered that child might grow up to become a great world leader and bring peace to the nations?" he countered.

"Does it matter what would become of them?" she said, the anger rising in her voice. "Nothing about that makes sense. If the woman has a child from being raped, it will be a constant reminder of what happened to her. Do you not think she would grow to resent her own child in that instance?"

"Do you think she could forgive her rapist?"

"No."

"Why not?"

"Because they would have committed the most violent, brutal act against a woman any man can commit. It is dehumanizing to do that to another human being. It's sick and violent, and I would forever resent anyone who would do that to me or to my daughter. Violence is never right, no matter the situation."

"And what of the violence in silencing the heartbeat in your womb?"

Stacy moved to speak, opening her mouth. There were no words she could form at this moment.

"You speak of a violent act against a woman, and indeed, that is the most heinous, despicable act a man could inflict upon a woman. No man should ever behave this way. But no one speaks of the violence required to tear a child from the womb. No one dares speak of the silent voice that never gets a chance to be heard. We cast our eyes away from this act. We pretend it doesn't hurt anyone. The truth is, that one simple act destroys the greatest gift a woman could ever know."

"But a woman can choose for herself, can't she?"

He nodded.

"And a woman can decide what she will do with her body, yes?"

Again, he nodded.

"Then there is nothing you can say that will persuade me to think otherwise. If a woman is violated by a man, that act of shame should never be rewarded by a child's life existing."

"You speak of so much guilt and shame surrounding this act. You condemn the violence one person enacts on another and wish to erase the memory of it by eliminating the result. But what if you could focus on the beauty that might arise from that act? What of the life of the child that would exist because of that act? Wouldn't you rather focus on the beauty of a child's laughter? Or the wonder in their eyes as they see this world for the first time?"

Stacy closed her eyes and shook her head violently. She plugged her fingers into her ears and began to recite gibberish. She stomped away from the Being and came to rest on a small rise in the land, just across the gravel road. As she opened her eyes, she became silent at the sight before her.

Hundreds of gravestones perfectly aligned stretched out far across the field. There were monuments, large stones carved into praying hands and smaller stones simply marking the final resting place of a loved one. She marveled at the expanse of markers spread out before her, the silence seeming to whisper to her soul.

By now the Being had walked to join her where she stood. He looked over the stones, himself filled with wonder at the sight. A soft moan emanated from his throat, a groaning she'd never heard before in her life. It sounded more akin to something heard in a horror movie. He shook his head before turning to look at her.

"Tell me, what do you think these people would say to you if they were able to speak to you right now?" he asked.

"There is no way for me to know," she said, her voice just above a whisper.

"Think carefully, child. What did these people regret before they died? Did they regret anything? Who did they leave behind and not make amends with? Was their death greeted by a hundredfold of friends celebrating a life well lived, or a smaller gathering of mourning and deep sorrow?"

"What does that have to do with my decision?" she said, closing her eyes once more and shaking her head.

"Do you suppose even one of the women buried here decided to end the life of their child because of that disgusting act against her?

Suppose you had the opportunity to talk to them. What would they speak to you now, if given the chance?"

"You continue to taunt me with these questions. Why do you do this?" she said, her voice cracking. She fell to her knees, her body limp from the depth of sorrow consuming her heart.

"I am not taunting you, as you say. Merely, I wish to provoke thought." He knelt beside her. "I want to be sure you understand the ramifications of your decision. If you decide to abort your child, she may not grow up to start the nonprofit organization we witnessed. Perhaps she would be the one to do greater things than you can imagine."

"But it would seem you're trying to persuade me to think as you do. I don't appreciate that at all."

"And what is life without persuasion?" he smiled.

Slowly, his eyes filled with grace and love as he gazed upon her tear-stained face. A peace drifted between them, soothing any fear she may have felt before. For a moment, her heart felt light and joyful again.

Chapter 7

Tori and Jason had retreated to what became their de facto neutral corners. He was ensconced in the lounge chair, immersed in typing on his laptop. She sat on the couch, trying in vain to distract herself with whatever selection was on television. She surfed through the channel guide numerous times and came up disappointed each time at having nothing to watch.

She was hesitant to say anything, seeing as how the last time she and Jason talked yielded nothing but the familiar anger they harbored for each other. Occasionally, she would look over at him, almost as if she were stealing a glance at a new lover. She closed her eyes and recognized that empty ache in her heart beginning to burn. She knew they had fallen out of love. But in a moment like this, she wished they could ignore their painful past and reconcile their hearts.

Suddenly, one of the machines Stacy was hooked up to began beeping loudly, sounding as if something terrible had happened. Lights flashed as a buzzing noise filled the air around them. Both Tori and Jason were jolted out of their stupor and looked at the source of the noise. Not knowing what to look for, they stared at each other first, then to the machines. The pair stood up and ran to Stacy's bedside, a frantic look in their eyes. They looked at each other again, then back to Stacy.

Just then, a pair of nurses came rushing inside the room and moved beside the bed.

"Excuse us," one of them said, pushing past Jason.

He stumbled backward, his hand rubbing across his forehead, a lost look in his eyes.

"What happened?" one of the nurses said, looking at Tori.

"I don't know," she said. "We were just sitting here minding our own business, and one of these machines started making that obnoxious noise."

The nurses hurried through their routine, checking tubes, pulse rate, looking carefully at every detail on the machines keeping Stacy in a comfortable state. One of the nurses reached up and turned a switch on a machine and the noise stopped suddenly. The only sound after that was of the two nurses hastily rechecking every tube and Picc line running to and from Stacy.

"What's wrong?" Tori asked frantically. "Is she going to be okay? Is there a problem? Talk to me please."

"Everything appears to be normal, ma'am," one of the nurses said. "I don't see any problems here. It might have just been a malfunction of some sort."

"A malfunction?" Jason asked, sarcastically. "Isn't that a problem by itself?"

"Mr. Kent, if you don't mind, we know what we're doing, okay?" the nurse said, giving a stern look as she spoke.

"Wow, what a bedside manner," Jason said, holding his hands up and backing away from the nurse.

The pair continued to triple-check every line and machine, ensuring everything was in working order. Satisfied there was nothing of great import to be concerned about, they stepped away from the bed.

"She'll be okay," the nurse said. "I'm not sure why this happened, but it's nothing to be concerned with. Let us know if you need anything."

She made a few more adjustments to the IV bag and various tubes connected to Stacy and exited the room.

Tori leaned in on the bed rail, reached down, and stroked Stacy's cheek gently. "I hope to God she wakes up."

"Me too," he said, a heavy sigh escaping his lungs.

"What if she doesn't, Jason? What if she never comes out of this? I can't bear that thought," she said, choking back her tears.

"Look." He leaned on the bedrails opposite Tori. "I can't stand that idea any more than you can. Right now, we must be strong and patient. We need to trust the doctors to tell us how she's doing, okay? We'll just have to wait and see."

They both stood silent, looking first at Stacy, then to each other. Neither of them were certain what to say anymore. It seemed useless to continue talking about it.

They both gave a shrug and returned to their previous seated positions. Soon enough, they fell back into the same routine as before, nearly oblivious the other was in the room.

As the Being and Stacy walked through the city of Easthaven, she couldn't help admiring the vibe of a city that seemed to be in constant motion. Bright neon decorated the skyline, mixed with the sound of traffic, busy snaking along its main street, which dissected the city into two halves. They had made their way through downtown and were now heading toward the outskirts.

Up ahead, Stacy saw a mammoth building and marveled at the size of it. The Being was beside her, and she nudged his arm, pointing to the building.

"What's that?"

"The Onyx Resort."

"Resort?"

"Yes, next to Lake Arrowhead, right over there."

He pointed to their right as they continued walking. Parts of the lake were illuminated by the numerous bars and restaurants built on its shores. A marina jutted out near the resort, lined with all shapes and sizes of boats. They ranged from a few large yachts, to smaller boats, all the way down to Jet Skis. Why the owners wouldn't take the Jet Skis home was anyone's guess.

The resort itself was comparable to any built in Las Vegas, only there was no casino. The city council was adamant if this resort were built, it would adhere to the family values the council promoted and not involve itself in gambling. From the looks of it, it didn't need a casino to keep it busy. The parking lots and the oversized garage were at full capacity with cars. The massive digital sign out front advertised the lineup of A-list entertainment and comedy acts coming soon, as well as several local events taking place in any one of the ballrooms. By any measure, this resort was a boon to the local economy.

"Why are we here? Doesn't this seem out of place compared to where we've been?"

"What better place to hold a celebration on election night than a 5-star resort?" He laughed.

"Election night?"

"Yes."

"How do we know who's being elected?"

"Just follow me."

The pair continued inside the lobby of the resort. As they walked, Stacy marveled at how clean everything was. The carpeting was spotless, the walls showing no obvious signs of wear and tear. The staff scurried about, smiles on their faces, helping anyone they came across. It seemed like a literal beehive of activity. Stacy laughed at the sight of such opulence and decency. Certainly, this was a better atmosphere than what they encountered at the Medallion.

They arrived at the largest ballroom and paused. The level of security in this part of the resort was demonstrably more prevalent than in other parts, although there could have been plainclothes officers among the general populace as well. Here, it seemed one couldn't walk two feet without running into a uniformed officer or someone in the Secret Service.

These men stood out by their mannerisms and constant surveillance of the people nearby. The ubiquitous wires leading from their ears to their suits were a dead giveaway they were serious about their mission.

Stacy tugged at the Being's arm. "Who are we here to see?"

"Just follow me." He motioned his hand forward.

They made their way into the main ballroom which was even more crowded than the exterior of the room. Along one wall, a makeshift stage had been set up, a podium occupying the middle front of it. There was a crush of people standing in front of the stage, laughing, and conversing with one another. Balloons hung in a net above the main floor, awaiting the arrival of a celebratory moment when they would be dropped. A DJ occupied one corner of the room, a small dance floor in front of his station occupied by those who wanted to dance at this occasion.

The problem was, Stacy still had no idea what the occasion was, and her curiosity was starting to get the better of her.

"Perhaps I should have told you. I don't enjoy crowds very much at all. Can you please tell me what's going on?" she said agitated.

"Just a few more steps, and we'll be there," he said, smiling.

He was right. Within moments, they found themselves in a hallway off the side of the ballroom. Gathered around a female were several more Secret Service men, a scowl fixed on their faces. This was more for show than anything else. As they neared the person in the center of it, Stacy suddenly smiled.

Olivia stood calmly among the Secret Service men, dressed in a beautiful white blouse, a black skirt, and a short-waisted coat. In one hand, she held several note cards. In the other, she held what looked like a picture. Stacy pushed her way through the crowd and stopped beside Olivia.

It was the same picture she had seen in every other scenario. A blurry picture of a woman and a baby. Stacy furrowed her brow, suddenly realizing this picture must be of some importance. Otherwise, why would it keep showing up in each of her dream states? She moved back to where the Being stood and shook her head.

"So this party is for Olivia?" she asked.

"Yes."

"To what office has she been elected?"

"Senator," he responded, smiling as he looked at her.

Her eyes became wide, a smile coming across her face as she felt a wave of pride like nothing she had felt before. Even tonight, after what she'd witnessed, this was by far the most triumphant accomplishment she could witness.

"A senator," she said, softly, shaking her head. "My daughter could be a senator. How simply amazing?"

"Well," the Being said with a shrug, "not so much when you consider what had to transpire before this moment."

"I guess so. May I ask you a question?"

"Certainly."

"I continue to see the same picture in each of these scenarios. Would you tell me what the significance of that picture is please?"

She looked expectantly at him as she spoke. For his part, he adopted a look of bewilderment. His eyes darted side to side as he shifted in his stance. Clearly, there was more to tell, and it wouldn't be a simple explanation.

"Let's just say, it's something of value that your daughter has chosen to keep with her at all times and leave it at that, okay?"

He glanced over at her and noticed the wounded look in her eyes. If she were expecting a better explanation, she wouldn't be getting it from him. At least not now.

All of a sudden, the volume of the music in the ballroom increased, and the buzz from the gathered crowd consumed the air around them.

"Okay, Senator Hamilton, are you ready?" a staffer asked her.

If Stacy didn't know better, it looked exactly like the man, Paul, she had seen just previously.

"Yes. I'm ready," she answered.

"Great," the man said, giving a thumbs-up gesture and moving off in the direction of the makeshift stage.

As he did, the crowd began cheering. The anticipation was palpable, and it showed in Olivia's mannerisms. She began nervously shifting in her stance, moving her weight from one leg to the other. She straightened her blouse and coat, smoothed out her skirt, and took several deep breaths. From what Stacy could see, it was the exact same breathing exercise she practiced for cheerleading events.

"Ladies and gentlemen, thank you all for being here on this momentous occasion," the staffer said onstage.

This brought even louder cheers from the crowd.

"This has been a long, hard campaign, and we couldn't have reached this point without your support, so thank you," the staffer said.

Again, the crowd cheered, only this time it lasted a little longer.

"I know you didn't come here to see me, so I won't keep you waiting any longer. Ladies and gentlemen, it gives me great pleasure to introduce to you… Senator Olivia Hamilton."

As soon as her name was spoken, the music kicked in louder than before, the balloons fell from the ceiling, and Olivia made her way from the hall to the stage.

Ascending the short staircase, she took a few steps on the stage and paused, waving to the crowd. She brought her hand to her mouth and blew a kiss to everyone in attendance. From where she stood next to the Being, Stacy recognized the same motion her mother made in blowing kisses to her.

Olivia strode in the direction of the podium, a broad smile affixed to her face. More than once during the cheering, she would bring a hand to her chest, mouthing the words "Thank you" to each person there. After several minutes, she stepped to the podium and leaned into the microphone.

"Thank you all," she said. "Thank you, thank you. If you would, I'd like to say a few words."

The crowd quieted, the music faded, and everyone stood in a hush, watching Olivia. There were no words to describe the pride Stacy felt in this moment. She stood in silence as tears fell from her eyes.

"Thank you," Olivia said. "I'm so proud to be standing on this stage tonight with a clear directive to serve the people of this great state."

The crowd erupted in cheers again, as more than a few held up campaign signs, the name Hamilton splayed across them. Olivia smiled and motioned for the crowd to quiet again.

"You know, I campaigned on the idea that if we genuinely love one another, we will work together. It is only when we lay aside any differences we may have and do what is right for the common good for all of us that great things are accomplished."

It seemed as if the crowd would cheer just about anything she said tonight as they raucously roared their approval.

"I intend to go to Washington with a clear mission in mind—to make our lives better," Olivia said. "Now, this will require each of us to take responsibility for what we do and how we act. I will need your help to maintain this ideal we shared throughout this campaign. Can I count on you to help lift this country to even greater heights?"

The crowd responded with a resounding and deafening, "YES!"

"I want to reassure you—you are not alone. You are not forgotten. No one will be considered greater or less than another. We all have something to offer, and I want to see what great things we can accomplish together."

More cheering from the crowd.

"Tonight I want to propose to you an idea I've had for some time now but haven't been sure how to articulate properly for it to be clearly understood." She glanced at her notes. "I propose we find a way to reach out to those less fortunate than us and help them develop a path to success. I know what it's like to see the homeless on the streets. I know what it's like to see the terror in their eyes at having been forgotten. I know what it's like to feel lost and afraid. That's why I'm going to work with business leaders to afford opportunities to these people and ensure we help them end the cycle of poverty in their lives."

The crowd roared its approval of this idea.

"I believe in the dignity of each person. I believe in kindness and care. I believe that only when we teach someone to become responsible for their own lives, we create better communities and better cities for everyone. Because there is dignity in earning a paycheck. There is dignity in owning your own home. There is dignity and pride when you work to earn your own living. This is how you build strong people, who in turn build strong communities."

Once again, the crowd roared its approval.

"I want to thank you all for coming tonight, and I'm sorry to cut this short. But right now, I've got a lot of work to do, so let's get started. Thank you."

As the crowd cheered and the music started again, Olivia stepped away from the podium, waving and smiling at the throng of people. She appeared deeply touched and humbled to be standing before her constituents, representing them at the highest level of government.

"This is surreal," Stacy said.

"Why do you say this?" the Being asked.

"Look at her." she pointed toward Olivia. "She's a state senator. This is unreal."

"Perhaps, but isn't it wonderful to imagine if this were real?"

Stacy paused before she spoke, suddenly realizing what she was told at the start of this journey. This was only one of many possible outcomes for her daughter. Either one of them could come true, or none of them would come true. She shook her head at the conundrum of being swept up in the euphoria of this moment and the realization it might not happen.

"You're wondering which, if any, of these scenarios might come true, aren't you?" he said smiling.

"Well," she started, "yes, I am."

By now Olivia had taken refuge in the back hallways of the resort, presumably retiring to a private room. The crowd continued its revelry as people began to dance. The bartenders stationed opposite the DJ stand were frantically trying to provide enough alcohol to the masses to keep the tips and the buzz flowing.

"What if I told you one of these scenarios were true? Would you believe me?" he asked.

"Will you allow me to know which one is true?" she asked, quizzically.

"Perhaps. Or perhaps I'll keep you guessing." He laughed.

"That's a very cruel thing to do, you know that, don't you?" she said. "Anyway, can we see what Olivia is doing now?"

"But of course."

He waved his hand in a circle, and the air became filled with colors again, swirling and melding from one shape to another.

Soon enough, they found themselves in one of the finer suites in the resort. Located on the upper level, it offered a beautiful view of Lake Arrowhead. Outside the suite was a balcony, offering a near panoramic view of the amenities offered by the resort. In daylight, one could stand on the balcony and take in the sight of the small hills surrounding the lake. Currently, this was only hinted at by the lights of the bars and restaurants on the shore and the homes ensconced on the hillsides.

Seated at the dining room table, Olivia was busy poring over numerous papers, a pair of dark-rimmed reading glasses on. Several of her staff members were seated around the table as well, comprising the bulk of her team.

The Being and Stacy stood near the entry to the balcony directly behind the table. This satisfied Stacy's curiosity to see what Olivia was looking at. She hated to be nosy, but she couldn't break this habit.

"Okay, Paul, how are we going to implement this?" Olivia said to the staffer who made the announcement earlier.

Stacy chuckled at seeing him in a different position than before.

"We've got a meeting with most of the top businessmen here in Easthaven next week," Paul said. "I've already sent them an agenda of how we'd like to go about hiring the homeless. Some of the leaders are hesitant about hiring people without any skill, but most seem at least curious."

"Okay, so how do we make them go from a little to all the way in?" she asked.

"Don't know." He shrugged. "I guess we have to hear their side of it before we work this out and put it into practice."

"Okay, at least we have something to go on. Richard, what do you have on the state-funding side?"

She looked over at the frail-looking man to her left and seated a few chairs away. Richard was older, seeming near the grave by his appearance. However, there was a fire in his eyes that indicated he had energy to spare.

"Governor Thornton has asked us to review the prison budget. I don't know why he can't do that, but maybe it's because he's so closely tied to the police force."

"Wasn't he on the force for a number of years?" she asked.

Stacy's ears perked up at hearing this name, curious if it might be the same officer who was on the scene of Tucker's death.

"Yes. In fact," Richard said, clearing his throat, "he was, uh, the officer who filed the report after your father's death."

Olivia recoiled at hearing this. She sat back, gently removing her glasses and setting them down on the table. She propped her elbow on the arm of the chair and placed her head in her hand.

"I'm sorry, ma'am. I didn't mean to bring up a bad memory," Richard said, himself looking sorrowful.

"No, no, it's okay," she said. "I just… I just never realized he was there when my mom filed the report."

Stacy's eyes filled with tears, and she buried her face in her hands. She was suddenly escorted back in time mentally. She could see the flashing lights of the emergency vehicles and the police cars. She felt the same anger and guilt as before, reliving the sight of Tucker taking his last breath in his car. The Being simply watched her cry, never moving to comfort her.

"Liv?" Paul asked. "You okay?"

She looked up, suddenly realizing she hadn't spoken in several minutes.

"Yes," she said without confidence. "Yes, I'm fine. Now let's move on. What's next?"

Tori found her way to the hospital garden to smoke, enjoying the warm afternoon air for a change. This garden had been constructed explicitly for the purpose of providing a calming respite for patients and family members during their stay. Located at the rear of the building, it overlooked a large wooded area that took up most of the acreage behind the hospital.

Through clever zoning, the city council deemed these woods a nature preserve, thereby preventing the hospital from expanding and destroying it. It was a sore spot for some of the hospital administrators they wouldn't be able to use this land, but they soon grew to appreciate its value. More than once, the staff had taken advantage of the jogging pathways the city constructed through the woods.

She took a drag on her cigarette, tilted her head back, and blew out the smoke. She held the cigarette gingerly in her left hand, her right arm across her chest. She shook her head, trying to clear her thoughts of all that had taken place.

She thought she and Jason had a moment of closeness together, but that turned out to be false. She was both grateful and resentful that Tonya had told her the news about Stacy's possible abortion. And she wondered when, or if, her daughter might wake up. Not to mention the scare they had just a few short minutes ago with the alarm sounding on one of the machines. Granted, there was nothing wrong, but what if there were?

She looked to her left and saw a family sitting near one of the small ponds in the garden. An elderly patient sat in a wheelchair, a haggard smile crossing his weary face. A few family members had gathered with him, sitting, or standing as close as they could to the old man. It was clear from their expressions they all knew the old man was in his last days.

Tori shook her head. Death seemed to be so final, so brutal in its expedience. Somehow it all seemed so unfair. She turned away, lowering her eyes to look at the ground. She brought her cigarette to her mouth and took a quick drag, exhaling the smoke slowly. And then it hit her.

What would she feel if the doctors told her Stacy would never come out of her coma? What if these were her last days too?

She felt the tears coming slowly, inexorably tracing a line down her cheeks. She sniffled and looked over once more at the family by the pond. They had gathered in a group hug around the old man, as one of the family members prayed through their tears. Tori couldn't help but notice they all appeared calm, almost peaceful in their demeanor. She wiped her cheek and wondered how someone could be so composed in the face of certain death.

She shook her head, grunted, and took one more drag on her cigarette. She slowly rose from the bench and turned to walk back inside the hospital. She walked the few steps over to the trash receptacle, extinguished her cigarette, and threw it away. She took one last look at the family, now smiling.

She couldn't shake the feeling they knew something she didn't.

Olivia was alone, seated at the desk in her hotel suite, her staff having retired to their own rooms. It was well past 2:00 a.m., and the soothing quietness of her suite was the perfect antidote to the raucous noise of the party downstairs.

Sleep eluded her, even as fatigue wrestled for control of her thoughts. Her emotions seemed to be delayed in the realization she'd won the election, as her heart raced with a mixture of concern and excitement. She shifted in the chair, moving to stand up. She stopped suddenly as she caught a glimpse of herself in the mirror.

She paused before she stood, studying herself carefully, as if this were the first time she realized she was an adult. She noticed the lines at the corners of her eyes, the way her mouth seemed to arch downward. She stiffened her posture, jutted out her chin, and wiggled her shoulders straighter than before.

"I'm a state senator," she said, almost whispering. "I deserve this. I belong here. There's nothing that can take that away from me."

She flashed a smile at her reflection and nodded her head, content in her affirmation. She stood up and moved toward the bathroom, reaching for her nightgown on the corner of the bed. Just then, her phone buzzed. Curious, she dropped her nightgown, picked up her phone off the desk, and looked at the screen to see who was calling. She let out a heavy sigh and shook her head, swiped the bar to answer the call, and pulled it to her ear.

"Hi, Mom," she said, the frustration evident.

Stacy took a few steps closer, straining to hear any part of the conversation, wanting to know what part she might have played in Olivia's success.

"No, Mom, it's okay. I understand... No, you don't need to apologize. It's all right... I know you needed to be there for Grandma. I didn't expect you to leave her alone... Yes, it was nice... Well, I'm flying to Washington this weekend. That's when my term starts... No, Mom, I don't need your help. I have a moving company to do that... Yes, they'll handle all of that... No, Mom, I have interns to help me unpack when I get there. I have a staff of people and everything..."

She sighed heavily and rolled her eyes.

"Yeah, Mom, I miss you too..." she said, hoping the sarcasm wouldn't betray her. "Okay, well, I'll try to call you sometime next week, but I've got committee meetings lined up most of next week too, so it's difficult to say when I'll call... Okay. Love you too... Goodbye, Mom."

She pulled the phone away from her ear and swiped it off. She held it against her chin and closed her eyes. She began her breathing exercise again, trying her best to calm down. After a time, she took one long, deep breath and exhaled slowly. She placed her phone back on the desk, picked up her nightgown, and moved into the bathroom, shutting the door behind her.

"What did I say to her? Why am I not allowed to listen to myself talk to her?" Stacy asked, looking wide-eyed at the Being.

"You continue to betray your own intentions," he answered.

"I do no such thing. I simply don't understand why I am unable to hear myself interact with my daughter. Why is this?"

"And I will continue to ask you, why are you so concerned about someone you don't wish to live?"

His voice, like his demeanor, was harsh.

"You continue to mock me yet never provide me an answer. Are you a coward, or are you trying to hide something from me?"

The anger in her voice was clear, the rage exuding from her eyes. He met her steady gaze even stronger.

"Mocking, you say? Is it mocking to tell the truth of your intentions? Is it mocking to simply point out what you have already spoken of and your desire of what you wish to happen? I think you need to reexamine your question before you accuse me of something like that."

She turned away at hearing this, once again realizing the folly in this line of questioning. She walked to the bathroom door, placing her hand on it and resting her head against her hand.

"I never realized it could be this way," she whispered.

"What could be this way?"

"Seeing what my daughter may become." She turned to face him. "I never realized being a mother could be so devastating."

He grinned. "Do you think this is how your own mother feels?"

"What do you mean?"

"Come now, young one," he laughed. "Surely, by now, you have to understand what you put your own mother through."

"What happens between my mother and me is no one's business," she shouted. "I would ask you refrain from bringing my mother into this conversation. This is about me and my decision. I'm the one who must live with the consequences, not her. I'm the one who must decide to carry this burden or not, not my mother. She has no bearing in this decision."

The Being crossed his arms, bringing a hand to his face, stroking his chin slowly. His eyes remained fixated on Stacy as he appeared deep in thought.

"What?" she asked, a hint of desperation in her voice. "Why do you look at me this way?"

"Perhaps we should continue here," he said, waving his hand in a circle again.

As she was accustomed to by now, the room became filled with brilliant colors and light, flashing and swirling around her. She closed her eyes this time, feeling as if she were on a roller coaster, her stomach feeling the same thrill of motion in navigating the up and down trajectory of the rails. The colors stopped after a few moments, and Stacy gazed around her, a look of surprise on her face.

The senate offices in Washington were as well appointed as she'd heard about in her government class at Oakwood High. Clerks and various officials scurried about the hallways of a large complex, a cell phone never far from their ear or out of their hands. The noise of conversation echoing from the ceiling and heels clicking against the ornate granite floors floated around her, blending into a mass of confusion.

"Where is Olivia?" she asked.

"Her office is down the hall, the last one on the left," he said, pointing.

"I need to see her."

"By all means, go," he said, waving his hand.

Stacy took a few steps toward the office then stopped, turning to look at the Being.

"Aren't you coming with me?"

"Not this time. You'll be fine, young one. Just prepare yourself for what you witness. It is a testament to who you are."

"What does that mean?"

"You'll see."

He smiled, knowingly, as Stacy shrugged and moved toward Olivia's office.

She stepped inside and was greeted by the sight of Olivia sitting in a plush leather chair, a manila folder opened on her desk. She shuffled the papers inside it nervously as two older men sat expectantly in the two chairs opposite Olivia.

They both wore what must have been expensive suits, one man with a full head of gray hair, the other with flecks of gray scattered among his thick, black hair. The man with gray hair sat looking at Olivia, bemused by the freshman senator's efforts to seem in control. The younger man fidgeted in his seat, hyperactively shifting his weight every few seconds. He had his eyes fixed on the floor, seemingly wanting to avoid eye contact with Olivia.

Standing in the corner and behind Olivia was a young female intern, arms crossed in front of her, clutching tightly to an oversized leather appointment book. She wore a simple, knee-length skirt and white blouse and a pair of low black heels. She reached up and fixed her brown-framed glasses, pushing them further up her nose.

"Senator Hamilton, this is really very simple," the older man said. "I don't quite understand your hesitancy."

"Senator Gilmore, I ran on a record of elevating families out of poverty. I don't understand how this bill helps them."

"Such a freshman," Gilmore laughed, "trying to be the knight in shining armor for her constituents. So naive."

"How is wanting to be ethical naive?" she asked.

"My dear senator, you don't get appointed to the chairmanship of a committee without a bit of larceny," Gilmore sneered. "While I appreciate your innocence, you'll find very few who will sympathize with you on the Hill. This is a game, and you'll play by our rules or get buried in obscurity."

Olivia narrowed her eyes, straightening her reading glasses and clearing her throat.

"Senator Gilmore, you obviously don't know much about me, do you?"

"I know what I need to know," Gilmore laughed, "and if you don't think I can keep you anonymous in this chamber, you're mistaken."

"I can't support this. I won't cosponsor this bill. I won't give in to your high-pressure tactics. It won't work with me."

Gilmore smiled, admiring her spirit. He sighed, ran a hand through his hair, and leaned forward in his chair. He looked down at the floor briefly, leaning his elbows on his knees. He chuckled and looked up at Olivia. "I was promised you were a tough sell, and I can see I've got my work cut out for me now. But there's something you need to understand."

He leaned back in his chair, crossing his left leg on his right and adopting a smug expression on his face. The younger man was still fidgeting in his seat, his eyes darting around the room. He seemed to be lost in contemplation, but it was hard to tell from the vacuous expression on his face.

"I don't think you fully realize what I'm capable of doing. If you did, you would've signed this as soon as I came in the room, no questions asked. My dear, I have a great deal of influence here. I'd like to keep it that way. I'm accustomed to working with colleagues I can trust and who do right by me, as I do right by them. But I don't tolerate fools lightly."

His eyes turned dark as he spoke, his gaze unnerving in its intensity.

"Senator Hamilton, I suggest you get on board with this bill. It will add to your résumé and allow you the prestige you so richly deserve. If you don't agree to this, I must warn you. If you so much as whisper a proposal in committee, it'll be buried as soon as you bring it up. I'd think long and hard about what you're saying here before you run off on some idealistic campaign of wanting to save people who don't deserve it."

It was Olivia's turn to fidget in her seat. She glanced down at her desk, straightening her glasses once more, trying to regain the composure that eluded her. She attempted to hide the fact she was shaking uncontrollably from the withering tone of Gilmore's voice. She thought she achieved this but took note of her shaking hands. She stood up from her chair, her knees wobbly and lacking firm support. Still, she did an admirable job of controlling her nerves and cleared her throat once again.

"Senator Gilmore, I appreciate your offer," she said, her voice thin. "But I don't think you understand me. I'm not signing this, no matter what you threaten. This bill is nowhere near what I believe in. In fact, it would further the poverty of families and lead to utter desolation in their lives. If the taxes you propose in this bill become law, these families will lose their pride and dignity. I don't care what you say about me, but I will not sign this. You can find someone else to try and bring on board, as you say. But you will not intimidate me. I think you need to leave my office."

Gilmore leaned his head back and laughed, loudly enough to be heard in the hallways outside. He glanced up at Olivia, a smile affixed to his face, and rose from his chair. He straightened his suit coat and stepped closer to the desk.

"Senator, you're everything I expected and more. I was told you were strong-willed and feisty. I can see I have my work cut out for me. But be forewarned." He leaned down on the desk and glared directly in Olivia's eyes, an evil glint she'd never seen before. "You will play by my rules. Sooner or later, you will fall in line. Be sure of that, my dear senator. Or so help me, I will find a way to have you removed from office. Do you understand?"

Olivia stood firmly in place, a smile crossing her lips. "Senator Gilmore. Feel free to do whatever you wish," she said softly. "I can't be bought. Just ask your friends who visited me on the campaign trail. They weren't successful, and you won't be either." She leaned in closer to Gilmore, matching his icy glare with one of her own. "I'll take your best shot and still find a way to win," she said, arching an eyebrow. "Do you understand?"

Gilmore's face registered his shock at hearing this. Clearly, he'd met his match. He stood straight, ran a hand through his hair, and nudged the young man still seated. He stood up quickly and straightened his tie.

"Senator, it's been a pleasure. We'll be in touch. You have a good day."

The two exchanged a firm handshake before Gilmore turned and left the office, the younger man following close behind.

Stacy watched in awe as Olivia stood toe-to-toe with what appeared to be a tough, no-nonsense senator. Her smile was as brilliant as the pride welling inside her heart.

"Look at her," she said, turning to the Being. "Look at how confident she is, how passionate. I never realized this could happen."

He simply smiled at Stacy, shaking his head and crossing his arms on his chest as he did. She got a confused look on her face.

"What is it you're not telling me?"

"You're too young to see behind the facade."

"What does that mean?"

"It means there's an element of selfish narcissism behind that smile," he said, nodding toward Olivia.

It wasn't until Gilmore was completely out of sight that Olivia finally exhaled loudly. She sat back down in her chair, propped her elbow on the arm of the chair, and rested her head in her hand. She breathed in heavily and sighed.

"Ms. Hamilton, is there anything I can get you?" her assistant asked.

"No, thank you, Mallory," Olivia said without looking up. "I just didn't expect to be bullied when I got here. This isn't what I bargained for when I ran for office."

"I'm sorry, ma'am," Mallory said, stepping closer to Olivia's desk and reaching inside her stack of papers. "I…uh, think you should see this, ma'am." She stood next to Olivia's chair, holding out a piece of paper in her hand.

Olivia looked up, puzzled. "What is it?"

"It's your schedule for the day," Mallory said, sighing. "You've got a meeting in half an hour with Senators Larkin and Neal."

Olivia reached up and took the paper, her eyes glancing up and down at the meticulously laid out plans. She shook her head, suddenly realizing she might have gotten into something she couldn't handle.

"What do they want?" she asked.

"I think you should read it for yourself, ma'am, but I thought you should be prepared for the worst."

"Why is this meeting the worst?"

"Because," Mallory sighed, "they want you to cosponsor a bill that would tax people on food stamps."

Olivia's eyes grew wide as she digested this information.

"Ma'am, this would almost ruin some of the people in your district," Mallory said. "I don't know much about where you're from, but I know enough to say it wouldn't be well received."

"You're right, Mallory," Olivia said, shaking her head. "It would ruin a lot of people's lives."

She suddenly became emotional, her eyes welling with tears. She reached up and wiped her cheeks, took a tissue from the box on her desk, and wiped her face.

"What is it, ma'am?"

"It would ruin my mother's life."

Stacy's mouth dropped open when she heard this. She took a few steps backward.

"No, no, she's wrong. No, I can't end up like that. She's wrong."

She turned to look at the Being, the anger exuding from her eyes.

"Tell me she's wrong," she practically screamed.

"Young one, you are only able to see what happens to your child, not you. I cannot let you see what happens here," he sighed.

"But she's wrong," she said, stepping closer to the Being, and taking hold of what passed for his shirt collar. "She's wrong! Show me what happens to me. Show me!"

"Stacy," he said in a curt, angry tone.

She stepped back suddenly, a look of surprise on her face.

"I explained the parameters of what you would and would not see on this journey. There is no amending the rules of this arrangement. You will only see what could, or could not, happen to your child. That is all you ever need know."

"But I must know, how do I end up on food stamps? How could I have sunk so low? Don't I go to college? Why would I not have a well-paying job and have a good life? How could this happen to me?"

He closed his eyes, turning away from her and waving his hand again. As usual, the colors around them became bright and swirled around them both.

A few moments later, they stood in darkness, again light shining only on the two of them. The Being had not turned to face Stacy. His shoulders were hunched over, his breathing seemingly labored, coming as it did in heavy bursts.

"Why do you not look at me? Why do you not turn around and face me? Is it because you are afraid?"

"Tell me, why do you seem disturbed?"

He turned around slowly, a look of stony resolve in his eyes. He took two steps towards her before he stopped, raising himself to his full height.

"Perhaps I was wrong," he said in a low voice. "Perhaps I shouldn't have made this bargain with you. You have done nothing to show me you understand the lesson you should learn. All you have done is demonstrate an arrogance for your own well-being and safety. You are curious enough about your child's life, yes, but somehow the conversation always comes back to you. Tell me, why are you so conflicted about your life if you've already decided what to do?"

She lowered her eyes and searched her mind for a reasonable explanation.

"You have no idea, do you?" He shook his head. "Young one, I would advise you to watch and learn carefully. There is a reason I'm showing this to you. To this point, you haven't shown me you know what the lesson is yet."

"But what can I learn by watching only my child? And who's to care if I ever give birth to this child? Why is it so important to you? You're nothing. You're an avatar, something conjured in my imagination, I know this is true. You said yourself, this isn't even real. You said yourself none of this could come true, didn't you? Why should I listen to you at all?"

The Being turned and walked to a bench that had suddenly appeared behind him. He sat down, slowly and carefully. He crossed his legs and rested an elbow on the armrest of the bench. He placed his chin in his hand and looked at Stacy, a warm glow in his eyes.

"You're finding it more difficult to say yes to ending your child's life, aren't you?"

"Why is this any of your concern? Why do you care so much about me? You don't know anything about me."

"Oh, but I do. I know far more about you than you realize. Why would I waste my time showing these things to you if I did not care about you?"

"Because all this is a sick joke. You don't want me to end this child's life, I can see it. You're the one telling me how wrong it is if I never have my child. You're so transparent. Of course, you care, but only because you want me to have this child."

He stood and walked slowly toward her. "And you haven't been listening carefully enough." He stopped in front of her, a finger laid across his mouth. "My dear, I have told you, only you hold the power of that decision. It matters little what I desire for you. All I am doing is presenting the possibilities of your child's life. You still must decide. If what I show you makes it more difficult for you to choose, so be it. But I will not enforce my will upon you. Have you not realized that yet?"

He gazed upon her lovingly, as a father would to his child in a time of need. She looked into his eyes and felt a warm glow in her heart. She failed to understand why this feeling washed over her, but it brought a peace to her soul as she looked in his eyes.

She turned away, falling to her knees. She reached a hand to her chest, feeling as if something were changing about her. She'd spent most of her young life laser-focused on what her future held with Tucker that she hadn't considered life without him. Now she felt as if she'd reached a crossroads. This was much more difficult than she realized.

He walked beside her and knelt, placing his hand on her back. His fingers gently raked across her back, much like a mother would to a child nearing slumber.

"Young one, you have yet to discover the potential locked inside your heart. There is so much to explore that it will take you nearly a lifetime to realize what impact you may have on others. Don't waste this opportunity to learn and grow. I believe in you, Stacy."

Something in the way he spoke soothed any fear she may have felt. She closed her eyes and buried her face in her hands. She didn't cry, but she suddenly felt if she gazed upon the Being, she would be blinded by the sight of him.

"What am I to do? What will I choose?"

"Your life with Tucker can never be, you know this. But you can still have a life for yourself and, if you so desire, for your child and with your mother. You are strong enough to know the truth, young one. Allow your heart to lead you."

Tori had made her way back to Stacy's room, walking in as Jason was walking out with a disgusted look on his face.

"What happened?" she asked.

"The doctor just left about a minute ago," he sighed. "He said they have to run more tests on her."

"What tests?"

"I don't know," he shrugged. "But it pisses me off they can't seem to find out what's wrong with her."

"Jason, just calm down." She reached out and stroked his arm. "They said she's okay and all her vital signs are positive. Let's just focus on that."

"Whatever," he said, stepping into the hallway. He took about three steps away from her before stopping and turning back. "You know, none of this would've happened if she didn't find those pills. It's your fault she's in this condition, Tori. Your fault."

She leaned against the doorframe and sighed as he began to walk away again. "Jason, for the last time. Can we just lay aside our differences and focus on Stacy right now? Or is that impossible for you?"

He walked back, stopping in front of her, an angry look in his eyes. "As long as I know the reason why she's laid up like this, no, we can't lay aside our differences, okay? Like I said, this is your fault. She dies, it's on your head, got it?"

The words were harsh, laced with a venom she'd never heard before. He turned away from her and stomped off down the hallway, headed for the elevators. She watched him disappear around the corner and leaned her head against the doorframe.

"Why can't we work this out?" she whispered.

Chapter 8

The dark gray walls of Silverbay Penitentiary were forbidding enough. The bleak overcast sky above only added a sense of dread for anyone who happened by here. Located about ten miles outside of Beckton, it was built hard against the Southern River. The walls of the prison were positioned purposely close to the riverbank to discourage anyone from escaping in that direction. A swift current was always evident on this wide swath of water, and the warden used this as a means of leverage against the population hidden behind these walls.

Built in the 1800s, it had been revamped numerous times over the years, adding some modern amenities, but maintaining its grotesque stature as one of the most closely guarded prisons in the system. Anyone sentenced to serve time here knew they would be in one of the harshest environments anyone could imagine. The cells were small on purpose, not affording much space between the bunk and the cell wall. While there was fresh lighting installed, this fortress maintained the dubious honor of being one of the darkest prisons around.

For Stacy, this was the first time she'd ever encountered something as sinister as this structure. Growing up, it was inevitable to hear reporters discuss men and women convicted of crimes and sentenced to prison. Even at her tender age, she was not immune to the morbid fascination of what led someone to a life of crime and ultimately to live behind bars. Of course, she never wanted to experience this for herself, yet it was something that aroused her curiosity.

As they made their way alongside the walls, she stared wide-eyed at the surrounding area. A dirt road led away from the massive iron gates that served as the main entrance. On either side of the entrance, twin turrets marked the top of the administrative offices. These offices jutted away from the main prison wall and were built in an almost-semicircular pattern around the main road. Guard towers were spaced evenly along the expanse of the main wall and occupied each corner of the prison.

Approximately twenty yards away from the prison wall, a long chain link fence lined the perimeter of the grounds, a tightly knit roll of barbed wire affixed to the top of the fence. It was perhaps thirty feet high at its tallest point. Spaced approximately ten feet away from this was another chain link fence of the same construction. In between the fences was a trench, filled with iron bars, the spiked ends facing the prison at about a forty-five-degree angle.

Clearly, the warden made any thought of escape as difficult as he could.

The Being strode slowly along the wall, seemingly unconcerned with the whereabouts of Stacy. He knew she would follow him, but at this moment, he appeared oblivious to her encroaching fear. For her part, Stacy kept a short distance between herself and the Being. For some reason, she felt the need to walk behind him rather than beside him.

As her head continued to turn side to side as they neared the entrance, she suddenly felt the urge to join the Being and walk beside him. She hurried to where he was, and they continued walking in silence. Finally, she needed to satisfy her anxiousness.

"Why have we come here?"

"Because this is where we need to be now."

"But what is the purpose of this? Please don't say my daughter could be here," she said, the fear creeping into her voice.

"She is."

If she was looking for any sign of hope, it was obliterated in those two words. She stopped walking and dropped to her knees, then to all fours, dry heaving as she did. The Being noticed her absence beside him and turned. He saw her body convulsing, the sound of her throat restricted in pain and walked back to her. He knelt as he arrived, placing his hand on her back and gently rubbing it. He looked off in the short distance away from where she was and waited patiently for Stacy to return to normal.

"No," she whispered, "no, my daughter can't be in prison. It's not possible."

"My dear, anything is possible."

She pulled her head up slowly, moving her body to a seated position and wiped her face.

"This is nothing I would wish on anyone. Who deserves to be treated like an animal? Why should anyone be forgotten this way and spend their life chained to this horrible place? Couldn't there be another way?"

Her voice sounded desperate, her words aching for truth. The Being sat down across from her and sighed. He rubbed his forehead and shook his head.

"There are all manner of reasons I could provide you why this may happen, but none of them would satisfy your question. But that's not why we're here."

She began practicing her breathing exercise again and fell into something akin to a meditative state as she did. Her eyes closed; she took long, slow breaths and exhaled in the same rhythm, each time calming her nerves and easing her mind. She took one last long breath and exhaled, opening her eyes as the last shred of breath escaped her lips.

"I don't know if I can bear to see this."

"Why?"

"Because I don't wish to see my daughter in pain."

"Pain, you say?" he said, a smile creeping onto his lips. "You don't wish to see your child in pain. That's almost laughable."

"Why would you laugh at this?"

"Surely you must see the twisted logic in your thinking."

"I'm afraid I don't understand, nor do I care to listen to you right now."

"So be it," he shrugged. "Are you prepared to see Olivia?"

She glanced up at the prison walls, appearing darker than before and shook her head slowly. "I… I don't know."

"If you prefer, we could pause our journey. Mind you, we will not be abandoning it, merely postponing the inevitable."

"If it is possible to break away from this madness. Please, I beg you, allow me time to gather my thoughts," she replied.

"But of course."

He waved his hand in a circle once more, as the colors illuminated the space around them. She closed her eyes, feeling the rushing wind blow across her cheeks, tossing her hair behind her. For a moment, she felt a smile on her face.

When the rushing wind stopped, she opened her eyes and discovered they had returned to the same meadow where they first met. The sunshine glowed around her as she turned her head in all directions, listening for the voices of children.

It was strangely silent.

"Where are the children?"

The Being strode a little distance from her, rubbing his chin briskly.

"They have been taken away," he said, crisply. "That is all you need know."

"Taken away? Where have they gone? Will they return?"

He stopped, drew in a breath, and turned. "No," he said, ominously.

She pushed herself off the ground and stood, her knees still feeling wobbly from having seen the prison just before. She tried to step toward the Being but found herself frozen in place. She was able to move her arms and head, but her feet remained firmly in place where she stood.

"What happened to them?" she said, beginning to quiver.

He strode with a purpose toward her, more shuffling his feet than walking. His face was dark and cloudy, his eyes fiery. He stopped two paces from her and looked directly at her.

"The evil one has come and captured the children who were here. They are gone forever," he said, the rage echoing in his words.

Stacy brought a hand to her mouth as tears began streaming down her face. The shock reverberated through her soul, and she felt as if she might vomit again. She dropped to her knees again, then finally rested one hand on the ground, her head low.

"Where has the evil one taken them and why can't we bring them back?"

"My child, there comes a time when evil consumes the heart, clouding over any sense of right and wrong. It tears away any ounce of concern, leaving only selfishness and pleasure in its wake. There is nothing that can be done to change the heart whose singular focus is to do whatever delights it. The heart is full of mischief, my dear. One must learn to harness its beauty and wonder if one is to live correctly."

As he spoke, her nausea was replaced by a righteous anger she'd never known before. She cursed loudly as she knelt, letting go an almost deafening shriek of pain and anguish. She rested now on both knees, arms outstretched, and head tilted back toward the heavens.

"Why is this? Where is this evil one? I wish to see him and confront him for what he has done for the souls of these children," she bellowed.

"My dear child." he held up a hand toward her. "This is not the way to overcome this truth. There is a much better way."

"Tell me," she said, standing on her feet and finding she could step toward him now. "Tell me, and I'll do it, I swear. No one should destroy a child, no one."

He cocked his head as he heard this, a smile slithering across his mouth. He began chuckling, slowly, then faster, until he was laughing loudly.

For her part, Stacy simply stared quizzically at him, thinking this was odd behavior. "Why do you laugh?"

He shook his head and wiped his forehead, regaining his composure. "Young one, you amuse me. If it were not for our mission, I would suspend this entire exercise and allow you to return to your life as you know it. However, since you have agreed to see this through, that will not happen."

"But why did you laugh at me again? Do you think me silly or evil? What is it?"

"Quite the contrary. You are one of the more intelligent souls I've encountered throughout my journeys. You have a sense of right and wrong, warped as it may be, but you still don't understand the ramifications of what you wish to do. Overall, however, I'm impressed with you."

"But you laughed when I wanted to go after the evil one and destroy him. Why?" she said, anger spilling from her eyes.

He adopted a sobering look as he noticed the rage in her eyes and inhaled deeply. "If you knew the power of the evil one, you would tremble. He is not one to be trifled with, nor to be taken on in singular battle. He is one who will taunt you, tease your mind, send you into fits of rage and despair, all in the hope of destroying your soul. Once this is accomplished, it becomes easy for him to lead you astray until you find yourself his prisoner."

He looked at her thoughtfully as she stepped back, her eyes wide and fearful.

"He is the personification of evil, my dear," he continued. "I pray you never fall victim to his wiles or his deception. For that is what you face now."

"How is this possible?"

"You do not wish to see the child in your womb live, is that right?"

"I can't. It would ruin my entire life."

"And you still feel this way after what you've seen, correct?"

"You've seen what evil may befall my child. The more I witness, the more I think I would be doing it a favor if I never let her live. Her life could be ruined. She could be in prison, as we saw. Why should I allow that to happen? It's unfair, both to her and me, to see her live this way. It's not right, and I want no part of it."

The Being began pacing back and forth, carefully placing one foot in front of the other, his eyes fixed on where he stepped. He held a finger to his lips, his head turning side to side. He paused, raised his head, and looked at her.

"So you wish to live your life as you choose, is that right?"

"Yes," she nodded, pulling herself upright, jutting out her chin.

"After all you've seen, what have you learned?"

"I've learned my child could be anything she wants, but that's a frightening thought. Why should I allow her to live and see her homeless or go to prison or be in a miserable relationship? Why would I want that pain inflicted upon her?"

"Tell me," he said, taking two steps toward her, "what of your own life choices?"

"What of them?"

"You made the choice to have sex with Tucker yet never once contemplated the outcome. Why?"

"That's none of your business. What I chose to do with him was between the two of us."

"Was it really?" he smirked.

"What an arrogant thing to say. Have you no decency?"

"Young one, to this point, you have done nothing but demonstrate mostly contempt for your situation. You vacillate between showing the qualities of a good mother and someone who is consumed by self. You have not made up your mind, much as you say otherwise. Your choices affect everyone around you, yet you choose to ignore this fact."

"No, it is you who ignore the truth of my circumstance," she yelled back. "My boyfriend is dead. I was supposed to spend my life with him. My mother and I don't get along. It's nearly hatred between us. My father isn't in my life often enough. He's too busy with his new girlfriend to care. My friends have plans for their futures. They will go to college, find good-paying jobs, and build a life I can only dream of without a child. Why do you ignore this truth about me? Is it because you do not care for me?"

Her eyes were burning with rage, the anger contorting her face into a mask uglier than she had known before. He stepped back, blinking his eyes in sheer amazement at this emotional outburst. He took a moment to compose himself, gathering his wits.

"So you believe your life will not be complete by having this child, am I correct?"

"No. It will be destroyed. I have plans I wish to see come to fruition. I have goals I wish to reach. A child will interfere in such a way I will not attain them."

"And what of other examples to the contrary?"

"I know of no examples," she replied, indignance covering her words.

"Have you not seen, young one? Many other women in your exact situation have overcome worse odds than you and have gone on to lead a fulfilling life. They've earned master's degrees, attained high positions in companies, and graduated with honors from college. They have gone on to have fulfilling lives despite their circumstance. How can you ignore these women?"

The shock in his voice was clear as he shook his head looking at her.

"I will never achieve such things. I don't believe you."

He began pacing again, shaking his head and whispering to himself, gesticulating as he did. Stacy watched this odd behavior and marveled at how clueless he looked, how utterly weak he appeared in this moment. She felt a modicum of satisfaction in having finally quieted talk of her possible success if she were to carry a baby to term.

He stopped pacing, snapped his fingers, and turned toward her. "There is something you need to see, something of which I hesitate to show you, simply because it goes against what this mission is about."

"And what is that?"

He looked around the meadow, the sun glistening off the blades of grass, shimmering as the wind blew across the field. He smiled and motioned with his hand. "Come. I'll show you."

Wordlessly, she followed him to a small hut, hidden in the shadows of the trees at the edge of the meadow. He opened the door and walked inside, closing it once they both occupied the cramped room. He pointed at what appeared to be a small screen, though it glowed from a puff of smoke in the corner of the room.

"Look, young one," he whispered, "look at what you have done."

She squinted her eyes as the mist cleared, her gaze growing wider as the hospital room she lay in at this moment came into view.

She saw her mother sitting beside the bed, her hands and head resting on the bed rail. Her mother's body shook as the tears came falling in waves from her eyes. Her father stood at a distance from the bed, a grim look on his face. He seemed frozen, almost statuesque, neither moving his hands or feet. He appeared devoid of emotion.

She looked at the machines she was hooked up to, the rhythmic tones adding a layer of solemnity to the scene.

The doctor and nurse stood at the end of the bed, both with sober expressions on their faces. It was clear they weren't there to provide happy news to her parents.

"Wh-what's happening to me?" she asked, her voice thin.

"My dear, you can only be in a coma for so long until your body shuts down and betrays itself. It's almost inevitable this will happen."

She turned to look at him, terror flashing in her eyes.

"I can't die," she whispered. "No, I can't die."

"And why is that?"

She turned back to look at the scene unfolding now, gazing wide-eyed at the sadness surrounding her near-lifeless body.

"Because there is much more I want to do with my life," she said, the words choking in her throat.

"And what of your child? Is it possible this is how they feel?"

His smile was tinged with sadness, as Stacy closed her eyes, bowed her head, and openly wept. He waved his hand, and the scene disappeared in a thick, misty fog, dissipating into the air. They stepped out from the cramped room and back into the beauty of the meadow. He moved to touch her shoulder, gently, lovingly, as became his custom.

"Young one, as I told you at the beginning of this journey, you have been given a unique opportunity. You have a chance to see what could be in the future, a future you hold in the palm of your hands. I cannot make this decision for you. In truth, no one else can make this decision. Only you can. I simply wish to expose you to the potential there may be if you decide to allow your child to live outside your womb. However, you hold the key to what will become of this child." He stood beside her, taking her hand in his and squeezing it. "This is no easy task, my child. I realize this feels like a burden only you can carry. But you must trust me when I say, there are many others who care about you and wish to see you whole. All you need do is reach out to them, believe them when they say they care for you and accept their help. Do you understand?"

Her breathing was shallow and came in quick, short bursts. The tears felt like rivulets of fire burning her cheeks. She reached up and wiped them away, sniffling hard as she did. She drew her hand away from him and stumbled a few feet away. She wiped her nose and shook her head.

"No. No. This is madness. This is absolute insanity. You have brought me here hoping I will change my mind. You want me to have this child, I can see it in your eyes and hear it in your voice. You do not care what is happening in my life right now. You don't know the pain I suffer when I think about the consequences of my actions. Who are you to tell me what to do? Why should I listen to you at all?"

He cocked his head to one side as he looked at her and gave a slight nod. "Of course, you're right. Why should you listen to me? Who am I to tell you what to do? Of course, you have every right to decide what your life will become. That's how it should be. So you must answer that question. Why are you listening to me?"

"I have no choice right now. I'm trapped in your maddening game until such time as you decide this is over. Isn't that right?"

"Yes," he smiled, "that's right."

"And when will this be over?" she pleaded.

He stepped closer to her, placing his hand gently on her shoulder. "My dear, I want to make sure you are fully prepared for what lies ahead. Life is never easy. No one guarantees you will be happy every second of every day. There are hard choices to make, decisions you will regret, and most you will find great joy in. You have an entire life ahead of you. You have only witnessed a portion of what potentially may come. As I have mentioned before, some of what you see may be true, or none of it may be true. But what happens in your future depends on you. Throughout this journey, you must ask yourself these questions. Do you believe you have enough information at this moment to move forward? If not, where do you turn? Do you trust others to help guide you and navigate past the snares that may entangle you? This is all I wish for you to learn. Does that make sense?"

She thought for a long moment, her eyes gazing around the meadow, hoping to find some logic in the emptiness around them. She sniffled once more and wiped her nose. Her eyes were red and puffy from her tears, as the fatigue from her emotional outburst crept in on her thoughts. She let go a heavy sigh and closed her eyes.

"I am fully aware of the gravity of my decision. I accept the burden of any future consequence. But it is my burden alone to carry, not someone else. And I must choose according to what I believe is right. If it is not what you want for me, so be it. If it is not what my parents want, I will not concern myself with their opinion. I will choose for myself, and what others may think about what I do is irrelevant."

He studied her carefully, looking for any hidden compassion in her soul. "Perhaps we should move forward," he said, his voice low.

Jason had sequestered himself in a corner booth in the cafeteria, nursing a lukewarm cup of coffee. His eyes were locked on his phone, scrolling through several text messages from his girlfriend, smiling occasionally at the sexual boldness of some of her comments. As a man nearing the heart of middle age, it felt good to be so sexually desired, something his marriage seemed to lack.

He sighed, wishing he could be with her instead of at the hospital, but his devotion to his daughter came first. He closed out the text message app and turned off his phone. He placed it back in his pocket and took a sip of his coffee, surveying the scene around him.

Sitting at a table near the cafeteria entrance, two young women were demonstrably animated in their conversation. They laughed and leaned toward each other, a clear indication this was a close relationship. He looked over at a corner table, where a group of doctors and nurses were enjoying their brief time away from their duties. Their laughter was even more raucous than the two women, as was expected. One does not work in a hospital without developing a mechanism to alleviate the inevitable pressure.

At yet another table, a young man dressed in bloodstained scrubs sat with his head low, a haggard look on his face, his eyes locked on the floor. It was clear from his body language his latest surgery was unsuccessful. The young man wiped his forehead and took a sip from his coffee.

Jason shook his head, not envying the pain this man felt. He marveled at how anyone this young could carry such a heavy burden on a daily basis, literally holding life and death in his hands. Jason took one more sip of his own coffee and realized it was nearly empty. He lifted the cup high until the last few drops slithered into his throat.

He sighed, ran a hand through his hair, and rubbed his eyes.

What if Stacy never wakes up? he thought.

He quickly dismissed the thought almost as soon as it entered his mind. He stood, pushing his chair behind him, and walked toward the trash can. He threw the paper coffee cup in the receptacle and headed to the exit. He took one last look at the young surgeon and hoped he never had to accept that same sullen gaze in his own eyes. The thought of losing his daughter was something he could never bear to think.

"I don't wish to move forward right now," Stacy said, crossing her arms. "I wish to remain here, where it is beautiful and peaceful."

"You wish to remain here?" the Being said. "I'm curious to know your reasons."

Something in the way he looked at her caused her composure to flee. She uncrossed her arms and looked down at her feet, straining to latch onto a coherent thought. She was left wanting.

"Please, enlighten me with your reasons why you wish to stay. After telling me you wanted to see what may or may not happen to your child, you suddenly wish to end our journey and remain in this space. Am I correct?"

"Y-yes," she said, her eyes darting across the ground, "I think."

He gently tilted his head back and laughed heartily. The sound echoed off the surrounding trees and shook the ground around her. She looked up at him, her eyes narrowed and tinged with anger.

"Why do you laugh?"

"You amuse me, child."

She stormed to where he stood, a rage filling her soul. "You continue to say this to me. How do I amuse you? Why do you mock me this way? I'm coming to despise you. Do you realize that?"

"Despise, you say," he chuckled, crossing his arms. "Pray tell, why?"

"All this time you've shown me nothing but lies, nothing but fabrications of a life that may never come to fruition. You continue to taunt me with these questions of why I wish to rid myself of this burden. And I continue to tell you why I can never be a mother. You refuse to believe me, yet you demand I listen to you. This isn't right." She stood in front of him, fists clenched, eyes raging.

The Being had a bemused look on his face as he surveyed her carefully. A smile crept across his mouth as he watched her. "If you recall, I said the exact opposite. Or have you forgotten?"

She stepped back from him, the rage lessening as she did. Her eyes stayed fixed on him as she unclenched her fists. Her shoulders slumped over in near defeat at being reminded of this fact.

"It's okay, young one. I understand why you're so angry."

"Do you? Pray tell, why?"

He began pacing back and forth in front of her, rubbing his chin again in the same manner he did when they first met.

"Up till now, your life has been simple. You woke up, went to school, socialized with your friends, attended your practice, and spent time with your boyfriend. You had a future planned for you and Tucker, a future as idyllic as any you could dream. You had your life planned out to the hilt, following your boyfriend to UCLA, where you would continue this fairy-tale life into eternity. Am I correct so far?"

She nodded, a sullen look on her face.

"You spoke of marriage, of having a family with Tucker and growing old together. Sadly, that can never happen now. We don't need to cover the details on this, do we?" He looked carefully at her.

"No," she whispered. "No, we don't."

"Yes, you and your mother may not get along, but you're to blame for part of that."

"I'm what?" she asked sternly.

He stopped walking, pausing long enough to look over at her. "Oh, yes. I forgot you don't realize such things at your age." He chuckled. "My mistake." He continued his pacing back and forth.

"What do you mean by saying, 'my age'?

"Don't take offense, my dear." He waved his hand. "I could tell you stories about your own mother behaving in a similar fashion when she was your age, but that's not relevant to the story we have yet to finish. Anyway…"

"Wait!" she interrupted. "What do you mean you could tell me stories about my mother? What does that mean?"

He suddenly stopped pacing altogether, his head low. He closed his eyes and took a deep breath, exhaling slowly. He shook his head, his lips moving, but there was barely any sound coming out. Stacy cocked her head slightly, trying to grasp what he was saying. Her ears strained to make sense of any coherent words he might be saying, but it was no use. It seemed as if his mouth were moving to the inner dialogue he was speaking.

Finally, he raised his head, turning to look at her.

"Forgive me. I spoke in error regarding your mother. It is of no consequence to our journey."

"You meant something by that. What was it?"

He sighed once more, closed his eyes, and shook his head. "Young one, have you not learned anything yet?" he said exasperated. "You have exhibited the qualities of a mother. You have tasted the emotions a mother feels in watching their child take flight in this world. You have witnessed the heartache of a mother whose child chooses to live contrary to how they have been taught. All this was never about your child though. Most certainly, you must have realized this by now."

Stacy's eyes grew wide, the shock evident on her face. She moved to speak, but words failed her. She brought a hand to cover her mouth, shaking her head.

"Yes, dear one. This journey is about you, not your child."

"But…but what am I to learn? How am I supposed to react to this now? I still don't understand," she said in a whisper.

He stepped toward her, stopping a few paces in front of her. Reaching out, he placed a hand on her shoulder. "My dear, you have spent your young life doubting who you are, nearly convincing yourself you can't trust your parents. You've fought them, become almost enemies with your own mother, without asking yourself why you should react in anger. I could tell you the many reasons why this may happen, but I believe you know the reason." He smiled and squeezed her shoulder. "You are much stronger than you know. You are capable of so much more than just being an object of someone else's fantasy, the way you were with Tucker."

"No, you're wrong," she said, pulling her shoulder away from his hand. "Tucker loved me. He wanted to be with me forever. He wanted to marry me."

"Are you sure? Did he ever tell you this, or did you just imagine he wanted the same things you did?"

"I-I don't know," she said, furrowing her brow.

"Think back to what he said that night. He wondered how you could speculate about a future together. He only spoke of playing football, of earning respect from the highest level of the sport. And after the most intimate moment two people could share, he told you he didn't believe he could be a father. What should that tell you?"

"But you said yourself, Tucker and I could have a beautiful life together." she pointed a finger at him. "It was you who told me we would have lived happily together. Why do you try to convince me otherwise?"

"Oh, yes, you and Tucker would have been happy together, there is no doubt. But it would not have been as idyllic as you think."

"How do you know this?"

"Child, I have shown you a possible future for your child," he sighed. "How do you think I am capable of doing this?"

She stared at him, a curious look on her face. She hadn't considered this question. She'd been so caught up in her own thoughts during this adventure she never bothered to ask how or why this was possible.

"Never mind that now," he continued. "Just know this. All that I show you is for your own benefit. Do you believe me?"

She shrugged.

"What don't you understand?"

"Well, literally all this," she said waving her hand. "This beautiful meadow where I heard children's voices. I felt happiness and joy. It was beautiful. But now, after watching my child, I'm frightened. How can I stand by and let these things happen to her? Why would I even allow her to live if I knew she would suffer in such a way? I would not wish this upon her at all. She deserves something more than what you've shown me."

"May I ask you a question?" he said.

"Of course."

"What have you learned from your own mother?"

"What do you mean?"

"I mean, child, watching her, listening to her, observing how she dealt with the circumstances of life. What did you learn from her?"

"I learned that relationships don't mean much of anything."

"Do you believe that?"

"Not entirely."

"Explain," he said, crossing his arms.

She sighed, closing her eyes, and gathering her thoughts. She hadn't expected this sort of cross examination. "My parents divorced when I was little. I don't remember much of them being together, and when they were, they would scream at each other constantly."

She closed her eyes and shook her head, coming close to covering her ears at the echoes of her parents' voices in her head.

"They would assign fault, blaming each other for the misfortune they found themselves in, about having fallen out of love. They spoke bitterly to each other, they acted cold and hateful toward one another. When I tried to find a reason for this hatred, they would tell me it was none of my business and I shouldn't worry about it."

"And you shouldn't."

"Yes, I should have," she answered, nodding her head. "I should have known what was going on. I should have understood why they decided not to love each other anymore."

"Why was this important, young one?"

She paused, looking first to the ground, then raising her head to look directly at him. "If I had understood, maybe I would've found a way to remove the anger I felt toward them both and cast it away. All I wanted was to be as far away from that pain as I could get. I wish I had run away and never returned to live with them. Instead, I was forced to watch as two people I loved the most in life argue over who was a better parent to me." She reached up and wiped her brow, shaking her head. "Why was I forced to choose?" she whispered.

The Being stood silent, carefully watching as Stacy searched her memory for a morsel of hope. Knowing this would lead to further despair, he stepped toward her again and stopped when he was in front of her.

"My child, don't do this. Don't allow yourself to become entangled in emotions you know nothing about. Your parents were once idealistic and brash like you. They, too, were teenagers, flush with hormones and desires, just as you are. If you understand this, you might understand why they arrived at the same conclusion at the same time."

She looked up at him. "And what conclusion is that?"

He sighed. "That neither one had the temerity to survive a marriage."

"But I thought it was supposed to be till death do us part. Isn't that part of the vows? Isn't that part of what you promise each other? That marriage is supposed to last forever?"

"Yes, child, it is supposed to be wonderfully complicated. But it is more about someone being the right person more than finding the right person."

"What does that mean?" she said, wrinkling her nose.

"Marriage demands sacrifice, a commitment to a common purpose at the exclusion of any other emotion. It requires transparency and support, something that is left behind far too often when the reality of a relationship becomes manifest. It requires all the effort in the world to give of yourself and never demand anything in return. It demands two people working to make it successful. It only requires one of them to derail it."

"But why is this important to what I am seeing now? How am I supposed to relate what I know of my own mother to supposedly becoming a mother myself? If I no longer want this burden for myself, why should I relate it to my mother?"

"If you choose motherhood, are you afraid you'll make mistakes?"

"Of course, I am," she sneered. "Who wouldn't be afraid?"

"Are you afraid you won't know the answers to your child's questions?"

"Yes. Why do say this?"

"Because your own mother believed the same thing. She believed she would fail, that she would not be good enough for you. Yet she found the courage to become a mother and still teach you as well as she was able. How do you suppose this happened? Think of what you've witnessed in your own mother's life that is good, and perhaps you'll understand."

"You don't know my mother," she said, angrily. "You have no concept of what she has done that causes me to hate her. You would do well to stop talking about her while we journey on."

"If you wish," he said, waving a hand in the air.

"I do," she said, her voice weak. "If you could only know how she would flirt with my male friends at school, how she dressed to make herself appear less like an adult, you might understand. She embarrassed me anytime she would visit my school. I hated her for trying to entice boys half her age to sleep with her. I despise her behavior."

"Well, she taught you at least one good thing."

"And what is that?"

"How not to behave as an adult."

"I suppose you're right."

He moved beside her, placing his arm around her shoulders and giving them a squeeze. "You must understand, I have your best interest at heart, child. I believe in you. You're a strong, confident young woman, capable of handling such a momentous decision as this and finding a way to rise above. Why else would I have proposed we take this journey together?"

His smile was warm, soothing in its effect upon her heart. She felt herself being able to smile back in response.

"However, I wonder, you still insist on me giving birth to this child. Why is that?"

"You're not listening." he shook his head.

"Listening to what?"

He stepped in front of her and placed his hands on her shoulders, looking into her eyes. There was a softness about him that allayed her anxiety, a warmth she hadn't felt.

"You hold the key. You must decide. No one else can tell you what to do. Only you can make the best decision based on the information at hand. Now, do I wish you would consult with those wiser than you? Yes, of course. You deserve to know every outcome your decision will have on those around you. You haven't even told your mother you're pregnant. You're hiding from her, as if you could keep this a secret. Nothing hidden remains in the shadows. Sooner or later, it is brought into the light."

He glanced up, looking to a point beyond where they stood. She furrowed her brow, turned, and followed his gaze. It led to the meadow. She recoiled in fear at what she saw, the suddenness of the display in front of her too horrific to bear.

Scattered among the field, rising skyward, were millions of tombstones, each with a name and date on them. A small picture of a child adorned each stone, a smile affixed to their faces or their eyes closed, as if their eternal slumber were suddenly exposed.

She stepped backward from the meadow, her hand covering the inaudible scream she felt welling inside, begging for expression. Her eyes were wide, darting in every direction, daring her mind to absorb such a horrible sight. She sank to her knees, unable to look away from the tableau before her.

"Why did you show me this?" she whispered. "Why must I see their names and faces?"

The Being walked toward the meadow, slowly gazing upon each stone, a sad, crooked smile on his face. His eyes couldn't contain the sorrow he felt at this sight, but he nonetheless moved toward them. He paused, turning to face Stacy.

"I show you this to convey the gravity of your decision," he replied, his voice somber. "What you witness is but a drop in the ocean of horrific choices made, each of them with probable cause for termination. None of them deserve this ignominy. Yet here they are, frozen in eternal memory."

"No," she shook her head, "no, this cannot be. Why would their memory remain?"

His eyes suddenly became dark and angry. "Do you think a child could ever be forgotten? Even in their most fragile state, do you believe they can be cast away into the sea of forgetfulness? How can the cry of an unborn child ever be silenced?"

Shrinking back from him, she could feel the rage in his voice overwhelm her. She turned away, closing her eyes as she knelt on the ground. She held up her arms, as if they were able to deflect the anger of his withering gaze.

"I wish to continue our journey now," she said, her words labored and soft.

"You what?" he said, cocking his head toward her. "You wish to see more?"

"Yes," she nodded. "Yes. Anything but this. Please. I cannot bear the sight of this."

The Being raised his hand, snapped his fingers, and moved toward her. As he did, the tombstones faded away into the air, once more returning the meadow to its more natural state. He stopped just in front of her, lowered his hand to her, and waited.

She glanced up, noticing his eyes were still troubled, but not enraged as a moment before. She put her hand in his as he helped her stand to her feet. She sighed, brushing her gown and straightening herself.

"Are you sure you wish to continue? You seemed nearly broken when we were about to enter the prison."

Stacy thought for a minute, a pensive look on her face. Finally, she jutted out her chin and nodded.

"Yes. Yes, I'm ready to face what will come. Lead me on."

"As you wish," he said, waving his hand.

Immediately, the air around them swirled with colors, the air rushing by them both. Once more, she closed her eyes and waited for the wind to stop blowing.

Chapter 9

When the wind stopped, Stacy opened her eyes to discover they were inside the visitors' room at Silverbay Prison. A long counter divided the room in half, the thick Plexiglas wall cordoned off by small partitions, just high enough to afford a semblance of privacy between inmate and visitor.

There were only a handful of inmates talking with their visitor. Some remained in shackles as they spoke on the clumsy phone receivers, barely able to reach a hand to their ear and hold the receiver. Why the prison didn't upgrade to having microphones on either side of the Plexiglas to make conversation easier was anyone's guess.

Several guards stood against the back wall behind the inmates, keeping a watchful eye. Each of them were mammoth in size, their bulging arms pressing tightly against their short sleeve blue shirts. Each of them adopted a scowl on their faces, a not-so-subtle hint to the inmates to rethink any shenanigans they might have wished to act upon while visiting.

The exchange between inmate and visitor was surprisingly cordial. Only the occasional curse word from the inmate allowed the impression of disgust. The most unsettling spectacle was the variance in age of the inmates. A grizzled older man, skin wrinkled and frail in body, sat talking to an equally older woman. Judging by the tears in their eyes, this relationship was far deeper than one could imagine.

Another inmate looked young enough to still be in high school. His brown hair was disheveled, and his arms were full of tattoos. He sat talking to a man dressed in a well-appointed suit and tie. It was obvious this was a lawyer going over details for a defense trial that must have been forthcoming.

Stacy watched wide-eyed as she absorbed the sight before her, wringing her hands and feeling herself shake nervously. Just knowing what each of these inmates must be facing daily was enough to set her on edge.

The Being stood close by, studying her reaction. A soft, awkward smile crossed his lips as he gazed upon her. Judging by his firm stance, he didn't appear distressed in any way by what he saw. He simply waited for the opportune moment to interact with Stacy.

Just then, the doors opened, and a woman visitor entered the room, following one of the guards. Stacy narrowed her eyes as she caught a glimpse of the woman. Her dark hair had been highlighted with frosty-gray streaks, and her deep brown eyes were tear-stained and puffy. No doubt this was a hard situation to be in. The guard pointed the woman to a chair somewhere near the middle of the row of visitors, followed by a nod of the head. The woman thanked the guard and dutifully sat down. She placed her elbows on the small counter in front of her and rested her head on her balled up fists. She was breathing heavy now, appearing on the edge of a nervous breakdown.

A few moments later, another door opened, this time on the side where the inmates were. Stacy's eyes grew wide as she saw the prisoner led into the room, and her tears came instantly.

Olivia was clad in prison-issue orange fatigues, her hands shackled near her waist, the chain leading down toward the shackles on her ankles. Her steps were halting and awkward, her shoulders hunched, and her back curved due to the weight of her chains. A female guard escorted her toward a seat opposite the female visitor who just entered.

Olivia looked frail, her body showing evidence of having lost weight. Her hair was disheveled, tangled, and matted in places. The dark rings around her hollow eyes gave her an overall macabre appearance. Whatever nightmare she was living in here, it was taking its toll.

For her part, the woman lifted her head, the noise of the door opening breaking her out of whatever trance she had been in. Her eyes followed Olivia across the room until she was seated opposite her. The guard leaned in close to whisper something in Olivia's ear and unlocked the shackles on her hands. After this, the guard stepped a few paces directly behind Olivia.

She feigned a smile as she picked up the phone and mechanically brought it to her ear. The woman reached up for the phone receiver, her hand shaking, and did the same. The two of them sat silent for several minutes, neither one finding a proper greeting for this moment.

"I'm glad you came," Olivia finally said. "I know my mom wasn't up to coming to visit. It means a lot you're here, Tonya."

Stacy's eyes grew wide, and a smile crossed her lips. Here was her dearest friend in the world coming to visit her daughter. Yes, the years brought about change, but Tonya still looked as beautiful as the day she drove Stacy to the clinic. Her face had become a little fuller, and she had gained some weight, but overall, she appeared in good health.

"I'm so sorry your mom couldn't be here, Liv," Tonya said. "I tried to talk her into coming with me, but she didn't answer when I stopped by to pick her up."

"It's okay," Olivia said, trying her best to sound calm. "I know this is hard for her."

"I'm just glad she trusts me to be with you."

"Me too," Olivia responded.

"Oh, I…uh, brought that picture with me," Tonya said, reaching down and pulling it up off the counter.

Stacy hadn't seen Tonya carrying anything and was surprised when she pulled it up and held it to the plastic windows. She stepped closer, getting a better look at the picture. As she suspected, it was the same one she'd seen before—a woman sitting with a small child, their faces blurry and unrecognizable.

Olivia's eyes began welling with tears, and she reached her hand up, touching the picture through the window. She lowered her head as the tears fell, dripping off her cheeks and forming a puddle on the counter.

"I know it's hard, Liv, but I know you wanted to see it one more time," Tonya said, her voice cracking. "I'm so sorry."

An awkward, deathlike silence fell between them, punctuated by the sound of them sniffling back more tears. Stacy watched the two women and walked slowly behind Olivia, wondering what could have caused such an outpouring of emotion. Tonya slipped the picture into her purse and looked back up at Olivia.

"Oh, and I'm so sorry I missed the funeral," Olivia said. "I'm sorry for everything."

Stacy froze, her breath trapped in her lungs, her legs unable to move. It was as if every function of her body was numb at the sound of the word *funeral.*

"Whose funeral is she speaking of?" she whispered.

The Being slowly rubbed his chin, inhaling and exhaling in almost the same rhythm.

"I'm not sure I should tell you," he answered, matching Stacy's tone.

"I deserve to know," she said, turning slowly toward him. "Whose funeral?"

He could see any attempt at stalling was fruitless. His mind raced with all manner of possible explanations and ways to define this moment but came up empty. Finally, he relented.

"It was your father's funeral," he said, his words frail and calm.

The room fell into a dreamlike appearance, bending and dancing at odd angles as Stacy watched Olivia and Tonya still talking. Their mouths were moving, but she couldn't hear any audible words either of them said. Her body was numb; any strength she might have had was replaced by a nothingness that frightened her. Nausea began welling inside her as she stumbled to lean against the back wall of the room, hoping to gain some semblance of normalcy in her ability to stand.

The Being came beside her, placing an arm underneath hers and propped her up.

"Stacy, you must understand, it was unavoidable. It is the natural order of things."

"I understand," she whispered, her eyes still shut.

She pushed away his arm, turning so her back was against the wall for support. She breathed slowly, clearing her mind and focusing on peaceful thoughts. She opened her eyes and stared at Olivia and Tonya, still engaged in conversation.

"I promised your mother I'd come visit as often as I could," Tonya said. "I mean, I feel partly responsible for you being here."

"No, no, no, don't do that," Olivia said, waving her hand. "You're not the one who's responsible for that old woman dying in the accident. Don't say that."

"But I saw you were drunk when you left my party, Liv. I should've stopped you before you got in your car," Tonya said, the anger in her voice evident.

"You couldn't have stopped me. I would've found a way to leave."

"I should've taken your car keys then. Any way you look at it, you shouldn't have left my house," Tonya answered.

"Well, obviously, we can't change what happened, can we?" Olivia said, sighing.

"No, we can't, Liv. But we can try to make a better future."

"What future?" Olivia sneered. "What kind of future do I have? I'm not getting out of here for another ten years. What kind of future is that? What do I have to look forward to?"

"Come on, Liv. You've got a lot to look forward to. Just give it time."

"All I have is time," Olivia snapped.

"Look, I'm sorry your mom was too embarrassed to come down here. I'm sorry I'm here instead, but I thought you could use some company."

"I'm sorry I snapped," Olivia sighed, rubbing her forehead. "It's just a lot to process right now."

"It's okay," Tonya said. "But how are you holding up?"

"I'm okay, all things considered. I mean, I've got a bed, three meals a day. Otherwise, it sucks."

Just then, a voice broke over the intercom system.

"All prisoners, report back to their cells for inspection. All prisoners, report back to their cells."

Olivia closed her eyes and took a deep breath, shaking her head.

"I'm sorry we didn't have more time, Tonya. Thank you for coming down and being here."

"Of course, Liv. I'll tell your mom you said hi."

Olivia smiled weakly. "Uh, yeah. Thanks."

The guards herded out most of the inmates in a hasty fashion, then moved closer to the inmates who remained, motioning for them to wrap up their conversations.

"Okay, I gotta go. Love you. Bye," Oliva said, hanging up the receiver phone and waving at Tonya.

She stood up, as the guard placed the shackles back on her wrists and locked them. She pointed toward the door and motioned for her to start walking. Olivia shuffled her way toward the door leading back to the cells.

Tonya sat watching silently as her best friend's daughter disappeared behind the steel door. She wiped a tear from her eye, glanced down at her purse on her lap, and stood up, pulling the purse over her shoulder. She straightened her blouse and made her way to the exit. She pulled the door open and headed off to the lobby, then finally, the exit of the prison.

Both the Being and Stacy remained in perfect silence, taking in the scene. As if on cue, the Being moved toward the door leading to the cells. Stacy followed close behind and soon found they were in a long hallway, steel bars lining either side. It appeared these might be holding cells, but Stacy couldn't be sure. They journeyed further on, making their way through a series of steel bar doorways, each leading deeper into the prison.

After a time, they arrived at a long row of cells, lining only one side of the hallway. The steel bars had seen better days, the cracking and peeling of each one indicating they were overdue for replacement. The Being grimaced as he walked, his eyes fixed straight ahead. He never blinked at the sight of each lost soul confined in their dank, musty cells.

Some inmates lay on their beds, staring at the ceiling. Some sat on the edge of the bed, their elbows resting on their knees, head lowered in defeat. Still others seemed to busy themselves with books from the prison library, reciting passages of long ago knowledge. The various ways the inmates passed their time here fascinated Stacy.

Unlike the Being, she couldn't help but stare at these inmates as she passed by the cells. Her eyes were wide, a mixture of wonder and fear welling in her soul. How anyone could survive in this environment was beyond her. She paused at a cell, staring at the inmate standing against the steel bars.

She cocked her head, mesmerized by the vacant look in this man's eyes. His face was haggard, his hair and clothes disheveled and worn. Dirt and dust seemed to be his closest friend as his fingers and cheeks were covered in it. He leaned against the bars of the cell, lazily smoking a cigarette, blowing the smoke slowly and succinctly in the air. It was as if this was the only nonregulated activity he could perform without a prison guard dictating to him.

The Being noticed her standing a few cells back from him and stopped. He narrowed his eyes, looking deep into her soul. He gave a tired smile and a slight nod of his head. He walked a few paces back to where she stood, stopping a short distance away.

"What is it you see, young one?"

"This man seems trapped inside a cage. He has nowhere to go, nothing to do. It's as if he's just waiting to die."

"Perhaps he has already died, and his body is simply waiting to be placed in the ground."

"How could he have died if he stands here now?" She turned to look at him.

"Death does not always arrive when the body no longer functions. It may come in the simplest fashion and readily abide until the soul accepts its presence. Once the mind has accepted the inevitable, the body slowly follows until the last breath escapes one's lips." His voice sounded tired and worn as he spoke.

"Does he deserve such punishment? How can it be that someone commits an act so heinous yet is treated with such contempt?

What if he were innocent? Why should the innocent suffer such a cruel fate?"

"You still haven't connected the dots, have you?" he half whispered, his eyes closed, his head shaking.

"What did you say?"

"Nothing. Come. We must find your daughter."

He motioned for her to continue. She took one last look at this man and shook her head. How could anyone survive such treatment and expect to behave normally?

She caught up with the Being just before they crossed a dividing hallway, running perpendicular to the one they were walking. The hallway was cut off on all sides by sets of double steel bar doors, a guard manning each side. Beyond the dissecting hall, they came across another row of cells, only this time they were occupied by women.

Stacy's breath came faster now as she stared into each cell, intently looking for Olivia. Again, the sight of a human being turning into nothing more than waste was more than she could handle. She would've wept, were it not for her desire to see her daughter.

Finally, the Being stopped in front a cell at the end of the row. Stacy came beside him and looked inside. She shook her head at the unmistakable sight of Olivia, sitting on the edge of her bed, arms wrapped around her stomach, rocking back and forth. She had a wild look in her eyes and seemed to be muttering something unintelligible. If ever there was a time Stacy wanted to rush to her daughter's side and hold her, it was now.

"Why does she do this?" she whispered.

"Routine is a part of human nature. Even things we may interpret as bordering on the psychotic become the norm in abnormal circumstances."

"Is she okay? Mentally, I mean?"

"Stacy, one does not commit a crime, suffer the consequences for it, and ever return to normal thinking. The ghosts of these hallways and cells linger in the imagination, always seeking to frighten souls at various moments in life. It's unavoidable to lose your sanity."

Assured by the doctor everything would be all right if she left, Tori made a brief stop at her condo to freshen up. She promised Jason she would only be gone for a short time and head back to the hospital as soon as she could. Besides, she needed to be away from him for a while. Her feelings of closeness notwithstanding, their arguing reminded her why they divorced. To stay married would have been too volatile for them both.

She stood in the bathroom, washing her hands when she looked in the mirror, and slowly blinked her eyes. Seemingly for the first time, she noticed the bags starting to form under her eyes. She reached up and traced a finger across them, as if her gaze would cause them to disappear. She felt a sadness creeping into her heart, a longing for the days of her youth.

I used to be so good-looking, she thought. *How did I get to be so old?*

She shook her head, cursing the disappearance of unfettered youth as well as the onslaught of middle age. She ran her fingers through her hair, searching carefully for any sign of grayness appearing. She saw a few strands starting to turn, but nothing serious to worry about right now.

I need to get this colored soon, she thought, sighing heavily.

She turned off the faucet, shook the excess water from her hands, and reached for a towel. She dried them off and wiped her face with it. Holding it against her face, she closed her eyes, breathing in the fresh scent of a towel recently washed. It was the little things that gave meaning to a moment. Odd that she would think of this now.

She replaced the towel, turned off the light, and walked down the hallway toward the stairs. Her phone began buzzing as she reached the top step. Pulling her phone out, she rolled her eyes upon seeing the name on the screen. She swiped her finger across the screen to answer the call.

"Rick, this isn't a good time," she said, walking slowly down the steps.

"Hello to you too. I was just calling to ask why you haven't returned any of my calls."

She reached the kitchen and sat down at the dining area table.

"I've been a little busy with Stacy being in the hospital, that's all."

"Sorry to hear that. Should I come down?"

"No, you don't have to. Besides, I don't think you'd feel comfortable."

"Why is that?"

"Because Jason's there too."

There was a long silence on the phone. The only sound Tori could hear was of Rick clearing his throat and sniffling loudly. He sighed a few times and let out a sarcastic chuckle as well.

"Rick? Are you okay?" she finally asked.

"Yeah, yeah, I'm all right. I just don't know how I feel if you're in the same room as your ex, that's all."

"You knew all this when we started this relationship, Rick. You knew I was divorced, and it was inevitable for me to see Jason. When it comes to Stacy, we're her parents, and we both need to be where she is when needed. You knew this about me when we met."

"Yeah, I did. Doesn't mean I like it though."

"I'm not asking you to like it. You just need to find a way to accept it, that's all."

"It's a lot harder than it looks, Tori. I'm sorry. You'll just have to give me time."

"Time?" she asked, her voice not masking her exasperation. "We've been together almost two years. How much time do you need?"

"I don't know, but I don't feel good about this at all."

"Rick, I'm a grown woman. Either you trust me or you don't. Either you believe I love you or you don't. I just hope you realize how difficult it would be if I didn't have your support."

"Look, I didn't call to get into a long-winded discussion about our relationship. I called to ask you to meet me for dinner tomorrow night."

"I don't know, Rick. Can we reschedule?"

"What is it now, Tori?" he sighed heavily.

"What do you mean?"

"There's got to be a reason you don't want to see me. Besides your daughter being in the hospital, I mean."

"Look, the reason I can't meet you is Stacy, and I need to get back to the hospital. I just stopped home to get a few things and freshen up a little. We'll talk later, okay?"

"Okay, whatever," he said and disconnected the call.

Tori stared at her phone for a few minutes, dumbfounded at how abruptly Rick ended the conversation. Feeling less than enthused about their relationship at this moment, she shrugged, stood from the table, and put her phone in her pocket.

She stood motionless in the kitchen, mentally checking she had everything needed to return to the hospital. She patted her front pants pocket, feeling her car keys firmly ensconced inside. She reached for her purse on the kitchen table and slung it on her shoulder. Pulling the keys out of her pocket, she headed for the garage.

It was free time at Silverbay prison, and the inmates milled about aimlessly in the main courtyard. Located behind the cafeteria, it contained a small area for weightlifting, eight basketball courts—each with a high fence around it—and an open space, perfect for walking, tossing a football or baseball, or just standing without purpose and staring at the prison walls that became home.

Olivia sat with another inmate on an old set of wooden bleachers, three rows high. She alternated between taking a drag on her cigarette and watching the activity around her. Time moves slowly in prison, and the only way to cope with it was to find a mental distraction.

The Being and Stacy stood near the bleachers, silently taking in the scene around them. Having never seen the horror of prison up close, her eyes were wide with fear. Knowing she couldn't be seen was little comfort at this moment, but she still did her best to hide behind the Being as much as possible. Her nerves were unsettled thinking of what led each inmate here. She closed her eyes, wishing away the horrific thoughts floating through her imagination.

As she opened her eyes, she saw a male inmate strolling toward Olivia. He was short, frail-looking, and seemed as if he could be broken in two pieces by any of the inmates here. The man stopped a few feet away from Olivia and looked at her.

Olivia looked up from where she sat, a lost look in her eyes. "What do you want, Lucky?" she asked.

"I still want to know if you've accepted Jesus Christ as your Savior, Olivia," he said, his voice as thin as his body.

Olivia sneered. "I ain't got time for that, Lucky. If God were real, he'd show up right now and get me the hell out of here. I've told you before, I'm not gonna buy into that religious crap, so take that story elsewhere."

"But, Olivia, he can set you free from your sin, don't you understand?" Lucky pleaded.

"Listen," Olivia said, standing up, "I've heard your story before, and I don't believe it. You honestly believe I can be set free? From what? Prison?" She shook her head. "Like I said, if God were real, he'd bust open these walls and set us all free. Until that happens, I don't wanna hear it. It's time for you to go, Lucky."

He closed his eyes and shook his head, a slight smile crossing his lips. "Olivia, if you only knew," he whispered. He turned and shuffled slowly away, headed for a group of inmates who'd gathered by the fence line. It appeared this was where the religious inmates gathered, judging by one man standing in the middle of a circle holding a Bible in one hand and waving wildly with the other.

"Liv, that was mean," the dark-haired girl sitting next to Olivia said.

She was small but wiry, her thin frame belying her muscular features. She had short black hair cut in a bob and tattoos covering her arms.

"I just don't want to hear it, Easy," Olivia said, sitting down. "That man bothers me."

"Why?"

"He's been on my ass about being a Christian since I got here. I just don't buy it."

"Yeah, he's talked to me a few times too. I don't mind him. He's harmless. I just think you should back off from being so mean, that's all."

Stacy turned her head in time to see a group of about five female inmates storming across the yard headed for Olivia. The woman in front of the group was just overweight enough to look intimidating. Stacy reached out and tapped the Being on the arm.

"What's happening?"

He slowly turned to look at the group of women and turned back to Olivia. "It's the way of prison," he said, mournfully.

Olivia looked in the direction of the group of women, now much closer, and shook her head.

"Damn," she whispered, as she stood up again, "I knew she'd try something."

Easy turned to look at the group of women, and she, too, stood up next to Olivia. The other inmates on the bleachers scattered, not wanting to be involved or to risk ancillary punishment from the warden. Everyone knew what was about to happen.

The group of women stopped several feet from the bleachers, while the heavyset woman in front continued. She stopped in front of Olivia, an evil glint in her eye, and swung at Olivia with what appeared to be a shank. Olivia instinctively put her arms up as the shank tore across her forearm.

Olivia screamed as the woman moved in closer, grabbing Olivia by the collar and raising the shank above her head. By now Easy backed away as the other women in the group had as well. Whatever issue was being decided here clearly involved Olivia and this woman, though it appeared Olivia didn't seem to want to fight back.

The woman brought the shank down into Olivia's shoulder, twisting it for maximum effect. She raised it again and shoved it into her bicep. By now Olivia had fallen to her knees, helpless to stop this woman. Several more times, the woman stabbed Olivia wherever her hand flew. It seemed she was intent on killing Olivia, regardless the punishment.

Suddenly, a siren rang out above, and the other inmates in the yard dutifully scattered toward the entrances of each cell block. Prison guards were sprinting toward the scene, hopeful they could stop a murder.

The group of women suddenly scattered in varying directions. Again, none of them wanted to be party to whatever punishment befell these two combatants. It was the way of the inmate.

The woman continued stabbing Olivia wherever she could, the blood spurting out on the ground and onto the woman's prison issued garb. The guards arrived en masse, tackling the woman and wresting control of the shank away from her. She was screaming as the guards lay on top of her, applying pressure with knees and elbows on her back while working to secure handcuffs around her wrists. Two guards lifted her off the ground to a standing position, their hands locked on the woman's arms. Forcibly, they led her inside where she would be dealt with properly.

Olivia lay on the ground, motionless, her eyes closed. Several of the guards began administering first aid as best they could, but it was clear from her wounds she needed to be taken to the infirmary. Though not life-threatening, the damage the woman inflicted was brutal.

Stacy was rendered speechless, her mouth open, eyes wide and overcome with fear. For his part, the Being stood stoically, his face a mixture of anger and pain. He hadn't flinched as this scene unfolded, as if he had witnessed this kind of act thousands of times before.

By now more security guards arrived, pushing the few inmates remaining in the yard back inside. Several more officers had gathered around Olivia, who was moaning while she lay on the ground. Though she expected this, it wasn't what she thought would happen.

"These two have tangled before, haven't they?" one of the female guards asked another.

"Yeah, I caught 'em once in the laundry room fighting. This one had a towel wrapped around the other girl's neck. She was turning purple by the time we got there," the male guard beside her said.

More than a few of the hospital staff had shown up now and were busy assessing the wounds. The two guards who had been discussing the relationship between Olivia and the other woman stood, breathing heavily. They stepped back a few feet from the group around Olivia and watched. Stacy moved closer to them, wanting to get some insight as to why this might have happened.

"Damn shame this happened. She's one of the good ones," the female guard said, pointing at Olivia.

The male guard nodded. "Yeah, but she's got a temper. You don't want to screw around with her, that's for sure."

"What started it all? Or do you even know?" the female guard said.

"Yeah, Gipson said something about there were some dirty looks from one of 'em or something. Who knows?" the male guard said. "You know how it is, these people get offended by the slightest things around here instead of letting stuff go."

A stretcher was brought out, and Olivia had been placed on it. The hospital staff lifted her off the ground and carried the stretcher toward the infirmary. The guards surveyed the yard, looking for anyone who would have disobeyed the orders to go back inside, but found no one around. Within minutes, they, too, had evacuated the yard, leaving it empty.

The Being silently looked at Stacy. She met his gaze, bewildered by the look in his eyes. It was a mixture of compassion, rage, and sympathy all at once. She furrowed her brow, trying to quickly assess what he might be thinking.

Wordlessly, he turned his head toward the infirmary and began walking toward it. Stacy remained behind for several minutes before hurrying after him. Why he wanted to go escaped her. But she preferred to be in his company rather than linger in the thought of inmates trying to kill each other.

Tori was on her way back to the hospital, fighting her way through traffic, becoming more disgusted with the way people drove as she went. More than once, she cursed loudly at any driver making a very risky or very stupid maneuver through traffic. Her steering wheel took the brunt of her anger as she delivered a severe beating to it the longer she drove.

Finally arriving at the hospital, she pulled in the garage and started her way up the interior ramps to find an open space. Once again, she allowed herself to curse at her luck in arriving at a time when every space seemed full. Turning down each aisle and driving upward only exacerbated her anger. At this moment, she wished she qualified for a handicap tag to achieve a more favorable parking space. However, with the proliferation of those tags being given out, she doubted it would've helped at all.

Finally finding an open space on the sixth level, she eased her car in, put it in park, and shut it off. She gathered her belongings and got out of the car, slamming the driver side door shut. It wasn't proper, but at least she could feel some of her anger ease away in the sound of the door.

She made her way toward the elevators when she noticed a couple walking the same way. She thought she recognized them but couldn't be sure.

"Tori? Tori Butler?" the man said.

She stopped, a confused look on her face.

"Do I know you?"

"Greg Hamilton," he said, extending his hand.

Tori obliged and shook his hand.

"You remember my wife, Brenda," he said, putting his hand on his wife's shoulder.

She exchanged handshakes with Tori as well. The three of them smiled.

"Yes, I remember now," Tori said. "I haven't seen you since the funeral, that's why I was confused."

"That's okay," Greg said. "Here, let's walk together, shall we?" He motioned for the three of them to head toward the elevator.

"How have you been?" Tori asked.

"We're doing the best we can," Brenda said. "We miss Tucker every day, but we know he's with the Lord now, so we can't be too sad about it."

Tori gave her a quick glance, as if this were an odd thing to say at time like this. "Yeah, that's got to be a good feeling," she replied.

"How's Stacy doing?" Greg asked. "I'm sorry we haven't been here until now. We've just been so busy with getting things arranged with Tucker and all."

By now they had reached the elevator bank and pushed the button to go down.

"She's holding her own," Tori replied, pushing the hair off her forehead. "She's been through several tests, and so far, she seems to be doing well."

"I'm glad," Brenda said, reaching out and squeezing Tori's arm. "We've been praying for her since the funeral."

"Thank you," Tori said, looking up at the numbers above the elevator door.

"How have you been? Are you doing okay?" Brenda asked.

"As well as can be expected," Tori shrugged. "My ex-husband is here, and he's been a great help, in some ways. I mean, we still have some bad feelings, but we're trying to put that aside for Stacy."

Just then, the bell rang, and the Down arrow lit up. As the doors slid open, a young woman wearing earbuds staring at her phone stepped off and walked past them. The three of them got in the car and pushed the corresponding button to the hospital lobby.

"Well, we've been praying for you too," Brenda said. "I'm so sorry you have to deal with so much all at once."

"Surprisingly, I'm okay. Jason and I have only argued once, maybe twice, but for the most part, we've kept our feelings about each other out of the conversation."

"Good. I'm so glad to hear that," Brenda said.

They rode in silence until the elevator stopped at the lobby. The doors slid open, and they exited into what was now a hive of activity. The lobby was nearly full of people, all with expectant looks on their faces. Some were in more distress than others. A few were silent as they sat next to each other, not even a glance exchanged between them.

As the trio walked silently through the noise, Tori gave a quick sideways glance at Brenda. It surprised her to see a slight smile on her face and a twinkle in her eyes. She and Greg were holding hands, looking every bit like two teenagers who just found their first crush.

Why is she so happy after her son died? she thought. *What is it with these two?*

They walked to another set of elevators, pushed the Up button, and waited again. They distracted themselves with the goings-on of the people in the lobby, bemused by their feigned reverence for all the suffering going on just above them in the myriad rooms.

The bell rang again, and the doors slid open, only this time the elevator was full. Once everyone exited the car, Tori, Greg, and Brenda stepped inside, pushing the button for Stacy's floor. The doors slid shut, silencing the cacophony of the lobby. Tori rubbed her forehead and shook her head. Looking up, she turned to Greg and Brenda.

"Okay, I have to ask. Your son died just recently, and yet you seem so calm and peaceful about it. Why is that?"

Brenda looked at her, a wide smile on her face. "Honey, when you have the Lord in your life, you can face anything."

"But you don't even seem disturbed by his death."

"Oh, believe me, we are," Greg said. "I can't tell you the number of nights I've cried while I pray to God about our situation. Don't be fooled, we still mourn his loss. But what makes it easier to bear is knowing he's with the Lord right now."

"We don't mean to push our faith on you, Tori," Brenda said. "It's just…that's what keeps us going. Our trust in Jesus that he will work everything for the good."

Tori looked befuddled at the couple. She moved to speak, but just then the bell dinged, and the doors slid open. Greg and Brenda were first off the elevator, followed closely by Tori.

"She's this way," Tori said, pointing down the hall.

As they walked, Brenda reached over and gently squeezed Tori's arm. "I hope we haven't made you uncomfortable by what we said."

"No, not at all. Thank you."

"Your daughter is a wonderful girl. We haven't stopped praying for her since we found out what happened," Brenda continued. "I know the Lord has his hand around her."

Tori put her hand on her mouth, closing her eyes and feeling the tears trickle across her cheek. Brenda put her arm around Tori's shoulders and gave a comforting squeeze. They remained silent the rest of the way to Stacy's room.

Olivia lay on the infirmary bed, eyes closed, breathing calmly. It had taken the surgeon the better part of two hours to clean and stitch up her wounds. She was resting as best she could, considering the circumstances. A blood pressure cuff was attached to her left arm, while an IV line was hooked into her right arm for good measure. There were handcuffs around her wrists, one part of them hooked to the bed rails.

The Being stood in the corner, his demeanor stoic, his eyes calm, steady, and fixed on Olivia. It was difficult to gauge what he might be thinking or even feeling for that matter. He seemed an expert at hiding his emotions. For her part, Stacy dutifully remained at Olivia's bedside. She stood leaning on the bed rail, her head down, hands clasped in front of her.

"Is she going to be all right?"

"Yes," he said, flatly.

A nurse entered the room and calmly walked to Olivia's bed. She checked over the IV line and the fluid remaining in the bag, glanced at the blood pressure monitor, and notated the results inside a chart. She took her time examining the stitches to Olivia's wounds, occasionally reaching out to touch them or running her fingers over the wounds. After about ten minutes, perhaps less, the nurse checked the IV bag one more time before she left the room.

"Why did this happen?" Stacy asked.

He exhaled, closed his eyes, and shook his head. He rubbed his forehead slowly and muttered something unintelligible. "Think, my dear, think. Why would anyone attack someone else?"

She grasped the bed rail tighter, her eyes still locked on Olivia. She rocked back and forth away from the bed, her face a mix of confusion and anger.

"I don't know. I just know she didn't deserve this."

"Deserve what?" He sounded tired as he spoke, as if he wanted to end this game once and for all.

"To be attacked. Look at her." She waved a hand at Olivia. "She's lying here because someone else decided to try and kill her. It didn't have to happen. She deserves better than this, even if she is in prison."

He leaned forward, a gleam in his eye. "You admit she is defenseless."

"Yes. Of course, she is. At least that's how she looked during the attack."

"Perhaps she did something to provoke the reaction from the other person. Have you considered that possibility?" He rubbed his chin.

Just then, the door burst open as a group of uniformed officers and other important men clad in business suits hurried inside. A doctor and a nurse stumbled in with the group of men but seemed out of place among them.

There were four uniformed officers and three men in business suits, each of them looking as if they should be sitting in an office performing calculations for an upcoming audit. Whatever role they filled here at the prison seemed below their station in life.

Stacy moved away from the bed as the group approached, a look of shock and fear on her face. Even though she couldn't be seen, she didn't want to get caught up in the confusion.

"Wake her up," one of the men said.

He was one of the men dressed in a suit, and as he stopped by the bedside, he put his hands on his hips, pushing his suit coat back. He had a flattop haircut, thin build, and his face was creased and weathered, the effect of too many years of smoking.

The doctor walked slowly to the bed and reached down to Olivia's shoulders.

"Wake up!" he shouted. "Hey! Wake up."

He shook her body until she made a noise with her throat. She opened her eyes and looked at the ceiling, then to the group of prison officials standing around her bed. She gasped as she saw them.

"What are you doing here?" she said, her voice frail.

"Listen to me," the man with the flattop said. "You've been nothing but trouble since you got here. Now, it's a damn shame you got attacked in the yard, but I don't blame the attacker for what happened. I blame you." He pointed his finger at Olivia.

"And you've been nothing but a lying, worthless piece of trash since I got here," Olivia shot back. She tried to move her hands, but the handcuffs prevented her from raising them above her body from the bed.

"We've been through this, okay, Liv?" the man in the flat top said. "I don't care what you think about me. I'm here to serve the county and take care of you scum while you're in my prison."

"Well, you need to take care of that fat lard, 'cause I might have to kill her," Olivia said, spitting out the words.

Stacy's eyes grew wide as she listened.

"Why did you come here?" Olivia asked.

"We're moving you to solitary," the man in the flat top said.

As he spoke, two officers moved wordlessly to unlock the handcuffs. They gripped her arms tightly as the other two uniformed officers took hold of her legs and moved her off the bed. The thought of a struggle didn't seem to enter Olivia's mind as she was made to stand on the floor beside the bed.

As this was going on, the doctor and nurse were busy unhooking the IV lines and checking over her stitches. Satisfied everything was in order, they gave the okay for Olivia to be moved.

A chain was put around her waist and fastened tightly, then the handcuffs were locked to the chain belt. This prevented her hands from being moved not more than a few inches from her body. The officers did a thorough check of the handcuffs and chains, ensuring there was no chance they would slip off. Satisfied they were secure, the officers once again took hold of Olivia's arms and escorted her out of the infirmary to solitary confinement.

Stacy looked at the Being and noticed a sadness in his eyes, the hint of a tear forming in the corner of one of them. She shook her head and wiped a tear from her own eye, sniffling loudly as she did.

"How can you witness such a thing and not be sad?" she asked.

He turned his head slowly to look at Stacy. "You think I feel no sorrow in watching someone suffering the consequences of their actions?" he said derisively. "My child, you have no concept of sorrow."

A glint of anger rose in her eyes as she walked to where he stood. She stopped a few paces in front of him and stared into his eyes.

"I have witnessed enough sorrow in seeing what my daughter could potentially go through," she said through clenched teeth. "Do not mock my pain any longer. I know full well what sorrow looks like."

"And yet you have not considered the ramifications of never allowing this child to see the light of day," he answered, shaking his head. "How can you possibly understand sorrow if you do not mourn the loss of your own child?"

There was a quiet sadness creeping into his tone, as she stood silent, shocked at hearing this, a fury growing in her heart she hadn't felt before.

All of a sudden, she saw the familiar flash of lights around them as the wind began rushing by her. Within a moment or two, she found herself standing in a darkened, cramped cell, a single shaft of light shining through a slit on the door. It took several minutes for her eyes to adjust to the darkness, and as she squinted, she thought she saw the shape of a person in the corner of the cell.

She turned to look at the Being.

"Is this Olivia?"

He nodded slowly.

Olivia had curled herself up in the corner of the cell, her chin resting on her knees as her legs were pulled up tightly to her body. Her eyes had a look of terror and sorrow like Stacy had never witnessed before. She was a lost soul, hoping she could be redeemed in some form or fashion.

Stacy knelt on the floor and gazed lovingly at Olivia, a sad smile crossing her lips. She noticed the knife wounds, still fresh on her arms, her shoulder and across her left cheek. She wanted to reach out, to touch her daughter and let her know she was there.

For a moment, Olivia looked up, directly into Stacy's eyes. Stacy could feel herself being drawn into that gaze, warm and tender. Olivia smiled, childlike and innocent. Stacy turned to the Being, not sure what to make of this.

"Can she see me?"

"Only in her imagination. But yes, she can see you."

Stacy turned back to look into Olivia's warm eyes. She felt herself awash in conflicted emotions. On the one hand, she was in love with this beautiful woman, even in her current state. On the other, there was a disconnect between her heart and mind.

Tori, Greg, and Brenda stood silently around Stacy's bed, each lost in thought. Jason had made his way to the garden space outside to get some fresh air. He told them he needed to stretch his legs, but in truth, it was to escape any chance of being drawn into a religious discussion.

"She looks so peaceful," Brenda said, a wry smile coming to her face.

"I suppose she does," Tori said.

"Have the doctors told you when she might come out of this?" Brenda asked, looking at Tori.

"No," she answered, shaking her head. "They're still waiting to see what will happen. They said she's doing well and everything is normal, but it doesn't feel like it."

Brenda patted Tori's hand gently. "Well, we'll continue to pray."

Tori wiped her eyes and turned to look at Greg and Brenda. She held her hand to her forehead and looked down at the floor. Finally, she cleared her throat and looked up.

"I've got something to tell you. I'm just not sure how to tell you."

"Tell us what, dear?" Brenda asked.

"When I got to the hospital and spoke to the doctor, he said Stacy is pregnant," Tori said, her voice thin and frail.

The shock registered with Brenda and Greg as they both looked wide-eyed at Tori.

"She's pregnant?" Greg asked, in a whisper.

Tori nodded.

"I can't believe it," Brenda said, wiping her eyes.

"They said everything is okay with the baby though," Tori said. "I'm sorry to tell you this now. I know it's not the best way to find out, but I thought you should know."

Brenda reached over and squeezed Tori's arm.

"It's okay, dear. Everything happens for a reason."

"What do you mean?" Tori said, her eyes narrow.

"Well," Greg said, raising a hand in the air, palm upward, "I don't agree with how this happened, but we're about to be grandparents. Why should that upset us?"

"He's right, dear," Brenda chimed in. "We can celebrate a new life coming into the world despite the circumstances that brought them here."

"You're not upset about this?" Tori asked, befuddled.

"Yes and no, dear," Brenda said. "The circumstances aren't ideal, of course, and I would have preferred they be married before this happened. On the other hand, we can look forward to being grandparents."

She gave a reassuring smile to Tori, then turned to look at Stacy. She reached down and squeezed Stacy's hand.

"Okay, I don't understand something," Tori said, closing her eyes and rubbing her hand on her forehead.

"What's that?" Greg asked.

"You both go to church. You both believe in God. You both live a certain type of lifestyle. Isn't this something that goes against what you believe?" Tori asked.

Greg moved from the other side of Brenda to stand near Tori.

"Yes, we believe in God. Yes, we would have preferred Tucker and Stacy waited until they got married to have sex, but this is where we are. We can't change what happened, but we can change what will become of our grandchild."

"But aren't you upset? Isn't this like a sin or something?" Tori asked.

"I believe this," Greg said. "What the devil meant for bad, the Lord will turn into good."

"You see, dear, when you give your life to the Lord, that doesn't mean everything will be perfect. It means you can be forgiven for the mistakes you make," Brenda said. "It was a mistake for them to have sex outside of marriage, but now we get to enjoy the wonderful gift of a grandchild. How could we not love them?"

Tori studied them carefully, lost in her preconceived ideas of what church people were like.

Greg noticed this as he glanced at her. "You seem a little disturbed. Is everything okay?"

"I don't know," Tori said. "It's just, I didn't expect you to be so calm about Stacy being pregnant."

"Why is that?" Greg asked.

"I thought people who went to church were supposed to be angry about this sort of thing. I thought this was something that got a person excommunicated or something."

"You know what," Brenda said, "let's go downstairs and get some coffee and talk. We'll be more comfortable there, don't you think?"

"Sure," Tori answered.

By now Stacy found herself standing on the outside of Olivia's cell door. The dank lighting and pungent smell attacked her senses with little concern. The Being stood behind her, silent and still. For some reason, she felt as if they were no longer allowed in the confined space containing her daughter.

"Have you seen enough?" he asked.

"Of this? Yes. Yes, I have."

"It's such a pity for your daughter to be locked away in this cell, isn't it?"

"Of course." Her voice was just above a whisper.

"You wish she were free, even to roam the halls of this prison, don't you?"

"Yes."

"But even more, you wish her to be free from this prison altogether, isn't that right?"

She closed her eyes, breathing in and out, slowly exhaling.

"I wish nothing but the best for her. You know this."

"Interesting."

She turned to look at him. "Why is that interesting?"

He smiled. "You wish to rid her of these prison walls and allow her to be carefree, yet you have expressed your desire for her to die in the prison of your womb, without concern for her well-being."

Stacy closed her eyes. She had no answer. Nothing she would say could refute this fact.

"I believe you need to reevaluate your motives, if you haven't already."

"I've told you," she whispered. "I can't have a child and expect to live my life."

"You still believe that, don't you?"

She opened her eyes, lifting her head to look at him. "It's the absolute truth. And nothing you, or anyone, says can change this fact." Her words were clipped and harsh. "I believe it is you who needs to reevaluate things."

"Are you sure of this, young one?"

She straightened herself, pulling her shoulders back and jutting out her chin. "From the beginning I've told you what I know to be true. You doubt me at every turn and try to convince me I should have this baby by showing me these horrible situations in which she would find herself. So I will ask you again, why should I allow my child to live such a life as what you've shown me?"

"We've still got more to see, my dear," he answered with a smile. "I believe we need to move on."

Chapter 10

Greg, Brenda, and Tori found a table near the front of the café close to the small pond extending into the main lobby. For being lunch hour, the café was unusually empty, though it seemed it was gaining occupants as time went by.

"Thank you for buying lunch, Greg," Tori said. "You didn't have to."

She took a bite of her roast beef sandwich, set it back down on her plate and wiped her mouth with a napkin.

"You're welcome."

He and Brenda ordered the french onion soup, and both were busy stirring the contents in their bowls as the steam drifted lazily in the air.

"Okay, I just need to understand how you can be so calm about your son committing a sin, yet you're okay with it. I mean, I don't understand that," Tori said.

Greg smiled. "Have you forgiven Stacy for this?" he sipped another spoonful of soup.

"Well, I guess I haven't thought about it," Tori answered.

"Can you forgive her for this?" he said.

"I need to find a way to get beyond the fact she didn't tell me about her being pregnant. I think that's what bothers me the most."

"See, Tori, the love of Jesus is exactly like that," he said. "He found a way to get beyond our tendency to hide our sin. He knows we're sinful people, and we need forgiveness, just like we need to forgive our kids. And yet, he still loves us despite that sin. It's a mystery I wish I could explain."

Tori looked at him, befuddled by what he said. It sounded right, but she couldn't grasp the full meaning of his words. She needed time to sort it out before she could understand it. Instead of engaging Greg with any further discussion about faith, she decided to direct the conversation in a different direction.

"I'm glad you came by." She reached for her sandwich and took another bite.

"Like we told Stacy at the funeral home, we feel like she's family," Brenda said. "We care about her as much as we care about Tucker."

"She's a fine young woman, Tori," Greg said, giving a wink over his soup spoon. "You and Jason did something right in raising her."

"Yeah," Tori said, her voice devoid of emotion, "maybe we did."

"All I know is, she made Tucker a better man," Greg said, wiping his chin with his napkin. He reached over to his coffee cup, lifted it to his mouth, and took a quick sip. "He was crazy in love with her, I'll tell you that."

"He was a good young man too. You both raised him well," Tori said.

"Thank you," Brenda said. "It wasn't always easy. It took a lot of prayer."

"Well, that and the idea of him using his talent in football to further his life," Greg said. "He was headed down a dark road, but I think football saved him in a way."

"If you don't mind my asking, what happened?" Tori asked. She took a bite of her sandwich, wiped her mouth, and sat back in her chair.

Greg sighed heavily and rubbed his forehead. "His freshman year, he got messed up with the wrong crowd at school. I'll bet Stacy never mentioned that, did she?"

"No," Tori said. "I'm not sure if they were dating by then, either that or it was still brand-new and she hadn't told me yet."

"Oh, Tucker was smitten with Stacy the first time he saw her," Brenda said giggling. "He came home one day and said, 'Mom, I just met the most beautiful girl in school today.'"

She and Greg laughed together as Tori sat with a smile on her face.

"He was over the moon about her," Brenda said.

"I'm so glad to hear that," Tori said.

"Did Stacy ever talk about Tucker?" Brenda asked.

Tori froze, her thoughts suddenly locking up on her. She moved to take a drink of her iced tea, hesitating before pulling it to her lips, then she set the glass down. She lowered her eyes to the table and glanced back up.

"We never really talked about him much. She and I don't get along well, for some reason. I wish I knew why."

"Well, all I know is, the group of boys he was hanging around with was nothing but trouble. He always wanted to play football, and I told him that if he didn't give up being friends with those boys, he wouldn't be successful at football," Greg said, his voice taking on a harsh tone. "Once he decided football was his way out of here, we never saw those boys again."

"Don't forget about youth group," Brenda said, touching Greg on the arm.

"Oh yeah," he said, "the youth at the church was wonderful. They invited him on every outing they could, made him feel welcome. Eventually, they led him to the Lord. What a great testimony." Greg shook his head in amazement as he remembered this event. He smiled, a tear starting to form in his eye, but he wiped it away quickly. "Once he came to Christ, his life changed," Greg said, starting to choke up. "He was something special."

He and Brenda began crying, both wiping their eyes with their napkins. Tori became misty-eyed herself and joined them in crying over the loss of a wonderful young man.

Wintervale was an up-and-coming city, one that had seen its footprint grow exponentially in the last five years. It had a thriving arts culture, a well-rounded collection of bars and restaurants, as well as a new arena being constructed for a recently granted AHL hockey franchise. The city seemed on the cusp of exploding into a major metropolitan area, on par with Philadelphia or Kansas City.

On the corner of West Fifth Street and Third Avenue stood the gleaming Buxton Tower, housing offices for numerous major corporations. The entire fifth floor, however, was given to the law firm of Hamilton, Parker, and Thorson.

The tower itself was adjacent to what locals referred to as their own Central Park. Though not quite as big as the one in New York City, it was the quintessential gathering place for families to have picnics or the physically active to sweat in a quaint, serene setting amidst the bustle of the city. To say it was well used was an understatement.

The Being and Stacy walked slowly along the tree lined pathways, filled with people walking their dogs or jogging. There was a trail specifically laid out for those who preferred to navigate the park on bike or Rollerblades. The park seemed as busy as the streets that lined the four sides of the park, though not quite as congested.

At this point in the venture, Stacy had given up asking the reason they would be in a specific locale. When the reason was to see her daughter, it seemed superfluous to ask questions. Though unsure of what would happen, she reasoned—logically so—she was merely along for the ride. The Being had proven by now he was in complete control of their circumstances. To ask a question now would be to test his patience, something she loathed to do at this point.

As they walked, Stacy couldn't help but feel this setting was familiar. Something about it brought back a flood of memories when she and her parents went camping at the lake. It looked almost like the meadow in her dreams, though it was quite a bit bigger than that.

Could I have been here before? she thought.

As she pondered this question, she looked ahead and saw the familiar face of Olivia. Seated on a park bench at the confluence of three separate trails, she was focused on her tablet, hastily scrolling and typing on it. She appeared unaware of her surroundings, as evidenced by a half-eaten egg roll resting on a napkin, sitting atop her black briefcase.

Stacy raced ahead of the Being, forgoing the courtesy of waiting for permission, and stopped within a few feet where Olivia sat. All she wanted was to be near her daughter, even if it were a dream she was living in now.

Olivia was clad in a smart-looking business coat and skirt, blue with light white stripes. Her hair was pulled up in a bun on top of her head, her dark glasses fixed firmly on her face. She was the picture of focus and determination at this moment.

Stacy looked over at the black briefcase sitting next to her, admiring the fine craftsmanship and gleaming gold accents. She noticed a legal document sticking partway out of the case and leaned in closer to see what it was. After carefully looking at it, she saw it was a divorce decree.

"My daughter could be a lawyer?"

"Yes," the Being answered.

Olivia typed furiously on her tablet, her laserlike focus on full display. Her phone buzzed, and she moved the egg roll, reached inside her briefcase, retrieved her phone, and looked at the screen. She rolled her eyes as she swiped her finger on the screen.

"Hi, Mom," she said, a hint of disgust in her voice. "No, I'm at lunch right now… Yes, I've eaten… I'm not sure I can make it… I've got a meeting with the Crenshaws this evening… We need to go over the divorce papers. Yes, divorce is a sad thing to deal with… Yes, Mom, I still believe marriage is a great idea."

She took her fingers on one hand, held two of them to her temple, and pretended to pull the trigger on her imaginary gun as she spoke.

"Mom. Mom! I'll call you later and let you know if I can make it, okay? Yes, I know it's Dad's birthday, although I'm not even sure why you're going… Because you've been divorced for a long time. Why do you still celebrate his birthday together? Wait, you WHAT? You're talking about getting back together? After all this time apart, you want to get back together? I don't believe you… Okay, look, Mom, I gotta go, okay, I'll call you later. Goodbye, Mom."

Olivia pulled the phone away from her ear, pushed the disconnect button, and shook her head. She lowered the phone to her lap, straightened herself, and began breathing in slowly. Stacy smiled, recognizing it as the exercise she learned in cheerleading.

Olivia moved the egg roll off the briefcase again, opened the top, and tossed her phone inside. Stacy caught a quick glimpse of the same picture she'd seen in all the other scenarios before. A mother and a baby, their faces blurred.

After she closed her briefcase, Olivia started to pull her tablet back up but paused. She caught a glimpse of a mother and her small child sitting on a blanket in the field. The two of them played and laughed together. The child would run at the mother and pretend to push her over. The mom repeated this action as many times as it took for her child to grow tired of this and move on to another activity.

Olivia smiled as she watched the pair enjoying each other's company. They were oblivious to the outside world. All that mattered was the simplicity of this moment they shared. Olivia marveled at the patience the mother showed, the kindness she bestowed upon her child. She didn't seem bothered by the repetition. She and her child were together, and nothing else mattered.

Olivia was broken out of her thoughts by her phone buzzing again. She jumped as she heard it and pulled it out of her briefcase once more. She looked at the number and stiffened. She swiped her finger across the screen as she answered.

"Hello? Yes, Mr. Rockwell, what can I do for you? Yes, sir. I just came down to Central Park to work on the Crenshaw divorce papers. Yes, sir, I know I've been gone longer than a half hour, but I've been working the entire time."

She shoved her tablet into her briefcase, closed the lid, and pushed the clasps in place, locking the case. She stood, grabbing the briefcase in one hand, her phone in the other. She suddenly realized the egg roll was now resting on the park bench itself. She shook her head, dropped her briefcase on the bench seat, and picked up the roll.

"Yes, sir, I'm on my way there now," she said, frantically searching for a trash can. "Right, Mr. Rockwell, I'll be there as soon as I can. Yes, sir. Thank you, sir."

She hurried over to a trash can not ten feet away, throwing the roll inside. She pushed the disconnect button again and hurried back to her briefcase. She paused, not sure what to do with her phone. She finally settled on putting it in the pocket inside her coat. Picking up her briefcase, she hurried back to the office, her heels clicking like a metronome on the pavement.

Stacy watched her walk away, a smile firmly planted on her face.

"Wow," she said breathlessly, "a lawyer."

The Being had stepped beside her now, his gaze fixed on Olivia as well. He glanced at Stacy, then back to Olivia, who by now had crossed the street and entered the building.

"Do you think this could be true of your daughter?" His voice was low.

The smile disappeared from her face, replaced with a look of confusion. "What do you mean?" she said, her voice nervous.

"I mean, do you believe your daughter could grow up and become a lawyer?"

"She can be whatever she wants. I've already told you that."

"Only if you allow her to live, Stacy."

He slowly turned his head to look at her. She didn't return his gaze and had no reply to his statement. Convinced he'd made his point, he made his way toward the tower, leaving Stacy frozen in place for the moment.

In the elevator ride back up to Stacy's room, Tori, Brenda, and Greg were silent, each of them feeling satisfied at having eaten an adequate lunch but dealing with Stacy's pregnancy in their own way. The elevator slowed its ascent and stopped at their floor, the bell ringing as it did. The doors slid open, and the three walked around the corner from the elevators, toward Stacy's room. As she rounded the corner, Tori took two steps then stopped, her jaw dropping. Brenda and Greg followed, curious as to what brought such a reaction.

Standing just outside Stacy's room, Jason and his girlfriend were talking. Tori recognized the sheepish look on Jason's face as the one he always got whenever she caught him doing something wrong. She watched intently as the girl gesticulated and pointed at Jason. The longer she went on, the weaker he became. Finally, she gave one last, sarcastic wave of her hand and turned away.

Her head low; she was heading for the very elevators Tori, Brenda, and Greg had just vacated. The girl looked up, caught sight of Tori, and stopped dead in her tracks. She held a hand up to her chest, looked back at the now-emasculated Jason, then turned back to Tori.

Jutting her chin out and holding her head high, she continued walking toward the elevators. Tori stepped to the other side of the hallway as the girl rounded the corner and reached the elevator doors. Ignoring Tori's stare, she pushed the button and waited. Thankfully, it only took about a minute for the elevator to arrive. The doors slid open, the girl got in, turned, and pushed the Lobby button. She glanced up at Tori, giving a sarcastic smile and wave, as the doors slid shut.

Tori stood still, her eyes blinking, unsure what to do or where to go. She looked down the hallway to Jason, who was leaning against the wall, his head buried in his hand. She turned to Brenda and Greg, unsure why, perhaps seeking moral comfort.

All she could do was imagine what led to this moment and why she was here as a witness.

The interior law offices of Hamilton, Parker, and Thorson reflected the exterior opulence of Buxton Tower. The finest nylon carpeting lined nearly the entire floor, its alternating squares of charcoal and light gray offsetting the white walls. Sleek, stylish furniture dominated the main floor, while a few old oak and mahogany desks could be found in certain offices.

Stacy followed close behind the Being, marveling at the overwhelming sense of affluence on display. The ornate light fixtures, the artwork hanging on the wall, the soothing sound of smooth jazz playing politely over the speaker system. All this caused her to believe this firm was one of the most expensive in town, catering only to the wealthiest clients.

The Being meandered toward a corner office with a large dark wood panel door. Naturally, it was closed. To the right of the door hung a name plate that said, "Olivia Hamilton, Attorney-at-Law," on full display. Stacy smiled, a reminder of Olivia being a lawyer. She drew in her breath and exhaled, a sound of satisfaction escaping her lips as well.

"Looks familiar, no?" he said, his eyes fixed on the nameplate.

"Yes, it does." She nodded, a smile on her face.

"She's not in here though. She's in a meeting." He pointed down the hall.

"I want to see it."

"Come."

With a wave of his hand, the pair strolled down the hall, Stacy becoming curious as to what she would witness. Within moments, they arrived at the conference room and walked inside.

Seated around a gleaming blacktop desk were the founders of this firm, as well as their junior partners who someday longed to have their own names listed on cover letters and stationary.

Olivia was seated at the head of the table. To her left sat Carter Thorson, a brash, almost-reckless young lawyer. Clad in the usual power suit and tie, his black hair was perfectly coifed and sculpted to give the appearance of authority. To Olivia's right sat J. Penrose Parker, the elder statesman of the three. His graying hair and shy smile belied his gruff demeanor. His blue eyes might have communicated he was approachable, but far too often, they reflected the harsh treatment he would dole out if something went wrong.

"Where do we stand on the charges of infidelity, Harper?" Olivia asked of the fresh-faced junior partner at the opposite end of the table.

Normally calm and collected in his actions, Harper Fields was rattled at being asked to speak up. He shuffled some papers, suddenly feeling himself perspire at having the spotlight put on him so early in the meeting.

"Well, we had a private investigator follow Mr. Crenshaw to a hotel over on the east side. Our guy said Crenshaw arrived at the hotel first, followed by a former stripper ten minutes later."

"Did he see her go into the room? Does he have pictures?" Olivia asked.

Her left elbow was propped up on the arm of her chair, her chin resting on her hand. She'd adopted a bemused look on her face as she listened.

"He got a couple, but they aren't clear."

"What do you mean, they're not clear?" she asked, a harsh tone to her voice.

Fields shuffled his papers, dropping a few on the floor. He started to reach down to pick them up, then turned his attention to the stack he held in his hand. Clearly, his nerves had been shaken.

"Well, ma'am, I mean, he took pictures, but the ones he got are a little blurry," he said, sheepishly.

Olivia shook her head, took off her glasses, and set them on the table. Thorson leaned in on the table, tapped his knuckles on the desk, and looked directly at Fields.

"Harper, we counted on you to deliver the goods on this one," he said, sounding every bit the scolding father. "And this is the best he's got for us? Blurry pictures?" He shook his head.

"You're gonna have to try harder."

"Yes, sir," Fields said, continuing to shuffle his papers.

"We'll have to try again," Olivia said, looking to her left and down the table. "Murdock, what do you have on Mrs. Crenshaw?"

Heather Murdock was a voluptuous brunette, her smoldering brown eyes matching perfectly with hair reaching just beyond her shoulders. It was an open secret she enjoyed seducing any male member of the firm. No one ever bothered to bring it into question because she was so good at getting any male witness to confess their sins, all brought about from her bewitching smile.

"It's no secret she has lesbian tendencies, Olivia," she said. "We've seen her with both men and women before, so she's playing it pretty dirty right now."

"My kind of woman," Parker intoned, his deep, baritone voice resonating around the room. This brought polite laughter from the group as he spoke, but nothing more.

"So why did she file the divorce proceedings?" Olivia asked. "I've been studying this for more than a month, and I still don't understand why she's claiming the divorce was his fault because of his being unfaithful, when all along we know she was too."

"She's covering up for herself, Liv," Murdock said. "If the truth came out about her, her social status would disappear. Being as influential as she is, it would destroy her if her circle of friends found out about this. And status is everything to that woman."

Stacy watched from the corner of the room, her mind a jumble the longer she listened to the remainder of the lawyers' conversation debating how to handle this case. The jargon used, the verbiage exchanged might as well have been a foreign language to her. She only understood parts of the conversation but was impressed at Olivia's ability to hold her own against the boys. The Being took note of Stacy's curiosity and moved to stand beside her as they watched the meeting go on.

"Quite a lawyer, wouldn't you say?" He pointed at Olivia.

"Yes," she nodded. "Quite."

"I see you're mesmerized by her," he said, a wry smile coming to his lips.

"How can I not be mesmerized?" she turned to look at him. "She's amazing."

"Where do you suppose she gained interest in the law?" he asked, crossing his arms.

"I'm confused. Why should I care where it came from? She's a lawyer, just as she could be a doctor or a CEO."

"Or homeless or a criminal…" he offered, his voice trailing off.

She looked at him, eyes smoldering and angry. She stepped close to him, looking directly in his eyes.

"Why would you say that, to mock me?"

"My child, I've told you, some of this could come true, or none of this could come true. Why take offense if something is not possible?"

"Yet you refuse to inform me which may be true or not. Why is that?"

The Being sighed, rubbing his chin. "My dear, haven't you figured it out? Life is not a guarantee. It is a series of consequences borne out of choices made or lost. It is sailing in a sea of doubt and insecurity, absorbed in a mass of confusion. There is no assurance in life, save one."

"And what is that?"

"No one escapes unscathed," he smirked. "Everyone has scars. Everyone has unrealized dreams and aspirations, waiting for their turn to be given a moment of recognition. Everyone is facing the inevitable ending they know is coming but feel wholly inadequate to embrace."

"Why do you tell me this? It seems irrelevant to what I see of Olivia's life now."

He moved closer to Stacy, both of them watching as the meeting broke up. The members of the firm gathered their belongings from the table and began returning to their appointed offices.

Olivia remained seated, her head lowered, eyes closed. Thorson was standing in front of the chair he occupied a moment before, busily pushing his papers and binders in his briefcase. He stared at Olivia as he did, his eyes seemingly harsh.

"What's your problem?" he asked.

Olivia looked up, caught off guard at the abruptness contained in the question.

"N-nothing."

"I hope you're not thinking about why I left you."

"Of course not." she slammed her pen on the pad of paper in front of her. "You were too much of an ass for me, and I couldn't deal with it anymore."

"Whatever," he laughed. He closed and locked his briefcase, set it upright on the table, and put a hand in his pocket. "You think we'll lose this case, don't you?" His voice was somber as he spoke.

Olivia pursed her lips, suddenly fidgeting with anything she could put in her hands. She looked around the room, her eyes vacant and sad.

"Carter, if we don't have physical evidence of Mr. Crenshaw cheating, we don't have a case. We need photographs to show the jury. If we don't have those, we can kiss this lawsuit goodbye."

Thorson picked up his briefcase with one hand and rubbed his chin with the other.

"We'll get them. Trust me, okay? One way or another, we'll get the evidence we need."

She looked up at him. "I hope you're right."

"We will." He gave a quick wink and a smile before heading out the conference room door.

Olivia locked her eyes on the pen resting on the legal pad on the desk. So much to consider. So much to be done before this case could be closed and they reaped the benefit of their labor. She gave one last exhausted sigh and stood up. She gathered her papers and pushed them into her leather satchel. She picked it up, slung it over her shoulder, and headed back to her office.

Tori made her way to Stacy's room, a curious look on her face. She could see Jason was wounded and decided not to add to his pain. Greg and Brenda followed behind, trying to figure out a way to avoid what they expected to be a contentious conversation. Brenda moved hurriedly beside Tori and pulled her arm to stop her walking.

"Listen, Greg and I decided to go sit in the waiting room. We don't want to intrude in anything," she said, looking quickly at Jason. "We'll join you in the room in a few minutes, okay?"

"Fine," Tori nodded, not sure what she was saying.

"Okay, dear, we'll be along in a little while," Brenda said, giving a pat to Tori's arm and hurrying off to collect Greg and find solitude in the waiting area.

Tori stood motionless for several minutes, studying Jason, gauging how she would approach him. Clearly, this wasn't the time for fireworks, but it wasn't her fault this happened. She never liked his girlfriend, so why would she feel bad?

She walked slowly toward him, wondering if he knew she was there. She stopped a few paces away and listened to him moaning incoherently about lost love. She cleared her throat and crossed her arms. He jerked his head up and seemed surprised she was there.

"What are you doing?" he asked, his voice low.

"Greg, Brenda, and I went to lunch, you know that. We just got finished and came back here."

"So you saw what happened, did you?" he smirked.

"Yes, and Jason, listen, I'm sorry about…"

"No, stop it right now." he held up a hand. "Let me calm down before you start saying 'I told you so,' okay? Just give me some time."

"Jason, I wasn't going to say that." She stepped closer to him. "I was going to say how sorry I am this happened now."

Tori reached out and stroked Jason's arm tenderly. He looked up and noticed her eyes reflected her concern as well. For a moment, he felt like he was going to smile. He straightened himself and pulled his arm away from Tori.

"Why don't I believe you?"

"Come on, Jason. Why would I do that to you right now?"

"Because I know you hated her. You never approved of her. It's like you said, she's barely older than our daughter. So you should be happy it's over."

"Jason, just because we didn't work out doesn't mean I want bad things to happen to you. Can you understand that?"

"I still don't believe you."

"You can think what you want. It's true."

He looked into her eyes and saw a tenderness he hadn't seen for some time now. It reminded him of those heady days when they first started dating. Back then, everything they did was based on pure emotion and carnal desire. He marveled at how quickly emotions could change.

"Look," he said, pushing himself from the doorframe, "I just need to be alone, okay? I'll be back."

He stumbled past Tori, his head low. He passed by the small waiting area Greg and Brenda had found, making his way to the elevators. Despite the hallways being somewhat busy, Jason appeared isolated from everyone else.

Nightlife in Wintervale had seen a near explosion in popularity, thanks in large part to a four-square-block referred to simply as The Quarter. The city leaders had the foresight to restrict vehicle traffic in this area, opting instead to allow foot traffic to be the modus operandi. With brick streets and old-time lamp posts, it gave off a quaint, old-world charm. This only served to accentuate the bright lights and sometimes raucous music emanating from several of the clubs lining the streets.

It was a Friday night after work, and Olivia had met her friends at Club Azure, one of the bigger hot spots in the area. Separated into four different rooms, each with a distinct theme, it catered to a relatively wide variety of patrons.

Olivia and her friends were firmly ensconced in what was called the Ambiance Room, a sleek, modern-looking section of the club. Dim red and blue lights accented the party-themed messages scrawled across the shiplap walls. Thin, silky curtains framed pictures of famous movie stars of all eras. The vibe here was dance hits spanning from the '70s through the 2000s.

Olivia was among a group of five women sitting at a table near the left side of the expansive dance floor, laughing and sharing Jaeger Bombs. They weren't here to meet anyone special, just out for a chance to forget about work for a few hours.

The Being stood next to Stacy, both of them leaning against the wall, not far from Olivia's table, soaking in the mood of the people. Stacy smiled as she listened to recognizable songs, both from today and ones her mother had played for her before. She swayed gently as the music pulsed over the speakers, encouraging the sweaty twenty- and thirty-somethings to fill the dance floor to capacity.

To her right, Stacy saw a man clad in a navy blue polo shirt standing about six tables away. He was alone, nursing a tall glass of beer and staring directly at Olivia. Something in the way he looked at her unnerved Stacy as she slowly stopped dancing.

The Being looked directly at her, curiosity getting the better of him.

"What's wrong, young one?"

"Why is that man staring at Olivia?" She pointed in the man's direction. "He appears angry. Why?"

The Being turned to see the man distracted for the moment by his cell phone. The man peered intently at the screen, the soft light illuminating his swarthy features. He furrowed his brow and his face turned stoic.

"He's nothing," the Being said half-heartedly.

Stacy took note of his facial expression, knowing there was more to the story. "No, you're lying. He's not nothing. Who is he?"

"You don't need to know," he said, curtly.

"If my daughter is in danger, I should know."

"Danger, you say? Do you really wish to keep her from harm?"

Stacy wasn't prepared for his sarcasm. She opened her mouth to respond but stopped herself short. Even though his comment stung, somehow she knew he was right. If there were one thing she'd learned while speaking to him, it was to be careful how she phrased anything about her daughter's safety.

Turning her attention back to the man, she noticed he was nervously pacing in small circles near the table. She watched as he'd fallen into a nervous routine of checking his phone, putting it in his pocket, taking it out, and checking it again. He repeated this same routine time and time again, serving only to unnerve Stacy. For reasons she couldn't determine, she decided to get closer.

She only took a few steps toward him, stopping when another man came to the table. The two men were busy conversing, leaning in close to one another as they spoke. With the music as loud as it was, talking directly into someone's ear was the only way to be heard. Unless one was as loud as the girls seated at Olivia's table were being.

Their squeals of happiness seemed to pierce the air around them, and somehow their voices could be heard above the din. Olivia moved off her stool and tapped the shoulder of her red-haired friend next to her.

"Hey," she shouted, "I'm gonna go to the bathroom. Come with me."

"Okay," the redhead nodded.

Olivia banged her hand on the table. "Hey," she shouted even louder, "watch our stuff. Heidi and I are going to the bathroom."

The other girls laughed and gave a thumbs-up as Olivia and Heidi made their way through the crowd. The two men watched as the pair left the table, both girls holding hands as they pushed their way through the cramped aisleways. Eyeing the girls' movements, the two men soon left their table and followed the girls toward the main entry of the room and out into the atrium.

All four rooms converged in this large, circular area, a fountain dominating the middle of the room, with wall-to-wall red carpet offsetting the sleek decor. From the Ambiance Room, the courtesy desk was to the left, dominating one wall of the atrium. Opposite the desk was the main entrance to the club. The other three room entrances were clearly marked by a marquee above their respective doorway. Two sets of restrooms were located on either side of the atrium, dividing the four rooms in half.

Stacy had followed the girls to the restroom and watched nervously as they made their way inside. Once Olivia and Heidi made their way into the restroom, which was currently not occupied, each girl stumbled their way to a stall, closing then locking the stall door. Olivia let out a heavy sigh as she sat down.

Stacy stood with her back to the entrance wall, folding her arms across her chest.

"You okay over there?" Heidi asked, her voice still at a high volume.

"Yeah," Olivia said, leaning her elbows on her knees and resting her head in her hands.

"Hey, Liv?"

"Yeah?"

"I think I'm drunk," Heidi said, laughing heartily now.

Stacy let out a gasp as she saw the two men enter the restroom. As silently as they could, they walked slowly toward the sinks, located opposite the stalls. One of the men reached over and turned on a faucet in the sink, letting the water run. Stacy's eyes grew wide with fear as she knew what was about to happen.

As soon as she heard the water running, Olivia jerked her head up. Her mind exited the fog of her semidrunken state, trying to calculate what was happening. She hadn't heard the familiar clicking of heels on the floor, indicating another woman was with them. As she listened to the water rushing from the sink, a sense of dread washed over her.

Without warning, there was a swift kick to both stall doors, the locks giving way to the force of the leg kicks from the men. Both girls screamed as each man grabbed ahold of the girls, dragging them out of the stalls. The man who grabbed Heidi stood behind her, his arms wrapped tightly around her torso. He had a lascivious smile on his face as he looked over Heidi's thin but voluptuous body.

Olivia tried to fight back, twisting her arms as best she could to free herself from the other man's grip. The man did an admirable job in maintaining his grip on her arms and managed to push her back up against the sinks.

He let fly his right hand, swinging it violently through the air, landing a blow against Olivia's left cheek.

"No!" Heidi screamed as she tried in vain to get away from the man holding her.

The man who hit Olivia grabbed her by a shoulder and pulled her face to look at him. His eyes were dark and evil, a scowl affixed to his face.

Just then, two other females entered the room, laughing and enjoying themselves. They stopped and gasped when they saw what was happening. The man holding Olivia shot a heated glance at the two women.

"Get out. Now!" he shouted.

The two women immediately left the restroom, and the man turned his attention back to Olivia. She was breathing hard, her cheek red and throbbing from the blow he administered. She could feel a slight trickle of blood from the corner of her mouth.

Stacy watched with tears in her eyes as this horrific scene unfolded.

"You put my brother in prison for the rest of his life," the man said through clenched teeth. "I miss my brother. I miss spending time with him. You stole this from me, do you understand?"

Olivia nodded, her breathing heavy and labored. Her eyes darted from side to side, trying to avoid direct eye contact with the man.

"You will not be safe any longer," he whispered, a sinister tone in his voice. "There are others like me who will make sure you live the nightmare I live now. How does it feel knowing you will look over your shoulder the rest of your life?"

He slapped her across the face again. She gave a loud yelp as he did, feeling her cheek become warmer with the pain of his blow.

"I will suffer for the rest of my life with the knowledge that you put a good man in jail to die. And now I think you should suffer the same fate."

He reached behind him, pulling out a switchblade knife. Both Olivia and Heidi stared wide-eyed at the knife. Heidi tried to scream, but it was muffled by the other man covering her mouth. The man in front of Olivia clicked the blade out, the sound echoing in the silence around them. He drew his hand back to strike, but it was stopped by a security guard from the club who had rushed into the room.

The guard twisted the man's wrist backward, allowing the knife to fall to the floor, causing him to loosen his grip on Olivia as well. She fell back against the wall and slumped to the floor. She brought a hand to her mouth, wiping the trace of blood from her face.

A second guard plunged head long toward the man holding Heidi, who threw her aside. He squared up to the guard, but it was no match. With ease, the guard tackled the man without issue. They fell to the floor, wrestling for an advantage. After a short skirmish, the guard pushed the man on his back, attaching handcuffs to the man's wrists. He rested the full weight of his body on the man, who was yelping in pain.

With both men subdued, the guards picked them up off the floor and led them out of the restroom. By now two other security guards entered the room to look after Heidi and Olivia, making sure they weren't severely injured.

Stacy exited the restroom, a hand over her mouth in shock, her body shaking at what just took place and what could've potentially happened. She felt the sting of a tear fall from her eye, then another. She was paralyzed in fear.

The Being sauntered over to where she stood, watching the comings and goings of both the patrons and the staff of the club. Heidi and Olivia were led out of the restroom by a team of staff members and security guards. They were whisked away behind a door to one side of the front desk, no doubt to calm their nerves but also to file a report and be attended to for any cuts or bruises they might have incurred.

"Why did this happen?" Stacy said, almost whispering.

"You heard the man. She was responsible for putting his brother in jail."

"But why would he attack her like that?"

"Retribution will cause a man or woman to do irrational things. It doesn't matter where, when, or how their vigilante justice is carried out. Those seeking their own form of justice will find a way."

"But who would expect it to happen here?" She waved a hand at the scene around them.

By this time the police arrived and were busy cordoning off the area and gaining control of the crowd as best they could. As the pair watched, curiosity ruled the crowd's reaction as they gathered tightly together, fighting for an advantage to see what happened. Admirably, the officers began their routine of asking questions to gather what evidence they could. The culprits had been taken into custody and led outside, leaving the crowd wanting in their efforts to capture any sort of action on their cell phone cameras.

"If she were a lawyer, would this sort of thing be common?"

"Not common, but not unusual."

"Not unusual," she repeated softly.

"Life is a chance, young one. Regardless of one's chosen profession, it comes with an inherent risk."

She turned her head to look at him. "But the risk could be minimized, could it not?"

"Yes," he nodded. "I suppose it could. But anomalies do occur. Sometimes more often than you think."

By now there was a marked lack of enthusiasm among the crowd in seeing anything of real import. The noticeable return to the distractions of the club came to the fore. Stacy shook her head, marveling at the expediency in which something such as this occurrence could be forgotten.

"Are you not curious what's happening with Olivia?" He stroked his chin.

"No," she answered, surprised at her lack of interest. "I suppose she'll be taken care of and will answer any questions properly."

He grinned. "So you have no desire to join her?"

She sighed, lowering her head and rubbing her eyes. "If none of this is true, why should I care anymore? If this is all something you've conjured to make me feel guilty about my choice, why does any of it matter? Why should I become emotionally attached to someone who may not even live these lives?"

The Being put an arm around Stacy's shoulders and led her gently outside the club. The cool night air brought a fresh respite from the recycled circulation inside. They stopped once they reached the opposite side of the street. The Being snapped his fingers, and at once, the cityscape disappeared, leaving them surrounded by what appeared to be movie screens. Each of them showed a continuous loop of a memory from Stacy's past. There was one of her and Tucker laughing on a park bench, sipping milkshakes. There was one of her and her parents sitting on the living room floor opening Christmas presents. There was one of her and Tonya talking on the bus after school

Stacy gazed in wonder at the scenes flashing before her, a smile crossing her mouth. It was comforting to see such happiness surround her. Emotionally, she bathed in the sight of all these delightful pictures. She felt herself becoming lost in this sudden burst of joy.

"This is wonderful, no?"

"Yes," she whispered. "Yes, it is wonderful. What is this?"

"Take a look around, young one. For this is the entirety of your life so far. These are the memories of your life. All that has happened to you."

He turned in a circle, his arms extended, waving his hands in a mystical fashion. More and more memories began to appear, each of them bringing a fresh wave of comfort to Stacy's heart. She felt outnumbered by them, scarcely able to see each one, before it became replaced with a new thought.

Slowly, her joy turned to doubt as she observed these thoughts. "Why am I seeing this?"

As quickly as they appeared, the memories disappeared, leaving behind something akin to a dark, gray sky. It wasn't quite black, but not as bright as it had been moments before. The air suddenly felt thick and heavy. Stacy folded her arms across her chest, her head turning every which way, trying to decipher what was happening.

"Your memories will remain with you always, child." She felt as if his voice encompassed every inch of air around her. "It contains all you wished to become when you were a child, all you desired for your life in the future, and precious moments locked away forever in your heart. Tell me, do you believe any of those fanciful dreams will come true for you?"

A little frightened, she turned in a circle, searching for evidence he might still be with her. She paused a moment, thinking she caught a glimpse of a shadowy figure in the distance.

"All that I wanted can't come true now. Tucker is dead. I can no longer harbor any dreams of a happy marriage with him. That future will not come true."

Just as suddenly as it appeared, the gray sky and wind disappeared, leaving behind a serene meadow beside a stream. The water slipped gently against the rocks, effortlessly wending its way wherever the path would lead.

She turned in a circle once more and saw the Being standing perhaps twenty feet away from her. He was peering intently into her soul, invading her thoughts. She could feel a presence in her heart she'd never felt before.

"Do you still imagine what a happy marriage would look like?"

He was leaning on a large wooden staff, crooked and shriveled like any tree branch would be after hundreds of years.

"I wish to be married, yes, though if it will not be Tucker, I can't imagine anyone else. Perhaps there is no one out there who would have me."

"So this dream of your life with Tucker won't come true, yet you still imagine what marriage would be like, no?"

She opened her mouth to speak, but paused, suddenly realizing she had never considered anything else.

"My desire to have the life I wanted died that night in his car. I hold no such hope now."

He walked agonizingly slow toward her, his feet barely moving forward. It seemed as if a weight had latched onto his back, bearing down on him with its massive size.

"Just as your life with Tucker shall never be, so the lives you see your daughter leading may never be. You are only witnessing the potential that lies within her if you choose to bring her to this earth."

"But what if she were to become homeless? Or be in an empty relationship? How could I stand by and watch this happen to her?" Her voice was choked back by her oncoming tears, emotion overwhelming her senses.

"Young one, you have witnessed a great deal of imagination. You have seen firsthand how quickly a once innocent child can become something much different as they grow. Once they achieve adulthood, you no longer lay claim to their choices. You must remain hopeful you have done your job well as a mother for them to avoid the pitfalls you have witnessed here on this journey. But." He stepped closer to her. "You have also seen how successful your child might become if given the chance."

A warm, soothing smile crept across his face, a glimmer of joy in his eyes. "But how will I know what she will become? How am I to be certain my child will make good decisions when they are on their own?"

"Remember." he placed a hand on her shoulder. "It's not about you anymore. It's about another life depending on you to lead them."

Tori sat disconsolate beside the hospital bed. Her gaze rigidly fixed on Stacy. It had been this way from the moment she sat down. How long she was staring, she didn't care. Brenda and Greg sat on the couch opposite Tori, alternating between closing their eyes in prayer and distracting themselves with the books they'd brought with them.

"My world is falling apart," Tori said, absentmindedly.

"Why do you say that?" Brenda asked, looking up from her book.

"Because it is. I'm alone in all this."

"Nonsense. We're here for you, as long as you need us."

"Thank you. I'm glad I've gotten to know both of you better. It makes me happier to know Stacy was with someone who came from a good home."

"And we're glad we can support you. After all, you and I will be grandmothers together. We've got a lot of planning to do to make this baby feel welcome."

Tori froze. She blinked her eyes rapidly, trying to digest what she just heard.

Grandmother, she thought. *I'm a grandmother now.*

"What's wrong, dear? You look a little sad."

"No," Tori said, shaking the weight of her thoughts from her head. "No, I'm just trying to grasp the idea that I'm going to be a grandmother. I'm not old enough to be a grandmother."

"It was bound to happen sooner or later. Might as well get used to it now."

The Being and Stacy stood in the corner of the police precinct, the buzz of activity around them seeming chaotic. There were prostitutes being checked in, drug dealers sitting alone, their handcuffs attached to metal chairs. There were even middle-aged soccer moms who'd been busted for drunk driving. The evidence of wrong decisions was all around them. Stacy shook her head and laughed at the spectacle of it all.

"You find this funny?" he asked, clearly perturbed.

"In a manner of speaking, yes."

"As you look at these people here, what do you see?"

"I see people who deserve what they get."

"And why do they deserve this? Did your daughter deserve the treatment she received when we saw her in jail?"

His voice was calm yet bitter as he spoke. She closed her eyes when she heard this, the idea her daughter deserving anything less than forgiveness suddenly falling into her thoughts.

"That…that was different," she said, her words halting. "She'd done nothing wrong."

"And these people have done something worthy of scorn? Do they deserve to be treated as lesser people for having made a mistake?"

Stacy was speechless.

"Young one, you must be careful in how you speak of those who make mistakes. There is punishment enough living with the pain of their consequences. Must it be compounded by a constant stream of ridicule and demeaning words from those around them?"

Stacy closed her eyes, almost willing this scene to end. She opened them just in time to see Olivia and Heidi exiting the lieutenant's office. Both women were still frightened by what happened at Club Azure. Now they had to walk back to the friends they called to pick them up here, fearful of the shadows.

Stacy could feel the pain of both women, their heads hung low, their faces red from crying. There remained a minimal reminder of mascara around their eyes, the tears having cleaned it from their faces. She was surprised at the overwhelming urge to run to them, to hold them both and comfort them. She furrowed her brow at this thought, watching as both women were escorted out of the precinct to their friends waiting for them outside.

Where did that come from? she thought. She shook her head, hoping it would free her thoughts of those emotions.

The Being took note of this and smiled. "Why are you confused?"

She turned to look at him, her eyes frozen in an empty gaze. "Confused? I'm not confused by anything."

He leaned in close to her ear. "Yet you wish to comfort your daughter as a mother would, don't you?" he whispered.

With that, he turned and walked away, heading out the front doors of the precinct. She watched as he walked outside, leaving her standing in the middle of the hive of activity surrounding her.

Chapter 11

The lower east side of Blackburn was reserved for the less fortunate among the population. Here, houses were worn down, their windows and rooflines showing obvious signs of neglect. It wasn't uncommon to see several older model cars or trucks in various states of repair, or disrepair, depending on how one viewed the situation. Trailer parks were not uncommon, though the city had begun to pour money into this section of town by repaving the roads throughout. It was the first sign they wanted to give the people trapped here a chance to overcome the poverty that was so prevalent.

Nestled at the corner of Malvern and Twain Streets was a dirty white double-wide trailer. The windows were caked in dirt, the shutters worn and broken, some of them hanging by a single, weakened bolt. Weeds populated the area around the wooden latticework at the bottom of the trailer, as vines wove their way around the wood. A concrete sidewalk filled with cracks led to a set of old wooden stairs leading to the front door of the trailer. One had to be careful when navigating the steps for fear of falling through them.

The pair had made their way here to take in the sights and sounds of the next phase of their journey. They walked in silence along the blacktopped road riddled with potholes. It was apparent the city had not yet reached every road in this section of town. Parked cars lined the street, some held up with a carjack, their tires resting against the car itself, while others showed clear signs of being taken care of by the owner.

"Is this where she lives?"

"Yes." He nodded, looking at her. "You no longer seem surprised by what you see or where we are. Why is that?"

"Perhaps I have become accustomed to our journey taking us to various locales. I don't believe anything will surprise me at this point."

"Be careful what you wish for, my child. It just might come true."

Within a few moments, an older red sports car squealed its way around the corner, heading to where they stood. They both turned to watch as it came to a stop at the trailer in front of them. The young man behind the wheel put the car in park, turned off the ignition, and stepped out from the driver side.

He was tall and thin, his gaunt face showing the signs of having consumed too much alcohol. His bloodred eyes masked their true color at this moment, and his long dark hair was a mess of tangles hanging down across his shoulders. He appeared angry as he shuffled a few steps from his car.

"Olivia!" he shouted, his voice booming. "Olivia, get out here now!"

He tried to stand straight, but it was clear the alcohol was having a negative effect on his equilibrium.

"Olivia, I said get out here now!"

The door on the side of the trailer opened, and Olivia stumbled onto the small wooden steps. Clad in a pair of shorts and a white T-shirt, she appeared as if she had just woken from a nap. A fresh cigarette hung from her lips as she reached up and lit it. She stared at the man standing in the street, an angry look in her eyes.

"What do you want, Gordon?" she sneered.

"I wanna come inside and see my baby," he said, slurring his words.

Stacy shook her head in surprise at hearing this, a wave of shock coursing through her body.

"And I told you, I got a restraining order against you. You need to leave right now 'cause you're too close to me."

"Aw, c'mon, baby." he held his arms out. "I didn't come here to make trouble. I just wanna see our baby. Is there something wrong with that?"

"Yeah, there is." she stepped down the wooden steps and onto the sidewalk. "I don't want you anywhere near my baby. You beat me, and you hit her too. Why should I allow that in my house?" Olivia's anger was rising the longer she looked at Gordon, who was laughing.

"Aw, man, are you still on that? That was one time, and she ran into me. It was an accident."

"No, it wasn't, and you know it, you jackass. That's not what the doctor said when I had to take her to the emergency room. You hit her!"

"Why would I hurt our baby, huh? What kind of crazy thinking is that, Liv?"

"It's not crazy thinking, you son of a bitch," she said, taking a quick drag on her cigarette and stepping closer to him.

She blew a stream of smoke from her lips and crossed her arms. Gordon laughed as he stumbled toward her.

"Aw, baby, you know I love you. Why can't you let me come back inside?"

"'Cause you're a no-good drunk. You need to leave before I call the police."

"Go ahead. I ain't doin' nothin'," he said, stepping closer to Olivia.

"Yes, you are. I got a restraining order on you, and you're violating it," she said, taking another drag on her cigarette.

Gordon's drunken gait was more pronounced as he stumbled toward Olivia. By now several other residents had stepped outside their homes to see where the shouting was coming from.

"Go ahead and call the cops, I don't care. You think they're gonna listen to you?"

"Yeah, I think they will."

Gordon stumbled even closer to Olivia, to the point she could smell the alcohol on his breath. She turned her head away and waved her hand in the air toward him.

"So you gonna let me see my baby, or what?"

"No."

She swung her hand at his face, hitting his cheek. His head turned sideways from the blow, and he reached up and rubbed his cheek before turning to look at her. Unbeknownst to both, a neighbor was on the phone dialing 911.

"You bitch," Gordon said, swinging his arm back and sending his backhand solidly against her face.

The force of the blow caused her to fall to the ground. She landed awkwardly against the sidewalk, the cigarette falling out of her mouth. Carefully, she propped herself up on one arm, rubbing her cheek with her free hand. She made no move to stand, fearing what might happen next. If it were anything like before, Gordon would be on top of her, hitting her mercilessly. He stepped near her prone body, reached down, and grabbed her hair, pulling her back up on her feet.

"No, Gordon, stop it," she whispered.

"I haven't even started with you yet," he said through clenched teeth.

"Hey! Leave her alone," a booming male voice said.

Olivia and Gordon both turned to see who yelled. One of the men who'd been watching from a few houses down started walking toward the pair. He moved quickly for a man as big as he was, his sinewy arms and taut legs looking like they were propelled by a motor.

"That ain't no way to treat a lady, Gordon, and you know it," he said.

Gordon released his grip on Olivia, practically throwing her to the ground, before turning to face the man. It was made more difficult by his drunken condition, but he did an admirable job at trying to look intimidating.

"You ain't got no business in this fight, Junior. Go on back to your home, and leave us alone."

Junior continued walking until he was close enough to push his barrel chest into Gordon, his glowering face hinting that any fight would be short-lived. Gordon's eyes grew wide, and he shrank backward, falling to the ground as he did. He looked up at Junior, his blurry eyes a mixture of shock and fear.

No one in the neighborhood knew much about Junior. He kept to himself and was hardly seen outside during the day. Throughout the park, rumors swirled about him, ranging from one saying he worked the overnight shift to another saying he was a psychopathic killer. For him to intervene in any situation was rare.

"I know a coward when I see one," he said, his baritone voice rumbling from the depths of his soul. "I know someone who beats a woman and needs to learn a lesson. Now leave her alone."

"She's my girlfriend, and I'll do with her as I want. You can't stop me," Gordon sneered. "Why don't you go on back home to your momma and leave us alone?"

Junior reached out a massive hand, grabbing Gordon by the shirt collar, pulled him off the ground and closer to him. Gordon's eyes were never more filled with fear than they were right now.

"I don't think you understood me," Junior said, his voice low and scary. "I said, leave her alone."

"Or what?" Gordon laughed, his drunken sense of bravado coming into play now.

"Or I'll personally see to it you'll never be able to have sex with anybody ever again. And that's a guarantee. Now leave the lady alone. Got it?"

Junior half threw, half placed Gordon back onto the sidewalk and laughed as he watched him try not to fall. Once Gordon regained some form of composure, he straightened his hoodie and brushed the hair out of his eyes. Suddenly feeling more sober, he looked up at Junior.

"All right, you win."

He looked over at Olivia, who was still sitting on the ground, rubbing her cheek. "I guess you don't need the cops this time, huh?"

As if on cue, the faint sound of sirens could be heard in the distance.

Gordon smiled. "Saved by the bell, right?" he sneered. He turned back to look at Junior. "You're lucky I don't have my Glock on me right now. There'd be pieces of your brain all over the sidewalk right now if I did."

The sirens were louder still, as the group estimated they must have just entered the trailer park. A few moments later, two police cruisers turned the corner and sped down the street toward the spot where Junior and Gordon stood.

The pair of cruisers, occupied by one officer each, reached the scene first. The sound of a third siren could be heard approaching the scene but wouldn't be on site for several more minutes. The officers got out of their cars and walked cautiously toward Junior and Gordon, neither having moved from where they stood earlier.

"Why am I not surprised to see you here, Gordon?" the male officer said.

As he approached the two men, he had one hand on his service revolver. Curiosity got the better of her, and Stacy peered intently at the officer, feeling as if she knew him. He appeared a little older, a hint of gray in his light hair and a few more creases around his eyes. Looking at his name plate, she smiled. It had the last name Thornton on it. She felt the same sense of protection and comfort she'd felt the night Tucker died.

"It's nothing, Officer," Gordon said, "just a misunderstanding."

"That's always what it is, right, Gordon?" Thornton asked. "How many times have we been out here before because of a, quote unquote, misunderstanding?"

"I don't know."

"Let me give you a hint. Your sister invited me to her wedding. That's how many times we've been out here," Thornton said.

The second officer stood about three paces behind Thornton, both thumbs shoved into his bulletproof vest, his wraparound sunglasses resting on top of his head. By now the third police cruiser had pulled in and stopped opposite the other two. The female officer got out of the car and walked toward the group, stopping far enough away to avoid a direct confrontation with Gordon.

"Are you okay, Olivia?" Thornton said, looking over at her.

By now she managed to rise to her feet and stand next to Junior, tears forming in her eyes. "Yes," she said softly.

"That's quite a mark he left on your cheek. Do you want to press charges?"

"No," Olivia answered, shaking her head. She looked down at the ground, crossing her arms tightly against her body.

Thornton pursed his lips and imperceptibly shook his head. He glanced over at Junior.

"Don't get to see you too often, Junior. What brings you out?"

"Just trying to help, sir," he mumbled.

Thornton gave a shrug and turned his attention back to Gordon.

"Why did you come back here?"

"Can't I just talk to my girlfriend?" Gordon said, slurring his words.

"Not when you're drunk like this. You know the drill, Gordon. You got someplace to go now, or do we have to put you back in jail?"

"I got someplace to go."

"Well, I think you need to get there, don't you?"

"Fine," Gordon said, a hint of resignation in his voice.

He started toward his car, fumbling for his keys in his pocket. Thornton took note of this and stepped closer to Gordon, reaching out a hand to stop him.

"I think you better walk this time."

"Nah, man, I'm all right to drive." he waved a hand at Thornton.

The other two officers stepped in closer now, surrounding Gordon.

"I'll be okay, man, leave me alone," Gordon said, swatting at Thornton's hand again.

"Don't make this worse than it is, Gordon, understand me?" Thornton's voice was suddenly more commanding in its tone.

"I said, leave me alone," Gordon said angrily, swinging his arm at Thornton.

All three officers converged on Gordon, grabbing for any body part they could.

"Man, get off me," Gordon shouted, struggling to break free. "Get off me!"

"Get on the ground. Get on the ground!" Thornton yelled.

With great effort, the officers wrestled him to the ground, the other male officer pushing a knee into Gordon's back. Thornton had his hands on Gordon's head, pushing it into the pavement. The female officer had pulled out her handcuffs and reached for Gordon's wrists.

"What are you doing?" Gordon shouted. "I ain't done nothing wrong. I just wanted to see my girlfriend."

Having gained control of Gordon's wrists, the female officer secured the cuffs and stood up. Thornton and the other male officer grabbed Gordon's arms and pulled him to a standing position.

"You okay?" Thornton said, looking at the other two officers.

"Yeah, no blood this time," the female officer said, looking over her arms. "Just a couple scrapes, that's all."

The male officer stood stoically next to Gordon, his eyes cold and dark. His hands were clasped firmly on Gordon's arm, and he began pushing him toward his cruiser. Thornton leaned down and picked up his hat from the ground before turning back to Olivia.

"Are you sure you're okay, Olivia?" he asked.

"I'll be fine." She wiped her nose and sniffled.

Thornton suddenly looked around, a curious look on his face.

"Where's Junior?"

Olivia looked up, noticing for the first time he wasn't standing next to her. She gave a shrug. Thornton scratched his head, letting out a sigh of exasperation. He chuckled and shook his head. By now Gordon had been placed in the back seat of the cruiser, and the male officer had returned to stand near Thornton. The female officer had walked to stand next to Olivia.

"Ma'am, do you need to go to the hospital?" she asked Olivia.

"No. I'll be all right."

Stacy watched as Thornton and the other officers discussed their follow-up plans and what would happen next. They spent time talking to Olivia as well as other witnesses nearby.

"Curious to know how this happened?" the Being asked, rubbing his chin and looking at Stacy.

"No. I've no need to find the answer. I only need to know my daughter will be all right."

"Look around," he said, waving his hand. "What do you see?"

She watched closely as Olivia's neighbors began to congregate near her trailer, offering a hug, a kind word of encouragement, or a smile to lighten the mood. The friendliness on display was refreshing, much more than what Stacy remembered of her own life. She found herself wanting to be part of something like this, a community that cared.

"Well," he asked expectantly, "what do you see?"

"She's well taken care of, that I know. But will she be okay in the future?"

"You ask about the future, about what's to come next for your daughter. Why do you care so much what happens to her?"

"After what I've witnessed, isn't it enough to hope for the best?"

"Yes. But what of your desire for now?"

"My desire for what?" she asked, lost in the sight of Olivia's neighbors coming to her aid.

"Your desire to rid yourself of this responsibility?"

She turned angrily toward him, a rage filling her eyes. "Why do we play this game? Why must I endure this constant torment you bestow upon me? It was you who told me I could see my daughter's future, yet you lied to me in what would transpire. Why do you taunt me with these images?"

The Being pulled himself to his full height, straightening his spine, pulling his shoulders back and jutting out his chin.

"Not once have I lied to you," he snapped. "Not once have I shown you something that is not possible. Answer me this: How can you deny the reality of this child growing tenderly in your womb? How can you ignore the reality of what's taking place right now in the unseen realms? How can you be so cavalier about choosing to terminate this child's life before it has begun?"

Her eyes flared with rage now as she wished to bore a hole in the Being's skull. "What I choose to do with my body is my right. What I decide about my future is up to me, not anyone else. No one deserves to tell me what to do with my body. Not you, not my mother, not anyone. If I choose to exercise my freedom of choice, who are you to tell me I'm wrong?"

Her body was rigid and cold as she stood defiantly before him. Her overconfidence in having laid waste to his questions was overwhelming her senses.

For his part, he lowered his head, the fire in his eyes becoming a soft glow. "Yes. I suppose you're right," he said slowly. "No one can force you to choose what you do with your body. You've been given that freedom from the day you were born. Yet I wonder…" He paused, bringing a finger to his lips.

"What is it?"

He looked up at her, a warmth in his eyes reaching into her thoughts.

"What greater regret can there be in deciding someone else's fate, without giving them the benefit of choice?"

Jason found his way to one of the jogging trails behind the hospital. As he walked, a calmness began washing over him. Within each step he took, it seemed the memory of his now ex-girlfriend became more distant.

What did I really see in her, except a nice body? he thought.

He chuckled at this and shook his head. He stopped walking, closed his eyes, and shoved his hands in his pockets. He inhaled deeply, the fresh air surrounding him exciting his lungs. He exhaled just as deeply and opened his eyes.

As he did, he saw a semi-well-endowed female jogging toward him. She was wearing tight, black leggings with half stripes of yellow across the thigh and a bright yellow spandex tank top. Her blond ponytail bounced playfully across her shoulders as she jogged. She smiled the closer she got to him, slowing her pace. As she drew even with him, she gave a wink and a smile then accelerated past him. He turned and watched as she continued down the pathway, a mixture of amusement and curiosity on his face.

Huh. Maybe I've still got it, he thought.

He gave a shrug and continued walking, his gait exposing his delight in being attractive to another woman.

"I don't think I'm ready to be a grandmother," Tori said. She'd moved to the lounger now, rocking back and forth nervously. Her gaze was fixed on the floor beneath her feet, her body rigid and tight.

Greg had fallen asleep on the couch, his body stretched across it, preventing anyone from sitting down.

"I'm too young to be a grandmother. This can't be happening," she continued.

Brenda stood a few feet away from Tori, wringing her hands.

"Tori, I'm sorry I said that. But it's true. There's no use fighting this. It's going to happen."

"No, no, it can't happen. Not my daughter. I taught her better than this."

Brenda rubbed her forehead, trying to formulate the right words. It was more difficult than expected.

"I'm sure you did everything you could to prepare Stacy for this life. Sometimes things don't work out. Do you think I like the idea that our son had sex before marriage? We raised him in church, we read the Bible together, we prayed together. I'm not happy with what he did, but I can't change that. The best I can do is be there for our grandchild now."

"Why can't she just get an abortion?" Tori said in a half whisper.

"What did you say?" Brenda leaned closer to Tori.

"I said, why can't she get an abortion?" Tori answered, looking directly at Brenda.

"Do you really think that's a good thing to do?"

Tori stood and straightened her shirt. "I believe it's an option, yes."

"So you don't see abortion is wrong in any way, is that it?"

"No, I don't."

"Do you believe it's murder?"

Tori was taken aback by this question. She stared at Brenda, her eyes blinking rapidly as she did. "I-I believe it's a woman's right to choose what to do with her body."

"What about the baby? Do they get to choose what to do with their bodies?"

"It's a woman's choice what to do," Tori repeated.

"That may be, but I happen to disagree when it comes to pregnancy. I believe every child is a miracle and should be treated with dignity, not thrown in a garbage can."

"Stacy can't handle this responsibility. You can't stand there and tell me she's old enough to be a mother. She's got her entire life ahead of her. If she has a child now, it could ruin her plans."

"And if she has an abortion, it's robbing you and I of showing this child the love it deserves. We're cheated out of teaching this child, of influencing Stacy in how to be a good mother. You don't see how this affects us?" Brenda was incredulous as she spoke, her tone a mixture of frustration veering toward anger.

Tori brushed her hair back and fidgeted with her shirt. It was clear she was fighting for something to say. She moved toward Stacy's bed, her gaze fixed on her daughter.

She's everything to me, she thought. *Why did it take this happening for me to realize that now?*

She reached out and took hold of the bed rail, nearly overcome with emotion. The anxiety of the last several days was finally catching up to her, and she began to shiver.

What if she dies? she thought.

She shook her head, clearing her mind of any negative thoughts. Finally, she looked up at Brenda.

"It doesn't matter about us," she said, her voice low. "It matters what Stacy decides, and I'll support her if she decides to have an abortion. I won't love her any less. Besides, she's too young." She looked down at her daughter's comatose body, tears forming a slow river across her cheek as she did. "She's too young."

The police had left the trailer park, and life returned to normal again in the park. Olivia was in the kitchen of her own trailer, washing the pile of dishes she'd let build up over the last two weeks.

I wish I had a dishwasher in this place, she thought.

The Being and Stacy found their way inside as well, standing across the room from where Olivia stood at the sink. The trailer was sparsely furnished, a worn-out couch sitting against the wall opposite the front door, a small coffee table nestled a short distance from the couch. The walls were nearly bare, save for a clock and a couple of pictures of Olivia that must have been taken by friends on a vacation.

Stacy took note of the clutter on a small end table at one end of the couch and noticed a curled edge of a picture resting amidst the various letters and bills.

She stepped closer, knowing she'd seen this picture before. As she got closer, she nodded her head. It was the same picture of a woman with a child, their faces blurred out.

Why do I see this in every situation? she thought.

"It's quite a picture, isn't it?"

"Yes. Only I wish to see who this is. Why can I not ever see their faces? Am I not allowed?"

"All in due time, young one."

Her curiosity was broken by the sound of a baby's cry coming from down the narrow hallway. Olivia paused, her head cocked in the direction of the cry. She was met with silence. Then another cry, this time louder. Olivia set the plate she was holding into the sink, dried off her hands, and headed toward her child down the hall. She let go a heavy sigh as she did.

Stacy's heart leaped for joy, her anxiousness to see her would-be grandchild overtaking her senses. She smiled, anticipating what she would feel at this sight of her daughter taking care of her child.

Suddenly, the air around her became filled with color as the wind rushed around her. Stacy covered her eyes, shutting them tightly and raising her arms to deflect the wind as best she could. A wave of anger and disappointment washed over her as the wind began to subside and the colors dissipated into the mist.

She opened her eyes to find herself standing on a beach, a warm, soft breeze brushing against her cheeks. The water was calm, soft waves roiling across the surface. So lazy were the waves it seemed to take an inordinately long time for them to reach the shore.

She turned to look for the Being, who stood some distance from her, his gaze fixed on a point far across the horizon. His face was a mask of indifference, a deep longing flashing in his eyes. Stacy furrowed her brow at the sight of him, seeming weak and frail.

"Why did you bring me here?" she shouted in his direction. "Why was I not allowed to see my grandchild?"

He turned ever so slowly toward her, his eyes narrowing as he did.

"You care so little about your own child, yet you wish to see your grandchild? Is that not the least bit insane?"

"And why do you refuse to tell me the truth? Is it because you are afraid of me?"

"Afraid?" he asked, suppressing laughter. "Me, afraid of you? Highly unlikely."

She stormed across the white sand to where he stood, her hands balled up in fists. "I've had enough of your games and your lies," she shouted. "Tell me the truth. Why am I not allowed to see myself with her?"

She stopped in front of him, her eyes shooting daggers through him. He turned his head away for a moment then turned back to look in her eyes.

"I will ask again, young one, what have you learned about your relationship with your own mother?"

"And I will ask you, why does that matter? My relationship with her is of no consequence in what I choose. It will make no difference to her what I do. She doesn't love me. She only loves herself. She's proven this time and again. Why won't you believe me?"

He turned to the ocean again, waving his hand in the air. Suddenly, the sky parted, and Stacy could see her hospital room once more. This time, it was not as sad as before. She saw Greg and Brenda sitting on the couch together, their heads bowed in prayer. She saw her mother sitting on the chair beside her bed, her head leaning into her hands, clasped against the bed rail.

"Tell me, child. If your own mother doesn't love you, why is she a permanent fixture by your side? Do you think she can change? Or will you condemn her to remain locked in the prison of your own hatred?"

Stacy's eyes grew wide. She had no way of knowing her mother had been so vigilant during this ordeal. She'd been so preoccupied with her own life she never took time to consider what her mother must feel about all this. She stared in disbelief at the concern her mother was showing at this moment.

Just as suddenly as it appeared, the sky returned to its natural blue state.

Stacy put her arm across her stomach, feeling herself become anxious. She wiped her face and stared at the waves inching closer to her feet. Somewhere, her mother was exhibiting a love Stacy hadn't realized could ever be possible.

"You've lived your life according to your own rules, child. You've ignored the very people hard wired to love you and keep you safe. You've shut out the ones who care for you and wish to help you answer the difficult questions of life. You've spent so much time running away from them you've never considered how you might feel if you run toward them."

Stacy closed her eyes. "What difference does it make?" she whispered. "My mother is consumed with herself. She lives to satisfy her own desires. She would never consider my feelings or listen to me if I tried to talk to her. What you've shown me means nothing."

The Being sighed heavily, shaking his head. "Why must she be so stubborn?" he muttered.

She looked over at him, curious who he might be talking to. Seeing no one, she considered he was even more unbalanced than she first presumed.

Jason walked into Stacy's room and stopped suddenly. A smirk came across his face, and he shook his head at what he saw. Greg and Brenda were on the couch, their heads bowed, whispering prayers to the Lord. Tori sat on the chair next to the bed, her hands clasped to the bed rail, her head resting against her hands.

And there was Stacy, motionless, her eyes still closed tightly. By now the machines she was connected to had become an almost-ubiquitous extension of her body. It was close to a full week of her being in this condition, and it wasn't any easier to see her this way. The uncertainty of her waking up added a layer of dread no one wanted to address.

Jason leaned against the doorframe, drew in a deep breath, and exhaled. He reached up and wiped his haggard eyes, realizing at this moment how tired his soul felt. Not only did he have to be in the presence of his ex-wife, but his daughter was in a precarious situation, his girlfriend had just broken up with him, and he was losing time at work. His boss had been understanding up to this point, but he had gotten a few e-mails in the last couple of days asking how soon he would return to work.

He opened his eyes and looked to his right, seeing Tonya standing next to him. She looked even more concerned than when she visited the first time. She turned to look at him and gave a half-hearted smile.

"I didn't mean to startle you, Mr. Kent," she said, in a low voice.

It seemed neither of them wanted to disrupt Greg and Brenda, who were still engaged in prayer.

"No, no, you didn't," he answered. "I was just taking a few minutes to calm myself down."

"How is she?"

"Still the same, I guess." He shrugged. "The doctors ran some tests on her a couple of days ago. I don't know what they were looking for, but they said she's still okay."

"Did they say when she might wake up?"

Tonya made a vain effort to hide the fear in her voice but was unsuccessful. Jason looked at her, reached over, and gave a slight squeeze to her shoulder. She turned to look at him, even as a few tears began tracing lines down her cheeks.

"Let's not worry about that until they say something for sure, okay?" He winked.

"Okay," she nodded.

They both heard Greg and Brenda say "Amen" and raise their heads. They smiled as they looked at Jason and Tonya standing in the door.

"Hi, Jason. Hi, Tonya," Greg said.

Tori raised her weary head when she heard this and turned toward the door. Her eyes were still slightly unfocused from her slumber, and she blinked rapidly, wiling them to function properly.

"Oh. Hi," Tori said.

She straightened herself in the chair, reached up, and brushed the hair out of her face and did her best to look presentable. Brenda stood from the couch and walked toward Jason and Tonya, meeting them halfway into the room. She reached out with open arms, pulling them to her. Jason and Tonya were caught off guard and awkwardly returned the embrace, each with an arm around Brenda.

"We've been praying for you, Jason." She released her grip on them and stepped back, a smile on her face. "We've been praying for all of us, really," she said, waving a hand around the room. "We've been asking the Lord to bring us the peace that passes understanding as we go through this time."

"Thank you," Jason said, a bemused look on his face.

"But most especially, we've been praying for Stacy's baby," Greg said, standing from the couch.

"What about it?" Jason asked.

By now Tonya had moved behind Tori and stood with her hands on the back of the chair Tori occupied.

"Jason, we're going to be privileged with being grandparents," Greg said, his face lighting up with a smile. "Isn't that wonderful?"

"I hadn't thought about it," Jason said, the realization of this truth just now penetrating his thoughts.

"We've been praying for a healthy child to be born and all the ways we can help her get through this," Brenda said. "After all, she's going to be a single mother and will need as much support as she can get."

Tori kept her gaze fixed on her daughter, her arms across her chest, one hand raised to her mouth as she nervously chewed on her fingernail. Tonya remained silent, absorbing the unease in the room. Suddenly feeling out of place, she began to wonder why she decided to come back for a visit.

"But I'll support her no matter what she decides," Tori said, her voice registering just above a whisper.

"What's that supposed to mean?"

"It means, Jason, that no matter what she chooses, I'll still love her," Tori said, turning to look at him. "It means, even if she decides not to have this baby, I'll be by her side. It's not up to us. It's up to her. Don't you agree?"

Something in the way she asked this question caught Jason off guard. He hadn't considered abortion as an option in this situation.

"I don't know. I guess I just assumed she'd have the baby and we'd help her out when we can. Isn't that what you thought?"

Greg and Brenda had returned to the couch, both deciding to stay out of the personal business Jason and Tori had to sort through.

"Jason, she's all alone. She doesn't have a place to live, she's going away to college next year, she's not ready to be a mother," Tori said, the exasperation creeping into her tone. "She can't handle this responsibility. She's not ready."

"Maybe." He shrugged. "Maybe we could help her though."

"Like how, Jason?" Tori said, standing from the chair and moving to face him. "How are we going to do that? We've got our own lives to live. We barely talk, except when I call you and remind you to deliver the money toward her college fund. How are we supposed to do this when we don't get along anymore?"

Olivia knelt on the ground outside the side of her trailer, tending to her small flower bed. She'd planted some roses, daffodils, and several other flowers that were in full bloom. She was busy pruning the small bushes that were planted in between each set of flowers. The sun shone beautifully in the blue sky, providing just enough warmth to be comfortable but not overly hot.

The Being and Stacy stood a short distance away, watching as Olivia set about her task. Stacy had a smile on her face, enjoying the sight of her daughter being so meticulous in caring for her flowers. She crossed her arms and held a hand up to her mouth, the pride welling up inside.

Just like my mom used to do, she thought.

She was distracted suddenly by the sight of Junior walking slowly, almost nervously, toward Olivia. His hair had been combed, and he wore a different shirt than before, tucked into his pants this time and buttoned all the way to the collar. It was clear from his mannerisms he had nothing but the best of intentions in speaking to Olivia. The Being glanced up and smiled at the sight of Junior, a twinkle in his eye as he watched the young man approach.

Olivia paused, leaning back on her legs, wiping her brow with her forearm. She set the pruners on the ground next to her and removed the wide-brimmed straw hat from her head, brushing the hair out of her face. From the corner of her eye, she caught sight of Junior, who had now reached the front of her trailer. A wry smile came to her face as she eased herself to a standing position, watching as Junior stopped in front of her.

"Hi, Junior. Can I get you something to drink? Lemonade or iced tea?"

"No. No, thank you," he replied.

"What can I do for you then?"

"Uh...well," he stammered, running his hand through his hair several times, "I just wanted to ask you something." He shuffled his feet as he stood, alternating between looking at Olivia and staring at the ground.

"What's that, Junior?"

"Well..." he gulped, "I-I was going to the movies Friday night. I wondered if you'd like to go with me."

She giggled, bringing her hand up to her mouth, covering her smile. "Junior, are you asking me on a date?"

"Well...uh..." He gave a sheepish grin as he looked at Olivia, then fixed his gaze on the ground. He nodded his head, then turned his gaze back up to Olivia.

"Junior, I'd love to go, but I'm already dating Gordon," she said, her voice sympathetic but firm.

"I know," he answered, again nodding his head. "But he's no good for you, Olivia. He hurts you a lot."

She crossed her arms, her eyes darting around the area, searching for a way to extricate herself from this conversation. "He-he doesn't mean it. He's under a lot of pressure since he's still on parole. He's been working hard to get out from under it, but he's been struggling. He's a good man, he just has his moments."

Junior's gaze returned to the ground as he moved rocks with his well-worn shoes. He shook his head. "A good man never hits a woman," he said softly. He raised his head and looked directly in hers. "I would never hurt you, Olivia. You shouldn't have to worry about being hurt by anybody."

"Look," she said, stepping closer to him, "you're so sweet and so kind, and I appreciate you coming over earlier to stop Gordon. But I just don't feel that way about you. I'm sorry to say that. You're such a nice boy, Junior, but I think you need to look to someone else." She reached out and stroked his upper arm slowly.

"I'm so sorry."

"I understand," he said, his voice soft. He looked up and directly into her eyes again. "Can I say something?"

"Of course," she answered, folding her arms again.

"I love you, Olivia. I've loved you from the first time I saw you, when you and Gordon moved in. But I could tell he was no good for you. He's mean to you. He hurts you, and you shouldn't be hurt, Olivia. I would treat you so nice if you'd be my girl."

Tears came to Stacy's eyes as she saw this unfolding. Her heart yearned for Olivia to give Junior a chance and make her daughter happy.

For her part, Olivia smiled and shifted in her stance, her head low. She cleared her throat before looking back at Junior.

"I had no idea you felt this way," she said, her voice low. "Why didn't you tell me this before?"

"Because Gordon was always here. I couldn't tell you without making him mad."

She sighed. "Junior, I've been with Gordon for almost five years. We have a baby together. I met him because he works for my grandfather."

Stacy was shocked to hear this, drawing in her breath in surprise.

"Do you love him?" he asked.

Something in the way he asked this question caused Olivia to take a couple steps back from him. Her mind was a jumble of thoughts as tormented emotions waged a battle for supremacy.

"You know, a baby needs a father," he said.

Olivia nodded.

"Is Gordon a good father?"

"I don't think that's any of your business."

"If you can tell me you love him and he's a good father, I'll leave you alone," he said, his words drawn out and slow.

Olivia opened her mouth to speak, but the words remained stuck in her throat. She turned away from Junior and squeezed her shoulders together. She wasn't prepared to have this discussion, let alone answer anyone truthfully of her feelings for Gordon.

For his part, Junior stood awkwardly, waiting for an answer. He suspected he might never get one, but he needed to know the truth, or what passed for it anyway. After several minutes of silence between them, she turned to look at him.

"Look, I appreciate you helping me earlier today. I'm grateful you stepped in when you did. But I just can't start over with someone else right now. I've got my baby to look after. I need to do what's best for her right now, no matter how much I don't like it. Do you understand, Junior?"

He cleared his throat and sniffed loudly for several minutes as he shuffled his feet, his head low. He nodded his head and looked up at her. "Yeah," he said, the pain evident in his tone. "Yeah, I get it. But you need to know this—you don't deserve to be treated the way he treats you, understand? He's a liar, he's a cheater, and he's no good for you. But me…" His voice trailed off as he turned away to start heading back to his trailer. He paused and turned back to look at Olivia, who was in tears now. "I know what people say about me," he said, his voice low. "I hear the whispers about me being stupid or a psychopath. I'm not blind to how people look at me. But if you'd ever ignore that, Olivia, maybe you'd see who I am. I always thought that's how you treated people. You were never one to believe what everybody said. But I guess this time it's too much."

His words were laced with pain, and he chuckled sarcastically. "I won't waste any more of your time, Olivia. You take care of yourself. Have a nice day."

He turned and walked with a purpose back to his trailer, his feet moving faster than he anticipated. Olivia watched him through tear-stained eyes, holding a hand to her mouth. She never expected to hear Junior say something like this, never imagined how he might feel about her.

As Olivia pondered the idea that she was perhaps giving in to popular opinion, Stacy moved in a circle around Olivia, staring in disbelief at what she witnessed.

"Go after him, Olivia," she yelled. "He's a good man. Go after him."

Olivia took two halting steps toward Junior, but it was too late. By now he'd reached his trailer and gone inside, slamming the front door behind him for good measure.

"Go get him," Stacy begged. "What's wrong with you? Good men are hard to find, and you just let one go. Stop it and go tell him you're sorry."

Stacy knew her words fell on deaf ears. It was useless to continue berating her daughter's decision. Olivia couldn't see her anyway as her tears were interrupted by the cries of her child in the bedroom. She'd left the windows open to hear any disturbance inside and respond quickly if needed. Olivia bent down, picked up her pruning shears, and walked disconsolately toward her front door.

Stacy was frantic, turning her gaze from Olivia to the Being and back again.

"What is she doing?" she yelled.

"She's doing what she thinks is right. She's chosen her path, and she's being faithful in honoring that choice."

"You mean, she wants to stay with Gordon? She knows he's no good for her. She doesn't love him, I know it."

"Isn't it her choice to decide who she loves?"

The question was just a little too smug for her liking, and she glared at him. "I understand she's making her choice. But it's the wrong one."

"And you think you could force her to make the right choice?" he laughed.

"Yes," she answered defiantly. "Yes, I do."

He began pacing again, stroking his chin as he did. He muttered to himself and waved his hands in the air. He looked smaller than normal, cutting such a slight figure Stacy believed he could blow away with one strong gust of wind. She shook her head, closing her eyes, realizing this was an illusion.

Suddenly, he stopped and snapped his fingers. He began to turn in jubilant circles, laughing and raising his hands in the air.

"Have you gone completely mad?" she asked.

He stopped dancing and walked to where she stood. "Perhaps," he said, leaning close to her. "Perhaps I'm just looney enough to think you'll understand why I brought you here."

He gave a sudden wave of his hand as the air around them filled with the bright colors and rushing wind she'd grown accustomed to during this trek.

Chapter 12

Tori and Jason found themselves walking slowly along one of the jogging trails behind the hospital. The weather was warm, the breeze soft and gentle, and the fatigue of staring at their daughter lying helpless in bed was beginning to wear on them. Neither of them spoke as they walked. Instead, they distracted themselves with their surroundings, taking in the view the woods afforded them. Finally, Jason cleared his throat.

"I wish you hadn't seen her break up with me."

Tori gave a soft chuckle and smiled at hearing this. "I'm sorry it happened while your daughter is in the hospital."

"Why don't I believe you're sorry?" He lifted a hand and rubbed his forehead.

"Jason, I already told you, I wasn't going to say anything to you about it. It's none of my concern what happens now. We're divorced. It kinda comes with the territory that I shouldn't care."

"Well, I still wish you hadn't seen it happen."

She gave him a quick glance and turned her head forward. "Well, you knew she was too young for you, right? I mean, what's that about?"

"I don't know," he chuckled. "Maybe I just wanted to recapture how I felt in college. You remember that, right?"

A sly, sensual smile crept across her lips. "Yeah, I do." She laughed. "We did have some good times, didn't we?"

"Yes, we did. Do you remember the song that played on our first dance? It was the spring formal, wasn't it?"

"Yes, it was. And I believe the song was 'The Lady in Red.' How could I forget?"

"That was a magical moment, wouldn't you say?"

He shook his head. "God, you were beautiful that night."

"Thank you." She blushed. "You were pretty sexy yourself."

"Aw, c'mon." He laughed. "I was a complete moron. I didn't even know what I was doing with a girl as beautiful as you. I was in way over my head."

"See, that's where you're wrong. If you'd bothered to look, you would've seen I'm just a simple girl."

"Guess I found that out a little too late, huh?" He glanced at her and gave a wink.

She giggled. "Maybe."

They returned to being silent and continued walking further along the trail. They stopped on a small bridge crossing over a shallow creek meandering through the woods. They both leaned on the side rail and watched the water rushing over the rocks in the creek bed. They fell into a blissful peace as they stared at the water, mesmerized by its motion. It was a perfect moment of rest during a crisis.

"You know, I never got over feeling inadequate about being with you," he said, breaking the silence.

"What do you mean?"

"I mean, you were this amazing girl, way outta my league, who liked me. I never figured out why you did, and I never bothered to find out. I got stuck trying to answer the question of what you saw in me the entire time we were together. I never found an answer."

Tori shifted nervously where she stood, clasping her fingers tightly together and laughing softly. "Jason, all I wanted was you." She stood up and turned to face him.

He reciprocated.

"You were enough for me. You didn't have to act a certain way or be a certain type of guy or look a certain way for me to like you. All I wanted was just who you are. That was enough for me."

"So how come we never got along? I mean, I know I was gone a lot, and you were home by yourself. It didn't help Stacy was brought into our lives while we were still figuring things out between us. It seemed like it complicated things. But you knew I was going to be on the road more than I was going to be home. You knew that when you married me."

"Yeah, I did," she nodded. "I guess I thought I'd get used to it and it wouldn't matter so much. Turns out, it made a lot of difference. As for Stacy, I wouldn't trade her for anything in the world. We may have our differences, but I love her. This whole situation has made me realize I need to be there for her more than I was before. I just hope I get the chance to tell her how much I love her."

"Yeah," he said, "me too."

They both turned back to look at the creek, leaning again on the railing. The silence seemed deafening between them. He cleared his throat and looked at his feet.

"When did we stop trying?"

She was taken aback at hearing this, unprepared for this line of questioning. "Do you honestly think we're going to figure that out now? When do you think it happened?"

"I think it was when I went to Florida trying to figure out why the Baker account blew up. Remember?"

"Yeah." Her voice was low, and she nodded her head.

"I found out you'd slept with your secretary on that trip and confronted you about it when you came home. We never argued as much as we did that night."

There was an unspoken sorrow between them now, a brokenness tearing at memories they were unable to repair. He chuckled and shook his head.

"I was so foolish. It wasn't like I fell out of love with you. I just did it. I wish I could take it back."

"A little too late for that, wouldn't you say?" she answered, her eyes fixed on the creek.

"What about you? What about all those young men you slept with while I was gone? Are we gonna ignore that?" He was feeling on edge the longer they talked.

"Aw, Jason, why are we doing this? We're rehashing everything wrong about our marriage, like we can fix it now. Why does it matter? We both moved on."

"Yeah, I know," he sighed.

An uncomfortable silence fell between them again as they both mentally retreated to whatever safe space they clung to as reassurance. Somehow it didn't feel right to try and work through something that was beyond repair. Jason cleared his throat and rocked back and forth on his heels.

"For what it's worth, I'm sorry," he said. His voice struck a conciliatory tone, and for a moment, she was caught off guard at his admission of sorrow.

"I'm sorry too," she said, reaching up and wiping a tear from her eye.

They remained this way, silent and purposely distracted by the creek, for what seemed hours, before deciding to make their way back to the hospital. They needed to return to Stacy's room and allow their past to drift away.

A smile crossed Stacy's face as she followed the Being down an old familiar road on the near west side of Blackburn. She'd driven this way many times before with Tonya to go shopping at Springs Mall. Her heart swelled with pride as they passed by landmarks she'd memorized when she was a child.

There was the Dairy Outlet, where her dad would take her for ice cream. Across the street was Hannigan's Food Mart, where her mom took her to shop for groceries. And then there was the mall, a seminal structure in a town such as this, but one of the busiest places in the entire city every weekend. Discussions had been ongoing about building a much-needed parking garage attaching to the mall, but talks bogged down when city council decided to fund the mayor's request for additional police and fire units.

Located on a small parcel in front of the mall was Gray Moon Café, a throwback burger-and-shake joint resembling a diner from the 1950s. Stacy remembered her parents talking about how they both worked here when they were teens. As a result of their shared time here, they learned a lot about customer service from dealing with the clientele who frequented the establishment.

"I can't believe I'm home," she said, her voice a mixture of wonder and emotion.

The Being turned back to look at her and smiled. "I knew you'd appreciate being here. I wanted to show you one final piece of the puzzle that may be your daughter's life."

"Of course. I presume she's employed at the café?"

"Correct."

"It could be worse. But I'm glad she has a good job."

"Any job can be good. It all depends on the attitude you bring."

She moved to speak but stopped herself short. It was of little consequence to respond, so she ignored the comment.

"Are you ready for the final scenario of this dream?"

"Yes," she nodded. "I'm somewhat saddened this will be the last time I see my daughter. She's amazed me with her abilities and resilience."

"Why should that surprise you?"

"After all I've seen of what could possibly happen, and not knowing if any of them will come true, I'm amazed how she's composed herself. She's a strong young woman."

"And where do you suppose she learned that strength?" He gave a knowing smile to her as she lowered her eyes and shook her head.

She exhaled loudly and shuffled her feet. If there was anything she'd learned so far, it was that this Being was persistent in pestering her with questions. It was better not to respond.

"I want to tell you something before we go inside," she said.

"And what is that?"

She looked into his eyes, a deep sense of respect and love exuding from her expression. "You have challenged me at every turn. You have opened my eyes to a wider world than I realized. Every possible scenario I've seen my daughter in has been enlightening. I realize this is not something everyone can experience, and I have not taken this journey lightly, though you may disagree. Simply, it has taught me well how humanity can behave. There is cruelty among us, and I still question whether it is wise to allow my child to be born into this world. It would kill me if I had to witness some of these events come true for my child. While I appreciate your efforts to the contrary, you have not succeeded in changing my mind. I hold fast to the belief that I am not able to care for a child on my own. I do not have the resources to depend upon to aid my situation. You have not persuaded me. Rather, you have simply hardened my resolve to do what's best for me, regardless of the outcome. Do you understand?"

He shuffled a few paces away from her, his head low. He clasped his hands behind him as he turned in a lazy circle. Stacy watched him intently, her eyes fixed hard in watching his every move. He seemed defeated, as if he had no recourse of action.

He paused and shook his head, his eyes screwed tightly shut. He let out an agonizing moan, one that caused Stacy to shiver when she heard it. He turned to look at her, his eyes a mixture of anger and sorrow.

"Have you not listened to me?" he asked softly. "Have you not understood what I have been trying to show you? Young one, this entire exercise was meant for your benefit, for you to ponder the ramifications of your behavior with your own mother. Yes, you have the power to decide. No one can interfere or stop you from making that decision. Not even me, much as it pains me to say that. It is without question your decision should be respected. But tell me this..." He walked agonizingly slow toward her, stopping a few feet from her. "If one has not given due diligence to every possible outcome, who is to blame for the consequence?"

"You believe I have not thought of every outcome? Haven't you already shown me every possible outcome? Or at least some semblance of my daughter's future? How can you say such a thing?"

"My child, this journey was merely a glimpse into your daughter's possible future. I never told you it was factually accurate. You know this. Why do you still behave as if you don't?"

She remained silent, searching for an answer. The harder she tried, the less she was able to find a plausible response. Better to be silent than to speak and be misunderstood.

"I did not tell you my thoughts so you may berate me," she finally said. "I'd prefer to get this over with and return to being normal again, if I am able."

He drew in a deep breath, paused, and exhaled slowly. He pursed his lips and narrowed his eyes, studying her heart and mind. Perhaps he'd bargained she was susceptible to persuasion and guessed wrong. The longer he searched her heart, the more he came to realize the stubbornness inside was impenetrable. Finally, he nodded his head.

"Okay," he said. "Okay. Then let us continue."

He waved his hand forward, and the pair crossed the street toward the café.

Parking was at a premium this day, indicating the popularity the ownership enjoyed. To one side of the building was a separate door, leading inside to the main café. This was for customers to place a carry-out order without having to wait in line with those wishing to be seated at a table. The line here stretched well outside the door. However, the service was relatively fast, and customers didn't have to wait long for their orders.

As the pair entered the dining area, they were greeted by a cacophony of sights and sounds. Buoyant music emanating from the jukebox in the far corner mixed with the sound of clanging plates and glasses. The patrons themselves brought another layer of indistinguishable sound by their conversations. The voice of one of the cooks behind the counter would occasionally call out an order number loud enough to be heard over the din, an impressive feat considering the compact nature of the dining area.

The walls were covered with vintage photographs of local celebrities and sports teams. There were a few pictures of Hollywood actors, but those were few and far between. Clearly, ownership showed a deep affinity for everything local. More than one high school jersey was hung prominently in large frames, neatly folded and accented with a single light shining directly on them.

Stacy found herself enraptured by the photographs hanging on the wall, smiling as she recognized some of the local dignitaries. She made her way past the photos of the political leaders and prominent businessmen to the corner where the photographs of athletes were displayed. She saw a few pictures of cheerleading squads that had won state titles and smiled, wishing her own team were fortunate enough to have ascended to that height.

Of course, no local sports display would be complete without a shrine to Quincy Baker. There was his trophy for winning the rushing title, another trophy for his academic achievements, and still another for leading his team to the state title in 1935, the only year his team achieved that goal. And then there were the Oakwood High School state champions from when she was in school.

She drew in her breath as she recognized each player on the team. In the picture, the trophy was placed front and center as the team captains sat on either side. Resting beneath the trophy was a jersey bearing the last name Hamilton. This was how the team honored Tucker's memory. He was every bit an important part of this team as anyone, and out of respect and love, the team included him in the photo.

Stacy's eyes welled with tears, the familiar pangs of love and loss overtaking her thoughts. She desperately missed him and wished they had one more day to spend together.

"His teammates loved him," the Being said.

She turned her head toward him, then back to the picture. "Yes," she nodded, "they did."

"Does it pain you to see this?"

"No," she shook her head. "I just wish we had more time. He shouldn't have died. Why didn't I simply take him home like the coach asked me too?"

"Sadly, that question will never find resolution. However, out of every loss, there can be victory if you search it out."

She turned to look at him. "What do you mean?"

"I mean, out of the loss of your boyfriend came something beautiful."

He winked, turned his head toward the café counter, and smiled. She followed his gaze and burst into a mournful smile herself.

Olivia had just come out from the kitchen area and was busy taking an order from a customer at the counter. Her hair was pulled back in a tight ponytail, her apron draped over her blue polo shirt and black jeans. She scribbled the gentleman's orders on her pad as fast as she could. She looked up when she was finished, flashed a brilliant smile, and pushed her pen and pad into a pocket on her apron.

Taking the menu from the customer, she turned and headed back to the kitchen, disappearing through the entryway.

"She's beautiful, isn't she?" he said.

"The most beautiful thing I've ever seen."

"And to think, she wouldn't be alive if it weren't for you and Tucker."

She absorbed this comment, reliving that moment with Tucker all over again in her mind's eye. He was so tender, so loving that night. She felt completely at peace with him. For reasons she couldn't explain, what they did never felt wrong.

"I suppose you're right."

"Tucker never had the chance to see your daughter. He never even knew she existed. His chance to be a father was ripped away from him in an instant. It's painful to see someone you love be taken away so quickly, isn't it?"

He leaned in closer to her, a curious look on his face. In reaction to this, she blinked her eyes rapidly and shook her head, hoping he wasn't implying what she should do about her pregnancy.

"Why did he think he couldn't be a father?" she whispered. "He would've loved her."

"In the same way you love her, no?"

"Again, you insist on taunting me."

She screwed her eyes shut and turned away from him. "You have done this far too often. I grow weary listening to you endlessly prattling on about love and respect and hope. None of that matters, do you understand? I am the one who will decide this, not you."

Her anger seethed from every syllable and caused the Being to withdraw slightly from her. He turned back to watch the goings-on of the café patrons, amusing himself with their boorish conversations. As he watched, Olivia came from the kitchen area carrying two cups. One had lemonade, the other looked like iced tea. She set the cups down in front of the appropriate customer and leaned down on the countertop, engaging the men in conversation.

Permission to see her daughter was unneeded at this point of the adventure, and Stacy took this opportunity to approach her daughter. She walked to the counter, curious what the three of them were discussing. She stopped at the end of the counter near them and leaned in closer to listen.

"Yeah, reminds me of the time me and Ethel went camping up there by the lake," one of the gentlemen said. "She sure hated trying to fish from that pier. The whole damn thing was rotten and needed replaced, but the park service is too cheap to pay for a new one, I guess. Anyway, she cast her line in, leaned too far forward, and fell in the water. It would've been funnier if she knew how to swim, so I had to help out."

"No, she didn't fall," Olivia said, laughing with the man.

"I swear to heaven, she did," the man said.

The other gentleman became preoccupied with his drink and turned his head away from the other two. He scanned the now full dining area, giving the appearance he didn't want to be involved in any more conversation.

"So how did you get her home? Did she have a change of clothes or something?"

"No, I had to drive a mile back to the cabin and get a towel to cover her seat in the car. Poor woman had to sit there by herself for about twenty minutes while I was gone."

"Aw, well, she's a saint if she didn't get upset waiting for you."

"Yep. She was surprisingly good at being patient," the man said, taking a sip of his tea.

"Well, I'm gonna go check on your food and see where it is. Do you need anything else?" Olivia tapped the counter with her knuckles and straightened herself as she spoke. A warm smile graced her lips.

The man looked up from his iced tea and smiled. "Nope. I'm okay, little lady," he said.

"Then I'll be right back."

She turned and made her way back behind the swinging doors that led to the kitchen. The man who had turned away while Olivia was there turned back to his friend and started talking about the incoming class of freshman at Granite Hills University and what impact they might have on the team next year.

Stacy moved away from them and moved to the kitchen, a hive of organized chaos.

There were the grill cooks wearing black T-shirts covered by an apron, tending to the hamburgers and various other meats sizzling before them. There were the managers clad in button-down gray shirts, shouting orders and setting the already prepared dishes on the expediting deck. There were the waitresses who would come and go frequently, balancing large trays with customers' orders or clutching tightly to several glasses of soft drinks in both hands. It was impressive to watch this mass of confusion coming together in a wonderful sense of deliberate intent.

Stacy scanned the faces of the employees here but didn't see Olivia. Curious, she moved through the kitchen toward the rear of the restaurant. There she saw the back door propped open and saw a puff of smoke dissipate in the air outside. She stepped through the door and saw Olivia leaning with her back against the wall, holding a cigarette in one hand and a picture in the other.

Stacy drew in a breath, her eyes wide with curiosity. Stepping closer to Olivia, she saw the same picture so prevalent in every other scenario before this one. The same pose from the mother and child, the same blurred-out faces. She cursed that she was unable to see the identity of the girl and child adorning the photograph.

Olivia sniffed loudly as she stared at the picture, closing her eyes and bringing the photo to her chest. She leaned her head back against the wall and sighed, bringing the cigarette to her mouth. She took a long drag on it and blew out the smoke casually. She took one more look at the picture and then shoved it into her apron.

Quietly, the Being had made his way outside and observed the way Stacy watched her daughter. His soul felt heavy as he measured the intent of her heart, knowing the quandary she was in and how difficult this time was for her.

"Shall I tell her?" he whispered, glancing toward the heavens, a sad smile crossing his face. "She's been through enough by now. She should know the truth."

He paused, as if waiting on some miraculous sign to appear above him. When none came, he shrugged, lowered his head, and watched as Olivia threw her cigarette on the ground, stepped a foot onto it, and ground it into the pavement. Within a moment, she was inside the kitchen, her focus returned to servicing the customers awaiting their orders.

Stacy watched Olivia walk back inside, a mixture of deep sorrow and anger coursing through her heart. She wanted to hold her daughter, just once, to see how it would feel. For a moment, the thought of eluding this burden disappeared, leaving the deepest sense of connection she'd ever felt in her life.

"Have you seen enough, or should we continue here?" he asked.

She turned in slow motion to face him. "Where does she live? Is she involved with anyone? Does she have children of her own?"

She was pleading now, her voice just above a whisper. A desperation clouded her eyes as she looked at him.

"If you wish to know the answer, I can show you."

She stumbled toward him, her motions appearing forced. She stopped in front of him and looked into his eyes. "You understand this is the cruelest exercise I've ever participated in, don't you?"

"Yes," he answered, "but I've noticed one thing."

"What's that?"

He drew in a deep breath, closed his eyes for a moment, and released the air in his lungs. "Each time you have seen your daughter, your desire to hold her and comfort her grows stronger. At her worst, you have longed to embrace her and kiss away her tears. At her most triumphant, you have applauded her efforts. You are experiencing the pangs of what it means to be a mother, in every sense of the word. Yet the struggle in your heart remains."

She lowered her head and brought both her hands across her stomach, clutching at her gown. She felt her eyes begin to well with tears, but she held them back.

"It would ruin my life," she whispered. "No matter what I may feel or what I witness, this burden is too great to carry. I can't do this alone."

He studied her carefully, measuring every nervous tic, each gentle movement of emotion locked in her soul. He realized she was conflicted, as she had been from the start, but considered the ramifications of this endeavor was worth the price of her discomfort.

He stretched out his hand and slowly turned it, the colors appearing around them once again. The rushing wind felt almost like a baptism of relief to Stacy as she clutched her stomach tighter. This only lasted a moment before she opened her eyes again.

She found they were in a part of town everyone referred to as the Bottoms. Although no one knew how this nickname came to be, it was understood this was a semidangerous part of town. No one intentionally moved to this section of town. Usually, three types of people claimed this area as their home. One, they were born here and found their way out. Two, they decided life wasn't going to get any better and resigned themselves to dying here. Or three, life had dealt them a harsh return and they had nowhere else to go.

As she looked around, to her right, Stacy saw a small ranch home that was built sometime in the 1970s. It had a one-car garage to the left of the front door, a bay window on the far right, and a small overhang above the front door. A porch light glowed directly to the right of the door, illuminating the front steps, but not much more.

There was a rusting pickup truck parked in the driveway, the rear fenders both appearing close to falling off. The driveway itself suffered from neglect as cracks checkered the entirety of the blacktop. On the street in front of the house was a used midsized sedan starting to show its age. It was clear the occupants were living on a shoestring budget.

"So is this her house?"

"Yes."

She surveyed the weathered home carefully, noticing its roofline needed repair and the paneling on the sides looking worn and battered. Appearances to the contrary, it was evident this home was built out of quality materials to have not fallen into complete disrepair.

She gave a shrug and chuckled as she looked at the house. "At least she's not on the street."

"Indeed."

He moved to stand beside her, a sign of comradery in his actions.

"What are we waiting for? Aren't we going inside?"

"Are you anxious to leave this nightmare?"

"Nightmare?" she answered, furrowing her brow.

"You seem surprised. You don't agree parts of this have been hellish?"

"Perhaps some of them were too harsh, yes. But what difference does it make? This is all a dream. None of this may come true, so why should I be emotionally invested? You've said so yourself."

Upon hearing this, he laughed heartily.

She looked to him, confusion in her eyes. "Why do you laugh?"

"Because you have witnessed the abysmal conditions your child may live in, and you wept. You have seen the accomplishments she may be capable of, and you were glowing. Yet you refuse to see the event that may transpire soon is despicable. Truly, this is a maddening exercise."

She took two steps forward, cocking her hand behind her, and swung with all her might at him. He ducked out of the way as her body twisted in a circle, causing her to fall to the ground. He laughed at this petty showing of anger.

"I hate you!" she shouted, banging her hand on the ground.

"Whether you hate me or not is of no consequence to me. All I wish is to see the best for your life, but you must be willing to accept it. If you refuse, there is nothing I can do to stop you from making the mistake you almost certainly will abide in." His voice was powerful, almost filling the air around her with its might.

She covered her ears as she heard him speak and drove her face into the ground. She screamed again, thrashing her arms and legs in the air.

All of a sudden, she felt herself nearly paralyzed, unable to speak or move. She was still aware of everything around her, but her movements had ceased. Only her head was able to turn, ever so slightly, to look at him. He stood firmly in place, his arm outstretched toward her, his fingers splayed out from his hand. His face was a white-hot light, his eyes like fire. He was cloaked in a white robe, a scarlet scepter in his hand.

"I do not take kindly to fools or imbeciles who refuse to listen to reason. I have brought you here to expose your heart to the wonder of your daughter, and you have treated this as nothing more than a game. You have dismissed the lessons I wished you to learn. You have failed to recognize the importance of how your life will impact others. When will you realize this is your child's life you're dealing with and not yours alone?"

The anger pierced her heart, his words almost menacing in their tone. His face turned black, but his eyes maintained their fiery-red appearance.

For the first time, Stacy felt her soul begin to quake. Clenching her eyes shut, she turned her head as best she could. Whatever spell he conjured was powerful enough to strike fear in her heart.

"Now, will you allow this journey to reach its conclusion, or do I need to remind you of who I am?"

As he said the words "I am," she cowered in fear, but not fear as to be terrified of a ghost. Rather, she found herself fearful of the strength in his character, his wisdom, and the power on display at this moment. She wasn't sure why she felt this way, but she realized a response was futile.

"No," she managed, her voice weak.

"Good."

Within moments, she found herself standing on the ground, her knees shaking. She wrapped her arms tightly around her stomach now, wishing she were safe in her bed.

"Once this is over, you shall return to your normal life," he said, his voice much lower than before. "However, you shall not forget what you saw here. Understood?"

By now he'd returned to his normal appearance, the scepter in his hand having turned to a staff. He cocked his head sideways, his eyes fixed on Stacy. She glanced up quickly at him and nodded her head. He gave a wide smile.

"Good. Let's continue," he said softly, waving his hand toward the house.

Wordlessly, they walked inside the house, entering what passed for the foyer. If the outside looked dated, the interior confirmed it.

To their left was the living room, with wall-to-wall shag carpeting. Behind that was a smaller room appearing to have been turned into an office, as a small desk, a cabinet, and a chair occupied the space. To their right was what appeared to be a playroom, as toys were scattered over the floor, the childish drawings on paper arranged on the wall in a haphazard manner.

Down the hallway between these rooms was the dining room. On the left wall halfway to the dining room was the doorway to the half bathroom. As the pair walked down the hall, they entered the kitchen, its dated appliances adding to the overall ambiance of a retro era. In the middle of the wall to their immediate right was a doorway that must lead to the basement.

Further to the right of the kitchen was the family room. Despite there being several windows on the back wall of the room facing the backyard, it was surprisingly dark. The only nod to an update was the carpet in this room, which was more tightly woven than the one in the living room.

There came the sound of footsteps from below as the door to their right opened, exposing the basement. Olivia stepped into the room, carrying a Crock-Pot, reasonably covered in dust and grime. She moved to the kitchen sink and placed it on the counter beside it. As she set about washing it, she started to sing. Her voice was melodious, gentle, and warm.

Stacy couldn't contain the smile on her face as she listened, enraptured by her daughter's beautiful voice. She closed her eyes, becoming lost in the purity of the sound. It was simply the most beautiful voice she'd heard in quite some time. It reminded her of Allison Krauss, but in a slightly lower register.

Though she was not in a concert hall or on a stage, Olivia sang with the conviction of a trained professional. In her mind, she was standing in front of twenty thousand people, all cheering for her and applauding her talent. As she sang ever louder, she closed her eyes, swaying to the rhythm of her voice, raising her hands and dancing in place.

It was quite possibly the most beautiful thing Stacy had ever witnessed.

The Being simply watched as mother and daughter enjoyed a spiritual, yet unseen, communion in this moment. Their souls were joined by time immaterial. He glanced from Olivia to Stacy and back again, his soul overflowing with pride at the simplicity of love on display.

"Why isn't she onstage somewhere?" Stacy finally asked. "She's wonderful."

"She gave up on that dream a long time ago," he said, stroking his chin.

"Why?"

"She determined that life wouldn't provide her the opportunity to pursue this dream. She settled here and determined this was as good as it would get for her."

"But she's so good," Stacy gushed. "Listen to her." She pointed at Olivia, now dancing in the kitchen, a wooden spoon filling in for a microphone.

"Yes. She's a natural at this. Where do you suppose that talent comes from?"

"Well, I was in choir for a year. I always liked it but didn't give much thought to singing as a career."

He smiled at her. "Now you're seeing the connection from parent to child. Well done."

Olivia had now danced her way to the living room, her gyrating seeming to be in perfect motion with her words. She jumped onto the coffee table and shook her hips side to side, one hand in the air, the other clutching her faux microphone. She was the picture of complete peace.

The sound of a car door slamming outside brought an end to her singing, and she suddenly froze. Her eyes became wide, and her body shook at what was to come.

The front door opened and was summarily slammed shut as the sound of footsteps pounding down the hall came closer. Olivia stepped off the coffee table and ran to the kitchen, placing the wooden spoon back in the utensil holder.

Stacy turned her head toward the sound of the footsteps, in time to see a man stalking toward Olivia. She was almost horrified to see it was Gordon.

"Is dinner ready yet?" Gordon roared. He stopped just a few paces away from Olivia.

"No, not yet. I was just starting it now," she stammered.

Gordon smacked the back of Olivia's head with his hand. "Get it done fast, bitch. The boys are comin' over to play cards, and I want to eat before they get here. Got it?" He glared at her, his eyes dark and menacing.

The fear on her face was impossible to hide now. "You know I'll get it done, Gordon. I always do."

"Yeah, you do," he sneered. He reached down and smacked Olivia's backside and laughed. "That's my good woman. Doin' what God created you to do, serve your man."

He moved to the refrigerator, opened the door, and pulled out a can of beer. He headed for the den and flopped down in one of the chairs facing the television. He picked up the remote from the end table next to him, aimed it at the television, and sat back in the chair. He cracked open the beer can and started laughing—at what, Olivia didn't know. She'd occupied herself with preparations for dinner at this point and did her best to ignore Gordon.

"No," Stacy whispered, "no, it can't be the same boy she was with before. This is impossible."

"Nothing in life is impossible if you believe it's the best you can do."

"What does that mean?"

"It means, you choose for yourself how your life will unfold. There is a myriad of examples of people who started with nothing yet achieved a great deal through hard work and determination. There are some who choose not to put forth any effort, and as such, they suffer in silence. Then there are those who have been gifted with a great talent, such as your daughter, who believe it isn't worth anything to anyone else. These people will suffer in silence as well. This is the life Olivia has chosen."

By now Greg and Brenda had left the hospital without notice to either Tori or Jason, who both sat sullen in their usual places in the room. The silence was nearly deafening, save for the machines hooked up to Stacy.

Just then, Dr. Blanton entered the room, carrying a manila folder. He was occupied with whatever information was inside it as he stopped near Stacy's bed. Both Tori and Jason stood from their seats and moved next to him.

"What is it, Doctor?" Tori asked, wringing her hands.

"It's good news. We've stabilized the baby and don't see anything indicating a problem. I'd expect everything will be normal as she goes along in her pregnancy."

Both Tori and Jason exhaled loudly, their concerns falling away, sinking into the abyss of forgetfulness.

"Thank you, Doctor," Tori said, reaching out and touching Blanton's arm.

"You're welcome. Is there anything I can get you?" he said, glancing from Tori to Jason and back again.

"No. We're okay," Jason said. "Thanks for the good news. I appreciate it. But…uh, do you have any idea when she might wake up?"

"It's hard to say. Anytime we're dealing with a coma patient, there's no one way for this to end. We may have to discuss what to do if she doesn't wake up, but that won't be for some time. Right now, we're keeping an eye on her, and she's responding well."

Tori groaned, leaned down on the bed rail, and lowered her head. "I don't think I can take this anymore, Doctor," she said, turning her gaze to Blanton. "It's been almost a week, and we haven't seen any sign she knows we're here. You said sometimes people in a coma can hear us, but I don't think she can."

"I said that it's common for people in a coma to hear their loved ones. I never said it was a guarantee," Blanton said, holding up a hand. "You've just got to trust that your daughter's a fighter. Let's not forget, she's got something to say about the outcome here too. We can only do so much to stabilize her and make sure she's comfortable. The rest is up to her."

Blanton tapped the folder in his hand, turned, and exited the room. Tori and Jason stood looking at each other, the fatigue and concern exuding from their shared glance.

Olivia sat rigid at the dinner table, her motions forced as she pushed her fork to her mouth and back to her plate. Internally, she was shaking, her heart beating faster now as she was hesitant to speak.

To her right, Gordon was preoccupied with the fried chicken Olivia made, biting off large pieces of the chicken leg on his plate. He made no pretense for decorum as small pieces of his food mixed into the stubble on his chin.

"This is good," he said, his words muffled as he chewed. "I always knew you could cook just like your mom."

Stacy's ears perked up, and a smile flashed across her lips.

"I'm glad you like it," Olivia said softly.

Gordon picked up his beer can and poured the last vestige of liquid into his mouth. He pulled it away from his lips and let out a satisfying sigh, shaking the can for good measure.

"Well, looks like it's time for another beer." He laughed. "You want one?"

"No. I've got more tea. I'm okay."

"Suit yourself."

He shoved his chair away from the table, rose from the chair, and half walked, half wobbled to the refrigerator, exposing the effects of already downing at least six beers before he arrived home. He pulled the refrigerator door open and bent down.

"Hey," he shouted.

Olivia jumped, closing her eyes. "What?"

He stood up, leaned on the door, and looked over at Olivia. "We're out of beer. Didn't I tell you to pick some up this afternoon, huh?"

He slammed the door shut and headed toward Olivia, who had visibly shrunk in her chair.

"No, don't hurt my baby," Stacy said, her hand reaching out as if trying to stop his progress.

The Being stood stoically nearby, a blank look on his face.

"I-I didn't have time, Gordon," Olivia stammered. "I was at my voice lesson, and it took longer than I thought it would, and…"

"And WHAT?" Gordon roared, pushing a chair to the floor. "What excuse is it this time?"

Olivia threw her fork on the table and stood up, facing him. "Listen! I gave up my dream to be a singer for you. The least you can let me do is enjoy my time at the studio, okay?" she shouted back at him.

"Oh, here we go again. You were gonna be the next Madonna or Beyoncé or whatever. That's all I've heard for three years. Well, you know what? You're nothing! You were nothing when I met you, you're nothing now, and you're always gonna be nothing," he screamed, waving his hands in the air as he stepped closer to her. "You're nothing but a meaningless waitress, understand?"

He turned and stormed toward the front door, leaving her in tears as she leaned against one of the dining room chairs. She watched as he walked to the door.

"Where are you going?"

"Out with the boys," he shouted, reaching for the doorknob. He paused, looking back at her, a scowl affixed to his face. "Don't wait up."

The venom was clear in his voice, piercing her heart with surgical precision. He pulled the door open, stepped outside, and slammed it behind him. Olivia remained leaning on the chair for several minutes, the tears falling hard.

Stacy was weeping openly at what she just witnessed. She looked from the front door to Olivia and back again. The Being remained silent, his head askance as he watched Stacy's reaction, carefully measuring her devotion.

"Why is she in such pain?" Stacy whispered.

"Imagine growing up surrounded by upheaval and dysfunction, my child."

"But my life is dysfunctional. It shouldn't be her life that ends up like this."

"Choices made in haste lead to regret, most times. Some choices may turn out well. However, without carefully weighing the outcome, one can become ensnared in a web of anger and pain. Sometimes, there is no way out of this."

He spoke calmly, his words measured and drawn out.

Stacy shook her head upon hearing this and sighed. "My daughter deserves much more than this. She deserves to be treated like a queen, not a servant, or a criminal. She's better than this."

"That very well may be," he said. He strode casually toward Stacy, his head bowed, and his hands clasped behind him. He stopped within a few feet of her, drew himself to his full height, and inhaled deeply, letting the air escape his lungs at the same rate. "But why concern yourself with someone else's pain if all you wish is to avoid it?"

"Jason, where did we go wrong?" Tori said.

She was rocking back and forth on the couch in the hospital room, nervously wringing her hands. Her eyes were wide, and she kept turning her head side to side, almost trance like.

Jason was just starting to fall asleep when he heard this and shook himself awake. He reached up and rubbed his eyes, yawning and stretching as he straightened himself in the lounge chair.

"Didn't we already talk about this?" he said, the fatigue evident in his voice.

"Maybe. But I'm worried about what comes next."

"What do you mean what comes next?" He leaned forward, his elbows resting on his knees.

"I mean, have we taught our daughter well enough to make a good choice about being a mother? Have we given her enough information to trust she makes the best decision for herself?"

"Tori, we've done best we could. We taught her what we know. So far, she's done well for herself and stayed out of trouble. All we can do going forward is be there when she needs us. Our teaching days are over. From here on out, our job is to just be advisers to her. We can't stop her from doing what she wants."

"I know that, but I'm scared."

"Look, we can't change what happened, can we?" He stood from the lounger. "This is where we are. These are the circumstances we're in, and we have to do the best we can for Stacy and help her with whatever she decides."

Tori stopped rocking and looked down at the floor. She closed her eyes and sighed heavily before looking up at Jason.

"What do you think about her getting an abortion?"

Jason leaned down on the bed rail, his eyes transfixed on his daughter. He chuckled. "Hadn't really thought about it."

"Would you be okay if that's what she did?"

"I don't know." he waved a hand in the air. "I mean, honestly, I'm not the one carrying the baby, so I don't know if I can tell her what to do."

"Jason." She stood from the couch. "This is our daughter. She's got a tough decision to make. Don't cop out on me and give me that crap. I want to know honestly. What do you think if she has an abortion?"

He glanced at Tori, confusion clouding his vision. He looked back down at Stacy and sighed.

"I-I don't know, Tori. If we're being honest, she can't afford to have a child and go to college. I mean, who's gonna watch her baby while she's in class? I'm on the road a lot. You're busy doin' whatever it is you do. She can't afford day care. It'll eat up most of the money we've saved for her first year. She can't hold a job, have a baby, and go to school and be a cheerleader if she wants to. I don't see how this is gonna work without our help, Tori. Do you?"

He looked at her, his eyes pleading for an answer he knew he wouldn't get. She returned his gaze, the pain in her soul exposed in her tears.

"I don't care if you disagree with me or not, but I'd be okay if she never has this child, Jason," she said, her voice above a whisper. "We can't be there to help her, and I doubt Greg and Brenda will be willing to be involved with her at all. They say they want to and are looking forward to being grandparents, but how much of that is just being caught up in the moment?"

"Yeah," he nodded, "I get that. But I think there's one thing we may be overlooking."

"What's that?"

He looked directly into Tori's eyes. "What does Stacy want to do?"

Olivia spent the rest of the evening cleaning up after dinner, finding time to read through her music books after filling the dishwasher. Even though she'd given up her dreams, she still wanted to improve for herself.

When did things change for us? she thought. *Did he ever really believe me about my pursuing a career in singing?*

She was seated on her couch, leafing through the newest songbook her vocal teacher had given her. It was a compilation of '80s and '90s songs, an era of music that intrigued Olivia. Her teacher very enthusiastically endorsed the idea Olivia learn some of the hits from this period, and the more she studied them, the more she grew to love the songs.

She stopped turning the pages when she arrived at a song by Whitney Houston, "I Wanna Dance with Somebody." She smiled, got up from the couch and went to retrieve her phone from her bedroom. Finding it lying underneath some junk mail, she quickly pulled up her playlist as she walked back to the living room.

She found the song on her playlist, plugged her phone into the speaker set, and pushed the Play button on the display screen. Within moments, the air inside the living room was filled with the buoyant sound of Whitney Houston at her best. Olivia began dancing around the room, singing at the top of her lungs.

Stacy laughed as she watched this scene unfold. The infectious beat wasn't lost on her as she began to bob back and forth to the rhythm. For his part, the Being simply smiled, the joy at watching mother and daughter sharing a dance together overwhelming his senses.

"Did you ever think maybe it's not up to her?"

Jason exhaled, putting his hands in his pockets. "Tori, I just told you. We can't live her life for her. If she wants an abortion, fine. We find a way to get it done. If she wants to keep it, we..." His voice trailed off as he shrugged his shoulders. "I don't know what we do, but we have to be there for her no matter what."

"That's what I said," she answered.

"Oh, sorry, was I not listening again?"

"Don't start with me, Jason. I swear to God, don't start with me again. I've had enough of your smart-ass remarks already, I don't need any more."

"Look. I don't care what she does, all right? She's an adult, and we must treat her like one. It doesn't matter what I feel or believe or what Greg and Brenda believe. It matters what she wants. And we can't force that on her. Only she can make this choice."

"God, you sound like you're running for office, Jason," she said, throwing her hands up in the air. "I think she should get it done. She can't have a baby while going to school. She'd flunk out and go on welfare or get food stamps or whatever. She's got a long life ahead of her, and she doesn't need the burden of a child hanging over her head."

"You don't think she can handle it?"

Tori crossed her arms and jutted out her chin defiantly. "No, I don't think she's capable of that yet. She can't even clean up her own room, Jason. What makes you think she can take care of a child?"

"I don't know," he shrugged. "Look, I don't have time to talk about this right now. About an hour ago, I got an email from Wilson saying they need me back at the office immediately. Apparently, we're close to losing the Gardner account, and they want me to get back there to do some damage control."

"So you won't be here if she wakes up?" she said.

"No. I'm afraid I won't be. I need to catch a flight within the next few hours and get back to the office. I'm sorry I won't be here, but this is what I need to do. Just let her know I was here, okay?"

"Jason, you can't just run out on your daughter like this. Your family comes first."

"Yeah, well, if I don't keep that account, I won't be able to provide for my family, so this has to come first right now."

Tori shook her head and lowered it into her hand. "Typical. Just typical."

"What's typical?"

"You. Running out on us, just like you did before our divorce. I should've seen this coming."

He reached down to the floor, picked up his backpack, and slung it over his shoulder.

"Listen, you can be mad all you want. But I've got a plane to catch in a few hours. I need to go. Just let Stacy know I was here, okay? Can you promise me that?"

"Yes. I'll let her know."

Time stood still as they looked at each other, their emotions darting in all directions at this moment. Neither of them knew what to say or if words were necessary. All they could feel was the awkwardness of a father leaving the bedside of a daughter in dire need of guidance only parents could provide.

"All right," he said, breaking the silence, "I gotta go. Text me when she wakes up, okay?"

"Sure," she answered.

"Okay. Take care."

He offered a weak smile and turned to exit the room. Within moments, he'd disappeared and was headed for the elevators. Tori kept her gaze fixed on the doorway, hoping against hope he would suddenly reappear and want to stay with his daughter.

The longer she watched the doorway, it became increasingly evident he wasn't coming back.

Chapter 13

Stacy found herself walking softly through the same forest as before. The sky was a deep, gunmetal gray color, the breeze providing a chill to her surroundings. She wore a long, flowing white gown this time, absent a crown. As if in slow motion, she moved mechanically toward the meadow, only she heard faint echoes of voices surround her.

She turned her head carefully, peering through the grayness around her to where the voices might be emanating. Seeing nothing, she came closer to the meadow, still bathed in sunlight. She could feel a hint of warm air blowing outward from the clearing, but it was insufficient in warming the remainder of the forest.

She stopped, suddenly realizing the Being was no longer with her. She turned in a circle, surveying the landscape around her, searching effortlessly for any trace of him. She furrowed her brow, curious as to what caused his absence. She turned once more, almost certain she would see him appearing out of the grayness surrounding her. She became unnerved he was nowhere to be found.

Grudgingly, she had learned to accept his presence, at times intolerable, other times supremely challenging. Indeed, she had seen more than expected, and her resolve in believing what she would decide had become less than ideal. Still, she couldn't shake the fact she would be better off without the burden of a child. After all, she had plans. She had goals to reach, accomplishments still within her grasp that would never come true if she carried this child to term.

No, she thought, *it is for the best.*

As she neared the meadow, she saw a streak of a child run by, a whimsical smile upon its face. In turn, her face exploded in joy. She would finally see the children she'd heard before and revel in their happiness.

She tried to run, to sprint the remaining distance, but she couldn't. Every effort she made to move quickly failed. She found herself feeling as though she were passing through a mass of tar for how slow she was moving. Her mounting frustration only served to push her to extreme agitation.

Just then, she caught sight of the Being dancing in the meadow, running away from a child. She couldn't make out the child's face from where she stood but was confident she would be able to partake in the happiness on display here now. She heard the child squeal with delight and looked to see the Being had picked up the child, swinging them through the air.

By now she managed to wade through whatever morass she was mired in and found herself standing once more at the edge of the meadow. To her left, she saw a mother, clad in a pair of denim shorts and a loose-fitting T-shirt. To her right, she saw the child running back to their mother, clad in a pair of shorts as well, with a dirty T-shirt. The Being clapped his hands as he watched the child jump into their mother's arms.

Slowly, he glanced over at Stacy, who by now was near tears at the sheer joy she saw in the mother's smile. He waved to her, and she returned the courtesy. He started toward her, more floating than walking, until he stood in front of her. The smile on his face couldn't be erased.

"Is this what you hoped to see earlier, young one?" he said, waving his hand behind him.

By now the mother and child were on the playground apparatus, their imaginations ruling their actions.

"Yes," she answered. "Yes, it is."

"Come with me for a moment," he said, motioning for her to follow.

He led her to the opposite side of the meadow, near the shanty where, previously, she was able to see her hospital room. They stopped at the rear edge of the shanty, overlooking a small creek, wending its way through the forest. The sound of rushing water was faint but soothing.

"My child, I must release you back to your home," he said, a sober look in his eyes.

"I can return to my life now?"

She clasped her hands together, bringing them to her mouth, as tears began flowing from her eyes.

"You are no longer welcome here," he said, the sadness evident in his words.

"Is that a bad thing?"

"Of course not. Like I told you before, this is a unique opportunity to see a future that may, or may not, come true. You have survived it and handled each situation with a great deal of composure for someone as young as you."

"I never once felt afraid as I walked by your side. Somehow I knew that if I followed you, nothing would harm me. You stayed true to your word. Thank you," she said.

"Of course."

"Only there is one question," she said, raising her hand.

"Yes?" He arched an eyebrow.

"I kept seeing the same picture, repeatedly, yet each time I could not see the faces of who it was. Why is that? You said it held some significance to Olivia, yet I was unable to determine what that was."

He broke into a wide smile. "My dear, some things are better left to discover on your own. It becomes more meaningful when the truth is found after you search for it on your own. Rather than have me explain to you the importance, I believe you will find your answer soon enough."

"Well," she said, shrugging, "I suppose that's as good an answer as any I'll get right now."

"I must confess something to you," he said, turning to face her as he rubbed his chin again.

"And what is that?"

"I'm proud of you, my child."

"Proud? Of what?"

"For facing your fear. For watching with a broken heart what happens to someone you love. For your desire to comfort and protect your child. Not everyone will want to care for their child as you would," he said, a twinkle coming to his gaze.

"Again, thank you."

"This could have been a much different story, you know?"

"What do you mean by that?"

"I mean, I could have shown you far worse things that could have happened to your daughter. As it is, this was a mild sequence of events compared to some of the horror I've witnessed."

"You? You've witnessed other stories?" she asked, the questions in her mind exposed in her expressionless face.

He slowly stroked his chin, stepping closer to her, his gaze occupied by his footsteps. He stopped in front of her and looked directly into her eyes. Something in his gaze caught her off guard. There was a warmth, a calming effect in the way he looked at her. She'd never felt more at peace than in this moment.

"You have no concept of who I am, do you?"

"Should I?" she whispered.

"Search you heart," he smiled. "Look deep inside your soul."

He waved his hand in a circle, only this time the sky turned to black and she found they were practically floating in space. Galaxies and planets rotated around her, the stars numbered in the millions and painted the canvas of the sky the brightest white she'd ever seen.

Breathlessly, she gazed in awe at the spectacle before her. Words couldn't form in her throat to define what she was seeing. There was nothing to do but become lost in the translucent glow around her.

"All that you have seen will be remembered as a dream," he said. "All that you witnessed will be nothing more than a faint glimmer in your imagination. Once you return to your world, you will think back to our time together and question its reality. I can assure you, this is very real."

He began fading into the surrounding darkness, a bright smile affixed to his face, his hands and arms outstretched from his body.

"Young one, never forget what you learned in this deep slumber," he said, his voice filling the air around her. "Never take for granted the lessons you will carry with you. Enjoy your life. Allow it to fill you with joy and sorrow. Embrace the pain as well as the goodness. Never forget, you are stronger than you realize. I have faith in you, child. Now, go."

With one flick of his wrist, the cosmos around her disappeared, and she felt herself floating through a black hole once more, only this time she was approaching a light. There were sounds she didn't quite recognize emanating from the light and pungent odors reaching her nostrils. There was also a hint of sorrowful tears.

Tori sat in the lounger, her head resting on her hand, propped up on the arm of the chair. She tried falling asleep, but rest eluded her, replaced with a familiar emptiness. She'd lost hope of any reconciliation with Jason. Save for a few glimpses of their past together, there was nothing more they could pursue as a couple. She embraced the reality her marriage was finally over.

She was startled out of her half slumber by the gurgling noise she heard. She jolted upright, her hand falling to her lap. Thinking the noise came from Stacy, she peered intently at her body, begging for a sign she was coming out of this nightmare.

Once again, there was a gurgling sound, only this time Tori thought Stacy flicked her index finger. She jumped up out of the chair and within two steps reached the edge of the bed.

"Stacy?" she yelled. "Stacy? Can you hear me?"

She desperately tried to rouse her daughter from the sleep she'd been in, to no avail. She turned toward the doorway of the room.

"Doctor!" she shouted. "Nurse! Somebody! I need you now!"

Just then, two nurses and the on-call doctor rushed into the room.

"What is it?" one of the nurses said.

She was pleasantly plump; her brown hair and tan skin belied her actual weight. She stopped next to Tori as the other nurse, a slim blond, rushed to the opposite side of the bed. The doctor, tall and muscular with boyish good looks, stood at the end of the bed.

"I heard her make a noise," Tori said. "I heard it. I heard her make a noise."

She was in a near panic as she watched the three of them check various lines, the blood pressure cuff, the heart monitor, everything needed to ensure this wasn't something imagined, something that wasn't happening. The urgent commands from the doctor came fast and hard as the three worked in tandem to make sure nothing was overlooked.

Stacy's body seemed to heave, a deep breath being drawn into her lungs. She flicked more than one finger again, and her head moved slightly to the left. Tori dissolved into tears as the signs of life were becoming more evident. The brown-haired nurse put her arms around Tori and pulled her backward, allowing the doctor and the blond-haired nurse enough room to carry out their appointed tasks.

Again, a deep breath from Stacy's body. Again, more finger movement, only this time it was on both hands. Her head moved side to side slowly. Her legs began to twitch, and her feet jolted together, then apart.

"Is she all right?" Tori cried out. "Is she okay? What's happening? Is she dying?" By now panic gripped her being, and she began shaking.

"Ma'am," the doctor said, turning to look at Tori, "it looks like your daughter is going to be okay."

He flashed a smile that allayed some of Tori's concern, but she was overcome with a mixture of anticipation and a macabre sense of doom.

"Thank you, Doctor," she whispered. She brought her hand to her mouth, her body beginning to tremble.

The urgent commands of the doctor began anew as the three continued their efforts. There were only one of two possible outcomes, and Tori refused to accept one of them as plausible.

Suddenly, she heard a cough, then another. She pushed her way to the bedside and looked down to see Stacy moving her hand toward her mouth, reaching for the tube one of the nurses was slowly, but effortlessly, pulling it out of her throat. Stacy's cough became louder and more pronounced now, and her body began to move in slow motion.

"Looks like she's gonna be just fine," the doctor said, smiling at Tori. "She's a very lucky young lady."

Tori could only nod as her eyes never left Stacy, begging wordlessly for her to open her eyes.

"Stacy," Tori shouted again. "Stacy, can you hear me?"

Stacy's eyelids fluttered, almost opening, but not quite. With a great deal of effort, her eyes started to open wider. She winced as the lights stung her eyes, shutting them almost immediately.

"Stacy, it's your mom," Tori said. "I'm here, baby. Open your eyes for me, Stacy."

"Ms. Butler," the doctor said, putting his hand up, "we need to give her time to adjust to what's going on. She's been sedated and in the dark for some time now, so it's gonna be a little while before she's back to normal. Be patient, okay?" He smiled as he spoke, reaching out and providing a comforting squeeze of her shoulder. He turned away, giving Stacy his full attention again.

The brunette nurse took hold of Tori's shoulders, once more pulling her a few paces away from the bed.

"But…but I want to see my daughter," Tori protested, turning her head between the nurse and Stacy. "I want her to see me when she wakes up."

"Ms. Butler, she'll be like this for several minutes," the nurse said. "Let's just wait here until we see for sure she's okay."

The blond nurse and the doctor continued working on Stacy, checking everything at least five times each, if not more. They continued to chatter back and forth, but Tori had no way of knowing exactly what they were looking at. Nervously shifting her weight from one foot to the other, she couldn't wait until the doctor gave the final okay for her to move beside Stacy's bedside again.

Tori positioned herself at just the right angle to see Stacy's head. Her full concentration was devoted to silently urging her daughter to open her eyes. Even though there were positive signs of Stacy waking up, it wasn't a sure thing until they could speak to each other. Until that happened, Tori remained on the edge of fear, begging God this wasn't false hope she was feeling.

Stacy opened her eyes a little wider this time, blinking them rapidly, and finally settled on leaving them half opened. She turned her head inexorably from side to side, trying to grasp what she was going through right now. It was little comfort the doctor and nurse were talking to her. She needed to hear a familiar voice and feel the tender touch of her mother.

Tori looked on in a tear-stained blur, a faint smile crossing her lips. She shook with anticipation, painfully waiting for that moment she could hold her baby again. The nurse standing beside her began rubbing Tori's shoulders, a soothing gesture amidst the combined emotions of panic and joy.

"Stacy," the doctor said. "Stacy, do you hear me?"

She squinted up at the doctor and gave a slight nod of her head. The doctor turned back to look at Tori, smiled, and gave a wink of his eye.

"She's gonna be fine," he said.

Stacy turned her head to where Tori stood. She blinked her eyes and opened them a little wider. As soon as they made eye contact with each other, they both smiled. An unspoken distance between them was suddenly bridged in the millisecond they saw each other.

Finally, the doctor turned and walked to where Tori stood. He stopped in front of her and reached out his hand, placing it on her shoulder.

"She's gonna be just fine," he said. "You can talk to her now, but it'll take time for her to get her strength back and she feels normal again. I'll give you a few minutes with her, but she's going to need to rest, okay?"

Tori nodded. The doctor and nurse stepped aside, close to the wall, and allowed Tori to pass by. She smiled as she approached the bed. She leaned down on the rails and reached for Stacy's hand, taking it in hers. She squeezed it tightly.

"Stacy, honey, I'm so glad you're all right," Tori said.

"What happened?" Stacy asked, her voice raspy and soft.

"It was an accident. We'll talk more when you feel better, okay?"

"Okay," Stacy answered.

"I'm going down to the cafeteria and get something to eat, then I'll be back, all right?" Tori said.

"Okay," Stacy whispered, closing her eyes, and moving her head side to side, slowly.

Tori turned to look at the doctor and nurse by the wall.

"How long do you think she'll be like this?" she asked.

"Why don't we go out in the hallway and talk?" the doctor said, pointing toward the door.

Tori nodded and followed the doctor outside, picking up her purse from the lounger as she did. They took a few paces away from the open doorway and stopped. The doctor turned to face Tori, a look of apprehension on his face.

"Ms. Butler, first, my name is Dr. Reddick. I just wanted to discuss what to expect in the coming days," he said.

She nodded.

"For her to open her eyes and talk like that right after coming out of a coma is somewhat of an anomaly. It's happened before, but not in every case."

"An anomaly?" she asked.

"The majority of patients who come out of a coma tend to have delayed speech and motor skills. It may take them weeks, sometimes months, to return to their normal routine. I don't want to give you any false hope on her recovery or even talk about the worst-case scenario. We'll be evaluating her over the next few days and make sure everything is okay before we know for sure if any of her cognitive skills were affected."

"Oh my god," she said, her hand coming to her mouth, "could she…could something be wrong with her?"

"Like I said, I don't want to make any hasty decisions. She literally just woke up, so it's going to be a while before we're able to determine that." He reached out and placed a hand on her shoulder. "Stay positive, Ms. Butler. We'll do whatever we have to do to make sure she's okay. I'll meet with Dr. Blanton later on, and we'll plan out a course of action for her recovery, okay?"

"But she seemed like she was normal just a minute ago," she said. "What if she…"

"Ms. Butler. Let's not jump to any conclusions here, all right? Let me and my team do what we have to do to make sure she's stabilized before we finalize a conclusion here," Reddick said. "Sound good?"

Tori looked at her feet, wiped her eyes, and clutched her purse to her side even tighter. "Okay," she said. "Just let me know if you run into any problems."

"I will," he said smiling. "Let me reach out to Dr. Blanton, and we'll get started right away. Now, why don't you go get that cup of coffee and cherish the fact your daughter is awake again."

"Thank you. I will."

She turned and started off toward the elevators. Walking was difficult when her insides were vibrating with anticipation and her legs felt wobbly. She reached inside her purse for her cell phone but stopped short.

No, don't call Jason, she thought. *He doesn't deserve to know right now.*

She withdrew her hand from her purse, arrived at the elevators, and pushed the down button. A smile crossed her lips. For now, her daughter was awake and seemed like she would return to being her normal self. The smile faded just as quickly as it came when she remembered the doctor saying he couldn't be sure Stacy would fully recover yet.

The bell rang for the elevator, and the doors slid open. She stepped inside the empty car, pushed the button for the lobby, and leaned against the back wall.

Why couldn't Jason be here now? she thought just as the doors slid shut.

Over the next several days, Stacy's improvement was markedly better. The doctors had determined there were no adverse effects to her motor skills or her speech. They were pleasantly surprised she had come through this ordeal relatively unscathed. Though she couldn't go home quite yet, her recovery was progressing well.

"How do you feel, honey?" Tori asked.

She sat on the lounger next to the bed. She had gotten them lunch from the cafeteria, chicken noodle soup for Stacy and a roast beef on wheat with lettuce for herself.

"I'm okay," Stacy said. "I'm starting to feel more awake though. How soon did they say I could go home?"

"Tomorrow. It can't get here fast enough," Tori said.

Stacy sighed. "Good. I can't wait to sleep in my own bed again. This one is ridiculous."

"Hospital beds are never comfortable. I wish I knew why." Tori laughed.

Stacy fished around in her bowl at the remaining noodles in her soup, gathered them on her spoon, and brought it to her mouth. She slurped it loudly as she looked at her mother, a twinkle in her eye. For her part, Tori was less than enthused at this behavior.

"Will you stop?"

"Sorry," Stacy laughed, "had to do it."

The gleam in Stacy's eye found its way to Tori's heart, and the two of them burst into laughter. A moment of bliss shared after hours of pain. Tori stood from the chair, the plastic container holding her sandwich almost entirely emptied. She reached over for the bowl on Stacy's bed tray.

"Are you finished now?" she asked.

"Yeah," Stacy nodded, placing the spoon back in the bowl. "Thank you."

Tori picked it up and placed it on top of her container, walked to the sink outside the bathroom, and set them on the edge. She turned on the water faucet to wash her hands and caught a glimpse of herself in the mirror.

She paused, noticing the lines around her eyes, her puffy cheeks, and the haggard look in her eyes. She shook her head.

Damn this getting old, she thought.

She chuckled, squirted some soap out of the dispenser, and washed her hands. She waved her hand in front of the paper towel dispenser, ripped off a couple of sheets, and dried her hands. She turned the faucet off, threw the towels in the trash, and turned to walk back to the lounge chair.

She stopped after taking one step. Stacy sat motionless on the bed, a forlorn, lost look in her eyes. Tori furrowed her brow. She walked over and stopped at the bed, leaning down closer to Stacy.

"Stacy, honey? Are you all right?" She reached out her hand and stroked Stacy's arm, a look of concern on her face.

Stacy turned to look at her. "Yeah. I'm okay. Only there's something I haven't told you. I'm not sure how you'll react."

"You mean that you're pregnant?" Tori said.

Stacy's eyes grew wide, and her head jerked backward as she looked at her mother. "How did you find out?"

"Dr. Blanton told me shortly after I got here. I have to say, I'm still mad you didn't tell me, but, honey, I support whatever decision you make about it."

"Well, I haven't decided yet," Stacy answered, shrugging her shoulders, "I think."

She looked down at the bedsheets and began fumbling her fingers on the corners of the sheets, mindlessly flipping them back and forth on the bed.

"Honey, we'll have time to talk about this when we're home, but if you want my opinion, you're not ready to have a child. You've got too much going on right now to have that kind of responsibility. I don't see how you can go to school full-time, be a cheerleader, and take care of a baby, not to mention try to have a job while you do it all."

"You sound just like Tucker." She gave a mocking half smile and shook her head as she spoke.

"What does that mean?"

"The night he died, I asked him what he thought if I got pregnant. He told me I should have an abortion and he wasn't ready to be a father. I know he would've been fine, but he didn't seem like he'd support me no matter what I chose. I was disappointed."

"I can imagine."

"I didn't wanna tell you and Dad 'cause I didn't want you to worry about it."

"Honey, we'd worry about you no matter what, okay? That's what a parent does, worry about what happens to their kids. You don't think it hurt me to see some of the things you went through? You don't think it hurt me to find you passed out on your bedroom floor? You think I didn't worry when you were lying here in a coma, not sure if you'd ever wake up again? It's a parent's job to worry."

A smile came to Stacy's face as she began to laugh.

"What's so funny?"

"You sound like something I heard in my dream."

"What do you mean?"

Stacy sighed heavily, closed her eyes, and gave herself a moment to collect her thoughts. "It was something that happened when I was in my coma that I can't explain."

"What was it, honey?"

"It felt sorta like a dream, but not really, if that makes sense," she whispered, her eyes suddenly fixed on a distant point beyond the room.

"Do you want to talk about it?"

"I guess, but it'd be hard to explain," she shrugged.

"Well, just try. It doesn't matter if makes sense or not. Sometimes talking about it helps it make sense," Tori said.

She sat down in the lounger and pulled it toward the bed, leaning in closer to her daughter. She had a feeling this would be a long story.

"Well, I dreamed I was in this forest. It was all gray and stuff. In the middle of it, there was this meadow, and the sun was shining on it. It was weird. I met this person, or something, there, and he told me he could show me my future."

"Your future," Tori repeated mechanically.

"Yeah," Stacy nodded. "But it wasn't my future. It was my baby's future."

Tori stared blankly at her daughter. "What are you talking about?"

"I know, like I said, it's hard to explain. He showed me all these different things that could happen to my child. Like all these different possibilities of who she could become. It was really strange."

"It sounds like it. But why did you mention something I said reminded you of this dream?"

Stacy began practicing her breathing exercises again, slowing her heart rate and calming her nerves. Moments such as this were a reminder of the benefit of having practiced this routine. She shifted her weight on the bed and pulled a pillow from behind her, placing it on her lap, slapping it as she did.

"Before I go on, there's something else I need to tell you."

"What?"

"I went to a clinic to talk about getting an abortion."

"I know."

"How?"

"Tonya came by to visit, and she told me. She said you were really scared to tell me about going. Honey, I just told you. I support you no matter what you decide to do."

"Seems like all my secrets are out then."

"Unless there's something more you haven't told me."

"No," Stacy said, letting out a sigh. "If it helps, I'm sorry I didn't trust you enough to tell you."

"We'll deal with that later. You were saying something about your dream though."

"Yeah. Like I said, it was strange. This person kept showing me what may or may not happen to my child but never said what was real or not. He only said there was the potential for these things to happen."

"What person?" Tori asked.

"Beats me," Stacy answered, her hands lifted palms upward. "I mean, I never knew who he was for sure. I just know I wasn't scared of him. It was kinda peaceful."

"So what kinds of things did you see?"

"I had a daughter. She was beautiful. He showed me she could be all these different people, like a doctor or a lawyer. It was really weird."

"And you didn't know if any of this would be true or not?" Tori said, her words slow and drawn out. It was clear she was playing catch-up in her mind.

"Yeah," Stacy nodded. "But there were some other things I saw I didn't like." Her face became dark and withdrawn as she remembered watching her daughter suffer the indignities that took place.

"Like what?"

"She was homeless in one scene. In another, she was in prison and got stabbed by an inmate. I mean, it was sick. I hated seeing that stuff."

"Oh my god," Tori said, pulling her hand to her mouth, "that must have been awful."

"It was. But the weirdest thing is, I kept wanting to run to her and hold her in my arms. I wanted to tell her she would be all right. I don't get why I felt that way."

"I do," Tori said, sniffling hard. "You feel like a mother."

"That's what this person kept telling me. It seemed like he was trying to convince me to have this child. I kept telling him it would ruin my life if I did."

"Maybe not ruin your life, but it would definitely be hard."

"I know, Mom. I just feel like I don't have anyone to help me."

"Look," Tori said, standing up and leaning on the bed rail, "whatever you decide, I'll be there for you. I promise."

"How can I believe you when you haven't been there for me before? You're not exactly the most trustworthy person, you know," Stacy said, anger flashing in her eyes.

Tori shook her head, raising a hand to rub her forehead. She looked at Stacy, a hint of disgust in her gaze.

"You know, since you've been here, I've done some soul searching, and I realized something. I know I haven't been the best role model for you. I know I can be selfish, and a lot of that I blame on your father. But I promise, I'll be here for you throughout this pregnancy, whatever you decide. You've got to trust me."

"I honestly don't know if I can, Mom," Stacy said, raising her hand. "I'm sorry, I just don't have a lot of confidence in our relationship."

Tori sighed, picked up her purse, and pulled it up on her shoulder, searching for a way to make it more comfortable.

"I'm sorry you feel that way. I'm sorry I wasn't there for you before. I just told you, I've done some evaluating about myself, and I thought you' be grateful to hear I'm ready to try in our relationship. But I shouldn't be surprised. You've always been ungrateful."

Tori banged her hand on the bed rail, shook her head, and sighed. She looked up at Stacy. "Look, I'm going home for the night. Dr. Blanton said it's okay if I leave you here alone tonight. I'll be back tomorrow to take you home. I hope this will give you time to think about whom you can rely on."

She turned and walked out of the hospital room without the courtesy of a goodbye. Stacy watched her mother leave the room, tears trickling down her cheeks.

"Thanks for nothing, Mom," she whispered.

On the way back to her condo, Tori's frustration grew. She alternated between grunting in disgust and cursing as loud as she could. More than once, the steering wheel took the brunt of her anger, rattling as she struck it repeatedly with her hand.

I need to get away from this stress, she thought. *I feel like I'm gonna lose it.*

Suddenly, a smile crossed her face. She reached over in her purse, fishing around for her phone. Successfully finding it, she quickly looked up her "Favorites" list and touched a name. The phone began ringing, and she straightened herself in her seat as she waited. On the fifth ring, there was an answer.

"Hello?"

"Hey, Rick, it's Tori. What are you doing right now?"

"Uh, nothin'. Why?"

"I wondered if I could drop by for a little, uh, you know."

There was a long pause on the phone. For a moment, Tori thought she lost the connection.

"Rick? Rick, are you still there?"

"Yeah. I'm here."

"So what do you think?"

"I'm not sure what to think, to be honest."

"Look, this doesn't have to mean anything, okay? We don't have to define why we do what we do. I thought we'd worked beyond that a long time ago."

"Yeah. Whatever."

"Okay. I'm about five minutes away. I'll be there soon. You better be waiting for me in the bedroom, got it?"

"Okay. Whatever."

"See you soon."

"Bye," he said and disconnected the call.

The morning after was always the hardest part. Tori had been through this routine countless times, yet she never found a way to stave off the emptiness that inevitably came calling. She'd decided a long time ago this was a small price to pay for a night of what she felt was well-deserved passion. She'd made her way back to the hospital and stumbled through the lobby. She managed to reach the elevators and waited for one to arrive.

Why did I do that? she thought. *I'm not in love with Rick. Why did I spend the night with him?*

She shook her head, a laugh escaping her lips. She looked back at the elevator, waiting for the doors to open. Within minutes, the familiar sound went off, indicating the arrival of an elevator car, as the doors slid open. As she entered, she made her way to the rear of the car, pressing the button to reach Stacy's floor.

She let out a sigh and leaned against the elevator wall, her head feeling thick and cloudy. She had yet to adhere to the promise of not overimbibing, telling herself the next time was the last time. Once again, she felt that familiar sting of alcohol raging against her good sense.

The ding of the elevator sounded like a church bell, and as the doors slid open, she moved cautiously out into the hospital hallway. Despite her hungover state, she had to find a way to gather herself together enough to get Stacy home in one piece. She was determined to make this work.

She shuffled down the hall toward Stacy's room, the bustle of the doctors and nurses becoming nothing more than a buzz in her ears. Despite her best efforts, she couldn't isolate herself from the noise. As she neared Stacy's room, she noticed Dr. Blanton standing just outside the doorway, talking with a colleague. She cleared her throat and straightened her blouse, brushed her hair back, and tried to stand as upright as her hangover would allow.

Blanton shook his colleague's hand and closed the chart in his hand. He slid his silver pen into his coat pocket, looked up and saw Tori, and walked to meet her. He was rubbing his chin vigorously, the same way a villain does in children's fairy tales.

"Ms. Butler," he said, extending his hand, "the day you've been waiting for has finally arrived, huh?"

She reached out and shook his hand, smiling. "Yes. It's been difficult, but I'm glad she's able to leave," she said, her words thick and foggy.

"I was just going over some details with the neurologist. We were comparing her readings from when she first got here to now. She's done a remarkable job of overcoming this hurdle. You should be proud of her."

"I am," she said, shifting her weight from one foot to the other. "I'm just glad she doesn't have any side effects from what happened."

"That's the other thing we were discussing," Blanton said. "It's not uncommon, but it's always a good thing to not see any ill effects from a coma. I'm only glad we could help get her well again."

"Well, thank you, Doctor, for all you've done."

"You're welcome, Ms. Butler. But take care of this young one. She's seen a lot." He smiled, a twinkle igniting his eyes. He winked as he turned and walked away, disappearing among the other white coats in the hallway. Tori stood dumbfounded, a sudden wave of awe and peace washing over her, as if she'd encountered something supernatural.

What the heck was that? she thought. She gave a shrug and walked into Stacy's room.

Stacy sat in the lounger, fully dressed, some of her personal items stowed away in a hospital issue plastic bag. Her left leg bounced up and down, and she was biting her fingernails.

"I just saw Dr. Blanton outside. Did he come in to see you?" Tori asked.

"No," Stacy said.

"Oh."

"Why?"

"Nothing. I just wondered. You ready to go?" Tori said.

"Yeah, I got the discharge papers, and the nurse said I can leave whenever I'm ready."

"Well, okay then. Let's go."

Tori led the way out of the room, followed by Stacy, clutching her plastic bag. As they walked down the hall, more than one nurse stopped them, letting Stacy know how proud they were of her and what a pleasure it was to be a part of the recovery team. Tori and Stacy took the compliments and tears in stride, anxious to head outside and get home.

After several stops and starts initiated by the hospital staff, they finally arrived at Tori's car, parked on the third level of the attached garage. They both got in, buckled up, and headed out of the parking space. Stacy leaned her head back on the cushion of the seat, a broad smile affixed to her face. It felt good to feel fresh air on her face again. Though it was a little over two weeks she had been here, it felt like a lifetime ago that she'd seen the sunshine.

"Are you feeling okay over there, honey?" Tori asked, glancing at Stacy.

"Yes," she answered. "I feel great."

She held her hand out the open window, allowing the breeze to brush across her fingers, breathing in the warm air and reveling in the sun shining on her face. She closed her eyes and reminded herself that these were the important moments in life to enjoy.

"Hey, is there anything special you want to do for dinner tonight, honey?"

"I don't know," Stacy shrugged. "I mean, I hadn't thought about it."

'Well, we could go out to Del Arini's, get some Alfredo. Or we could go to Hannigan's for some burgers. Your choice," Tori said.

"How about we just order a pizza and eat in?"

"Okay," Tori nodded. "If that's what you wanna do, we'll do it."

The pizza delivery turned out to be the perfect antidote to a steady diet of hospital cafeteria food. Tori and Stacy sat together in the kitchen, laughing and talking. For the first time in a long time, they were genuinely happy to be in the same room with each other. It seemed they'd reached a turning point in their relationship.

"Are you full? Want any more garlic bread? More pop, anything?" Tori asked.

"Oh god, no. I'm stuffed," Stacy said, throwing a small piece of crust from her last piece of pizza onto her plate.

"Honey, I'm so glad you're home. I've missed you."

Stacy picked up her glass of pop and took a drink. She adopted a curious look on her face as she kept her eyes on the table.

"Is something wrong?" Tori asked.

"No," Stacy said. "It's just…this is so weird."

"What's weird?"

Stacy sighed, brushing the hair out of her eyes. "You and me. I mean, we've fought for so long. We always used to argue, and now we're sitting here like best friends or something. Why is that?"

Tori took the final bite of her extra meat pizza and reached for her napkin. As she chewed, she wiped her hands clean of any crumbs or grease. She reached for her glass of wine and took a sip, then placed the glass back on the table. She didn't let go immediately.

"Like I told you, I've done some soul searching. I had time to think about our relationship, and I realized we need to do some things differently. This whole ordeal has really made me reevaluate what's important."

"What's so different from before? Why the sudden change?"

Tori's eyes darted around the room, her head following their direction. Finally, she closed her eyes and rubbed her hand over them before she looked at Stacy.

"There's something I never told you," she said, her voice low.

"What?"

Tori drew in a deep breath. "Before we got married, your father and I used to talk about raising a family. We both wanted children so much. We tried and tried, but nothing happened. We went to doctors and clinics, and nothing helped. We didn't know what was wrong until we visited a specialist, and he told us something we never expected to hear."

"What was it?"

Tori sighed, looked at the table, then up at Stacy. "Your father and I were unable to have children."

The words fell out of Tori's mouth, violently crashing against Stacy's ears. She blinked rapidly, her head shaking in disbelief.

"What? What are you saying?" she stammered.

"I've got something I want to show you. Hold on a minute."

Tori stood from the table and walked into her bedroom. She was gone for several minutes, allowing Stacy enough time to try and digest the news she just heard.

What is she talking about? she thought. *This is nuts.*

A few minutes later, Tori emerged from her bedroom, clutching a picture to her chest. A tear formed in the corner of her eye as she sat down. She picked up her wine glass and took a much longer drink this time, nearly emptying the contents in her mouth. She set it back down and wiped her lips.

"Since we found out early on that neither of us could have children, we were forced to look for other options. We argued over what to do and nearly split up because we couldn't decide what to do."

"So why did you stay together?"

"Because we settled on adoption."

The words hung in the air like dense smoke in an airtight room. Thoughts became a blur, emotions riding wave after wave of anticipation and fear.

"Adoption," Stacy whispered. "I'm…adopted?"

"Yes."

Stacy turned away, looking out the window to the parking lot just outside. Much like the pavement, her thoughts were fractured and pockmarked with questions.

"Why didn't you ever tell me?"

"We, we just never took the time to tell you. We always thought there'd be a better time someday. But after what you've just been through, I don't think there's a better time than now."

"So why do you have a picture?"

Tori glanced down at the photo, closed her eyes, and drew in her breath.

"This is a picture of you and your birth mother. I've held onto it so I could remember her too. We only met her once when we signed the papers. She was such a sweet girl, and we really felt a connection to her. But here, it's time you see this."

She handed the picture across the table to Stacy.

Stacy hesitated as she took hold of the picture. She looked to her mom, then back to the picture. As she held it in her hand, she felt herself moving in slow motion. She carefully brought it up to look at it and gasped as soon as she saw it clearly. Her hand came to her mouth, covering it in utter shock.

It was the same picture she'd seen in her dreamlike state, only this time the faces were crystal clear. Her mother looked young, perhaps the same age as Stacy, with vibrant blue eyes that sparkled with life and energy. Her wavy hair fell softly across her shoulders.

Stacy began to cry as she stared at her infant self, so frail, so precocious. A contented smile was on her face as she rested in the arms of her mother, as a child does when they're too tired to stand. She gazed in wonder at seeing the peace she and her mom appeared to have in this moment. Her entire life lay before her, and she didn't even know it.

"This was taken a month before the car accident that claimed your mother's life," Tori said. "We didn't know it, but she'd signed the paperwork finalizing the adoption shortly before this picture was taken. As soon as we found out she picked us to be your parents, your father and I didn't hesitate to make the arrangements to bring you home."

"She…died?" Stacy said, forcing the words out of her mouth.

"Yes."

Stacy reached up and rubbed her forehead, absorbing every detail of this picture. It was the most beautiful sight she'd ever seen. She smiled and shook her head.

"Mom, you're not going to believe this, but I've seen this picture before."

"What? How? I never showed it to you before."

Stacy looked up from the picture. "I kept seeing it in my dream. Every scenario with my child, she had this picture with her. The most unsettling part was, I couldn't see the faces. They were blurred out. What do you think that means?"

"I don't know," Tori shrugged.

Stacy laid the picture on the table and stood, clutching her stomach, rubbing her hand gently across her belly.

She took a few halting steps, reaching out for the sink, placing her hand on the edge, and propping herself against it for stability. Her knees felt weak, her mind completely devoid of cogent thought, as too many questions invaded her soul. She was numb.

"Stacy. Are you okay?"

"In my dream, this person kept telling me my life was no longer about me. He kept telling me that it was about my child. He kept asking me all these horrible, wonderful questions. He kept badgering me, asking if I were certain I wanted to terminate my pregnancy. I was shocked at seeing what could happen to her. In a way, it was unsettling to watch her deal with some of the situations she was in. If I'm being honest, it would be better if she didn't live. The things I saw almost convinced me to end it. I wouldn't want anything like what I saw come true for her."

She turned to face Tori, leaning her backside against the countertop.

"And then he said the dream was more about my relationship with you than with my child. That there are things I could learn from how we get along."

"I don't understand, Stacy. You'll have to explain it to me."

Stacy lowered her head, reached, up and rubbed her forehead again, letting out a heavy sigh. "I don't quite understand it myself, Mom. I mean, I kept feeling like I wanted to hold her, to talk to her and tell her how to be a good person or point out when she was making a mistake. And every time, this person would ask me how I got along with you or what I did to make your life hell by not listening to you. He said what I chose would affect my child, just like what you chose affected me. I didn't understand what he meant by that. I just ignored it, honestly.

"But I kept telling this person I can't have this child, I don't have anyone who can help me, and that my life would be better off without a child. After seeing all those possibilities, I can't bear the thought of my child seeing this world for what it is right now. I can't do this alone. It would interrupt my life. And I still think I'm right."

Tori stood and walked to stand in front of Stacy. "Honey, I know this is a lot to sort through right now. I'm sorry to tell you about your adoption this way. But when you were in that coma, I didn't know if you'd make it back to me. Now that you're here, I want to make sure we're honest with each other. As far as your pregnancy, I'll support you no matter what you do. I think you're too young to have a child, especially with all you have planned right now. There's just no time for a baby. Doesn't that make sense?"

"Yeah, it does," Stacy nodded. "That's exactly how I feel." She shifted her weight and stood up straighter now. "How old was my mom when she was killed?"

Tori stepped backward a few paces, a look of fear and compassion in her eyes. "She was your age," she whispered.

Stacy nodded, looking away for a moment, then turned her head back to look at her mom. "Is that why you told me, or was it something else?"

"Stacy, I told you because you deserve to know. And yes, your being in a coma made me realize that things happen we don't expect. I just wanted to be honest with you and see if we could build a relationship with each other, the kind we both want but haven't had. Does that make sense?"

"Yeah, I guess so. But there's something I still don't understand."

"What's that?"

"My mother gave birth to me and arranged for me to be adopted. She wanted a better life for me, right?"

"Yes," Tori answered.

"And I'm pregnant at the same age as my mother, and I can either give my child a better life or decide to terminate it now." Stacy looked up at her mom, her eyes heavy with questions. "Right?" she asked.

Tori nodded.

Stacy looked at a far point in the kitchen, her eyes staring at nothing and everything simultaneously. She remained quiet for a long time, her thoughts darting in all directions about her past, her present, and her future. She remembered her dream, how beautiful her daughter was, surprised how she reacted in each situation. Then there were the myriad questions the Being asked her to consider.

What of her own lack of asking for help when she needed it most? Could she rely on her mother? Only time would tell.

She closed her eyes, practicing her breathing exercises. As she continued, she felt the tension begin to drift away, the questions as murky as ever but seemingly more navigable in her mind. She opened her eyes, looked at her mother, and smiled.

She knew what she had to do.

ABOUT THE AUTHOR

Dan's core objective is to dig deep within his own heart, search the corners of his mind, and commit to paper some of the questions he has about his own faith. Sometimes, it becomes a matter of questioning a long-standing practice of a denominational body and if that is the best way to win people's hearts. To Dan, it's all about exploring the nuances and quirks that make up how we interpret this life in Christ. And there are a lot more questions than answers at this point.

His desire to use the gift of writing to honor the Lord compels him to provoke thought at Christian practices and explore his faith as it encounters difficult situations. Though some of his stories may step outside this overt message, there is still an element of faith in each one.

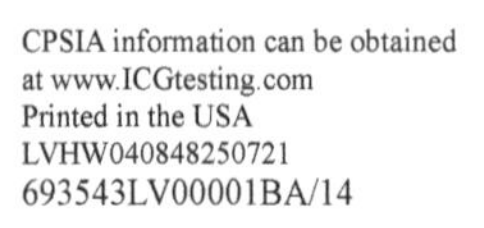

CPSIA information can be obtained
at www.ICGtesting.com
Printed in the USA
LVHW040848250721
693543LV00001BA/14